ODE TO DEFIANCE

ODE TO DEFIANCE

A BRAINTRUST™ UNIVERSE BOOK

MARC STIEGLER

DISRUPTIVE IMAGINATION

LMBPN Publishing
PMB 196, 2540 South Maryland Pkwy
Las Vegas, NV 89109

First US Edition,

ISBN: 978-1-64202-190-5

ACKNOWLEDGMENTS

This time out I'd especially like to thank Chris Peterson, my favorite pharmaceutical guru, and Bob Schumaker, who was a beta reader for me decades before the term "beta reader" came into being.

For Leslie Gerald Stiegler, antiaircraft gunner on the *USS Storm King,* who survived the kamikazes though too many of his companions did not.

Ode To Defiance Team Includes
JIT Beta Readers - My deepest gratitude!

Micky Cocker
John Ashmore
Dr. James Caplan
Dr. Erika Everest
Jeff Eaton
Misty Roa
Paul Westman
Mary Morris

*If I missed anyone, **please** let me know!*

Fashion Consultant
Judith Anderle

Editor
Lynne Stiegler

SHIPS OF THE BRAINTRUST ARCHIPELAGOS

The BrainTrust main fleet:

Argus: Manufacturing ship specializing in the manufacture of isle ships, but performing diverse manufacturing tasks including the manufacture of rocket boosters for SpaceR.

BTU: Ship hosting BrainTrust University, also known as BTU.

Chiron: Medical ship catering to medical tourists, i.e., people needing medical care who want to avoid either the long lines or the high costs of Western countries. One whole deck is now devoted to Dash's rejuvenation patients.

Dreams Come True: Isle ship filled with startup companies.

Elysian Fields: Tourist ship, also known as the party boat.

FB Alpha & Beta: Two of the original four BrainTrust isle ships, mainly hosting FB employees but also leasing space to other companies.

GPlex I & II: Two of the original four BrainTrust isle

ships, mainly hosting GPlex employees but also leasing space to other companies.

GPlex III: GPlex isle ship filled with compute servers.

GS Prime: Goldman Sachs financial services ship, mainly hosting GS employees but also leasing space to other financial services companies.

GSDC: Goldman Sachs Data Center ship.

Haven: Residential isle ship built by billionaires for billionaires.

Heinlein: Modified isle ship used as launch pad for SpaceR rockets. Kept at a safe distance from the main fleet, often moves closer to the equator for launches.

Helios: Manufacturing ship belonging to SpaceR, primarily tasked with the manufacture of Kestrel Titans.

Hephaestus: Factory ship where operations involving toxic and explosive materials take place. Nuclear reactors are built here. The ship is kept at a safe distance from the main archipelago.

Warenhaus: Logistics ship which also contains a silicon chip foundry.

Wells Morgan: Joint venture of Wells Fargo and J.P. Morgan, hosting diverse financial services companies.

The Fuxing fleet/archipelago

Stationed at the intersection of territorial claims of China, Taiwan, and the Philippines:

Mount Helicon: School and residential ship.

Taixue: School and residential ship, the flagship, the

first home of new students, employees, and families from around the South China Sea.

Zhaozhou: Manufacturing ship.

The Prometheus fleet/archipelago

Stationed off the coasts of Nigeria and Benin, a few miles south of the Benin capital of Porto Novo:

Al-Zarnuji: School and residential ship.

Archimedes: Manufacturing ship

Mount Parnassus: School and residential ship, the flagship.

CAST OF CHARACTERS

Aar Singh: BrainTrust peacekeeper.

Abshir: Somali twenty-something, cousin of Diric.

Admiral Edwin Beck: of the US Navy, charged with becoming an expert on the BrainTrust.

Alex Turner: Chief Engineer of the *Argus*.

Amadin: gigantic thug who runs things in the Benin patrol boat that is used as a prison for pirates

Amanda Copeland: Director of the Chiron medical department, current Chairman of the BrainTrust Consortium, Dash's supervisor.

Astri Dewi: Dash's cousin.

Ben Wilson: Aging venture capitalist

Brandy: SpaceR boss of launch operations

Cameron Ballard: Acting Assistant Director of the FBI Weapons of Mass Destruction Directorate.

Chad Duncan: leader of the Lab Rats, healthy young people mostly from America who volunteer as test subjects.

Chance Dixon: Intern for Dash, Doctor of Medicine.

Chen Ying: Son of the Chinese Politburo, student on the *Taixue*.

Ciara Thornhill: Mission Commander for the Prometheus fleet, daughter of Lenora.

Colin Wheeler: BrainTrust resident

Dash: Dr. Dyah Ambarawati, medical researcher, polymath

Dawn Rainer: New head of the Rainer social media conglomerate. Daughter of Anne Rainer who died undergoing rejuvenation therapy.

Dennis Gordon: Independent trucker specializing in delivering goods to California from out of state who lost his truck in a California seizure.

Diab: Palestinian engineer and leader of refugees.

Diric: Somali teenager, pirate, student on the *Mount Parnassus*, cousin of Abshir.

Dmitri Mikailov: Russian oligarch residing on the *Haven*.

Fan Hui: Daughter of the Chinese Politburo, student on the *Taixue*, one of the founding investors in the first major new corporations of the Fuxing fleet that mines manganese nodules from the ocean floor.

Fleet Captain Graysen Ainsworth, commander of the Fuxing fleet.

Gao: Chinese Air Force Captain and squadron commander.

Gary Schott: Employee of SpaceR at the Hawthorne rocket factory.

Gina Toscano: Wife of Matt Toscano, Vogue model.

Gleb: Bodyguard for Dmitri, assassin who attempted to kill Dmitri, employee with the Prometheus fleet subsidized by Dmitri.

Guan Jian: Son of the third member of the Chinese Standing Committee, student on the *Taixue*

Han Chunlan: Captain of the Chinese cruiser *Renhai* stationed near the Fuxing.

Hart Baddeley: Security Chief for the Fuxing

Hilaal: world-class virologist from the American University of Beirut, currently working with Doctors without Borders

Jam: Pakistani commando, peacekeeper on the BrainTrust, Expedition Commander for the Fuxing fleet.

Joshua Pickett: BrainTrust mediator, stationed on the *Chiron* and then the *Haven*.

Jubair: world-class virologist and researcher from the American University in Beirut

Julissa: Hukou peasant girl, student with the *Taixue*, serving as interpreter and companion for Expedition Commander Jam in China.

Jun Laquan: Hukou peasant boy, student on the *Taixue*, inventor of the scuba bot Jacques and co-founder of Oceanic Mining Unlimited.

Keenan Stull: Goldman Sachs financier

Khalid: Brilliant Sunni born in western Iraq trying to escape the endless violence.

Kuo Lim: Baotong villager, husband of Shu Shi, father of missing daughter Liling.

Lambert: Lieutenant Jeremy Lambert, adjutant for Admiral Beck

Lenora Thornhill: Mission Commander for the Fuxing fleet, co-founder of Accel, mother of Ciara.

Levinsky: Captain Levinsky, commander of an Israeli

patrol boat tasked with ensuring Palestinians do not violate the limits on their fishing rights.

Lindsey Postrel: Owner/editor of Cogent News.

Marcos Ford: Peacekeeper for the Prometheus Fleet.

Matthew Toscano: CEO of SpaceR, husband of Gina Toscano.

Nuan: Elder and unofficial leader of the village of Baotong.

Oziegbe: gifted leader of development projects from Senegal by way of Benin.

Ping: Peacekeeper for the BrainTrust, Security Chief for the Prometheus fleet.

Putu Arnawa: Peacekeeper for the Prometheus fleet.

Qi Ru: Hukou peasant, escaped to attend Oxford, venture financing broker for the Fuxing.

Rhett Woodson: Nuclear engineer and designer for the primary isle ship reactors.

Rodrick Sprague: Acting Commissioner of the Food and Drug Administration.

Sabaah: Best friend of Khalid, supporter of ISIS, later went to the American University in Beirut to become a software engineer with a special focus on both hardware and software for driverless vehicles.

Shu Shi: Baotong villager, wife of Kuo Lim, mother of missing daughter Liling.

Shura: Brilliant young girl from the Dahomey region of Benin, whose hands were amputated by the Benin Beloved Chief Advisor for Life.

Simon Bingham: Director of the CDC in Atlanta, boss of Velma Highwalker

Song: Brilliant older hukou peasant from the Loess Plateau, father of Tai.

Sonia Manning: Exotic dancer and organ replacement research scientist.

Soup: Suparman Herianto, peacekeeper for the Prometheus fleet.

Tai: Son of Song, hukou peasant diagnosed with web addiction.

Ted Simpson: Teenage developer of advanced homebrew copters.

Toni Shatski: Israeli Air Force Captain, engineering student at BTU, daughter of the Israeli Prime Minister.

Uwais: One of Khalid's two closest friends, ex-Hezbollah member, went to the American University in Beirut specializing in aeronautical engineering and rocket science.

Vasily: Bodyguard for Dmitri, takes orders directly from the Russian Union Premier.

Velma Highwalker: CDC scientist of Cheyenne ancestry, famous for her hot temper and opposition to various policies of the Chief Advisor and President for Life.

Werner Halstead: Chief Engineer for SpaceR

Wolf Griffin: BrainTrust peacekeeper.

Xiu Bao: Hukou peasant girl, student on the *Taixue*.

Yefim: Bodyguard for Dmitri.

Zhang: Chinese Army Major commanding troops near the Loess Plateau.

PREFACE: HISTORY OF THE WORLD

Many years ago, shortly before the United States President accepted the heavy burden of becoming the President for Life, he initiated a critical program officially designated as "Deportation Phase II."

A key goal of the program was to rein in the Sanctuary States, run by Blue governments who opposed the President's Red party. To impose his will on the Great Blue State of California, the President dropped the 101st Airborne into Silicon Valley to round up and expel all the foreign engineers.

Two of the leading Valley companies, GPlex and FB, saw this coming and commissioned Colin Wheeler to build the first "isle ships," oversized cruise liners designed to operate indefinitely without returning to port. Thus, when the soldiers arrived in the Valley, the foreigners had already boarded the isle ship fleet, which had then sailed into international waters just off the coast of San Francisco.

Once the ships had anchored and interconnected themselves by large gangways allowing people, bicycles, and driverless vehicles to flow easily to and fro, the fleet became in effect an archipelago of island/ships, each holding about ten thousand residents. Silicon Valley engineers of American citizenship, who stayed behind in California, could take ferries and helicopters out to the fleet to hold meetings with the expelled members of their project teams.

This archipelago, already occupied by many of the smartest engineers from America, attracted an ever-growing number of the best and brightest from all over the world, just as Silicon Valley had done prior to Deportation Phase II. The archipelago came to be known as "the BrainTrust."

Meanwhile, across the rest of the world, autocrats and regulatory bureaucrats slipped into ever-higher positions of ever-greater authority, stifling with ever-greater efficiency all innovations that might threaten their status quos. The BrainTrusters, excessively clever yet few in number, became the source of an increasingly higher percentage of the world's best inventions. Notably, they rapidly developed General Purpose Robots with considerable compute power and opposable thumbs, which were outlawed throughout Western civilization for fear they would send unemployment soaring. On the BrainTrust, such bots performed virtually all the manual labor.

Alas, the President for Life was no spring chicken and did not get younger as the years passed. He became a figurehead, giving a speech each month to his adoring fans while the real power flowed into the confident hands of his Chief Advisor. The Advisor fretted with increasing alarm that someday the President for Life would pass away and the restive populace would demand an election.

Around this time, a brilliant medical researcher (and all-around genius, who developed new inventions in every field from rocket science to nuclear engineering), Dr. Dyah Amabarawati, known to everyone as "Dash," came to the BrainTrust with a proposal that could in theory partially rejuvenate the elderly and make them years younger. Upon arriving, she learned that a team under the supervision of Amanda Copeland had developed the CRISPIER, a machine that supported genetic editing and molecular engineering. The CRISPIER used techniques evolved from the CRISPR technique devised in the years around 2017. The CRISPIER dramatically accelerated Dash's rejuvenation research.

The Chief Advisor needed Dash's rejuvenation therapy so desperately to keep the President for Life functioning that he started making attempts to snatch the young woman for the Needs of the State (*Harmony of Enemies*). His first attempts failed, yet he continued to pursue this course of action with unceasing vigor. The Premier of the Russian Union, himself getting on in years although he remained frightfully shrewd, made similar attempts on Dash, and occasionally teamed up with the Chief Advisor, who viewed the Premier as a great friend, to capture Dash together.

These attempts to take the good doctor were often thwarted by her two best friends. Jam and Ping, both peacekeepers, had mad martial arts skills. Jam was a former Pakistani female commando, and Ping was an itty bitty young woman of Chinese descent who'd spent over half her life in Chicago, although she was wanted in China for reasons one could only suspect.

Jam and Ping were reliably backed by Colin, who'd become the BrainTrust's informal strategist, playing the archipelago's enemies off against each other. They also had the help of Amanda, who was not only the ongoing boss of the *Chiron's* medical facilities but who was also doing a temporary stint (that kept getting longer, despite her wishes) as the Chairman of the BrainTrust Consortium.

The BrainTrust thrived despite the disparate forces arrayed against it, and the fleet grew. They built the *Chiron*, a medical tourist ship, where people from the nations of the West came for health care when their own medical systems either tried to charge them too much or waitlisted them for too long.

An entire deck of the *Chiron* was eventually devoted to Dash's rejuvenation therapy. The therapy had a fifty-fifty chance of rejuvenating any randomly selected person, killing those it did not help. The Dark Alpha series of AIs, using algorithms outlawed in the West in 2018, was able to distinguish winners and losers. They became a part of the rejuv program so that only candidate patients who would benefit were accepted. Chance Dixon, who had started her BrainTrust career as Dash's intern, had become her partner in managing and improving the rejuvenation process.

The *Dreams Come True* housed an enormous diversity of startup companies. *BrainTrust University*, aka *BTU*, supplied the elite education needed to engage in the most extreme engineering enterprises. *Argus* was the BrainTrust's manufacturing ship, and it used its advanced 3D printers to build, among other things, more ships. *GS Prime* and *Wells Morgan* offered regulatory respite to financial services organizations. *Elysian Fields* supplied a playground for visitors and tourists.

Additional enterprises and fields of engineering continued to move to the BrainTrust. When the Governor and Attorney General of California decided to seize SpaceR's assets, Matt Toscano, the new CEO, moved its operations to the archipelago (*Crescendo of Fire*).

With the help of the BrainTrust, SpaceR diversified in many directions. They built their own manufacturing ship, the *Helios,* to produce next-generation rockets. Their first spaceport ship, the *Heinlein,* was joined by other spaceport ships off the coasts of Europe, New York, China, and Africa to form the Global Express network. A suborbital Titan rocket from any spaceport ship could deliver passengers to any other such ship within two hours.

SpaceR also built the Starry Night satellite cell phone system, which, when combined with BrainTrust cell phones using BrainTrust computer chips (which lacked the legally required back door to allow government surveillance) enabled anyone anywhere to contact anyone else and talk in complete privacy.

Eventually, the BrainTrust expanded into multiple fleets. The Fuxing fleet anchored off the coast of China. The Prometheus fleet anchored off the coast of Africa, below the bulge of West Africa, west of Niger and south of the much smaller nation of Benin. They planned to search the impoverished hinterlands of these areas and collect those with brilliant minds who had no hope of advancement due to poor nutrition, poor education, and prejudicial cultures and governments. These potential geniuses were given high-speed immersive STEM educations using the Accel computer-based education system, which was able to maximize the student's learning rate by abandoning the lock-step one-size-fits-all teaching approaches of the West.

Lenora Thornhill, one of the three founders of the Accel Corporation and the world's foremost expert in education and testing, became Mission Commander for the Fuxing archipelago. From the main BrainTrust fleet, she stole Jam to become the commander of an expedition into the backwaters of China, collecting people who had passed the Accel phone-based test to qualify for Brain-Trust residency (*Rhapsody for the Tempest*). Lenora's patience was constantly tested by the frightfully competent Liu Fan Hui, a college student on the Fuxing university ship *Taixue*. Since Fan was the daughter of a member of the Politburo, she belonged to that elite cadre referred to by outsiders as the Red Princelings. In the years since the Chinese President had declared himself President for Life, he and the Politburo had also declared all high-ranking political positions hereditary, thus guaranteeing that one day Fan would ascend to a position of nearly unlimited power. All too often, Fan acted as if that day had already arrived.

Ciara Thornhill, daughter of Lenora and nearly her mother's equal on matters of education and testing, became the Expedition Commander for the Prometheus fleet. Just as Lenora had taken Jam to be her Expedition

Commander, so had Ciara taken Ping to be her Security Chief.

Another industry that had been snuffed out by dirtside regulatory fervor was copter/flying car tech, but the Brain-Trust had allowed advances in this arena to flourish. Facilitated by the power and flexibility of the 3D printers on the *Argus* that could be leased by anyone, entrepreneurs from all over the archipelago built homebrew copters to use in the periodic laser tag competitions. The copters would dodge amongst the isle ships, blasting each other with low-power lasers, and computer-determined hits would take copters out of the game until a winner emerged. Copter design evolved at a fierce pace under this competitive pressure.

As a teenager, Ted Simpson became a leading copter builder, and when Matt Toscano became his angel investor, he upped his game. His copters flew ever faster and farther. Eventually, Dash introduced him to materials science engineers on the *Dreams* who helped him build a stealth copter, useful for many applications to which local dirtside authorities might object. During one crisis, Ted applied the stealth coating to a Titan rocket, which came to be known as "the Black Titan."

Alas, Mother Nature had not been kind as the Brain-Trust rose to prominence. When West Antarctic Ice Sheet C broke off, floated to the equator, and melted, not only did it raise sea levels enough to reduce the state of Florida to the Everglades Territory, but it also wiped out the biggest port and the capital of Benin. Benin became a failed state, and its Navy turned from fighting pirates to conducting piracy. The Prometheus fleet had already had to fight a Benin patrol ship, and had had the misfortune of capturing the decrepit vessel. This rust bucket served as a prison, where Ciara and Ping housed the former pirates who once operated it.

This was the state of the world when the apocalypse began.

1

MISSING

The next epidemic could originate on the computer screen of a terrorist
   — Bill Gates, 2018

The first evidence of the impending apocalypse revealed itself on the BrainTrust through the absence of a number.

Chance studied the number on her tablet. "Where could it be?" she asked the universe in general.

Dash, who was examining wallscreens displaying the vitals for one of the rejuvenation patients on board the *Chiron* medical isle ship, asked distractedly, "Where could what be?"

"The CRISPIER we were using for this wing of our deck." They were on the Wenara Wana Monkey Garden deck; all the passage walls and most of the walls of the patient rooms were decorated like the lush jungle forest that grew into and meshed with Ubud in Bali.

Recently someone with more time than sense had gotten overly clever with the program that generated the renderings, so instead of a static display across the walls and ceilings, animations now enlivened the scenery. A monkey kept trying to reach out from the wall to grab Dash's glasses, to no avail.

Chance glared at the monkey as if it were responsible for the missing equipment. "We're missing CRISPIER serial number A32958."

Dash studiously disregarded the virtual simian assault on her eyewear. "And it's nowhere on the deck?"

Chance shook her head. "I had our bot wrangler send bots all over, looking for stray CRISPIERs. It's nowhere to be found." She pulled out her cell. "Hey, *Chiron* Security? Could you review the vidcams for the last couple of days for a machine that wandered off?" She pointed the phone at a CRISPIER down the passage and zoomed in. "It looks like this." Chance nodded. "Cool. Call me when you find it."

They strode into the next patient's room. All these patients had been pre-checked by the brand new Dark Alpha 43 to ensure they would successfully receive at least some years of rejuvenation from Dash's therapeutic injections. Each had consequently received a patient-specific cocktail of pseudo-viruses that would reconstruct their telomere chains, among other things. No patient had died, or even developed any serious side effects, in months. These would be no different.

After a quick check of the displays and a few words of encouragement for the man shifting irritably on the bed, they left the room again. Chance's cell phone rang. "Hey, man. Did you find it? *What?*" After listening a bit more, Chance explained to Dash, "Two guys dressed like lab techs wheeled it out of here, down to the dock, and onto a small yacht."

Dash asked, "Don't the CRISPIERS have trackers on them?"

Chance reiterated the question for Security, then turned back to Dash. "The thieves wheeled the machine up to a second one, disconnected the tracker from one, and moved it onto the other." She listened some more. "The trackers are pretty deeply embedded. Whoever snatched the CRISPIER apparently had some serious electrical engineering skills."

Chance spoke on the phone again. "See what you can find out about the guys who stole it, OK?"

Dash asked, puzzled, "What would someone outside the *Chiron* do with a CRISPIER, anyway?"

Chance stared at her. "Well, it would be a wet dream come true for a molecular biologist or a geneticist. I mean, they don't have anything like it dirtside." The CRISPIER was used for manufacturing the rejuvenation cocktail, among other things. Dash and Chance were the most advanced, most skilled users of the machines at this point, but other medical researchers on the *Chiron* were moving fast to catch up and apply it to other purposes.

Dash nodded briefly, frustrated. "Yes, but we haven't actually had time to write a formal manual for programming it yet. How could anyone use it without instructions?"

Chance shrugged. "I'll bet you could figure it out without instructions. In some sense, you did." Dash had been one of the two first serious users of the machine; the other had died a while ago. "They'd have to be as smart as you, though."

Dash would have blushed had she been a pale Caucasian rather than a native of Bali. "Or you," she insisted.

Chance scoffed. "Just you, Dash. As smart as *you*."

Dash hated these kinds of compliments. "Hmph."

Off the west coast of Africa, Ping hopped out of the hovering copter onto the rear deck of the one-time Benin Navy patrol boat that had more recently been commanded by pirates working for the Benin dictator. Ping had had the misfortune of accidentally capturing the decrepit warship over a year earlier and, lacking better ideas, had turned it into a prison for its erstwhile operators. The time had come to do something more sensible with both the prisoners and the boat.

Abshir cut the copter's engines and got out on the pilot's side.

They were immediately confronted by Amadin, an enormous beast of a man with maniacal rage in his eyes. Ciara had been collecting vidcam footage on the events taking place on the ship ever since the Prometheus archipelago wound up with *de facto* ownership of the vessel. The boat had suffered a total engine failure while attempting to attack the Prometheus isle ships. Since then, Ciara as Mission Commander of the archipelago had sporadically sent bots over with food, water, and tiny vid drones that scattered throughout the vessel as they approached.

Usually, the pirates on board destroyed the bots and as many of the vid drones as they could get their hands on after taking the food, although occasionally they allowed the bots to take an injured crew member over to the *Mount Parnassus* for medical assistance. Most of the injuries needing such assistance had been inflicted by Amadin. No one had actually died yet, but close calls were growing in number. Invariably, the pirates brought to the *Parnassus* begged not to be sent back, at least not until someone did something about Amadin. Killing him was the universally recommended solution to all the problems on the boat.

Ping had been training Abshir in hand-to-hand combat, and this was his final exam.

Amadin lurched toward Ping, his eyes glowing with his crude imaginings of what he would do with her. Abshir swept out a foot, causing Amadin to trip into the space where Ping had stood a moment before, then jumped on Amadin's back and banged his face against the deck repeatedly.

It took a lot of banging. By the time Amadin stopped struggling, Abshir was panting heavily. Finally, he stood and faced the dozen other pirates who had formed a loose circle to watch. None of them had tried to accost Ping, tiny and harmless though she seemed. Apparently, word had leaked from the ones who'd received medical treatment on the Prometheus fleet's flagship, all of whom had been allowed to watch her practice martial arts with her peacekeepers.

Ping clapped her hands as Abshir straightened and

barked at the pirates, "Now, listen up! You have a new captain." She pointed at Abshir.

Abshir looked back, startled. He started to point at himself questioningly, then realized that would not be very commanding and stood straighter to look every pirate in the eye.

Ping continued, "Salute your new commanding officer, or become shark chum the same way Amadin will once I get him back to the *Parnassus*." She toed the hulking, unconscious body. After handing Abshir a pair of hand-cuffs, she spoke softly. "Abshir, have your men load this body onto the copter." More to herself than to Abshir, she continued, "Hope the copter can still fly with this giant lump on board."

Abshir barked the commands and the pirates did as he told them with remarkable cheerfulness, much enhanced by the opportunity to get rid of the maniac who had terrorized them.

Ping watched the way the men sorted themselves out and was not surprised to see a pattern. Ciara had been analyzing the vidtapes of the crew interactions since the first vid drone had survived long enough to capture some action.

The Accel testing systems Ciara used to identify people with the brilliance, grit, and integrity to receive BrainTrust membership were derived from much older algorithms from the 90s, which had in their day been very reliable at identifying people with advanced leadership skills. Ciara had updated those algorithms and fed them the vidtapes. Two of the pirates demonstrated the ability to forge men into teams. As Ciara had predicted, those two took their cues from Abshir and ordered the men around until Amadin was lugged aboard the copter.

Ping pointed at those two. "You are officially Abshir's lieutenants. You will not only receive the basic needs of a sailor—food, water, and uniforms—you will also receive…" she paused to let everyone experience the rush of anticipation, "paychecks."

She waved her hand across all the men. "You can all receive paychecks if you work hard and obey the captain. If not, you can join Amadin on his upcoming deep-sea expedition. Questions?"

There were no questions.

Ping dug around in the space behind the copter pilot's chair and pulled out a tightly wrapped, crisply pressed blue shirt. The standard BrainTrust peacekeeper's uniform was black pants with a yellow shirt; the new Navy uniform would be the same, except for the color of the shirt. She handed it to Abshir, and he wordlessly pulled off his peacekeeper shirt and put it on. It fit perfectly, of course, having been printed specifically for the dimensions of his body just that morning.

Ping then reached into her pocket, pulled out a pair of shoulder boards, and attached them. "I hereby declare you to be the Captain of the BrainTrust Patrol Ship *Storm King*. Good day, Captain," she barked before climbing back into the copter, "I'll be sending people, equipment, and bots tomorrow to get this tub operational again. First thing will be to strip out the dead diesel engines and put in one of the new beta batteries for power. Today, get your men organized and ready to work."

Abshir, in a fit of enthusiasm, saluted her. "Thank you,

uh, Boss."

Ping shook her head and saluted back before spinning up the props to fly home. Halfway back, Amadin groaned; she snapped a quick fist to his temple and knocked him back out. "Just don't need the hassle of you waking up until you're in the brig. Whatever are we going to do with you? Ciara won't actually let me use you as chum for the sharks, darn the luck."

She sat back and continued to mutter. "And now I have a Navy. What the hell am I going to do with a goddam Navy?"

On board the *Taixue* university isle ship of the Fuxing archipelago southeast of Hong Kong, the guest of honor finally arrived at her surprise party.

When Jam walked in, she found an enormous orange-raspberry cake on the conference table; Security Chief Hart was cutting the last of the pieces. Jam exclaimed, "Sorry I'm late. What's going on?"

Lenora walked up to her and put a hand on her shoulder. "Congratulations, Jam! You're fired."

Jam stared at her. "I'm *what?*"

Julissa hugged her. "You worked yourself out of a job. A couple of the kids from Baotong and I can handle it from here." Baotong was a tiny village from which Jam had rescued the people *en masse*.

Lenora gave more details. "Your idea for holding testing fairs outside the web addiction clinics is working brilliant-ly." In China, a popular myth had gained traction that people who spent more than six hours a day online suffered from web addiction, and they were sent to rehabilitation centers with no computers but plenty of barbed wire. Jam had realized that many of the best and brightest of the peasantry would wind up incarcerated in such places and suggested focusing the resources for recruiting Brain-Trust residents on them. This worked great for the Brain-Trust and the "web addicts," albeit not so well for the people who ran the centers.

Jam, who knew most about how unhappy those business owners could get, objected. "But what about the angry rehab bosses?"

Fan Hui, a Red Princeling whose father was a member of the Politburo, answered. "When they have a problem, Julissa flies me in, and I speak with them."

Jam nodded. Fan probably didn't talk explicitly about firing squads for objectors, but images of such events surely entered the minds of those to whom she spoke.

Lenora continued, "We've filled both the *Taixue* and *Mt. Helicon* with residents, and we're working on a third ship."

Song, an elderly but remarkable mechanical engineer and one of Jam's first recruits, added, "And we've got new businesses springing up all over. Hardware, software…you name it." He rubbed his hands together. "I have a team now."

Jam smiled but remained uncertain. "So, what do I do next?"

Lenora chuckled. "I've been talking to Ciara. Now that we have things working pretty well here, we both think your skills would be better exploited doing something similar with her."

Jam's eyes lit up. "With Ping?" Ping was with Ciara, and she and Jam were old friends, having first met on their way to the BrainTrust.

Lenora nodded. "With Ping."

Jam put her hands together, not quite clapping. Then she frowned. "I still have some things to finish up, though."

Julissa nodded. "You certainly do. I have a list of stuff you need to do for me, among other things."

Lenora smiled lazily. "Take your time. But as soon as you can leave, you're out of here."

Captain Levinsky, commander of the Israeli Super Dvora Mk-III patrol boat that had just made an unlikely contact, gawked at the vessel to which his XO pointed. "What the hell *is* that, anyway?"

The ship, four stories high and rocking slightly in the mild chop, was a most unlikely agglomeration of concrete and plastic. The entire superstructure had a slight glossy sheen in the noontime glare. He thought he could see bare pieces of rebar reinforcing the sides of the vertical metal culvert that seemed to be functioning as a smokestack near the tail of the ship.

On the top deck amidships, a gawky gantry-like skeleton of shiny steel rose slightly, strapped down with ropes. Of the whole the ship, this odd gantry was the one part that looked well-built and carefully engineered. The words *First Chance* were crudely written on the hull above the waterline.

You had to watch the ship carefully to conclude it was

making headway. The captain suspected that, if they made it to the ocean and it got caught in the Atlantic Gulf Stream, it would slide backward.

The XO shrugged. "I sure don't know what it is, Captain. And our intel people, watching the Gaza Strip peasants build it well outside the port, don't know what it is either. Nor do our spies in Hamas."

The captain brightened. "Oh, right. I recall the briefing." He chuckled. "We thought about blowing it up on general principles when it was under construction, but then we got word that Hamas was considering blowing it up too. We figured that if Hamas didn't like it, we'd just let it go."

The XO went back on point. "Well, now it's our hot potato. It just breached the three-nautical-mile limit on Palestinian fishing boats."

Levinsky peered at the ship. "Doesn't look like any fishing boat I've ever seen." He pondered for a moment. "I don't suppose they have someone on board casting a line, do they? That would make it easy." If there were a flyfisher aboard the oddity, Levinsky could just blow the strange vessel to hell and gone and leave it at that.

But the XO shook his head. "Not that easy, I'm afraid."

The captain sighed. "OK, tell them to heave to. I guess we have to board them."

<hr>

Khalid watched as his two closest friends—really, his only friends—practiced trying to kill virtual renditions of the two deadly opponents they would one day have to defeat.

Wall to wall, brilliant fluorescent lighting made the

windowless room feel almost like it was bathed in sunshine. The light splashed unevenly from the rock walls and patches of reinforcing concrete.

The stench of partially dried sweat filled the still air as the fighters shifted to and fro in a flurry of strikes and counterstrikes. Finally, Sabaah accelerated from an already nearly-invisible whirl of speed to reach past the even skinnier arms of his opponent, completing a throat strike. He had once been a skinny little computer science geek specializing in driverless vehicle hardware and software but had turned martial artist to meet Khalid's needs.

Meanwhile ex-rocket-scientist Uwais, taller and stronger than Sabaah and as graceful as any gymnast, grappled his virtual enemy before being slammed to the ground by his full-feedback haptic sensor suit. His virtual opponent danced up to his side.

Khalid killed the virtuality after the haptic feedback kicked Uwais twice in the kidneys. He turned to Sabaah. "So, you think you can take her in real life?"

Sabaah wiped his brow. "Of course I can. Don't try to fool me. I know the real person is slower than this virtual simulation." He shook his head. "She has to be. No one could really be that fast."

Khalid frowned. "And yet, you were even faster for a couple seconds at the end. Allow me to repeat: I'm not augmenting these simulators. You must be able to defeat these simple renderings since the real people will be just as fast and far more cunning."

Khalid held his hand out to Uwais, who reached from the ground to let Khalid help him up. "And you."

Uwais' chest heaved. "I don't get it. She's not as fast as

Sabaah's opponent, but…she doesn't just anticipate your next move. It's like she can see the future." He smiled, a lopsided horror since he'd lost much of the musculature in the right side of his face in the missile strike years earlier. "Sort of like *you* can see the future. Are you *sure* you shouldn't be the one to take her?"

Khalid shook his head. "I'll have my hands full with other things. You have to get as good as she is at seeing the future."

Sabaah spun to strike at Uwais' shoulder; Uwais casually swung his forearm, deflecting the blow. Sabaah spoke confidently. "Don't worry, Uwais. You're getting there."

Khalid walked to the corner of the room that held the first aid kit, where he filled a syringe with a translucent green fluid.

Uwais shifted to offer his shoulder. After the injection, he rolled his arm around. "Dare I ask what that is?"

Khalid smiled. "A little something I cooked up based on some research by one of the professors on the BrainTrust. Accelerates the firing of the synapses in your muscle tissue a little bit. It should give you an edge." His voice turned stern. "Once you can anticipate as well as she can."

Sabaah offered an alternative. "We can beat them as a team. Once I take out the little one, we can take out the other together."

Khalid, who had planned to start them training on team tactics in another day or so, nodded. "Well said. As a team, no one has ever defeated us, and no one ever will." He paused. "But they have trained together as well. It still won't be easy." He looked at Uwais again. "And you still have to get better at one on one."

Uwais shook his head as if to clear it. "Again, then."

Khalid was about to flip the virtuality back on when Sabaah gestured.

"Khalid, who are these whores, anyway?"

Khalid spun sharply, angry. "Never call them whores. I thought we were past that kind of disrespect." He looked at Sabaah, who was laughing softly, and Uwais, who had joined in the laughter, and relaxed. "Ha-ha. Yes, you both know how to pull my strings. Well done, I guess." His voice turned harsh once more. "But one reason never to call anyone a whore is that it leads you to underestimate them. You must *never* underestimate these two. Never."

Sabaah pressed him. "You still haven't told us who they are."

Khalid pondered the request. He would have to fully brief them someday, so there was no harm in a little knowledge. Before flipping the simulation back into action, he answered briefly. "Their names are Jam and Ping."

Diab, the nominal captain of the giant Palestinian floating tub, stood slightly hunched before Captain Levinsky. Levinsky knew that Diab knew that the lives of everyone on board depended on the outcome of this encounter.

Diab could not help the bit of pride that filled his voice as he spoke of his vessel. "I know the *First Chance* does not look like much, but she really is seaworthy."

The captain decided to let that go and looked at Diab almost sympathetically. "Any terrorists on board?"

Diab scowled. "There better not be." He continued more cheerfully, "About half my residents are children, and half of the rest are mothers."

Levinsky grunted. Just because they were children did not prove they were not terrorists. Still, the more he extended his current line of thinking, the less he cared if they were terrorists. "We have to search the boat."

Diab nodded; he had clearly expected this. "I personally checked for guns and RPGs coming on board. You won't find anything like that here."

The captain waved to the commander of his Marine detachment. "Good. I don't want trouble any more than you do."

Diab stayed skeptically silent at this claim.

As the Marines scattered through the ship, Captain Levinsky walked to the bow, signaling Diab to come along. He pointed to the west, across the Mediterranean that stretched, glimmering in the sunlight, beyond the horizon. "Just exactly where are you going with these women and children?"

A soft glow entered Diab's face, a glow the captain had trouble recognizing on a Palestinian. It was a glow of hope. "I'm bringing my family and my friends and their families to the BrainTrust."

The captain barked a laugh. "How are you ever going to get to San Francisco?"

Diab shook his head. "We're heading to the Prometheus archipelago."

After a moment, the captain nodded. "Of course. Just go around the bulge of West Africa, and you're there." He paused, puzzled. "Are you sure they'll let you join? I hear they have very strict vetting processes before admitting new members. All their cabins are reserved for the best and brightest the world can offer." He looked skeptically at a boy and a girl kicking a soccer ball along the narrow deck. The captain figured the ball would go over the side any moment, but somehow, the players evaded this fate again and again.

Diab chuckled. "But we aren't planning to board their ships." He patted the gunwale. "The *First Chance* meets all the standards required to be a full-fledged isle ship. We're bringing our own cabins, in effect."

The captain gaped at him, then spluttered, "But...but...this is nowhere near big enough to be an isle ship. And nowhere near..." His voice faded before he finished the sentence. *Nowhere near elegant enough, or seaworthy enough, or shipshape enough.*

Diab's chuckle turned to laughter. "She's not very beautiful, is she? But that's not a requirement. The main structural requirement to be an isle ship is to have a spec-standard gangway that can hook up to the gangways on the other ships." He moved to the port side, pointing up to the skeletal structure on the top deck that the captain had noticed from a distance. "That up there is a fully conforming gangway. Their own policies state they have to let us hook up." His voice turned glum. "Assuming we can afford the attachment fee." His voice became determined. "I'm sure we can negotiate something."

Captain Levinsky craned his neck to look skeptically at the gangway structure. "It looks well-built," he confessed before muttering, "Unlike everything else about this tub."

Diab looked like he was struggling to decide how to respond.

But no response was necessary. For the captain, that gangway and the care that had gone into its construction was enough. It all made sense in its own desperate way. He was glad he wouldn't be there when...if...the *First Chance* reached the Prometheus fleet. He spoke on his radio. "Men, wrap it up. We're leaving."

When the Marine lieutenant in charge of the search returned, the captain asked, "Find anything?"

The lieutenant shook his head. "No, sir. Lots of women and children, just like he said."

The captain grunted, then turned and shook Diab's hand. "Good luck to you, sir."

When Levinsky returned to his ship, his XO gave him a puzzled look. "You're letting them go?"

The captain shrugged. "Not our problem anymore. If they get where they're going, they'll be the BrainTrust's headache." He pursed his lips. "But I doubt it will come to that. With that tub, they'll capsize and drown before they reach Gibraltar. Either way, not our problem."

US Navy Admiral Edwin Beck, making a futile attempt to blend in with the crowd, stood outside by the transparent gunwales of the main promenade level of the isle ship *Elysian Fields*. He watched with dark hostility as the laser ice show danced across the sky and Enya's *Orinoco Flow* soared from immense speakers on all sixteen of the interconnected isle ships.

The admiral wore civilian clothes—black jeans and a flannel shirt, protected from the weather by a crisp cream-colored waterproof jacket with a thick layer of insulating pile. His wife had presented him with the jacket years earlier so he could stay warm and look somewhat spiffy even when out of uniform. His look of command, however, even without the uniform, sometimes inspired even nonmilitary men to start to salute before checking themselves.

Tourists crowded the deck, all gaping and cheering as the laser beams, every color of the rainbow, bounced from the tiny shards of ice blown hundreds of feet into the air by the powerful pumps of the isle ships.

Oddly, the crowd did not press too close to the admiral, perhaps because he kept clenching and unclenching his fists as if contemplating whom to strike next. A small circle of empty deck space surrounded him, with only one person standing close enough to shout into his ear as the rhythm changed. Queen's *We Will Rock You*, known locally as the Founder's Song since they had played it when the first isle ships first left port for the open seas, now blasted across the archipelago.

Lieutenant Jeremy Lambert, his adjutant, yelled above the cheering, "Much more sensible than fireworks for a shipboard display, I'd say. Much better control, and no risk of fire." He licked his lips, already chapped in the bitter wind. "And the way they operate the lasers to generate scenes against the ice is remarkable as well. The isle ship renderings are excellent, but the scene of homebrew copters playing laser tag, using the lasers to generate images of lasers being beamed between battling copters, is, well, elegantly recursive."

Beck clenched his fists again. "Doesn't anyone besides me understand this is not so much a celebration as it is a practice exercise for advanced weaponry?"

Lambert pursed his lips. "Well, sir, I suppose fireworks were also weaponry when they were first used for celebrations. And this is November second, Autonomy Day, after all. The day the original isle ships crossed from America's territorial zone into international waters. Pretty much the biggest celebration on the BrainTrust calendar."

He swept his hand across the scene as the whole archipelago participated in generating the ice spouts, the laser art, and the throbbing music. "And it's the only celebration everybody aboard shares, when you get down to it." The BrainTrusters came from all over the world, bringing the oddest celebrations from the most obscure cultures. Just about everyone also celebrated some sort of Winter Solstice, although the entire archipelago had pretty much adopted Christmas as the time to exchange presents, regardless of religion or ethnic group.

The admiral shook his head. "Still, if we had to engage these supposedly unarmed ships in combat, what could those lasers do? See how the lasers shift frequencies continuously? Can they melt our missiles with infrared? Kill our pilots with gamma rays? How are they even doing that?"

Lambert shook his head. "Free-electron lasers, sir. They can shift the frequency of the output by modulating the transverse magnetic field strength of the undulators." He rubbed his hands together. "They can certainly beam infrared, but unless they've made a breakthrough, the frequency modulation tops out in the x-ray spectrum, so there's no danger of gamma-ray weapons."

Another symphonic work, *Exodus*, burst from immense speakers on all sixteen of the interconnected isle ships. Lambert shouted even louder, straining his vocal cords, "But I doubt these lasers are strong enough to be dangerous, even though they can go infrared. We have the most advanced military laser research in the world, sir, and even ours have severe limitations."

Beck answered softly, yet somehow his voice could still be heard over the din. "Why would you doubt they finished the job we started? These people make breakthroughs all over the place."

Lambert responded respectfully, if doubtfully. "Not really sir. If you look at all the technological advances they've achieved, they invariably deal with making a profit or living on the sea. There's no evidence they've developed any tech that's useful only for military applications. There's certainly no budget for it in the Consortium's records."

"Hmph. Well, let's hope we don't find out the hard way that they've squirreled away a military R&D effort."

"Indeed, sir. A war with the BrainTrust would be unfortunate, even if easily won."

Admiral Beck did not respond to this. He was pretty sure that war with the BrainTrust was pretty inevitable. That was the reason, after all, that he was here studying their oversized cruise liners. The Chief Advisor had demanded it.

The grand finale began as the BrainTrust's anthem saturated the air: Katy Perry's *Firework*.

2

PROS AND CONS AND PIRATES

Fail early, fail often, but always fail forward
   —John C. Maxwell

Dash stood with Ted on the top deck of the *Chiron*. The wind whipped at her, and she kept shaking her head to get her hair out of her eyes.

Three man-size drones whirred above them, struggling to hold position against the gusting air. Ted watched them mournfully.

Dash shook her head. "Bring them in, Ted. I think we've learned as much as we need to."

After bringing the drones back and stowing them, Ted followed Dash glumly to her office. He fingered her jade Ganesha statue as she delivered the final verdict. "I'm sorry, Ted, but as the simulations suggested, they just can't draw enough power from a satellite."

Ted had come to Dash with an idea for a much longer-range copter. Despite the advances the copter engine designers had made in fuel efficiency, there were still places on Earth it was hard to get to. This bugged Ted because he wanted to build a copter for Matt that could go all the way from the BrainTrust to his spaceport in Texas without stopping. Dash similarly wanted to build a copter for Lenora that could get her teams into northwestern China with neither muss nor fuss.

So Ted had dug up some old research on beaming energy from satellites to see if they could power a copter from space. He'd gotten rather excited…more excited than was justified, perhaps. He got even more excited as he read about the ancient experiments with the Stationary High Altitude Relay Platform, SHARP, that had flown in the 80s with 500kw of microwave beams from a ground station.

Dash had thought it was worth investigating, so she'd worked with the satellite engineers on the *Dreams* to build a couple of small prototype power satellites, unfolding large but featherweight and cheap mylar mirrors once in orbit to power free-electron lasers. Matt and SpaceR had chipped in a free launch to Low Earth Orbit (piggy-backed on the launch of a much larger satellite) in exchange for a handful of shares in the venture if it succeeded. Ted had built the prototype drones with his own money.

The drones were quite odd in appearance, with a large top surface covered in multi-junction solar cells that could collect at high efficiency just about any frequency of elec-tromagnetic radiation from low IR to UV-B. The surface sprouted numerous dipole antennas to serve as a basic rectenna for collecting microwaves.

The drones and the satellites communicated not

only about the position of the respective systems but also about the efficiency of transmission of different parts of the spectrum. In the face of cloud cover, for example, the system focused on beaming microwaves. Depending on other atmospheric conditions, the best frequencies could be found in infrared, light, and UV wavelengths.

But as this test had shown, nothing worked very well. The microwave beams spread too wide, while the UV beams scattered too much in the atmosphere. Beaming too much power in the high infrared tended to cook the recipient.

Ted mumbled, "I'm just sure it would work if we could use a carbon nanotube optical rectenna." With such a nantenna, they could get tremendous efficiency in the visible light spectrum.

Dash shook her head. "Perhaps. But we'd need more than a square centimeter of it, and that's about all we could get at the moment."

Ted rose to depart.

Dash sent a few hopeful words after him. "We can't scale it up enough to drive a passenger-carrying copter, but it works moderately well for the lighter drones, especially if we give them more lifting surfaces. I can't think of an application offhand, but there's real potential here."

Ted stopped in the doorway. "If people would just let us plant power-beaming stations here and there on the ground, it would work too. If people could just get along with each other, it would be easy."

Dash had the same thought quite often about many problems, not just this one. But she had been acquiring a disturbingly practical bent since working with Colin. *Fix the problems you can, and leave the others for someone else.*

Still, she suspected the satellite-powered drones could solve the problem…if she could just figure out what the problem was.

Ciara looked over the cast of new candidates for residency on the Prometheus archipelago. Every day a couple of barely seaworthy boats showed up with exhausted yet hopeful recruits.

Most of them had come because they'd passed the preliminary Accel test on their cell phones that suggested they could qualify. Since the preliminary test had evolved into something quite reliable, most of those people easily passed the full rigor of the final test to start new lives as students on the *Mount Parnassus* educational ship. An immersive education in STEM subjects was the first step to becoming productive residents.

Some of the people on the boats came because someone else had told them they'd pass the tests on the BrainTrust for no good reason Ciara could determine. A few of these achieved residential status anyway, usually the ones who had fought their way out of the middle of the Congo, thus demonstrating the kind of relentless determination—the grit—that the BrainTrust prized as much as engineering genius.

This time, one fellow had brought his wife and small son aboard even though he had failed the Accel preliminary test. He pursed his lips stubbornly. "I just know I can be valuable here. I've proven my worth every other place I've ever lived. Please just give me a chance."

He pointed in a direction that made no immediate sense to Ciara. "The men wrangling the bots that clean the passageways. They aren't well-coordinated; they spend half their time cleaning things another of the crew just finished cleaning." He looked down. "Well, not half, but there's an opportunity to make it better. Put me in charge for a few days and let me show you."

Ciara blinked slowly. "So, Oziegbe, you're claiming some sort of exceptional management/leadership talent?"

Oziegbe smacked his hands together. "Yes! Please, just let me demonstrate."

Ciara sighed. "Come with me to the testing facility. I'll put you through the full assessment." She led him down to her offices on the Kentucky Derby deck.

Here the artists in charge of the passages had rendered the walls with gently rolling terrain covered in bluegrass. Horses roamed across verdant valleys, and in one section, a small train of camels angled across the landscape. People who thought they knew Kentucky generally objected to the camels—until they saw the framed photo on the promenade of the actual camels in the actual Kentucky. Ping had just laughed when she'd seen it, explaining to Ciara that she had gone on a camping trip through Kentucky once, sleeping in the bed of their pickup truck, and seen camels just like the photo.

And speaking of the devil, as Ciara and Oziegbe walked along, Ping caught up with them.

While the *Parnassus* had been filling slowly but surely with new members, the fact was, even with only four peacekeepers, they were overstaffed. Ping needed some action, and she clearly kept hoping Ciara would find something for her to do. New candidates made a toothsome opportunity. More than one testing failure had become unruly upon finding he did not qualify.

After Ciara introduced Ping, Oziegbe looked at her in puzzlement. "So, you're the security chief." He hesitated, clearly afraid of being inadequately tactful. "Do you only deal with shipboard trouble? I confess, I'm surprised you haven't gone into Djeregbe to clean things up. They're doing terrible damage to your reputation."

Ping focused on Oziegbe like a hunting tiger that had just caught the scent of prey. "Who's that? What's Djeregbe?"

Ciara at least knew that much. "It's the city—well, the dilapidated town—just north of us that is the closest jump-off point to get here. The original town on the oceanfront was destroyed by floodwaters, of course, but it's experienced a rebirth of sorts as a kind of BrainTrust waystation."

Oziegbe shook his head. "But it's nothing like the BrainTrust. It's…well…it's full of fraudsters and hucksters."

Ping glowed. "How awful!"

Ciara glared darkly. "It's a part of Benin. It's not a part of the BrainTrust, and not within our jurisdiction."

Ping said placatingly, using a Ping variant of the concept of being placating, "Yeah, you're right, but I should probably go see. You know, get eyes on the ground; just a little investigation to see if there's anything we could do that would make it easier for the right people to find their way to us."

Ciara rolled her eyes as she realized she could not stop

her security chief if said chief decided to go. "Investigate *only*. Understand?"

Ping smiled radiantly.

The testing system used to select BrainTrust residents was oriented toward finding people who would succeed as engineers and scientists, but it was based on much older systems that had been designed to identify people with excellent leadership skills. While the preliminary test you could download as an app for a cell phone did not do significant leadership testing, the full system aboard the *Parnassus* did.

When the full assessment was concluded, Ciara nodded, satisfied. "OK, Oziegbe, you win. You're in charge of the ship's cleaning crew until we find something more suitable, a place where you can actually earn your keep. Keep an eye open, since you're as likely as I am to find your real position in this fleet." She tapped out a message on her tablet. "And my mom needs to know that we need to put a section into the Accel testing app to do a preliminary check for top one-percent leadership skills. Truth of the matter is, we need more people like you, Oziegbe."

Oziegbe breathed a sigh that blended both relief and pride, and Ping shook his hand in congratulations.

Ciara pursued her mission to the next step. "Do you happen to have any relatives with your skills? Or ones that might pass the tests to become engineers? We're always eager to explore the possibility of giving a chance to friends and relatives who could arrive on board with a solid social foundation and someone to vouch for them."

Oziegbe shuddered and put up a hand in a halting motion. "My family all died in different terrorist and military raids, and my wife's whole family, hundreds of them, share a widespread belief system best described as a 'cultural kleptocracy.'"

Ciara looked puzzled. "'Cultural kleptocracy?'"

Oziebge nodded. "To describe it the way it works in practice, if you start a new business, you have to hire relatives so they can steal from you. And if you get hired into some other business, you have to get jobs for all your relatives so they can steal from your employer."

He shuddered again. "Under no circumstance should you hire my relatives." He whispered, as if terrified of being overheard, although they were alone, "I would appreciate it if you would tell my wife, however, that it was your strict policy against relatives that left me unable to get them on board."

At this moment, Oziegbe's wife and son chimed in, shouting from far down the passageway as they approached. Oziegbe cried out with glee, "We're in!"

Both the wife and the son hugged him. "Thank you, thank you," they said to Ciara in their limited English.

Then the mother squatted in the middle of the deck and pooped. The son dropped his trousers and followed her example.

Ciara stared. Ping laughed, head shaking. Oziegbe buried his face in his hands. "We're originally from Senegal, you know. The air in that part of the world is, as one Peace Corps doctor described it, 'a fecalized environment.' They're just doing as they were taught."

Ciara muttered. "We need another module in the Accel 'Introduction to the BrainTrust' topic about the proper use of toilets."

Ping pursed her lips speculatively. "You keep telling me that we must support a great diversity of native customs. Celebrate the multicultural clash of ideas. We could just assign a bot to each one, with a pooper scooper attachment, to follow them around."

Ciara reiterated decisively, "Another module in the Accel Introduction."

The sun scoured Khalid's face as he sat down in the open market area to eat. He tugged his keffiyeh farther over his head; something in the motion stirred the air enough to give him a strong whiff of the delicious biryani on the rude table before him. It was too much; his eyes glazed and he sat motionless for a while as the waking nightmare washed over him.

Sometimes the nightmares came at night; sometimes they came when sparked by his environment, like now. He suspected he suffered from severe PTSD, although he had never bothered to get an independent diagnosis. Certainly the events of his life that had shaped him were worthy of a little post-traumatic stress disorder.

Today his waking nightmare was about his last day with his father.

They had lived in a small town just outside Rawah, deep in the Sunni-dominated western region of Iraq.

Khalid had spent the whole afternoon helping repair the decrepit truck that belonged to his neighbors. In exchange for his services, the neighbor let his father borrow the truck from time to time. At the age of six,

Khalid was already the best mechanic in the village and the only one who could keep that truck operational, although he usually needed someone to handle the tools for him. He usually partnered with a sixteen-year-old who was not too bright but had longer arms with much strength. Today Khalid's father helped him.

Evening came, the truck fired up, and they went in to dinner. As Khalid, his father, and his mother ate his mom's delicious biryani, an old argument broke out. His mother quietly insisted that Khalid should get a better education, that he was too smart to be kept here fixing trucks. His father, with growing anger, shouted, asking what she expected him to do about it. Finally, he rose from the table and scourged her, something he had been doing all too often since he'd returned home from the Iraqi Army, from which he'd been dumped by the Americans, along with all the other Sunnis.

A truck pulled up outside their house, the sound of the engine clearly announcing that it was a much newer truck than the neighbor's.

"Get up! Rise and shine!" a harsh voice shouted, followed by harsher laughter. "Time to pay for your sins!" The roar of a long burst of machine gun fire set Khalid's heart pounding in a way the cruel voice never could.

Half a dozen men charged into their home and dragged all three of them into the street.

The cruel men—a Shia death squad, clearly—formed a semicircle around them and forced them to kneel with their hands behind their backs. A good-natured argument arose over who would get to execute the heretics this time, but eventually, the winning soldier raised his rifle and aimed.

Khalid never forgot that rifle—the rifle that destroyed his life and saved him. Years later, when weapons became important to him, he found its designation: an American M16, one of the rifles given to the Iraqi Army after the conquest.

Putting the butt of the assault rifle against his shoulder and taking casual aim, the designated executioner fired. He clearly intended to hose them down.

But he'd barely started firing when the gun jammed. This too Khalid understood, years later. The M16 was a fragile weapon of war, requiring methodical maintenance, the kind of maintenance well-trained, technologically sophisticated Americans performed as a matter of course, which was hopelessly beyond the capabilities of the typical Shiite soldier.

The executioner stood there shaking the rifle, then banging it on the ground.

A radio crackled, and another man answered. After the call ended, he announced, "Enough. We have to get back to base."

Another man objected. "But we aren't done yet."

The apparent leader shrugged. "Good enough."

They continued to squabble as they climbed into the truck and departed.

Moments later, Khalid's mother knelt and wailed over the bloody ruin of his father, who lay in a pool of dark crimson that looked black in the dying light.

The Republic of Benin had had a complicated history long before the arrival of the Prometheus fleet of the BrainTrust Consortium. The tortuous history of dictator Kerekou, who had reigned in unrestrained glory from 1972 to 1991, lavishly exemplified the trials and tribulations of the nation he ruled.

Kerekou had first announced that Benin would transcend all the foolish political persuasions of the time, from capitalism to socialism. In effect, this resulted in personal control by the autocrat, unfettered and impervious to error. Shortly thereafter he declared himself a Marxist, which lasted until he announced he had become Muslim... which lasted until he realized he was a Born-Again Christian. Along the way, he took full control of the educational systems of Benin into his own uniquely capable hands, resulting in the departure of almost all qualified teachers from the nation.

A fully functioning democracy emerged at the turn of the century, and the future brightened. Then West Antarctic Ice Sheet C snapped from its anchorage, sailed majestically into the ocean to warm up and melt down, and lifted the sea level everywhere, including Benin's densely populated coast.

Porto Novo, the nominal capital, and Cotonou, the effective capital and largest city, hunkered at sea level at opposite ends of Lake Nokoue, which was itself mere spitting distance from the Bight of Benin branch of the Atlantic. Both cities sank into the ocean, although Porto Novo, with high plateaus to the north, offered reasonable relocation opportunities for anyone with enough money to build anew…which was to say, almost no one. Still, the official capital moved slightly north and noticeably higher to become the actual capital, in practice as well as in theory.

Little existed south of the Porto Novo Highlands. Nothing, really, except for one saltwater swamp where the destitute and hopeless huddled in the mud. This swamp was built on the remains of the town of Djeregbe, south of Lake Nokoue, a shanty port transformed into a disintegrating, disease-saturated ulcer of a town that viewed itself, with much contemplative mirth, as the Venice of Africa.

Ping muttered as their copter approached, "Mos Eisley, a most wretched hive of scum and villainy."

Diric shook his head. "Mos Eisley was much nicer. At least it was in a clean desert." He swept his hand across the shantytown. "I don't think we can land. Every piece of ground with dirt mounded up high enough to offer a dry spot has a building on it, and we can't set down on a roof because not one of those buildings is strong enough to survive a copter landing."

Ping ran an exasperated hand through her hair. "This copter's supposed to float, although I don't think anyone's tried it lately." The only case where she knew of someone trying to land a copter in the ocean was when Dash had been rescued from kidnappers, and the copter had flipped and sunk. That hardly counted as a good test, though, since the copter was full of bullet holes at the time. That had no doubt caused some modest damage to the copter's seaworthiness along with its hull integrity.

Ping guessed it was time to test the limits of copter tech

once more. "Put her down there, on the water by that pier. We'll see what happens."

They landed. Ping strapped on her batpack, while Diric strapped on his more ordinary day pack. She then fiddled with the release on the storage compartment hatch of the copter and left it open.

They rented a ride on a rowboat between the mounds of dirt that offered dry footing, and eventually they reached the mound that held the tin-roofed wood-planked stall wherein Uteteh's Surefire BrainTrust Admission Training engaged in business.

Before they reached their destination, Ping halted. "Diric, why don't you go ahead and see what he's selling? Before I burn the place down on general principles."

So, Diric came unto Surefire alone and innocent. Slouching slightly to get underneath the tin roof, he smiled wide-eyed at Uteteh. "Can you really guarantee me a place on the BrainTrust?"

Uteteh nodded vigorously. "You look like a smart young man, so I can certainly make you a resident. Let me give you a little test first. Some people need a bit of extra prep work to qualify." He pulled out a deck of flashcards covering a wide diversity of topics. He flipped them at Diric at high speed, jotting down notes about Diric's answers from time to time.

At the end, Diric tapped the cards. "I've heard the BrainTrust tests candidates too. Is it like this?"

Uteteh nodded again. "Yeah, man. I got these cards straight from the archipelago when I was a resident. Before I came back to help people like you. This is the real deal." He frowned. "Now, I have mostly good news."

Diric clasped his hands together prayerfully. "Can I make it?"

"Yeah, yeah. The good news is, you're almost good enough. The bad news is, you're not quite ready. You'll need to study." He slapped a fresh deck of flashcards on the table. "Study diligently with these for twenty-four hours, and you'll be good to go. Only twenty bucks, man, and you'll be using the gold toilets on the BrainTrust in no time."

Diric stood flabbergasted for a moment, a silent pause that Uteteh was more than equipped to fill. "And more good news. I have a charter boat going out to the Brain-Trust day after tomorrow. The boat is almost full, but I have one reservation left. Thirty bucks for the trip, but you better buy it now. I'll be sold out if you wait."

Ping came around the corner, having listened to all this with a bemusement that had slowly simmered into hot anger as she thought about the people this jerk had ripped off. She smiled brightly. "Oh, you're way overbooked already. In fact, you're out of business."

She shrugged off her batpack, which she had filled with suitable supplies for this expedition, jumped lightly over the countertop that separated Uteteh from his customers. "If you had a mediation agreement with the BrainTrust, I'd have to take you to them. But you're in luck; you're going to get off lightly. Give me all the cash you stole from your customers—which is to say, give me all your cash."

Uteteh bunched his fists indignantly. Ping just laughed. "Don't."

Assessing the confidence that confronted him, Uteteh decided the better part of valor was to play along. As

Uteteh handed over his ill-gotten gains, Ping turned to Diric. "Please pull the gas can out of my pack. We're going to build a bonfire."

Uteteh lurched to the front of the shack and screeched out five names. Ping responded by bouncing him off the wall, which unfortunately damaged the wall more than it damaged Uteteh. Indeed, the second bounce smashed the wall out, leaving Uteteh sprawled on the ground beyond the shack. The building now looked a little more modern, approximating the shape of an asymmetric A-frame.

Ping grunted and ducked under the awning.

Diric pointed into the distance and muttered, "Trouble."

Ping followed his finger and immediately cheered up. "Excellent. The local police. I needed to get them all together so we could talk."

The local police force consisted of five large thugs wearing the nondescript rags of their profession.

Ping approached them, waving her new-found wealth. "Guys, I have a job for you."

The nominal leader called, "Actually, it looks like you have money that belongs to us."

Ping stuffed the cash back in her pocket. "Ah, a hard negotiator. Cool." As the men settled into a circle around her, Ping leapt toward the nearest one, and kept running from one to the next faster than the thugs could keep track.

A few moments later, the five thugs lay in five piles of meat.

Ping stopped to take a breath. "Five men in one minute. Could Jam do that? Maybe, but I can do better too. My speed can definitely be improved upon."

Ping went around the circle again, inspecting their

injuries. She kicked one. "Hey, nice elbow to the eyeball." She touched the bruise under her eye.

She kicked another one. "And good kick to the knee. Almost got me." She stepped away and put her hands on her hips. "You'll all do for the moment. Like I said earlier, I have a job for you."

The men slowly sat up. The leader, in pain, whispered, "What job?"

Ping waved her hand around the ruins of Djeregbe. "You're going to go to all the rip-off places like Uteteh's and collect all their money. If they give you trouble, tear their stores down. I'll leave you the gasoline. Any questions?"

The leader asked the obvious question. "How will we know who all the rip-off joints are?"

Ping pointed dramatically at Uteteh, who was holding onto a corner of his ex-storefront for support, wobbling as the building made repeated efforts to fall down. "Uteteh here will point out all his competitors. Right, Uteteh?"

Uteteh recognized a boss when one hit him on the head. "Yeah, that's right."

The men's eyes lit up as they thought about the payday they would get.

Ping waved a finger back and forth. "No, no. I can see what you're thinking. Don't make a mistake. You're going to collect the money and give it to my representative when he gets here." Seeing the sly expressions on the faces, she continued, "No, no. I can see what you're thinking." She pointed into the sky. "See the giant dirigible up there loaded with telescopic cameras?"

The men peered up. The leader mumbled, "I don't see nuthin'."

Ping nodded. "Exactly. You're under continuous surveillance, and you can't even see where it's from. But look here." She fiddled with her cell phone, brought up a real-time view of their little circle, and held it in front of each man so he could see himself being recorded. "You can't move an inch without me seeing it. Try to steal from me, and you'll be sensationally sorry. You'll be my example for everyone in town." She gesticulated with some carefully crafted insanity. "Everyone will enjoy the show."

After the former thugs and the former con artist shuffled off to their new duties, Ping called the BrainTrust. "Ciara, I've got a fine project for Oziegbe. He was right; this place needs a wholesale makeover. It makes sense for us to have a station here for the people who come in hopes of joining us, but it needs to be built from scratch. Send bots. Lots of bots. And let's get these people hooked up with Accel, see how many of them we can put to work for us here in Djeregbe. Who knows? Maybe we can even pick up a resident or two." Ping listened with surprising patience as Ciara objected. "A part of Benin? Look at the pics I'm sending you. Benin abandoned this place decades ago. No one's going to fight over this swamp full of sewage. Trust me."

After a few more words that led to a tentative agreement, Ping snapped her phone shut. As she and Diric returned to their copter, Diric asked, "Why'd you let them go? They're thugs. Was it really wise to give them jobs?"

Ping shrugged. "You know, I wasn't entirely joking when I called them the local cops. They clearly work for some kind of local business association keeping order, or they'd have ripped off Uteteh themselves. The main problem is, they don't shut down the frauds and scammers like full-fledged policemen would. But it seems likely that most of them are trainable."

Ping brightened as she had a thought. "I'll put Gleb in charge." Gleb was an ex-Spetsnaz commando with whom the BrainTrust had a complicated history. He was now working at an ill-suited job with the Prometheus, subsidized by the Russian oligarch he had tried to assassinate. "He's a little too rough-and-tumble for peacekeeper work on the Prometheus archipelago, but he might work out here. Certainly he can teach them discipline."

Diric looked into the sky and asked one last question, wonderingly, "Do we really have a dirigible hovering overhead so high we can't see it?"

Ping laughed lightly. "Not a technology we offer quite yet. No, when we got out of the copter, I released a bunch of mini-vid drones, the same kind we used on the *Storm King* before Abshir took command. I just wanted our new employees to think the cameras were invulnerable so they wouldn't get any bright ideas about knocking them out." She chuckled. "I think it worked, don't you?"

Ping watched Djeregbe shrink in the distance as Diric flew their copter home. Suddenly an excited voice burst forth from the radio. "Hey, Boss, this is Captain Abshir. We've just spotted what looks like pirates grabbing a girl in the middle of the ocean. I've brought the *Storm King* up to full speed, but we're pretty far away. Can you get to her sooner?" He quoted a set of coordinates.

Diric veered toward the conflict and gunned the engines. Ping answered Abshir, "We're on our way! Can you slow 'em down?" Over the radio, she heard the distinctive sound of the 50mm firing.

Abshir sounded smug. "That rattled their cages. We dropped one off their stern, and their boat's bouncing all over the place." He yelled, off-microphone but loud enough for Ping to hear, "Nice shooting!"

Then he growled. "They're back up to speed. And I'm afraid to fire again since they're too close to the girl."

Diric pointed out the cockpit. "I see them."

At first glance, it appeared that the old speedboat with four men aboard was trying to rescue the girl. She was all alone on a piece of wood about the size of a boogie board, nine miles out to sea. One would presume her to be a survivor from a sunken boat. But looking more, carefully Ping could barely discern some sort of paddles on her hands and fins on her feet, suggesting, insanely enough, that she was out here intentionally. Swimming to the BrainTrust? Crazy as it seemed, Ping knew of other cases of people going through more horrific trials than this to get to the place where hope for a brighter future still existed.

Meanwhile, the way the men on the boat were laughing and taunting her and the way the girl veered away from them to try to escape, waving them off from time to time, clearly indicated that rescue was not the men's primary goal.

Ping bit her lip. "We're still too far. Hey, Abshir, have

you kicked in the supercapacitors?" The *Storm King* had been one of the first platforms to receive the new graphene power storage systems to soak up excess power during normal operations, which could be used to augment operations in an emergency. The supercapacitor had an energy density comparable to a lithium-ion battery, but a power density a thousand times greater. It could pour out electricity in an unbelievable torrent when required.

Abshir snorted. "Of course. That was the first thing we did. It's working great, and we're at forty knots, but it's still not good enough."

"Well, that girl will just have to hang tough." Ping continued to peer at the boat, wondering if Abshir wouldn't need to rescue the men as well. The speeder was not really designed for ocean waters, although it was apparently more or less adequate here in the Bight of Benin…if you were foolhardy enough.

The men—the pirates—dragged the screaming, struggling girl on board, cheering now and giving the finger to the *Storm King* since they knew the BrainTrust patrol boat could no longer shoot at them once they had a hostage on board. They accelerated away, then, as they saw Ping's copter approach, angled away from the copter and shook their fists in the air.

Ping stayed focused on the girl. "There's something wrong with her arms," she muttered. Her eyes were pulled away by a change in the movement of the *Storm King*. The ship was slowing down.

Abshir swore over the radio. "I pushed too hard and wiped out our emergency power too quick. Very inefficient of me. If I'd done this right, the power would have lasted a lot longer, and we'd have gone almost as fast. Sorry." He paused. "I don't think we can catch that speedboat at all on standard power. Looks like it's up to you."

Ping smiled wickedly. "It's like Disneyland here today, just going from one fun event to the next. Not a problem, Captain." She looked at Diric. "Drop me into the middle of that boatload of idiots please."

Diric frowned. "If they've got guns, they'll blast us on the approach."

Ping peered at the boat again, then shook her head. "These are low-end pirates, Diric. I think they're armed mostly with knives."

"I guess we'll find out." Diric soared in low, and sure enough, no machine-gun fire greeted them.

"OK!" Ping shouted, "Yippee!" She dropped into the boat, falling slightly to starboard as the vessel veered to port to try to avoid her landing.

Four men stood up on the dinky ship to confront her, causing the boat to sway wildly in the choppy seas. As Ping had predicted, they were armed mostly with kitchen knives.

But the man on the tiller had a rusty old pistol. He fired twice.

Ping twisted out of the way of the first shot, clearing the way for the bullet to strike the man closest to her as he tried to stab her with his knife. Ping jumped to the rail of the boat to dodge the second bullet, but it was unnecessary: the bullet jammed in the pistol's chamber and exploded in the wielder's face.

A perfect storm of simultaneous events followed. Ping tipped the boat by standing on the rail. The pistol owner rocked the boat further as he staggered blindly around. The man hit by the first bullet stumbled into the starboard side, and a gentle wave wobbled the vessel from the port side. Altogether, they managed to lurch the ship far enough to capsize.

The girl in the bow screamed and thrashed as she went into the water. The men screamed as well, but Ping paid no attention, swimming smoothly around the pirates to reach the girl.

Finally Ping got a good look at the girl's arms, which had looked so odd from a distance. What had looked like paddles from a distance *were* in fact paddles strapped to her arms, extending all the way from her elbows to her hands...except she had no hands.

The sight was jarring, even incomprehensible for a moment. Finally Ping realized that this girl was a victim of one of the several amputation campaigns that had swept through Africa over the course of the years. Ping had heard of this, but some part of her mind, some civilized part, hadn't really believed it despite all the horrors she had witnessed.

Ping shook her head. "Hold on..." she started to tell the girl before realizing that holding on was not something she could do. "Wrap your arms around my shoulders. Don't choke me, but don't let go." Then Ping realized that, with her phone and translator app underwater, the girl probably didn't understand English either, so she started to pantomime.

But Ping had underestimated her new charge, who responded, "'K," and complied. Ping turned to the pirates.

The one who had owned the pistol, still blind, was

simply flailing in the water, screaming. The one who had been shot had disappeared; Ping thought a small cluster of bubbles might mark the location of his passage. The other two had abandoned their knives, along with any attempts to attack Ping or grab the girl as they struggled to right the overturned speedboat. Success evaded them with deft surety in the chop.

Ping put some distance between herself and them nonetheless. Shortly, the *Storm King* arrived and threw a rope net over the side. Ping eased up to the net and spoke once more to the girl, whose teeth were now chattering behind blue lips, "Hold on really tight. Just another minute more." The girl nodded, and Ping climbed slowly up the side of the ship.

When they reached the deck, two of Abshir's crewmen wrapped them in blankets. They paused for a moment at the sight of the girl's arms, then finishing the wrapping process as if it were nothing out of the ordinary. It occurred to Ping that in this part of the world, her ex-pirate crew had seen it before.

A second team of sailors started hauling up the net. Ping was about to order them to halt, but Abshir beat her to it. "Leave the net down. We'll rescue the other four," he bellowed.

One member of the team squinted out to sea. "Only two left, Captain."

Abshir threw his hands in the air. "OK, we'll rescue the last two."

"Aye, aye, Captain," the net handlers responded morosely.

One of the handlers shook the net vigorously. "They're having trouble hanging onto the rope," he announced.

Abshir's second in command hung over the rail with the rusty old knife he'd cherished since his pirating days, presumably in case the surviving kidnappers had any fight left in them. "Ow!" He held up his hand, letting blood drip from his palm into the ocean. He snuck a furtive glance at Ping. "Knife slipped."

Ping growled, "That blood'll attract sharks. Better get those two out of the water fast."

The net handler shook the net again. "They're still having a lot of trouble holding on. Not quite sure why."

The second in command muttered, "My blood hardly makes a difference. The sharks are on their way anyway, what with the way the two dead ones are bleeding out."

At that point, screaming started from over the side of the ship—the kind of screaming that comes from yelling as hard and as fast as you could draw breath.

The net handler shook his head. "Too late," he announced.

The second in command offered a few words of comfort. "Captain, Miss Ping, it's really all for the best. I mean, sure, we were all pirates before you took us on, but we were just trying to feed our families." He pointed over the side. "Those guys were rapists and murderers—a wholly different kind of beast. They really *were* bad guys."

Ping glared at the men, trying to decide how angry she should be. Abshir shook his head. "And there you have it, Boss. The moral high ground on the high seas of Africa."

Ping turned her glare on her captain, then on his second in command. She sighed and said quietly to Abshir,

"Could you at least get him a better knife? If he's gonna cut himself like that often, it would be good if he didn't get tetanus or a fungus that'll eat his insides out."

Abshir shrugged. "I'll try, but he's very attached to that knife." He paused, thinking about alternatives. "I can probably get him to grind off the rust and oil the blade, anyway."

Ping just rolled her eyes.

3

BIG DEALS

It's not the size of the dog in the fight, it's the size of the fight in the dog.
—Mark Twain

At the clack of high heels on the marble floor, Gina Toscano put down her jasmine tea and rose from the booth she had commandeered in the *Haven*'s "business" cafeteria. Most of the cafeterias on the *Haven* had plush surroundings that absorbed sound and allowed quiet conversation, but the business cafeteria had gone the extra mile: noise canceling speakers rose inconspicuously between all the booths and tables, turning them into islands of privacy where guests could discuss the most sensitive of topics, from product release dates to quarterly revenue shortfalls. And of course, to get into the place, you had to either be a resident or be accompanied by a resident. While every ship in the archipelago was required to have a main public promenade connected by gangway to the main promenades of the adjacent ships, the business cafeteria was ever so private.

A tall blonde woman in her late thirties, wearing a severe white sheath with pearls swaying from her neck entered the room and narrowed her eyes as she searched for someone. Gina waved warmly to her, and she smiled, more or less, and came over. "Gina," the woman said graciously.

"Dawn." They pecked each other on the cheek. "Thank you for seeing me." As they sat down, Gina continued, "You're looking well." Gina only barely knew Dawn, having initially met her at the First Launch party thrown by Ben Wilson. Now they both lived on the *Haven*. Gina had moved there with Matt after the California government had assaulted SpaceR, and Dawn had come a few months later after Cogent News broke the story of the list of billionaires targeted for civil forfeiture.

Dawn's media empire, which she'd taken over running when her grandmother Anne Rainer was stricken with dementia, was in the middle of the list of forfeiture targets. Gina had been surprised at first that Dawn wasn't at the top of the list—she had one of the largest fortunes in the world, enough to keep California afloat for months if not years—but the editor of Cogent had explained it. While Dawn had plenty of money, she also had plenty of political pull, since her media empire could make or break the typical ambitious politician.

So the California government had chosen caution in the beginning, but now that Dawn was on the BrainTrust, they were too late to do anything except mourn the lost opportunity.

Dawn responded to Gina's ever-so-correct compliment on her looks with surprising vehemence. "Oh, please, Gina. You're a Vogue model. You know better. I look worn and drawn. The family business is killing me." She took a moment to order espresso from the server bot, then continued, "If we were sitting down with a gaggle of vicious social climbers ready to spill half-true gossip about everyone missing from the table, you'd be saying the right thing." She shook her head. "But you said you wanted to talk business. I require more truthfulness than that from my business partners."

Gina felt the tension fall from her shoulders. "Oh, thank God, Dawn. And yes, you do look a little the worse for wear." She took a sip of tea. "When Matt looks like you do and I tell him, he always thanks me and says he needs to do a better job of delegating."

Dawn gave her another smile, sincere this time. "And does he follow his own advice?"

Gina shrugged. "Sometimes. Usually. Eventually."

"Well, I shall try to do as well as your husband." Her espresso arrived, and she took a sip. "What did you want to see me about?"

Gina lifted her tablet onto the table and turned it so they could both see the screen. "Ships."

Dawn raised an eyebrow. "Ships? Isn't that a bit outside your area of expertise? Mine too, for that matter."

"Yes, but when Matt muttered about having a little spare capacity on the *Helios*, and I mentioned it where Colin could overhear, he hooked me up with Alex Turner on the *Argus*." The *Argus* was the ship-manufacturing vessel of the BrainTrust archipelago, and the *Helios* was the rocket-manufacturing ship for SpaceR.

"According to Alex, the *Argus* is also coming to the end of its current run, with the deployment of the last of the five spaceport ships for Matt's Global Express." Gina's eyes gleamed with excitement. "It's time to build a new kind of isle ship—a mostly-residential ship like the *Haven*, where people can buy cabins larger than the standard BrainTrust issue, but more affordable than the *Haven*. Not so ridiculously..." She searched for the word.

Dawn supplied it. "Ostentatious?"

Gina shrugged. "Close enough."

Dawn shook her head. "These isle ships are incredibly expensive. It needs to be as upscale as the *Haven* to pay for itself."

Gina smiled in triumph. "Not anymore. Alex has been teaching me about the newest features." She flipped pages on the tablet to display her numbers. "The *Haven* was built in San Diego using the same methods and materials used in the original isle ships. Even without the gold-plated bathroom fixtures, it was wicked expensive. But here on the BrainTrust, they've been driving the costs down kind of frenetically. The hull is made from calcium carbonate with magnesium rebar, all locally produced from the sea. The superstructure is again mostly salt-water-extracted magnesium, and the labor costs have fallen by a factor of ten as they've standardized the ship-building process and programmed the bots more effectively. For general-purpose manufacture, a bot wrangler typically manages a swarm of ten bots, but with the standardized programming, a single wrangler can handle a swarm of forty."

Dawn studied the numbers. "OK, I see how the costs have fallen since the first ships were built—by well over half. But they're still expensive." She rolled the screen some more, looking deeper into the numbers. "The reactors are still a big factor even though their costs have fallen too, I guess because of the mass-production assembly line they created after they started selling the reactors commercially."

Gina looked at Dawn with mild astonishment and considerable approval. Anne Rainer had had three children and a host of grandchildren, so Gina realized it shouldn't be a surprise that the one placed in charge of the family empire should be frighteningly smart. "That's what Alex says, but it's better than that. The reactors turn a profit."

Dawn raised a skeptical eyebrow.

Gina continued, undeterred. "The new line of beta batteries Dash and Rhett developed are so popular, there's a waiting list two years out to get them." The beta batteries, using Sr-90 as the energy source, had been invented just over a year ago. Even Dmitri Mikhailov—the Russian oligarch who was, if not the BrainTrust's most important resident, certainly its most grandiose—was getting his yacht retrofitted, replacing the *Buccaneer*'s diesels. "The critical ingredient is the strontium, which has to be bred in a nuclear reactor. So we breed and sell the strontium to pay for the nukes."

Dawn pursed her lips as if irritated at the smooth flow of answers, but the corners of her mouth curled in a smile, and a twinkle lit her eyes. "The titanium for plating all the exposed magnesium is also quite dear."

Gina laughed. "Manganese phosphate is a well-known anti-corrosion coating. The Fuxing archipelago is mining manganese from the ocean floor so successfully that the manganese market is at risk of crashing. We use almost no titanium in the new design."

Dawn scanned the numbers. "You think you can cut the cost in half again?"

"At least," Gina agreed.

Dawn shook her head in amazement. "So, how would this work? I put up the money, you oversee the operation?"

Gina huffed. "I'm putting up some money too." She pointed at the existing list of investments, including her own. She watched Dawn's eyes light when she spotted small amounts from both Ben and Dmitri.

Dawn stayed focused on Gina's investment, however. "I'm astonished that you have this much capital." She continued reluctantly, "Honestly, I've been surprised you could afford your mortgage on the *Haven*." The mansion-cabins on the *Haven*, designed for billionaires, were breath-takingly expensive—the most expensive real estate on the planet.

Gina sighed. "It was a struggle when we first arrived. Matt had just become CEO, and I'd semi-retired. But there wasn't anyplace else to stay, and Ben gave us a good deal on his." Which was to say, Ben had barely doubled his money. "But that was then, this is now. With the Starry Night satellites operational and the Global Express running to five space-ports, our stock is way up, and Matt's awash in bonus money."

After a pause, Gina added, trying not to sound too proud, "Most of this investment is mine, though. I've done pretty well myself, with my own SpaceR stock and a couple other little undertakings." Matt had just about gone through the roof when he'd learned that Gina had invested half of her own money in SpaceR when the stock had crashed during the battle with the California governor. As Matt had explained in a voice that did not quite scream, they needed diversification, not even more dependence on a single financial bet! She'd done well and gotten out, but he still grumbled about it.

Dawn laughed, and her whole visage seemed to relax. "Speaking of investments, you do realize this will hurt the value of our homes? Even if it's not quite as aristocratic as the *Haven*, it'll soften demand."

Gina had been afraid of this, so there was no point trying to lie about it to Dawn. "Yes, of course. I'm OK with it if you are."

Dawn nodded. "As Andy Grove, the CEO of Intel, used to say, 'Eat your own children before someone else eats them.'"

Both of them sipped their drinks. Dawn finished first. "Next question."

Gina laughed in response, guessing what was coming. "Customers. Demand."

Dawn laughed once more. "Exactly."

Gina flipped the tablet to another page. "As it happens, a lot of SpaceR people are looking to get out of the cramped quarters they're in. The archipelago never fully absorbed the influx of people when SpaceR moved out here, so I've got about half the ship's cabins reserved already." She pointed at the list.

Dawn just shook her head. "I give up. But there's still a problem." She started modifying the numbers on the sheets. Gina's eyes widened.

Dawn explained, "Please understand that my investment requirements are a little different from most people's. The ships are now cheap enough, but I would have trouble justifying an investment in just one ship. It's too small an amount to allow reasonable tracking. We will need to build at least two." She stuck out her hand for a handshake and Gina took it.

After Dawn left, Gina whipped out her phone. "Roberta! Hey, you surviving the real estate crash in California? Pretty awful? Yeah, I thought it might be like that. Pack your bags, girl. Have I got a deal for you! Real estate...yeah, real estate on the BrainTrust. I need a pro realtor out here ASAP."

<hr>

The girl with no hands lay on a hospital bed in the med bay of the *Mount Parnassus*. She still looked a little blue, but at least her teeth had stopped chattering. "My name is Shura," she declared in her little girl's voice. "I would like to apply for residency on the Prometheus archipelago."

Ciara looked upon her with eyes that glistened with unshed tears. "Application accepted. Request granted. I'll be giving you some tests to explore your strengths and weaknesses so you can get a fast start, but you're in. As soon as you're discharged, one of your new roommates will show you to your room."

Shura's eyes closed and her whole body relaxed in relief. "Thank you."

Ping chimed in, "You were kind of out of it when we rescued you, so I thought I'd mention that the thugs who assaulted you have been taken care of. They won't hurt anyone ever again."

Ciara looked at Ping appreciatively, as if surprised by such a tactful explanation that a bunch of people had been killed.

Shura held up her arms. "They were hardly the most terrible people I've met." She pursed her lips. "The Benin Beloved Chief Advisor for Life's army did this to me before he became the Beloved Advisor. When he came through my home town in the Dahomey region." She shuddered. "When I was a little girl. "

By most standards, she was still a little girl, but no one commented.

Shura continued, "My mom refused to marry any of the soldiers, so they did this to me, then killed her."

Ciara looked at Dr. Donald Giesen. "This brings us round to the next and bigger question. What can you do for her, Doctor?"

Dr. Giesen was Canadian by birth. The Canadian medical system, run top to bottom as a government fiefdom, had developed an unorthodox solution to the problem of doctors who threatened to make enough money to make it look inadequately socialistic: they had set an upper limit to the amount of money a doctor could make.

So Dr. Giesen and his wife had embraced the system the way a number of other doctors had: they worked hard for about eight months of the year, then slipped off to the Bahamas to sip margaritas for the other four.

When the BrainTrust first started seeking medical professionals willing to telecommute, it had been a natural segue for them to sip fewer margaritas while continuing to give medical care over the web. And when Canada changed its policies to allow full-time doctoring, they decided to forgo the opportunity to labor continuously in wintry Canada and turned to BrainTrust telecommuting from the beach full-time.

But even life in paradise grows old for some people. Donald and his wife (who was also a doctor) had thought in their youth about doing a stint with Doctors without Borders but had never taken the plunge. It had grown into a regret, so when the Prometheus fleet set sail for Africa, the advertisement for a medical team to join the fleet caught their attention. They could get paid, live in a safe place, and still do some good for people for whom top-of-the-line treatment for a gunshot wound was a clean rag.

The Giesens' first satisfying success had been Abshir, who should have died on his trip to the Prometheus archipelago while crossing the heart of Africa from Somalia. His had been an exciting case.

Shura, however, presented an even more extreme problem. Donald shook his head at Ciara. "The BrainTrust does of course have a couple of bionic hands in advanced prototyping, but they're shockingly expensive. And honestly, Sara and I are not qualified to attach them."

Shura piped up, "I don't really need hands. I can run

Accel on a tablet with a stylus and a mechanical gripper I've designed." She spoke more softly, uncertain but hopeful. "I will need someone to help attach the stylus to my arm, and I'm hoping I can use the 3D printers to make the gripper." Her voice fell to a whisper. "I don't have a tablet, either."

Ciara patted her shoulder. "All problems easily taken care of. At least that can get you started." She pursed her lips. "We'll have to think about what to do about the bionic hands."

Ping, of course, knew exactly what to do about the bionic hands. Moments after departing Shura's hospital room, she called Dash.

Once upon a time, Khalid remembered, he had had dreams. Many different kinds of dreams: some flying, some laughing, some...happy.

For some time now, he had primarily had nightmares. Four nightmares in particular. He'd stopped trying to escape them. Tonight was his mother's night.

At the tender age of nine, Khalid had become a book-keeper in nearby Rawah. His customer base had grown at an astonishing rate as word spread throughout the merchant community that there was a child who could do your books not only more quickly and more cheaply, but at least as reliably as anyone else. His name was frequently mentioned at gatherings as an example of the speaker's generosity in helping the poor.

The fact that no one could imagine a nine-year-old

engaging in embezzlement didn't hurt the growth of his customer list either.

His mother insisted on spending a ridiculous amount of the money on books—textbooks on math and science. He enjoyed the books, which he considered light reading, but wished his mother would let him buy her new clothes more often. And maybe an occasional ice cream cone.

Then one day a dozen pickups had roared into Rawah from the west, with men shooting their rifles in the air. "You are liberated," they exclaimed joyfully. "You are now a part of the Daesh Caliphate."

Khalid had heard of the Daesh, of course. They'd been roaming and conquering in northern Syria for a while now and were called ISIS by Westerners.

While the Daesh were not murderous heretics like the Shiites, they still had a bad habit of killing anyone who objected to their rule. Khalid half-walked, half-ran, home, pounding the dusty road with sandals ill-suited to the pace.

Upon arrival, he breathlessly commanded his mother, "We have to leave now. Daesh has come."

His mother knew the stories as well as he did, and her eyes grew wide. But she clutched her hijab and said, in a strangled mixture of fear and hope, "I'm sure they'll leave us in peace. They aren't Shiites, after all." She shuddered, clearly remembering the death of her husband.

Khalid shook his head. "Mom, listen to yourself. You know better. They burn even Sunnis alive for no identifiable reason."

A pair of pickups roared through the village and stopped in front of Khalid's house. Khalid couldn't stop shaking with his memory of the last time this had happened, but he was the man of the house now. He took a deep breath and went out to meet them.

One of his customers, surrounded by Daesh thugs, pointed at him. "That's Khalid. He's the one who's great with numbers."

The apparent leader nodded brusquely. "Get in the truck. We've been capturing oil wells as often as we can, millions and millions of dollars' worth, and we need an accountant we can trust." He opened the door to the lead pickup for Khalid.

His mother came running out, wailing. "You can't take him like this. He's just a boy."

Two of the men leveled their weapons and opened up on her, leaving her more bullet-ridden than Khalid's father had been. Khalid stared at them, stupefied, and again the shapes of the weapons stuck in his mind. More American M16s, undoubtedly captured from the Iraqi Army when Daesh had slaughtered all the soldiers at a depot.

Khalid launched himself at one of the men, too blinded by rage to think at all. The leader grabbed him by his collar, however, and hoisted him into the truck. "It's OK," the man said soothingly. "You're with us now. It's probably better this way."

Khalid sat in the truck, staring with glazed eyes into the distance and breathing raggedly as the miles slipped by.

Long before dawn, in the inky blackness before anyone with a cell phone cam could see, a helicopter emblazoned with the crest of the Great Blue State of California slunk up to land on the helipad of the GS *Prime*. As the copter blades spun down, Keenan Stull stepped forward to personally greet the VIPs. Hunched over in their dark gray suits, holding their hands up as if to mask their faces from an importuning camera, they hustled after him as he led them off the open roof and down the ramps to the Cherry Blossom deck.

Normally Keenan enjoyed bringing his customers to the Babylon deck, where his own office resided. But the scene of the Tower of Babel was, honestly, a bit proud, or even arrogant. He was pretty sure these guests would not appreciate the display of the Triumph of Man. His guests themselves were as arrogant as any he had received, but they didn't like anyone else feeling equally proud. Hence the cherry blossoms.

The cherry tree renditions on the passage walls, depicting paths through Washington DC, were unrealistic. In the GS *Prime* representation, both the Yoshino cherry trees with their single white blossoms and the Kwanzan trees with clusters of double pink blossoms were in full bloom at the same time. Nature didn't work like that; in the real world, one set of blossoms died before the other came to life. Goldman Sachs, of course, tried to achieve these kinds of results with all the blossoms open all the time. Once in a while, they even succeeded.

Keenan turned left before reaching the Lincoln Memorial and entered the Jokichi Conference room. The fragrance from the National Cherry Blossom Festival permeated the air.

They seated themselves around the conference table, and Keenan offered to get the coffee for them himself since they had explicitly requested no witnesses, not even an administrative staffer. These particular guests would surely take offense if he used a general purpose butler bot.

As Keenan brought them the cups, he finally turned to business. "First of all, thank you for coming to us for your financial needs. We are, as you know, a full-service provider. Governor, Attorney General, how can we here on the GS *Prime* assist you?"

The AG leapt directly into the explanation. "No one will give us a decent deal on a bond issue. Here we are, sitting on the richest state in the richest country in the world, and no one will give us a loan without trying to rip us off." The AG's words came out in vicious bursts. "It's not like we're fiscally irresponsible. We ran a surplus last year, for heaven's sake. How many states can claim that?" He half-rose from the table as if preparing to attack the man offering to be their savior.

Keenan had seen it before. The more desperate and afraid the customer, the more viciously he assaulted the only people who could save him. Keenan was confident he knew the general outline of the request. The public records told the story of California's financial predicament, and the recent government-backed referendum to overturn California's balanced budget law told its own story.

Keenan was frankly surprised they'd bothered with the referendum. The paths to circumvent the legal constraints were numerous, and California had used almost all of them on its journey to its current situation. One of the lunchtime games played on the GS *Prime* was, "What's the cleverest way to raise lots of cash on behalf of governments hamstrung by balanced budget laws?" The best ideas were cataloged for later use; California was not the first government entity to come to GS for assistance, after all. Immense fortunes had been made, and would continue to be made, facilitating society's guardians in their desperate efforts to bypass their own regulations.

Keenan spoke soothingly. "Don't let them worry you. The people you've spoken to up to this point have a rather simplistic understanding of finance." Of course, Keenan, with a Harvard degree and a background in the rough-and-tumble world of commodities futures, thought almost everybody in the financial world had a simplistic understanding of finance. "We just need to get you into more sophisticated instruments than the kinds of issues offered by a small-town PTA to fund its cheerleader squad."

The AG seemed mollified. Too mollified, Keenan realized. If the AG were too complacent, he might quibble about the cut GS would take. "But let's be clear. We have some work to do to make your paper attractive." He gestured for the wallscreen to come alive. "Let's take a look at the problems you have so we can come to a shared understanding of the project."

Both guests squirmed in their chairs at this but nodded acquiescence.

Keenan began, "Of course, the proximate reason you're here is the rather dramatic loss of revenues that has occurred since your remarkable surplus of last year. But that's not all. You had immense long-term obligations before this recent hiccup."

This time the governor objected. "But we've run balanced budgets for generations. We have no debt. Until recently, it was illegal!"

Keenan chuckled. "I didn't say you had debt, I said you had *obligations*. Take the state employees' pension fund, for example. You're looking at several hundred billion in obligations, against which your annual budget currently applies less than two billion. For an investor looking for a reliable income stream, these obligations represent extreme risk. What are the chances that the courts will find the guarantees made to the lenders higher priority than the demands of the retired union employees?"

Keenan popped numbers and figures on the screen until his guests' eyes glazed, as he had intended. The goal in this part of the discussion was to make the client acutely aware of just how desperately he needed GS's unique expertise, and how reasonable the profits GS would accrue seemed in the face of such a daunting undertaking.

He switched tracks. "So that's what we're up against. Fortunately, we here at GS have had decades of experience with these dilemmas, and we can design a suite of instruments just for you." He flipped to a new page on the wallscreen. "First, we'll reduce your visible obligations to make it clear that, despite the revenue shortfalls, you're actually pulling out of the hole. This will make your eventual offering much more attractive."

The AG shook his head in disbelief. "You can reduce our debt?"

Keenan did not answer directly since he did not want to have to distinguish between *obligations* and *visible obligations*. Instead, he told another truth. "We'll undertake what's known as a cross-currency swap using off-market rates. You'll put the money we lend you for the swap into the pension fund, demonstrating your management excellence." He took a breath. "This is where another of your assets comes into play."

The governor looked at him in astonishment. "We have assets?"

Keenan nodded. "Of course. Specifically, CalPERS, the pension fund itself. If you make CalPERS into the lead buyer of your bonds, others will follow. Despite being dramatically underfunded, the California Public Employees' Retirement System has an enormous pool of funds with which to buy California state bonds. And once they buy in, proving it's a good deal, you can play the same game with CalSTRS, the teachers' retirement fund."

The AG laughed with glee, and the Governor stuttered, "But wouldn't that be illegal?"

Keenan chuckled. "Oh, if you were a private company, they'd throw you in jail for a century for investing the pension fund in your own stock. But you're not a company; you're a government. What we're discussing here is pretty much the same deal as what the Feds do when they force the Social Security Administration to buy Treasury bonds. It's all perfectly legal."

The AG smacked his hands together. "Sounds completely reasonable."

Keenan continued, "Then, as the final enticement to buyers, we'll issue the bonds with a sliding interest scale ending in a modest balloon payment some years from now."

The governor frowned. "Balloon payment?"

Keenan continued smoothly, "And of course we'll give you our Best Customers deal: no interest for the first three years." Known historically as the 'teaser rate,' the Best Customers deal had come to be known among Keenan's friends who regularly did these types of government deals as the "sucker punch."

The AG's ears perked up. "No interest?"

They had lunch, dining on filet mignon and Cajun blackened salmon while the computers dotted the i's and crossed the t's on the detailed workup. The Governor and the AG had relaxed to the point where they even allowed Keenan's assistant to bring in the food.

As his admin cleared away the dessert tray, now empty of all chocolate mousse, old-fashioned paper spat from a slit in the tabletop. Keenan drew a line on the paper to mark the beginning of a pair of columns of numbers. On the left, in a large, elegant font, was the sequence of repayments if the swaps worked well. On the right, in a smaller font, was the sequence if the vicissitudes of fortune proved unfavorable. "This will be your schedule of payments," he explained.

The first numbers were quite low in both columns, and, being monthly, stayed low for the entire first page. Given the short duration of the politicians' attention span, they lost interest before they came to the place where payments started growing at an exponential rate. Keenan finished by pulling out the last, blank sheet of paper and writing in large, bold script the amount of money they'd get immediately to start spending. The paper he wrote upon was a soft, luxurious vellum, proven via scientific testing to hold the recipient's attention in a soothing way.

The Governor sat up straighter as he looked at the rather magnificent amount of money California would get from GS upon signing the deal. "Impressive. I had no idea we could work it out this well."

Keenan smiled. "We are here to serve." The smiled turned sober. He moved to their side of the table and pointed at a dark circle by the wallscreen opposite them. "Now, please look up at the certifying vidcam while we run through a couple of perfunctory corporate policy requirements." These requirements had been imposed by the executives years earlier to mitigate the legal issues from certain kinds of scandals resulting from misunderstandings. "First of all, you do understand that, in order to pay off the later parts of the loan, you will have to ensure that the State of California recovers, to create surpluses capable of covering these debts?"

The AG waved his hand dismissively. "Of course. Our newest program, the Affordable Child, Worker, and Consumer Protection Act, is going great. The rate at which it's spending money—"

The Governor interrupted. "Investing. It's investing—"

"—the rate at which it's investing money is just fabulous. It'll surely pay off long before these loans come due."

Keenan nodded with the same sober sincerity he would have displayed had he actually taken this explanation seriously. "Excellent. Finally, I need you to acknowledge that you are sophisticated financial investors, fully capable of understanding the intricacies of complex contractual relationships, and that you thus understand the agreement we have here?"

The AG snorted. "Of course. Everybody in the State of

California knows we're smart about financing. They wouldn't have authorized us to do this otherwise."

The enormity of this assertion held Keenan transfixed for a moment, but no hint of his reaction clouded his features. The vidcam was capturing his expression, after all, on an unalterable legal recording now embedded in the SmartCoin blockchain. He nodded gravely once more. "Of course. As I said, this is just a formality."

As they climbed onto their helicopter, the AG clutched the paper Keenan had given him and chortled. "What a bunch of suckers, giving us that much easy money with so little hassle."

The Governor was not quite as comfortable with the deal as the AG. "He's right, you know. We have to make sure the economy recovers so we can repay this loan. We could really use some new corporate giants paying taxes and buying real estate." He waxed philosophical for a moment. "Wouldn't it be interesting to know exactly what the characteristics of a state are that stimulate great innovation? The birth of new businesses? The creation of whole new multi-billion-dollar industries?"

The Attorney General snorted. "Who cares? All I know is, whatever makes a state great, we've got plenty of it—more than anybody else."

The Governor's failure to acknowledge the certainty of this claim hung in the air.

The AG waved his hand dismissively once more. "Besides, what's the worst case? Even if the economy recovers more slowly than expected, that balloon payment won't come due until your last term is over. It'll be the next guy's problem."

The Governor cheered up. "Good point."

Keenan called the GS CEO, Larry Winters, after washing his hands in a futile attempt to remove the stain from them. Keenan enjoyed working on the BrainTrust tremendously. Not only did he make a lot of money, but he knew he'd done well by doing good. He felt enormous pride in the work he'd done to help SpaceR get new projects off the ground, and some of the projects on the Fuxing archipelago promised to be just as rewarding. He loved working with people who knew what they were doing.

But helping governments spend money their taxpayers didn't have always left him feeling tainted.

Larry apparently didn't notice. "I see you were quite generous with the upfront disbursement."

Keenan grimaced. "The AG was hooked minutes after they walked in, but the Governor was suspicious. I figured some shock and awe would help. The last thing we needed was for them to go traipsing over to the *Wells Morgan* and asking some random passerby over there for other offers. No one ever wins in those kinds of bidding wars." This reminded Keenan of why it made no sense to feel guilty about working with politicians: when a fool has money, you have to hurry to be the one who parts them.

Larry grunted. "So you sweetened the pot rather than risk competition. Good call."

Keenan voiced his concern. "We want to get flat on this offering as soon as possible, of course." In financial parlance, "flat" was the state in which GS, as the market-maker, had long positions and short positions that balanced out. It was the moral equivalent of a gambling house with respect to a game of poker; the house didn't care who won and who lost since they took their cut in the entrance fee or a percentage of the pot. At the moment, GS owned a lot of paper betting California would make its payment schedule and was committed to selling more. "Selling the against positions should be easy, but…"

Larry offered comforting words. "We have lots of customers interested in non-correlating hedge opportunities, even if the risk is pretty wild. Shouldn't be a problem." Larry asked the question Keenan had been dreading. "I don't suppose you can entice any of your BrainTrust customers into getting in on this action?"

Keenan tried to visualize himself explaining these bonds to Ben. Or Matt. Or Amanda or Colin or Qi Ru. "Not a chance. They're not morons."

Ping was sparring with Marcos, one of the other three peacekeepers with the Prometheus fleet, when her phone rang with a blast of music from the Trans-Siberian Orchestra. "Gleb! How's the new town coming?"

The sound of gunfire—probably AK-47s—came over the line. "Somebody just showed up claiming he owns this place. They sort of have uniforms, so they might be Army. It's kind of hard to tell around here. Anyway, my guys all ran for cover. We hadn't yet let any of them have guns, for good reason, and this new guy has a team fully loaded."

More shots were fired. "I might be able to take them myself, but they've also got a technical." A *technical*, in this part of Africa, was typically a pickup truck with a .30 caliber machine gun anchored in the back. "I figured I'd call before I went after them in case you wanted to send backup." He paused. "Or in case you wanted to come for the fun of it."

Ping contained her desire to jump up and down and yip with glee. "Good thinking. With a bunch of machine guns blasting the countryside, no telling if someone might get hurt accidentally. We're on it."

She turned to Marcos. "Get Putu and Soup. We punch out for Djeregbe in ten minutes." She hit speed dial on her phone. "Abshir, time for us to explore the utility of Naval power in a coastal engagement. Head for town, full speed. Yeah, kick in the supercapacitors—but calmly, Abshir. Keep a little power in reserve." She laughed. "Who knows, the guy who thinks he owns our town may have a navy too."

Thirty minutes later, the full military power of the Prometheus archipelago assaulted Djeregbe. Ping watched from her copter as Abshir turned the *Storm King* to starboard and slowed to a minimal cruising speed, gracefully slewing the 50mm gun to keep pointing in the town's direction.

She spotted a series of flashes from a point a little northeast of the town; the technical was firing at her. "How charming," she said to Putu as he wheeled the copter a little higher and westward while continuing into town. "They have no idea what their effective range is."

She peered at the vehicle a bit longer. "And they have no idea how to drive, either, apparently. Looks like it's stuck in the mud." A handful of men were trying to hoist the truck out of a bog while the machine gunner fired, resulting in a spray of gunfire that seemed more likely to hit one of the men in the bog than one of the copters overhead.

As Ping and Putu zoomed over the town, a cluster of men with machine guns waved them in the air, firing almost as wildly as the technical in the bog. Putu glanced down. "Oh, no, they're pulling down your pretty sign."

Ping growled. Oziegbe's first project upon setting forth to reconstruct the city had been to replace Uteteh's Surefire BrainTrust Admission Training with a crisp white three-story concrete building named Ping's Surefire Brain-Trust Admission Testing—Free!

Ping had complained that the name was ridiculous, even though it was truthful marketing. They *had* installed a complete facility for doing BrainTrust admittance testing. People who passed the free test got free ferry rides out to their new homes on the archipelago.

Ping had thought the building was a great idea, but demanded they change the name. Oziegbe had been adamant. "We did a lot of A/B market testing, and this name is a winner. In the local community, 'surefire' is a very positive adjective, not a scam word. And Ping, well, the word 'Ping,' is now a hot brand. It stands for honor, justice, and the crushing of sleazeballs."

She'd insisted they change the name anyway, but Ciara

had insisted they keep it. "Use what works," Ciara had said, "And consider it penance for dragging us into this undertaking."

Given that history, Ping now considered letting the new arrivals tear the sign down unmolested. She sighed. Oziegbe would just make another one, no doubt with the word Ping in even bigger, bolder letters.

And speaking of Oziegbe, she saw him several dirt mounds away from the Surefire mound. Gleb accompanied him.

Ping considered leaning out of the copter with her sniper rifle and plinking a few rounds at the shooters below, but the copter was not stable enough for real sniper work, and if she hit the Surefire building, Oziegbe would undoubtedly complain. Instead, she pointed at Oziegbe and Gleb on the ground. "Let's get the team together."

Soon both copters had landed in the swampy water near Gleb and Oziegbe. Ping, Putu, Marcos, and Soup hopped onto the muddy land.

Gleb stared at Ping in puzzlement. "I thought you'd bring your Big Gun."

Ping rolled her eyes. "For what, six guys and a pickup? Please, a little finesse." She hoisted her McMillan TAC-50 sniper rifle, known as a Big Mac, and tapped it. "See? Finesse." She put it down. "Besides, I brought the *Storm King* in case we need a little more oomph."

After a brief discussion, they left Oziegbe behind and abused their copters by using them as boats, floating through the channels with their canopies down and guns up to the far side of a mound adjacent to the one holding the Surefire building.

Reaching dry land, they circled around a crude grocery market on the top of the dirt heap, telling the man and woman therein to stay down. Over by the SureFire, the enemy soldiers spotted them and fired a few rounds. Ping's men retreated across the peak of their mound, dropped to the ground so just their heads and rifles appeared over the crest, and shot a few rounds over the heads of the enemy. The enemy took positions on the far side of the crest of *their* mound that mirrored Ping's deployment.

The leader yelled, "Are you Ping? You trying to take my town? This is *my* town. This is *my* building." He spat on the ground. He waved at the technical in the distance. "Come on, show them!"

The men on the technical surely could not hear but got the message nonetheless. They started firing.

Ping yelled at the leader, "Tell them to stop! Someone could get hurt!"

The leader gave her a wide grin missing only three teeth.

Ping pursed her lips in exasperation. She set the Big Mac at a new angle and snapped off a shot.

The man in the back of the technical firing the machine gun fell backward off the truck.

The leader stared at the tactical, then pointed at Ping. "You killed my man! You can't kill my men!" He leapt to his feet. "You can't kill me! If you kill me, my brother will cut off your hands! And cut off your head! Then feed you to the sharks! Ha!" Apparently an ever-so-slight speck of doubt about the quality of his brother's revenge caused him to hunker back down after waving to the technical.

Putu observed philosophically, "I've always been

puzzled by threats like that. I mean, if he cuts off your head, why would you care if he feeds you to the sharks?"

On the technical, another man rose to take the place of the dead gunner. The goons' boss shouted again, this time from a prone position over the crest, "Shoot another of my men, and we'll open fire for real!"

Ping rubbed her temples. Should she just shoot the goons' boss? It would surely end this confrontation. She muttered to her team, "Anybody have any clue who his brother is?"

Gleb snorted. "When that idiot first showed up, Uteteh ran off shouting, 'Now we're done for! Now we're done for!' His brother's probably some dipshit gangster in Porto Novo." He pointed to the technical still stuck in the bog, unable to reach the town. "Honestly, who cares? Our village here has many disadvantages, but it's certainly defensible."

The technical still barked occasional bursts that threatened to hurt innocent bystanders, if not any of the hunkered-down members of the team. Ping spoke to Abshir, who was dialed in through her earbud. "Abshir, you see the technical off in the distance? Would you please ensure that they cease and desist?"

Moments later, the dim boom of a small cannon firing far across the ocean preceded a large splash behind the truck. A second boom sounded. The third boom came, not from the ocean, but from the location of the truck, after which there was no more truck.

Ping muttered to herself, "OK, so *that's* what I'm going to do with a Navy." She yelled at the goon boss, who was still gaping at the place where his truck had been, "Go home and don't come back." She curled her lip, thinking about what Ciara would say, and added, "Please."

Her opponent, rather than responding politely to her polite request, leapt up and gesticulated wildly. "You can't do that! You can't do that!" He stomped across the mound toward them.

Ping sighed. "I give up. Gleb, Marcos, which one of you did best in your last sniper practice?"

Marcos frowned. Gleb thrust a finger into his own chest. "I did."

Ping slid the Big Mac over to him. "Finish this."

The Brother To Someone Important was still yelling at them when Gleb finished it.

The five surviving soldiers lay over the crest, unable to decide what to do.

Ping shouted, "Throw your guns down. Hands in the air. Stand up and walk this way." As they hesitated, she continued, "Or I'll have my ship blast you the same way it blasted the technical."

Putu whispered, "Uh, Boss, you can't really do that. You'd damage the SureFire."

Ping shrugged. "How could they possibly know that?"

Abshir suddenly broke in on her earbud with an edge of panic in his voice. "I'm under attack! Both of the other two Benin patrol boats are bearing down on us."

Ping's heart leapt in her throat. Apparently the boss she'd just shot did indeed have a Navy, one twice as large as her own.

Repeated sounds of artillery fire came through from Abshir's end. After a long pause, Abshir spoke more calmly. "You know, it really makes a big difference to have your gun slaved to a radar-guided rangefinder. Looks like they're surrendering. I think we have two more ships." He paused. "Make that one more ship. The other one's pretty much gone already."

While this was going on, the men who had worked for the goon with the navy came out with their hands up.

Another short trip through the channels, still ignominiously using the copters as boats, brought Ping's team to the prisoners. Ping spent the time stewing and wondering who the idiot she'd just had Gleb shoot was.

At this point, Uteteh ran out of the building. He looked down in horror at the dead leader. "Oh, no," he wailed. "We're dead for sure now. No, no, no!"

Ping stared at him. "Why? Because of his brother? Who the heck *is* his brother, anyway?"

When Uteteh told her, she slumped.

Gleb offered philosophically, "Well, I was right. His brother *is* a dipshit gangster from Porto Novo. More or less."

Ping groaned. "Ciara's just going to love this," she observed mournfully.

4

ENOUGH IS ENOUGH

Men should be either treated generously or destroyed, because they take revenge for slight injuries - for heavy ones they cannot.
　　—Niccolò Machiavelli

Khalid stood in the comforting warmth of the shower, soaping up after examining the corpses of the newest batch of dead mice. He didn't touch the mice, of course—they were sealed in the biosafety cabinet—but working with them always made him feel a need to get clean.

He dropped the soap. "No," he whispered as another waking nightmare found him.

He stood with his wife Anjum in the shower, gently rubbing her distended belly with soap. "I can feel our daughter kicking," he whispered in her ear.

Anjum kissed him. "I'll just bet you can. I'm sure that's

the only reason you're taking so long. My tummy is now the cleanest thing in all of Palestine."

Khalid had escaped from Daesh not long after the Americans started taking out the leadership with precision-guided munitions from drones in the sky. As chaos descended on the organization, he undertook three tasks. First, he started laying aside large piles of cash that he believed he could use for worthier purposes than genocide. Second, he tracked down the two men who had opened fire on his mother. This took a lot of time; his memory of their faces was crisp, but he had neither names nor paper trails that might give him a clue as to their whereabouts.

He was not exactly sure what he was going to do when he found them. He was not a murderer. Far from it. While he had learned far more about weaponry than Daesh realized while going through a little basic combat training, he remained uncomfortable with guns.

The issue turned out to be moot. He found the men together in a pile of bodies taken from a cavalcade of trucks hammered by Hellfire missiles.

Before he left Daesh, he had to figure out where to go.

Khalid had made a friend, Sabaah el-Vaziri. They'd spent a lot of time together. Almost all their time, actually, because the leadership had assigned Sabaah as Khalid's keeper to make sure Khalid didn't forget his enforced loyalty. One reason they'd picked Sabaah for this duty was, he too was mathematically gifted, and while not an off-the-scales genius like Khalid, the leadership figured he had a better chance of noticing any accounting irregularities if Khalid got naughty.

Sabaah had come from Palestine to join the cause—to

help build the Islamic State predicted by the Koran and to participate in the prophesied great battle in Dabiq where the Muslims would route the Christians, thus marking the beginning of the end of times.

But as Predators roamed freely across the skies, blotting out targets with careless certainty, Sabaah had grown increasingly despondent. It became clear that the leader of Daesh was not, in fact, the Mahdi, that American firepower could not be overcome with prayer and dedication, and that the battle in Dabiq would have to take place in a more distant future when the Muslims would stand a fucking chance.

Khalid had encouraged Sabaah's despondency. Eventually, Sabaah had suggested they escape together. Khalid had agreed reluctantly to the plan for which he'd carefully laid out all the pieces for Sabaah to assemble.

So, after faking their own deaths at a level of detail so glorious even Khalid was convinced they'd been martyred, he'd wound up in Palestine, introduced to Sabaah's community as a brave and true fighter for Muslim justice and supremacy.

With his many millions in funds quietly lifted from Daesh coffers, Khalid for the first time had the opportunity to think about what he wanted to do with his life. When an outbreak of cholera struck Bani Suheila, he went to help. He learned many things. One thing he learned was that medicine was clearly his calling; he loved saving people in that way. Another thing he learned was that, in at least some plagues, death was the result of stupidity. In the face of cholera, a simple pallet of Gatorade could keep a family alive until they recovered.

One such family he'd helped had a daughter, Anjum, who worshiped the ground he walked on for saving their lives. One thing led to another. While he started planning to go to med school, she started planning the wedding. One thing led to another. He postponed his education for a while longer, until after the baby would be born.

So they were in the shower together when an American-made Israeli F15 roared overhead, shaking the windows. He wrapped his arms around his wife, gripping her tightly in a desperate effort to protect her.

As he later learned, the Israelis had identified the location where a number of high-profile Hamas leaders were planning a terrorist attack. They had swooped in and launched an American Joint Direct Attack Munition guided bomb. These bombs were precision weapons like the Hellfires launched by Predators, but on this particular bomb, one of the guidance fins locked up and the pilot lost control. It spun down too far from Hamas to damage the target, but close enough to Khalid to destroy everything.

Khalid still didn't understand why he had survived. The blast had lifted both him and Anjum off their feet, spun them apart like toys, and dropped multiple walls upon them. One wall crushed Anjum. Two walls crashed into each other above Khalid, leaving him in a triangular hollow from which a team led by Sabaah rescued him unscathed.

Sabaah took him home, fed him, and tried to make him feel better. "It is a gift from Allah," he explained. "You are here for a purpose. You are destined to do great things."

While lying trapped in helpless darkness under the building, Khalid had moved beyond rage. His mind had turned cold and clear, and his extraordinary analytical powers pursued new solutions to problems he'd never before acknowledged in their entirety.

So when Sabaah'd told him he had a destiny, he had responded with quiet determination, "Enough is enough. They all must go." He took a sip of the Faygo root beer Sabaah had supplied. "Intolerant Shias, intolerant Sunnis, the Jews, the Christians, and above all the Americans—all the corrupt leaderships of all the world. The entirety of modern evil civilization. All must burn." He'd closed his eyes for a moment. "I have a plan."

"Allahu akbar," Sabaah responded reverently.

Khalid had watched uncomfortably as Sabaah silently mouthed the word, "Mahdi."

Of one thing Khalid was sure: he was not the Mahdi, the foretold spiritual and temporal leader who would rule before the end of the world and restore religion and justice. He might be the herald of the Mahdi, he supposed, but he honestly had no real use for such labels anymore, if he had ever had.

Well, actually, he *did* have a use for such labels. His plan required becoming well enough known to establish an elite core of true believers. So he did not correct his oldest— nay, his only—friend. The Mahdi they wanted him to be? Herald of the Mahdi he would become.

Back on the Kentucky Derby deck of the *Mt. Parnassus*, Ping stepped into a small conference room and plunked herself down in a chair next to Ciara. Through the door of the room, they could see a chunk of a public open area where the Kentucky Derby racetrack was rendered on the wall. The horses stirred in their starting positions, then, as they sprang forth, a huge cloud of dust churned upward, covering the track in a light-brown cloud.

Ping offered the people in the room a sickly smile. "I'm really sorry."

Ciara's eyes glowed with unholy green fire. "Do I remember you? Are you the one who said, 'Oh, Benin abandoned this place decades ago? Nobody's going to fight with us over it, trust me?' That was you, right?"

Ping winced.

Oziegbe, on the other side of the table, offered some perspective. "She wasn't lying, you know. Benin really *did* abandon the place for decades." He wilted as Ciara turned her stare upon him. "But, uh, as we've now learned, they got interested in it again when it became the waystation for reaching the Prometheus archipelago. There was apparently enough money to be made for, uh, people to reconsider its value."

Ping threw her hands in the air. "How could I have known that jerk was the brother of Benin's Beloved Chief Advisor for Life?"

Ciara put her hands out in front of her as if she were trying to strangle someone. "You could have asked him before you blew him away. Did you consider that?"

Ping blew out a breath. "Yeah, OK, but honestly, I don't think it would have made a difference. The guy was nuts. It's a miracle nobody got killed." As Ciara opened her mouth to object, Ping continued, "Nobody anyone would care about, anyway."

Ciara pounded her fist on the table and jumped up to

start pacing. "'Nobody anyone would care about?' Except for Benin's top dictator!"

Oziegbe interrupted again. "Ping really did have to stop him. He was defacing her sign."

Ciara turned away. A sound like the tortured hybrid of a snort and a gurgled laugh came from her. Nonetheless, by the time she turned back, she had regained her stern visage. "Do we have a plan? Other than watching the entire Benin army descend on Djergbe?"

Ping looked at her feet. "Could we offer to make reparations? I could go meet him in Porto Novo, see if we could maybe cut a deal."

Ciara blinked. "Reparations? Money? Would that work? It's his brother we're talking about here."

Oziegbe nodded vigorously. "It could certainly work. For the Beloved Advisor, gold is thicker than blood." He winced. "It might take a lot of gold, though."

Ciara winced. "How much?"

Oziegbe winced again, gave her a guess, and winced a third time as he watched Ciara wince again.

Ping threw her hands up. "At the end of the day, it's not *that* much. Maybe I can get him to agree to stop his Navy from pirating everybody, while we're at it."

Ciara slashed with her hand, striking that idea aside. "His pirates we can handle. Actually, I think we already own his entire Navy at this point, after Abshir's little scuffle." She pursed her lips. "But it would be good if you could get a deal for a better price. Don't lead with our final offer, OK?"

Ping gave her a rather fine facsimile of a salute. "I'll negotiate a better price. You can count on me."

The CEO for CalPERS answered her phone, "Marlene Beane speaking."

"Marlene, good to hear your voice. This is the Attorney General speaking."

Marlene rolled her eyes. What did this nitwit want? "Yes?"

The AG's voice was ebullient. "I have a great new investment opportunity for you guys. We have a new bond issue."

Marlene had feared the possibility of getting this phone call ever since California had passed the referendum allowing the government to officially go into debt. "No. I'm not going to tie the retirement funds of all the state's employees to the success of the government's policies. It would be a legal nightmare, for one thing."

The AG turned on as much charm as he could muster. "Don't worry, Marlene. I have it on good authority there's no problem."

Marlene pulled out her tablet. "Who told you this?"

A long pause ensued, as if the AG were reluctant to tell her. "Keenan Stull on the GS *Prime*."

Marlene turned away from the phone and screamed into her fist.

The AG continued, "I'm sending you the details now. Take a look. If I understand it correctly, it's a sweet deal. Should help you with your underfunding problem."

Marlene started reading the terms of the deal. Unlike the politicians, she was hobbled by a deep understanding of mathematics. She shouted, "Send the money back now! Cancel this deal! Please, Attorney General."

The AG turned stubborn. "We're already spending the money. Couldn't pass up a deal like this." His voice became strident. "And you're by God going to support us by buying some of these bonds." He named a number.

Sweat broke out on Marlene's brow.

"Do it," the AG commanded, and hung up.

Marlene stared at her tablet. She could refuse; technically and on paper, CalPERS was an independent entity. But in reality, the relationship between CalPERS and the California state government was more complicated than that. At the end of the day, she knew, the AG and the Governor had the juice.

If she quit, they'd just get someone else, someone incompetent enough to think this was a good deal. She could raise a media stink, but what good would that do? Everybody loved the Governor these days.

In the end, she called Keenan Stull. Here she found someone she could actually talk to intelligently, even if he was nominally her enemy in this matter.

By the time she got off the phone, Keenan had her personally well positioned in the derivatives trades associated with the California bond issue. The government might go to hell in a handbasket, but if it did, she at least would do quite well by it.

Khalid set the test tubes into the centrifuge and watched them spin. The smooth, nearly invisible motion mesmerized him. "*Allah yil'an ibleesik/il-shaytan!*" he exclaimed in fury at himself. He knew never to watch the centrifuge spin, but he had been working day and night to prepare the first nation-scale experiment. His concentration had slipped.

He tried to lift his eyes to look at something else, the CRISPIER perhaps, but it was too late. The spinning centrifuge led to the waking nightmare.

From Palestine, Khalid had gone to Lebanon—to the American University in Beirut, a well-known and excellent medical school. As he had planned before his wife's murder, he went into medicine to study virology and become the world's foremost expert in the field. It was all the same, and yet so different. His final goal was now a nearly perfect mirror reversal of the goal that had driven him when he'd first learned how to deal with cholera epidemics.

Khalid was blowing through the curriculum at a pace never before seen by the medical professors. He was nominally a sophomore, but such terminology no longer applied; he was also taking senior and graduate-level courses simultaneously. Had he taken an exam to become a certified doctor, he would have passed easily.

At the moment when the whole building shook and the windows broke, he was watching his test tubes in the centrifuge spin.

Beirut had once been a tolerant, cosmopolitan marvel. Sunnis, Shias, Druze, diverse Christians…in total, eighteen different government-recognized religious sects lived in harmony. They had gotten along quite well for years on end.

Then things changed, for reasons much debated.

Hezbollah, a Shiite organization, developed a combat power comparable to that of the official Army with the help of weapons and training from Iran. Most people didn't fear them too much—most of the time—because Hezbollah viewed the Israelis as their main enemies—most of the time.

While Khalid watched the centrifuge, an elite Hezbollah action team in a building down the street planned a hit on an Israeli elementary school. The Israelis learned of it, and flagrantly violated Lebanon's sovereign airspace with a pair of American F35s that poured American Maverick missiles into the place. The precision-guided missiles struck true, but the overkill the Israelis had felt necessary to ensure everyone involved was eliminated caused considerable collateral damage.

While Khalid knew nothing of the Hezbollah planning, he suspected the missile strike might afford an opportunity he had awaited. He grabbed the medical bag he occasionally used when traveling to poorer sections of the nation to practice his skills and raced to the scene of destruction.

He performed triage and fixed people with minor injuries until he came to a tall fellow with a smashed face. The injury was terrible, making identification difficult, but despite that, Khalid recognized the victim as one of several university students he had been watching for recruitment.

A shadow blocked the sun overhead. "Sabaah, help me get him out of here."

Sabaah looked at the unconscious man doubtfully. "You know he's almost certainly a Shiite heretic."

Khalid closed his eyes and counted to three. "And that makes a difference how?"

Sabaah reached down and grabbed the man's shoulders. "You grab the legs," he recommended. "Where are we going with him?"

Khalid took this as an acknowledgment that being a Shiite made no difference. "Almost anywhere away from here for now. If they pick him up and take him to the hospital, he'll almost certainly be interrogated for involvement in some Hezbollah plot or another, and they'll probably figure out that he is indeed a Hezbollah operative."

As they carried the man away, Sabaah raised an eyebrow. "And you know that how?"

Khalid shifted his arms to rebalance the load. "Trust me." He added just a little bit more, "His name is Uwais."

So they carried the giant into one of the medical buildings that had sufficient equipment for Khalid to operate on him.

Uwais stirred on the cot in the classroom where Khalid had hung a sign saying, "Fumigation in progress. Please move all classes outside."

Khalid checked his pupils. "Can you hear me?"

Uwais nodded slightly.

"You're in a place where no one will find you, so don't worry about the cops." Khalid licked his lips. "I've worked on your face. After a couple more surgeries, I'm confident you'll have no visible scars, but I was unable to repair all the damage to the underlying muscles. I'm terribly sorry."

Uwais gave him a hint of a shrug.

Khalid dove into his sales pitch. He knew it was premature, but he felt a certain impatience to be moving forward on additional parts of his plan. "Uwais, I know several things about you. I know you are studying aeronautical engineering with a focus on rocketry. I know you're a combat-trained member of Hezbollah."

At this moment, Sabaah appeared on the other side of the cot. "But there are several things we don't know as well."

Khalid frowned at Sabaah. "Would you be interested in striking a serious blow for Islam? I don't mean more stupid raids on the Israelis, I mean a vast, shattering blow that would prepare the way for the Mahdi?"

Uwais gave another barely recognizable nod, but his eyes opened wide at last and gleamed.

Sabaah insisted on getting his question into the mix. "Even if it means working with Sunnis? Khalid here and I are both Sunnis, you know."

Uwais shifted to look Sabaah up and down. Another small nod followed.

Ping strolled through the Darby O'Gill Deck of the *Parnassus* in search of the small park where Shura hung out. Leprechauns lurched through the fields rendered on the passage walls, hauling cauldrons of gold. A double rainbow arched away just off to Ping's left, almost within touching distance. As she walked, the rainbow slid along beside her, and when she jumped at it, the rainbow jumped away as well, forever just beyond reach.

Ping gave up trying to touch the rainbow after three tries, and Ciara sidled up to her. "She's off the charts, you know."

They turned a corner and saw a statue of a white-furred pooka, mostly in the shape of a unicorn, just inside the park. A small child straddled the pooka's back, delighted to be seeing all the land from so high up.

Ping raised an eyebrow. "Shura's off the charts? Intelligence?"

Ciara nodded.

"So, how off the charts is she? As much as Dash?"

Ciara barked a rueful laugh. "I have no idea. Dash absolutely refuses to let us test her." She frowned. "Not even when we tell her it's for science. She just goes off on a meticulous explanation of how, when J.P. Guilford did a factor analysis of intelligence, he found over one hundred different kinds of intelligence, of which I.Q. only measures eight." Ciara shrugged. "She's right, of course. And though we do a lot better than the old I.Q. tests, our protocol still leaves a lot to be desired. We undoubtedly reject people who would be great BrainTrusters if the testing were better, but for the sake of the survival of the archipelago, we have to be conservative."

Ping shook a finger at Ciara. "Ha! You and your scientific pretensions. You can't fool Dash."

Ciara shrugged. "She seems so nice, so quiet, so accommodating. But there's this hard core that won't budge."

Ping pumped a fist in triumph. "Yes! Jam and I have taught her something after all." She grudgingly continued after a moment, "Although she might have been like that before. Hard to tell."

They came upon Shura. The girl was sitting at a picnic table, bent over her tablet, tapping it furiously with her stylus. Sounds murmured from the device as she achieved various educational goals. Eventually a particularly conclusive note sounded. Shura sat up, stretching her back. She blinked at her visitors, slowly focusing her eyes. "Hi."

Ping smiled. "I just came to see how you were doing. Pretty well, it looks like." She nodded at the gripper on one arm, a mechanical contraption sufficiently complex that Ping could not deduce its operation, not even when Shura flicked it to shut off the tablet.

Shura gave them an excited thirteen-year-old smile. "This is great! I love it all, though I especially love the biology. Especially molecular biology. I have a bunch of ideas." She looked sharply at Ciara. "Do we have a CRISPIER on board? I've heard we do, but I haven't found it yet."

Ciara laughed, glancing at Ping with a "See what I mean?" look. "We do, as it happens, but the documentation is pretty rudimentary."

Shura shrugged. "I can probably figure it out." She turned to Ping. "What's up?"

"I know you spent some time in Porto Novo. Surprisingly few of our people have been there. I was wondering, if it wasn't too upsetting, if you could tell me a little bit about it."

Shura smiled. "Thank you for asking. I hear you're going to visit the Beloved Advisor." Her eyes grew haunted. "You're going to give him money?"

Ping thought about asking her how the hell she'd found

that out, but decided she didn't want to know. "Yeah, but I'm under strict orders to negotiate a good deal."

Shura's eyes grew darker. "I told you his men did this."

Ping nodded. Prior to his ascension to Advisorhood, the Advisor had been the leader of the Islamic State Benin Province, an offshoot of Boko Haram, one of the most brutal terrorist organizations in the world. While the West was fixated on ISIS in Syria and Iraq, Boko Haram cut a far bloodier swath through Africa. The reason ISIS upset Westerners more was marketing: when ISIS performed an atrocity, they posted the video on YouTube. Boko Haram preferred a less public style.

In any event, when Benin found itself caught between rising seas to the south and declining rainfall and drought to the north, the soon-to-be Beloved Advisor saw his opportunity and brought his men to Benin.

The first buildings of the new capital had hardly gone up when Islamic State Benin Province declared itself the government. In a hard-fought but swift campaign against the demoralized Benin Army, the ISBP reminded the world that one could sometimes compensate for poor equipment and worse discipline by being sufficiently brutal and bloodthirsty.

Once in office, ISBP raised their standard of excellence in fomenting terror to new heights, prominently featuring a campaign of hand amputations.

Shura continued in a near-whisper, "I went to Porto Novo to see if I could figure out how to kill him. And the others." She stared wide-eyed into the distance. "All the ones who were there when they killed my mother. I shall never forget their faces."

Looking into her eyes, Ping could see them moving from one soldier to the next as she relived the scene. Ping shivered.

Ciara coughed. "I understand your desire, but, much as I hate it, we have to make a deal with him. Perhaps you could help with the layout of the capitol and the soldiers, and anything you learned about the Advisor while studying him that would give Ping a better chance of getting in and out of a meeting with the Advisor without being, uh—"

Shura completed the sentence. "Without being tortured and murdered."

Ping nodded. "Yes, I'd like that. Quite a bit, actually."

Shura smiled sunnily again. "I can help you with that. You must certainly not just call his secretary to set up a meeting. That would be very risky. Since you killed his brother, he might very well take whatever money you offer him, then kill you." She looked away. Her eyes turned dreamy. "You have to make sure that part of the deal is ongoing, so he has an incentive to leave you alive."

Ciara murmured, "Iterative cooperative game theory. I can't wait until you get to that module."

Shura's eyes went from dreamy to hard in a blink. "I am happy to help you, but I have a condition."

It was Ping's turn to blink. "What would you like?"

Shura's expression turned pouty; for a moment, she was an ordinary thirteen-year-old. "You have to take me with you," she blurted. "I want to look him in the eyes." Her expression flickered between sly and shy. "I will be your conscience."

Ciara snorted. "Ping's conscience is quite healthy, actually."

But one of the consequences of Ping's version of a conscience was that she felt guilty about cutting a deal with the man who had done this to Shura. She figured the least Shura deserved was a chance to see the man at the epicenter of her rage if that was what she wanted. "Deal."

5

LET SLIP THE DOGS OF

Been reading up on the DIY creation of transgenetic chimeras. Amazing how approachable the once difficult techniques have become. Very interesting!

—David Gagliano, software engineering alpha geek, with no particular knowledge of molecular biology, Facebook post, 2018

The Abdeen Palace in Cairo is considered one of the most luxurious palaces in the world, with five hundred suites and more antique clocks, most of which are decorated with pure gold.

The design is simple and functional: a long white block, two stories tall. Each floor contains windows in parallel running into the distance with a machine-precision regularity normally associated with parts coming off an assembly line.

The Beloved Chief Advisor's palace was modeled on

Abdeen, although it was somewhat humbler. It was only half as long, with only two hundred fifty suites. It housed more people, however, because half the suites had been turned into barracks to bunk soldiers for the protection of the Beloved from his adoring populace.

The crisp white facade of the Porto Novo Palace had also experienced some modification as reinterpreted for Benin's capital. It had been enhanced with edging of colorful LED lights, perhaps placed there to draw the eye away from a small flaw: the building of the palace had been directly overseen by the Beloved Advisor's brother, who knew little about construction and less about concrete. Errors in the mixing of the concrete had led to dramatic premature aging in the rather wet and always salty air of Novo Porto Highlands. The brilliant white exterior had evolved, therefore, into a mottled gray that showed to its best advantage under overcast skies on the brink of a rainstorm.

One aspect of the original palace had been improved upon quite dramatically. At Abdeen, the fence to separate the palace from the peasants had been black wrought iron. Technology had moved on, driven forward as usual by the Americans. So the barrier around the Porto Novo Palace was constructed from the same beautiful rust-colored thirty-foot-tall steel slats as The Wall built by the United States along the Mexican border. The Beloved Advisor liked to think of himself as a trend pimp, having been the first among dictators everywhere to not only copy The Wall but indeed to buy the panels from the very company that had manufactured The Wall in the first place.

Ping muttered as the guards escorted her, Gleb, and

Shura through the gate, "You know, with twenty bucks' worth of rope and PVC pipe, I could turn that thing into a climbing wall for children."

Gleb answered cheerfully, "But not with a hundred guys with machine guns watching you."

Shura observed more analytically, "The fastest way over is to go up in a cherry picker and rappel down the far side on a rope. In my practice runs, I made it in twenty-three seconds." She looked down her arms. "Using special tools, of course."

Ping looked down at Shura once more. The girl wore elegant clothing from the BrainTrust. After much discussion with Ciara, they had all agreed that Ping and Shura should look resplendently wealthy, in hopes of persuading the Advisor that he could make more by agreeing to a regular plunder timetable rather than just killing the woman who'd whacked his brother on the spot.

Ping of course wore the Versace strapless, fully beaded thigh-length dress covered in Warhol icons that Dash had bought her for First Launch, complete with the Vivienne Westwood diamond necklace so long it fell to her hips. Shura's only jewelry was a rather odd necklace, with a pendant consisting of a long curved piece of lacquered wood, thickly wrapped in tight, black and gold and red string. Ping hadn't had the heart to tell her it wasn't quite appropriate. "For my mother," Shura had explained the piece when Ciara offered her something with rubies instead. That settled the discussion.

When they reached the outer office of the Beloved Advisor's inner sanctum, a lithe woman wearing robes of rich red and gold welcomed them and performed a very thorough check for weapons.

In the end, the admin sent them on to the Beloved Chief Advisor for Life, who awaited them. As they approached his office, they could hear him cheering as if watching some kind of game on TV, rooting for the team that had just scored.

Upon entering the room, the first thing Ping saw was guards stationed in each of two corners. Gleb moved instinctively to take a chair close to one of the guards. Shura, oddly enough, moved with equal speed to take a chair close to the other.

The Beloved sat in the chair in the middle of the conference room, watching with excited joy the game on the wallscreen behind Ping. He tore his gaze from the screen and stared at her. "Huh. You don't look like someone who could kill my brother." He twisted his lips around. "Of course, my brother was never the sharpest edge on the bayonet."

Ping lowered her head submissively, then started bouncing ever so slightly on her toes. "It was a terrible misunderstanding. As my boss explained on the phone, we are happy to make reparations."

The Advisor slapped the top of the table. "And pay you shall!" he roared. "Put the first installment on the table!"

Ping leaned over and laid the USB chip laden with SmartCoin before him. "As you discussed with Ciara, we will also make a comparable payment at the end of the year."

The Advisor slapped the table again. "Every year! And all your ships will become a part of my fleet!" He eyed Ping in her exquisite dress and brilliant jewelry. "And you shall be my mistress!"

Ciara and Shura had both explained that the Advisor would likely make ridiculous demands as part of the negotiation. Forcing herself to remember this, Ping worked to become calm enough to answer this with a proper negotiator's counteroffer.

Her efforts were interrupted, however, as the Advisor turned back to the screen. "Ha! Look at that one. Very funny!"

Ping turned and looked at telecast running behind her. It took her a long moment to comprehend what she was witnessing.

In Afghanistan, some months before 9-11 and the American invasion that followed, the Taliban had found themselves in desperate need of a large open arena with much seating for public service activities. They had repurposed the Kabul soccer stadium, transforming it into the place where the Taliban conducted executions.

When an American journalist expressed outrage, the Taliban spokesman had suggested, with gleaming eyes, that if the Americans didn't like it, they should pay for the construction of a separate execution field. Then the Taliban would turn the soccer field back over to the soccer players.

In the end, it didn't work out quite as the spokesman had planned.

The Beloved Advisor had gone one better. The Porto Novo soccer field had been transformed into a place for performing amputations.

Ping stared for a moment, then started pacing back and

forth, keeping her mouth clamped shut so she would not scream.

As she paced passed Shura, the curved wooden ornament fell from her neck into Ping's hand, where it fit perfectly like a handle. Shura touched that handle, and the curved blade of a *wakizashi*, a very short samurai sword, popped out.

Ping stared for only a moment. Then another sound of horror came from the wallscreen, and Ping moved swiftly to stand beside the Beloved Advisor. *Snick! Snick!*

One hand fell on the table, one hand fell on the floor.

The guards in the corners of the room had not expected this, and took a moment to respond. Gleb, however, knowing Ping, had not expected the sword, but had nevertheless understood that the Beloved Advisor's lifespan could now be measured in heartbeats. Gleb had already primed himself to spring.

Shura, of course, had known exactly what was coming and was already standing as the surgical strikes took place.

So Gleb grabbed his guard's rifle with one hand while grabbing the guard's neck with the other and slammed the fellow's head against the wall with all the force a Spetsnaz commando's training and power could deliver.

Shura ran to the other guard as if to hug him, reaching up with her arms. A muscle in her arm twitched, and the harmless stylus extended, straight into and through the guard's eyeball, to bury itself deep in his brain.

A strange tableau held everyone in place as they tried to digest what had happened. Then the Advisor started screaming. Having lived in a bubble of unreality of his own making for many years, he could not recognize hard truth when it arrived, and fought it. "You can't do this! You can't do this! I am the owner of a nation! I am a sovereign recognized by the UN! You can't attack a sovereign!"

On the wallscreen, another horrific moment came and went. Ping clenched her teeth, then stretched one hand into the Advisor's mouth and pulled out his tongue.

Snick.

The Advisor started shrieking anew. This stimulated Gleb to take action, tapping the Advisor against the wall until he stopped complaining.

Shura giggled.

Ping tried to prioritize her problems and failed. She suspected she might be in shock; if this was what it felt like to be a pawn in someone else's plan, she needed to avoid such situations in the future at all costs.

Looking down at the blood on her gown, she muttered, "That stain is never coming out. Now I understand how Jam felt when the shark bit her dress."

Realizing this was not important, she turned and looked at the guard Gleb had manhandled. "You crushed his skull." She frowned. "Unnecessary. This is why you can't be a peacekeeper on the BrainTrust." Still not important.

She looked around the room. The wallscreen was still showing nightmares. "How do we get to that field? We have to stop them," she demanded, controlling a desire to shriek.

Shura answered calmly, "I've got this." She drove her killer stylus into the wall, and it retracted to normal length. With her clamp, she pulled out her cell phone, and in moments she was speaking. "Rubinelle, it's a go. Soccer field first."

Moments later, on the wallscreen, women in bright red uniforms flowed onto the field from the far side. Gunfire erupted. The women did not spray the field; rather, they took carefully aimed single shots, leaving a scattering of ISBP bodies across the neatly mowed grass.

The ISBP had not fought an actual battle in a long time. Within moments, they were as demoralized as the Benin army had been during the ISBP conquest of the nation. They started running, most of them dropping their guns in an effort to run faster.

Shura's face glowed. "Kill them all," she muttered.

Ping stared at her. "Shura, snap out of it."

Shura turned back to Ping. "I'm sorry, it's just…I've dreamed of this for so long."

Ping twitched her nose. "I'm afraid to ask this, but do you have a plan for getting us out of here? Your people may have stopped the soldiers at the soccer field, but a big chunk of the army is still here."

Shura waved her arm. "Not a problem."

Ping turned to Gleb. "What do you think? Should we try to fight our way out, sneak our way out, or believe the kid here?"

Gleb stared at Shura for a moment, then shrugged. "She seems to have things under control."

Ping blew out a breath. "Yeah, that's what I'm thinking."

Given that they had a way out, what was the next thing she needed to do? She hunched her shoulders as she realized her next task was far scarier than fighting her way through an army.

She pulled out her phone. "Uh, Ciara? Hi. Yeah, I'm here with the Beloved Advisor. Um, things haven't gone exactly the way we planned. Let me tell you the good news first." She snatched the USB with the SmartCoin off the table. "We've negotiated a much better deal."

Khalid manipulated the miniature bots in the sealed biosafety cabinet, guiding them through the process of transferring the lime-colored powder from the test tubes to the dispersion units.

The lime powder was incredibly fine, so fine that the slightest jarring of the tube caused the particles to dance in the bright ceiling illumination of the room. The dance continued for minutes on end, even in the absence of further stimulation. The Brownian motion of the air kept it aloft like dust hovering in a beam of sunshine. So beautiful, so delicate.

The dispersal units were even smaller than the test tubes. Shaped like PEZ dispensers, these brightly colored boxes had stickyback sections you could peel off to affix the unit to a wall or a ceiling. You could in principle pop the top and let the Brownian motion do its job, though the unit did have a tiny vibrator to facilitate the process and a miniature timer to specify the pop time.

And of course a normal person, popping the normal top without the appropriate special twist, would get a peppermint-flavored PEZ-like candy. Sugar-free, naturally.

Khalid then performed the other careful dance of removing the PEZ dispensers from biosafety and sterilizing their exteriors. Really fine powders like this were a pain to work with since the powder tried to adhere to the plastic surfaces, but eventually, he was done. Meanwhile, Uwais and Khalid stuffed the dispensers into a pair of battered suitcases.

Khalid talked as he worked, half to himself, half to his partners. "We really are living in a blessed moment, you know. While the CRISPIER and other advances have made it possible for scientists to develop cures for diseases faster than ever before, the very same tech has enabled the creation of new pandemics at an even greater speed. Now that we have our first killer virus from which to develop variants, we can enhance it and deploy new ones at least ten times as quickly, at less than a hundredth the cost. We can easily churn out a half-dozen deadly diseases while our enemies are still struggling frantically to cure the first."

He realized there was an analogy that Sabaah, with his background in software, would appreciate. "We are being protected from our enemies by an economic asymmetry somewhat similar to the one that protects computer-virus writers from computer security developers. In that field too, a lone hacker can outrun and outperform the multi-billion-dollar industry built to stop him."

Sabaah muttered, "Not a coincidence that the Herald of the Mahdi should be born into this place and time. It was ordained."

Khalid rolled his eyes. "Maybe. And please, Sabaah. Within these caverns, I am still Khalid."

Uwais offered good-naturedly, "Particularly since Khalid is still a Sunni heretic."

The last of the PEZ containers were stowed. Khalid looked at his friends. "You're all set?"

Sabaah nodded. "Passports, plane tickets from Cairo to Canada. From there we'll head south. Should be simple."

Khalid gave each of them a double kiss on the cheek, and they headed out the tunnel. Khalid went back to work on the next-generation virus, although he would not finish it until he got the results back from this first large scale test.

Ping sat in the conference room with Ciara, Shura, and Gleb. She stopped twirling her Aeron chair back and forth and stared at Shura. "Amazons? You're kidding me!"

Ciara put her hand to her forehead, still not quite able to believe what had happened. "All too true. Once upon a time, the Kingdom of Dahomey, which overlapped the nation now known as Benin, maintained an army contingent known as the Dahomey Amazons. The women warriors actually predate the Kingdom, and are also known as *minos*."

Shura smiled shyly. "My grandmother was their queen, and my aunt was next in line."

Ciara shook her head. "But it became only ceremonial long before the turn of the millennium." She frowned. "Which was considered to be a good thing at the time. The historical accounts of how the Amazons used their prisoners in training are both graphic and appalling." She rolled her eyes. "That was why the Europeans started calling them Amazons in the first place, naming them for the characters of Greek mythology."

Gleb pointed at Shura. "If the Amazons were reduced to purely ceremonial activities, what were they doing slaughtering soldiers on a soccer field?"

A look of triumph filled Shura's face. "After those soldiers murdered our people when I was a child, Rubinelle decided we needed to be reactivated." She held up her arms. "I, of course, could not join, but I would have." She waved at everyone in the room with her new stylus—one Ping had carefully vetted to ensure it did not extend into a rapier. "We had prepared in secret for many years but had to wait until we had someone who could be acknowledged by the people as a righteous leader. Someone you could believe in for bringing not only wealth and power but also justice, all in one." She pointed at Ping. "We didn't find anyone who really qualified until you came here."

Ping groaned. Her mind drifted back to the escape they'd made from the palace.

They'd followed Shura's instructions. First, they'd waited for the general in charge of the troops in the palace to come rushing in, requesting authorization to deploy more men to the soccer field. Upon encountering the Beloved Advisor in a semi-comatose and incoherent state with his wrists wrapped tight to slow the bleeding, the general found himself forcefully urged by Gleb to go ahead and deploy all the troops.

Once the troops had departed, Shura led them down to the garage where the Advisor's limousines resided. As Gleb drove through the gate in the Fence, Rubinelle met them: tall, thin and stiffly formal. She saluted Ping. "Colonel, good to meet you. We, the minos, are at your service. If I may, let me suggest you allow us to escort your vehicle out of the city to your copters."

Ping agreed to this but soon found the escape had turned into a celebration. Word had gone viral that the Advisor was out and the heroine Ping, who had killed his brother in the Battle of Djeregbe, had overthrown him. So while Rubinelle marched to a slow beat in front of the limo, and her troops marched proudly to the sides, the people came into the street and threw flowers.

Meanwhile, inside the limo, Shura kept staring at the general who had been in charge of the palace troops, her eyes gleaming with unshed tears, while she popped her stylus to its full killing extension, then retracted it, then popped it again.

Watching this, Ping rearranged the seating so that she sat between Shura and the general, at which point Shura whispered, "I remember. He's the one who held my mother down."

Ping thought about moving the general back next to Shura but refrained.

When they reached the copters, Rubinelle saluted crisply again. "We are tracking down the bandits as we speak. I will keep you apprised. If there's anything else you need, please command us, Colonel."

Ping slowly came to the dreadful realization that when

Rubinelle said "Colonel," she meant Ping. Colonel Ping. She shuddered.

As the copters lifted off with Ping, Shura, Gleb, and the Advisor included for medical attention, Colonel Ping muttered wearily, "And now, apparently, I have an army. What am I gonna do with a goddamn army?"

The urgent ringing of Ping's phone with a swatch of Gilbert and Sullivan's *Modern Major General* brought her thoughts back to the present. "Rubinelle, how can I help you?"

"Just giving you a heads-up, Colonel, that I've arrived with the new generals for your army." As she finished speaking, Rubinelle entered the conference room with three prisoners and two guards.

Ping hung up the phone and stared in bewilderment. "My new generals?"

Rubinelle saluted. "Yes, Colonel. The Advisor's generals were recalcitrant and died, but their seconds in command," she kneed the closest one in the back, "were open to taking a new oath." She unlocked their handcuffs. "Kneel."

The new generals knelt.

Ping's phone rang again, the caller a dirtside news service she'd never heard of. She sighed and decided that the better part of valor required her to put the call on speakerphone.

A stranger spoke. "Ah, Colonel, or, uh, Beloved Advisor—"

Rubinelle interrupted. "She is *not* a Beloved Advisor."

The voice stuttered, "N-no, certainly not. Uh, I'm the editor in chief for the Benin National News site. Could you please tell me what the news is today?"

Ping looked around the room at her compatriots, but none offered any help. "Uh, isn't the news just the news? Whatever important facts have come up since yesterday?"

The voice trembled. "But...we don't publish just anyone's facts. We need to publish *your* facts. Whatever you say the facts are."

Ciara clamped her teeth over her curled index finger and shrieked softly.

Rubinelle raised a finger. "If I may?"

Ping handed her the phone. "Go for it."

Rubinelle solved the editor's dilemma. "We are in the midst of a critical ceremony. When we are done, I will call you back and inform you of today's truths."

A relieved editor thanked her as she hung up.

Rubinelle, demonstrating her elemental nature as an unstoppable force, proceeded to the next item on her agenda. The prisoners—or rather, the generals—swore an oath of fealty. Rubinelle knelt beside them. "Your army is now complete, Empress."

Ping found herself staring dumbfounded again. "Empress? No. No. Just no."

Shura giggled, Gleb smirked, and Ciara turned an interesting shade of furious red that clashed with her sea-green hair.

Diab held his breath as the specially-designed gangway on top of the *First Chance* slid gracefully over to mesh with the gangway from the *Mt. Parnassus.* There was a loud click—too loud. Had something gone wrong?

Apparently not. A young Western woman with green hair and impossibly pale skin (*does she live in the bowels of her ship all day every day, never seeing the sun?*) led the way, followed by a middle-aged man probably from Western Africa, and a college-age kid possibly from the Congo. As they came across the gangway to his ship, Diab went up to meet them, girding himself for negotiation.

He had been pleasantly surprised earlier when they simply acknowledged him on the radio and allowed him to dock like a real isle ship, but he knew that the discussion of connection fees had to follow shortly. And his ship, he also knew, presented more than one nonstandard problem.

The first one was hooking up electricity. He couldn't keep using the *First Chance*'s diesels, so he would have to persuade the leader of the Prometheus fleet to hook power to him. The fleet had power to spare, he knew, it shouldn't be a problem. But he would have to pay for it, and he wasn't quite sure yet where he'd get the money. Or, to be more honest with himself, he had absolutely no clue where he'd get the money.

Ciara introduced herself as the Mission Commander, Oziegbe as her executive manager for liaison for the *First Chance,* and Asemote as her most brilliant student in the field of ship engineering.

Asemote's eyes went wide as he tried to take in everything at once. He reached out and touched one of the near walls. "You coated all the exposed surfaces with plastic? What did you use?"

Diab explained, "We looked at all the cheap plastics floating in the ocean, disintegrating slowly or not at all, to identify which would make good coatings. We chose PET plastic—the stuff from which plastic bottles are made—which was slow to degrade and easy for us to get."

Asemote nodded. "Good idea, and good enough to get you here, but eventually PET breaks down given both sunshine and saltwater. With the recent fall in prices, manganese phosphate is still better with respect to lifecycle costs." He frowned. "For interior walls, it might still be a great idea."

Ciara murmured, "And the most important thing we have to do is replace those diesels with beta batteries."

Asemote responded impatiently, "Yes, yes, of course." He looked up at the rebar-reinforced metal culvert serving as a smokestack. "Nothing useful there."

Diab was quite puzzled by his guests, who hadn't yet said a word about money. He felt his anxiety growing as he led them down into the ship, where a group of children was painting the passage walls.

Oziegbe rubbed his hands. "This makes sense, particularly for a ship with more families. Let the kids paint the walls. Honestly, the programmably-rendered walls on the *Parnassus* are a ridiculous waste of money."

Asemote shook his head. "Not as expensive as you might think, but you're probably still right. No reason to change the way they do it here." He looked down at an exposed wire running the length of the passage. "And this is entirely unacceptable."

Diab winced. "I know the wires shouldn't be exposed, but we were rushed, and some of the wiring we needed didn't get planned in."

Asemote waved the explanation away. "Of course. We'll do better when we 3D-model it first and manufacture the bulk of the interior with 3D-printed magnesium." He frowned. "That's not the issue. The opportunity here is to replace all this copper wiring with graphene wiring. It's more conductive than silver, you know, and way more corrosion-resistant than copper. Particularly on a ship where the leads get exposed to sea air. We'll replace all that copper with locally manufactured graphene."

Diab had had no idea that graphene made better wiring, but he suspected he could trust the young man's assessment.

After a few more assertions about what needed to be changed and what could be kept and what was a wondrous improvement in cost-effectiveness, Diab could contain his concerns no longer. "Look, I appreciate the assessment and the plans for all these replacement parts, but we cannot afford them. How much is it going to cost us to join you? Do you have any jobs we could do to earn a place here?"

Asemote stared at him in puzzlement.

Oziegbe laughed, then placed a gentle hand on Diab's shoulder. "My apologies. We've been running roughshod over you in our excitement."

Ciara continued. "Your ship here is a miracle, you know. Oh, it's an elephant all right, but it's still remarkable when the elephant dances."

Diab frowned, waiting for an actual explanation.

Oziegbe tag-teamed him. "We've been talking about

building a next generation of isle ship, probably smaller, and certainly a whole lot cheaper. There's a project on the main BrainTrust to build a new series of ships that are also cheaper, but they're still way too expensive for mass production." He licked his lips. "It's clear that between your people and Asemote, we have enough new ideas to reduce the cost even more."

Ciara made the offer. "So I'm hoping that in a few minutes you'll come on up to the *Parnassus* and look over a contract we've drafted. We'll pay your people both ongoing fees and a slice of the profits for engineering help developing a radically less expensive isle ship. And we'll make you a loan for the beta batteries for your ship. And a loan to build a new agricultural reef a bit southwest of here. The reef will give you something your people can do that will not only increase your self-sufficiency but also give you your first exports. This should tide you over until you come up with more ideas for products and services to offer."

Her smile broadened. "Given the inventive spirit you showed here, I have no doubt they'll follow shortly."

Her smile turned wicked. "I also expect you to make a new home in the first next-gen ship to come off the line, which will surely have kinks that need fixing." She looked around sadly at the ramshackle vessel of which Diab was so proud. "Because, let's face it, you deserve better."

Feeling relief flow through him, Diab stood straighter. He started wondering if he should name their next home *Second Chance*.

Sound asleep in his snug little cabin aboard the *Chiron*, Mediator Joshua Pickett vaguely heard his phone ring. He put his head under his pillow until it stopped.

Then it started ringing again. He grunted, rolled over, and clumsily scooped the blasted device off the side table. "Joshua here. It's five in the morning. This better be good."

A shy voice, almost a little girl's voice, greeted him. "I'm so sorry. I just couldn't wait any longer."

Joshua shook his head, trying to figure out who it was. His brain finally processed the data well enough to draw a conclusion as unlikely as it was dreadful. "Ping?"

The voice sounded relieved. "It's me." A pause ensued. Then she continued, with the same level of humility that had made her voice difficult to recognize in the first place, "I'm really sorry. I just...I've done something terrible, and I thought you could mediate."

Adrenalin pulsed through his body. He leapt from the bed and ran to the desk where he sometimes worked—and sometimes brooded—over ongoing mediations that did not yield to simple analysis.

He was sure that whatever Ping had for him, it would leave him brooding. "What have you done?" What could she have done that would leave her sounding like a little girl? Had she sunk an isle ship? Would even *that* cause this level of contrition?

"Joshua, I...hurt a man. He's a very bad man, but...I hurt him really bad." She told him what she had done to the Beloved Advisor.

Joshua worked hard not to throw up. "What on earth made you think this was a good idea?"

"It's what he does to other people. A lot of other people.

I just couldn't keep thinking straight when I fully realized what was going on."

Joshua remembered, in one of his early encounters with Ping, that she had given a similar reason for killing an incapacitated man. Joshua had given her a very light punishment because, based on the evidence, her action bordered on justifiable.

He shuddered, wondering if he could bear to look at evidence that would lead him to conclude that this too bordered on justice. He closed his eyes, wishing he did not have to ask the following question. "Do you have photos, videos, or anything documenting the events surrounding this…this event?"

"I thought you might ask. I have a lot of stuff. You have a wallscreen there?"

All too soon Joshua was looking at the photos of the Beloved Advisor before and after, at Shura and her stylus and her clamp, and at the video taken at the soccer stadium that day. As he looked at the first photos of the Advisor, he wanted to wring Ping's neck. But after looking at Shura and the video, he started wishing, quite unprofessionally, that she'd carved off more parts.

Eventually the nightmare scenes stopped. Joshua rubbed his eyes as he wondered how much of this would turn into frequent nightmares. When would he sleep well again? One thing was certain; he wasn't going back to sleep after Ping hung up.

On to the big question. "So, Ping, this is all horrific, and I'm glad I don't have to live with the choices you've made, but what exactly do you want me to do?"

At this point, they'd upgraded the phone call to a video

call, and he watched her frown. "I'd like you to mediate, Joshua. What compensation do I owe him? How should I be punished?"

Joshua rubbed his eyes again and shook his head. He spoke gently. "I'm not a priest, Ping. If you want to do penance and receive forgiveness, you need someone else."

Ping sighed. "I'm an atheist, Joshua. You're the closest thing to a priest I have."

Joshua lay back in his chair and stared at his ceiling, where the rendering of the night sky with Orion prominently displayed was fading in the rendered beginnings of dawn.

In its own peculiar way, he understood Ping's point. He passed judgment and meted out punishments, and after the punishment was complete, the perpetrator was nominally absolved.

But he was *not* a priest, dammit. "Even if I wanted to help, your Beloved Advisor is not covered by a mediation agreement." He pondered the matter. "One alternative would be to turn yourself over to the authorities in Benin, but they'd probably just execute you on the spot, or—" he gestured at the pictures of the soccer field "—even worse."

Ping winced. A coloration arose on her face that might have been a blush. "Uh, the problem is kinda the opposite from that."

Joshua raised an eyebrow.

"They, well, they've started calling me 'Empress.'"

Joshua's eyes bulged.

"Joshua, I'm afraid I may, like, have a country."

Really? Empress Ping? The mind boggled. Perhaps—

please God—perhaps it was not actually true. "Well. Let's not be hasty. Does *everyone* call you Empress?"

Ping sighed. "Pretty much."

Joshua pursed his lips. "But the army doesn't report to you, does it?"

Ping slumped. "The generals all swore an oath to me."

Oh, this sounded bad. "Is there any state news media? Surely they object."

Ping rolled her eyes. "Every morning they ask my second-in-command, Rubinelle, what to publish."

Joshua opened his mouth to ask a last desperate question, but Ping already saw it coming. "And I have access to all the government bank accounts. Including the ones the Beloved Advisor had declared his own personal accounts." For the first time she smiled, though a vicious satisfaction marred the expression. "Shura persuaded him to hand over all the account codes."

Joshua now faced a dilemma. In normal mediations, he granted compensation to the victim. Under those rules, he would now say, as part of Ping's compensation to the Beloved Advisor, that she had to return his accounts to him.

But he was pretty sure that in a regular court of law, after taking a decade to think about it, they'd conclude that the money really wasn't his, but had been stolen from the country he'd run.

Well, at least one form of penance he could require of Ping was now clear. "So you've got the army, the news media, and the money, in addition to popular support. Yup, you've got yourself a country, all right."

Ping groaned.

"I have one proposal for appropriate compensation, but I still can't require it. The nation of Benin doesn't have a mediation agreement with the BrainTrust."

Ping waved the objection away. "If I'm Empress, I can sign the agreement, right? Consider it done."

Joshua breathed a sigh of relief. This was starting to feel more like familiar territory. "I hereby require you, then, to fulfill your duties as Empress with excellence, justice, and compassion."

"What?" Ping cried in a strangled voice.

"Ciara will identify sets of Accel educational modules on economics and law that you must complete in a timely manner. And there's an obscure academic paper from the last century, *The Digital Path*, I want you to go over with Lenora."

Ping just looked dazed. "But—"

"And I don't know what the current state of the art is in bionic hands, but you also need to get the very best such tech for the Beloved Advisor."

Ping swallowed hard on this one. She seemed about to object, then gave him a different kind of smile—the one that Joshua immediately recognized as foretelling a complication. "OK, Joshua. But could I get new hands for the people the Beloved Advisor hacked up first?"

Joshua thought for a moment, then returned the smile. "Oh, by all means. How many people is that, anyway?"

"About a quarter million."

The number was just too large to comprehend. Joshua turned away, suppressing a need to run to the bathroom to throw up. "Yes, make him the last in line. You are authorized and required to use the financial accounts that once belonged to the Beloved Advisor to build a factory to manufacture bionic hands."

He exhaled sharply as he had a further thought. "You may want to turn it into a business. These quarter-million people will receive their new hands as compensation, but once you've got the factory, there are probably more people in the world who need the tech. You may want to talk to some of the big investors, like Ben Wilson, about turning it into a joint venture."

Ping settled back into a state of shock.

Joshua's eyes gleamed. "Do you feel better now? You wanted to do penance. I think competently running a country will serve as a fine form of reparation."

Ping blinked her eyes and muttered, "So, now I have a country. What am I going to do with a goddamn... Never mind, I refuse to ask the question."

Tiny dots of snow swirled around Sabaah and Uwais as they squinted toward the south. A vast expanse of white-frosted pine trees beckoned them, stretching across the invisible border utterly heedless of the political ramifications.

Uwais looked at the map on his tablet, then at the scenery to the southwest. "You can see the West Wall." The West Wall, made from the same rust-colored steel slats as The Wall, blocked off casual tourists from the uninhabited region that had once been the state of Washington, now known as the West Coast Waste.

Sabaah groaned. "You know, we could have waited a

few months until it was spring, and then we could have just walked across." He pursed his lips. "Better yet, we have people in place here already, don't we? Why not just let them do this?"

Uwais considered that carefully. "I think Khalid wants to keep them as sleepers until the Big One. It would be too bad if they got picked up before we had the final solution." He pounded his ski pole into the light powder beneath their feet. "And besides, then we never would have had this exceptional opportunity to learn how to cross-country ski and snowshoe."

Sabaah was unimpressed. "Since when have you wanted to learn to ski?"

Uwais watched as his exhaled breath turned steamy. "Since I found out we could. Really, Sabaah, you need to learn to take the opportunities as they come."

They took off down the slope at a slow but accelerating pace. Sabaah nearly wiped out on a pine tree.

Uwais yelled, "Embrace the flow!"

Sabaah scowled. "I'm more likely to embrace a tree trunk!"

Eventually they made it out of the forest and back into civilization. A careful search of FB media had identified an isolated house belonging to a retired couple of snowbirds who took their RV to New Mexico for the winter every year; Uwais and Sabaah had had their suitcases shipped there. They took the couple's spare car to the next town, then, when night fell, they told the self-driving vehicle to return home.

Uwais clapped his hands on Sabaah's shoulders. "I guess this is where we part ways."

Sabaah frowned. "I still don't get why we're doing this. I mean, the current virus isn't all that lethal. Seems like a waste of time. A dangerous waste of time."

Uwais shrugged. "Hey, you heard Khalid. The virus may not be as lethal as you'd like, but the Americans will help it achieve its full potential." Uwais offered Sabaah a sly chuckle. "You should know this better than I do. Unless I miss my guess, Khalid already had you help the Americans along the path, didn't he?"

Sabaah did not quite acknowledge this with the merest hint of a smile. "Off to Boston with you. I'll bet I can make it from Portland to San Diego before you can make it from Boston to Philadelphia."

Uwais shrugged. "It hardly makes a difference. We have to set the timers all to go off at the same time anyway."

Sabaah smirked. "I'll bet you a pizza."

Uwais' eyes lit up. "Deal."

Shura trotted along with Ping walking on one side and Ciara on the other. She was taking them to the elevator, thence down to the upper of the two agricultural decks where the *Parnassus* grew fresh fruit and vegetables.

Ciara had authorized Shura to section off a swatch of the deck for a set of experiments. Shura had been cagey about what she wanted agricultural space for, but Ciara had concluded after some consideration that it was probably safer to have her experimenting with plants than with, say, autonomous killer robots—though with Shura, that was not necessarily true. Which was why Ciara was glad Shura had volunteered to take her to see the project.

The deck's elevator stopped and they got out in the vestibule, where the gas masks and flashlights hung on the walls. Ciara grabbed a mask.

Shura raised her arm with the clamp in a halting gesture. "No need."

Ciara stared at her. The ag deck ran an atmosphere with a thousand times higher concentration of CO_2 than normal atmosphere, and it was lit by narrow-frequency LEDs emitting light at only the two frequencies (one red, one green) where chlorophyll had maximum absorption. Walking in there unequipped would leave you dying in a sickly yellowish glow.

Shura explained, "My section is right next to us, and I separated it from the rest so it could have normal air and sunlight." She opened the door.

They confronted a dozen or so trees so short they might better be classified as bushes. Bright red and orange seed pods larger than a man's hand mingled with white flowers to cover the trunk and the branches of each tree.

Ping tapped one of the pods. "Chocolate?"

Shura gave a little yip and jumped in place. "The best chocolate ever!"

Ping grabbed one and tugged it. "This sucker really doesn't want to let go, does it?" She touched the sheath strapped to her waist and grabbed her chura—the Pakistani knife with a wickedly curved blade, originally developed for attacking knights in armor—that Dash and Jam had gifted her with long ago.

The chura cut easily through the stalk anchoring the

pod, then again through the thick skin of the pod to reveal a dense pack of cocoa beans embedded in white pulp. "Gold!" Ping cried. "Well, better than gold, actually."

Ciara blinked at the revealed beans. "You've genetically engineered the cacao tree?" She reached up to the top of one of the trees, which she could touch with her outstretched fingers. "Aren't these supposed to be thirty or so feet tall?"

Shura nodded vigorously. "With my trees, you don't need any equipment to reach all the pods. And the pods are packed closer together."

Ciara shook her head in sharp astonishment. "I can hardly believe you did this in the short time you've been here."

Shura shrugged. "You're familiar with the Middle Eastern date palm? The Israelis bred it and engineered it to be short like this, and to produce ten times as many dates. And they didn't have either an existing example, like their date palm provided to me, or a CRISPIER to speed up the experimentation to go from an experiment every growing season to an experiment every day." A look of alarm crossed her face as she realized she had just explained away her own contributions. "But it was still pretty hard. I still think I earned some bonus merit reward tokens."

Ciara and Ping just laughed.

Shura continued mischievously, "But the shorter height and the denser pods are not the best part."

Ciara easily guessed the next part. "Your cacao plants are drought-resistant and need less water."

Shura jumped ahead to the application. "We can grow plantations of cacao trees in Benin." She looked at Ping and giggled. "The Empress can start a new business. A really big business."

Ping covered her face with her hand. "I'm trying to remember my history here. If I recall correctly, most of the world's chocolate used to come from around here, right?"

Ciara told the rest of the story. "The Ivory Coast and Ghana produced over seventy percent. They had a near-monopoly, even though the cacao plant originated in South America." She reached into the pod Ping held and squiggled out a bean. "In those days, chocolate was so cheap that everyone could have it all the time. But cacao trees are very sensitive to climate and need lots of reliable water, so as the climate dried out in the places cacao grew, the trees died."

She rubbed the bean lazily between her fingers. "Ghana and the Ivory Coast still produce seventy percent of the world's supply, but the supply is a tiny fraction of what it used to be. Which is why even on the BrainTrust it's used primarily on special occasions."

Ping smiled mischievously. "Except on the *Haven*, where they serve hot chocolate for breakfast every day."

Shura's eyes widened. "There's a place where they have chocolate every day?"

Ping laughed and rubbed Shura's head. "If this experiment of yours works out, we'll *all* have chocolate every day."

The little girl ran her fingers over the cold gray tombstone. The name on the stone said Louise Hall Goldstein.

Her mother knelt beside her. "And Willa, this is your great aunt. She was in the Navy, just like your father and me."

Willa touched the stone for a few more moments, then looked off to her right side. "Why did they put her in a park?"

Her father laughed. "This isn't exactly a park, kiddo." He pointed to the left, where row upon row of tombstones lay. "This is the Los Angeles National Cemetery. There are a lot of people like your great aunt here."

Willa was distracted as she continued to look to the right, where a vast field of neatly cut grass rolled into the distance but no graves or their accompanying tombstones had yet been placed. "But it's a park," she exclaimed and went running through the open space.

Her mother shook her head. "I guess it's a park."

The father wisely agreed. "Indeed."

A look of concern crossed the mother's face. "We should go. She felt feverish when she got up this morning."

The father scoffed. "You worry too much. She's had all her vaccinations. It can't be too serious."

At that moment, the child ran back to them. She pointed at a red rash on the back of her hand. "Mommy, what's this?"

Her mother inspected the skin. "I don't understand." She looked up at her husband. "It looks like measles, but it can't be." She tapped her daughter lightly on the head. "We're taking you home, little girl."

6

BACK IN THE US OF A

Never fear quarrels, but seek hazardous adventures
— Alexandre Dumas, The Three Musketeers

What are the consequences of requiring from one's employees a personal guarantee of loyalty above all else, casting aside characteristics such as intelligence, competence, and any sense of morality?

Statistically, of course, the preeminence of loyalty requires a reduction in such secondary virtues. But given a large enough pool of candidates, sufficient selectivity can overcome these obstacles. You can have a sycophant who exhibits superior intelligence, for example.

But...what impact does rabid loyalty have on critical thinking skills? It seems reasonable to guess, for example, that an extreme loyalist would be more inclined than normal to suffer confirmation bias (facts supporting one's loyalty remembered, others forgotten) and various association fallacies—halo effect, wherein things and people endorsed by one's liege receive a glossy sheen—and guilt by association, a tarnishing of any positive qualities for friends of people who oppose him.

At the moment in history when Khalid unleashed his first plague, no good research existed on this topic. This gap in human knowledge would not be closed until a team of researchers and grad students assembled by Lenora Thornhill completed their seminal investigation decades later.

Be that as it may, Cameron Ballard, the Acting Assistant Director of the FBI in charge of the Directorate for Weapons of Mass Destruction, presented all the symptoms of these critical thinking failures.

Ballard read and re-read the report detailing the thousands of deaths throughout the coastal cities with mounting excitement. At last he'd get a chance to demonstrate his skills!

He'd been chomping at the bit for some action ever since he'd gotten the promotion to AAD. Now *that* had been a stroke of good fortune, when his boss, Phil McMullen, had gotten crushed in a freak car accident: a self-driving car had swerved into him just out of the blue while he was walking down the sidewalk on Wisconsin Ave., having just left Crumbs & Whiskers. Phil was still in the hospital and was likely to remain there, possibly until retirement.

But Phil was a feisty old coot. If anyone was curmudgeonly enough to survive, he was.

Phil was an antique holdover from the days before the President had humbly accepted the heavy burden of running the country for the rest of his life. In a shocking display of near-treason, when their leader had ascended to his lifetime status, Phil had refused to take the Oath of Personal Loyalty to the President.

Phil should have been fired, except that the personal oath was not yet quite a legal requirement, and the Blues had done a ridiculous amount of whining about it. So the President's people had laterally-arabesqued Phil into control of the WMD directorate, which at the time was quiet and uninteresting to the President.

Cameron Ballard had been delighted to take the oath; he was a fan, after all. The President's decisive action had been the only thing that prevented a socialist takeover of the country.

Regardless, it was critical for Ballard that he excel in his acting director position before Phil cranked himself out of the bed where he now lay hooked up like a puppet. If Cameron could show his skills, he was sure they'd force Phil into retirement even if he survived the accident.

But showing your skills when in charge of the department that investigated bioweapon attacks was not as easy as it sounded. The most excitement his team usually got was a letter containing white powder sent to a federal worker. Everyone always leapt into action when that happened, and Ballard made sure the media got wind of a possible ricin attack.

But half the time the powder turned out to be sugar topping from a donut, and the other half it was a puff of cocaine.

So this new measles outbreak was important. According to his reports, the epidemic violated all the laws of dispersal for natural phenomenon, and it was immune to the standard measles vaccine. They were looking at a bioweapon attack on the largest scale.

At last, some action! And he knew just how to get started. Shucks, he already had a list of the most likely suspects. Conveniently, they were all on their way to get together in the same place; rounding them up would be child's play.

It was fortunate for the nation, Cameron realized, that Phil had been put out of the way in time for him to take control of this crisis. Among Phil's other old-fashioned curmudgeonly attitudes, he was the quintessential embodiment of the old-school FBI stereotype: intelligent but not very creative, careful but slow, and relentless as a Caterpillar bulldozer but loyal only to the search for truth and justice.

In this moment of crisis, America needed someone faster, more creative, and willing to cut the necessary corners. The right person had gotten the right job at just the right time.

Ballard figured on having a confession in forty-eight hours.

Dash was in the cafeteria finishing a scoop of raspberry gelato when her cell went off. "Yes? Dr. Bingham. How can I help you?" She looked at Chance, who looked back quizzically. "It's Simon Bingham, the chief scientist of the CDC." Dash listened on the phone in growing horror. "Are they insane? Yes, of course, I'll help. Give me a few minutes to figure out what to do."

Chance pointed a fork at her. "Crisis?"

Dash still looked horrified. "That measles outbreak they notified us about? It's appeared in most of the major coastal cities in America. Virtually simultaneously. And it's not measles; the measles vaccine has no effect." She shook her head. "But that's not the big problem."

Chance put down her fork, half-rising from her chair as if to start taking action, then sitting again when she realized she didn't know quite what action to take. "That's not the big problem? There's a bigger problem than a continent-spanning epidemic with no cure?"

Dash nodded. "The FBI thinks a scientist at the CDC is responsible since they're the ones with the means to create such a virus. So the FBI has locked down the buildings at the complex where they do the most sensitive virus work. Dr. Bingham saw the FBI vans swoop into the parking lot as he was arriving and turned around just in time to avoid getting caught. He can't raise anybody in the building."

Chance rose with swift determination. "I'll go get him. I can take one of Matt's Global Express spaceships and be offshore in less than two hours. I'll have Dr. Bingham safe before nightfall." She thought about the distances involved. "Well, before tomorrow morning, anyway."

Dash shook her head as she too rose. "You and I have more important things to do. With the CDC locked up, it's up to us to figure out this epidemic." She paused, reluctant to make her next statement, with all its horrific implications. "It's surely a bioweapon attack."

She gasped as she realized the connection, and she and Chance said at the same time, "The missing CRISPIER."

Dash dialed her phone. "I'll call Amanda. And Ping and Jam."

Chance shook her head. "I'll call Ping. And Wolf or Aar, whichever one answers first."

Dash added. "And Matt. He needs to have Kestrel Titans ready to launch." She laughed mirthlessly. "He's going to enjoy this—*him* charging *us* a premium for emergency services for a change."

Chance finished talking to Wolf on the phone. "Who's going to pay for it?"

Dash turned grim again. "I'm sure Dr. Bingham will reimburse us eventually...if he lives. If he's not in jail." She dialed Amanda. "I think Amanda can get the Consortium to pay for the moment." She became even grimmer. "Or barring that, I will pay for it. One way or the other, it has to be done. We have to stop this disease now, not just to keep it from sweeping across America, but—"

Chance finished the thought, "—before it reaches the BrainTrust."

———

Jam had finally finished tidying up all the details of her work as Expedition Commander for the Fuxing, and she boarded the next scheduled Global Express ship heading to the Prometheus archipelago.

She'd been fascinated listening to the tales of Ping's exploits, up to and including her acquisition of an entire country. Jam was uncertain whether she was sorry to have missed that episode or not. Surely it would have turned out differently had she been along, but whether it would have turned out better was uncertain. This Shura girl seemed to have had them all wired and dancing like puppets.

Jam heaved a sigh of relief as the ship left zero-g behind and regained gravity for the descent. She really didn't love this form of transportation, though some of that might just be residual anxiety since the first time she'd been on a rocket, she'd gotten shot down.

Anyway, she was glad when the noise of the engines cut out and the ship bounced gently on the deck of the Prometheus archipelago's spaceport ship. She sat for a moment, letting the other passengers depart while she made sure her organs had settled properly back into place.

As she got up to depart, Ping hopped through the hatch and dogged it shut.

Jam watched with alarm. "Ping! What're you doing?"

Ping gave her a huge grin, which Jam watched with a sinking feeling. "Gotta go! Buckle up; we're outta here as soon as we're refueled."

Jammed looked around at the empty cabin. "What about the other passengers? And where are we going?" Her heart leapt in her throat. "Is Dash in trouble?"

Ping half-pushed her into an acceleration couch. "Sort of." She explained about the measles-like epidemic in America and the takeover of the CDC by the FBI. "So we're going to America to rescue Dash's friends and everybody else we need to help fight the virus."

The engines started rumbling. Jam grumbled, "Just when I thought I was done with freefall."

Ping laughed. "Isn't it great?"

Soon they were weightless. Jam tightened her belt, while Ping released hers.

Jam watched her. "Stop bouncing off the walls."

Ping looked at her from midair quizzically. "What do you mean? I'm perfectly calm."

Jam frowned. "No, you're not. But I meant, stop bouncing off the walls."

Ping was hurling herself from one side of the cabin to the other, literally bouncing off the walls. She just laughed.

Eventually gravity returned, and Ping muttered, "Alas. All good things must end."

Ping jumped from the acceleration couch as soon as the engines stopped blasting. She started pacing in front of the hatch. "Hurry up, hurry up," she muttered. She banged on the hatch. "Let me out!" She swung her fist at the hatch again—

And almost hit Wolf in the face. "Easy, Empress," he said with a huge grin, a mighty sweep of his leg, and a bow that would have made any member of the French court proud.

Ping glared, then jumped into his arms. "You galoot!" Then she whispered loudly enough for everyone to hear, "Call me that again and you're fish food."

Aar waved her forward. "Let us hurry," he urged. "The copters are ready, and the sub's already on its way."

As they ran for the copter deck, Jam spoke to Aar. "Your turban."

Aar stroked his uncovered head and pointed at her. "Your scarf."

Jam spoke decisively. "I've studied Muslim practices around the world, and I do not believe Allah requires such covering. " She paused as they turned a corner. "And besides, on a mission like this, it's best to blend in."

Aar touched his head again. "As a Sikh, I am allowed to go without my turban in an emergency when lives are at stake." He climbed into a copter ruefully. "Millions of lives are certainly at stake here. It was a painful decision, but not hard."

Wolf took the controls of Aar's copter; Ping took the controls of Jam's copter. Both machines were black, clearly stealth versions derived from the ones for which Jam had been the test user.

It was interesting to ponder why they had stealth copters on the commercial SpaceR spaceport ship that normally anchored off the coast of New York. Ping presumed a number of businessmen preferred to get to America without the hassle of the New York Customs office, which was notorious for making travelers, even Americans, suffer.

Before they closed the hatches on the copters, Jam asked, "So who knows where we're going?"

Ping and Wolf answered in unison, "I do." It turned out they'd both been to Atlanta, where the CDC had its head-quarters. Wolf finished smugly with, "So Ping may know her way around the town, but I know where the doctor is hiding out."

A look of irritation covered Ping's face. "How'd you find out?"

Wolf laughed easily. "Found out after we landed. You were still in zero-g."

Ping continued to grumble as they closed the copter

canopies and skimmed over the water from the spaceport ship down the coast toward Georgia.

Doctor Simon Bingham hunkered morosely in a clump of trees and bushes outside the parking lot of The Big Chicken restaurant. Ping rustled the bushes. "Hey, Doc, what's up?"

Simon jumped in alarm, then turned to greet them as he calmed down.

Dr. Bingham was short for an American and on the pudgy side, with only a few wisps of hair left to him. But his eyes were bright, and his carefully tailored Oxford shirt would have given him a professional air...had he not been huddled in the bushes, wrinkling everything. He brushed the dirt from the knees of his crisply pressed pants with a certain touch of dignity.

Ping apologized for startling him. "Sorry. Dash sends her best, by the way."

The doctor looked around a little wildly. "Did anybody follow you?"

Wolf answered, "Unlikely. No one particularly knows who we are. Ping and I are just as much American citizens as you are, and no one knows our relationship with you through Dash. We rented a pair of vans and came directly here."

The doctor's whole body relaxed. "Thank God." He pulled out a kerchief and wiped his brow.

Jam started the discussion of strategy. "We cruised past

the CDC's Roybal office complex where you told Dash everyone was being held."

Bingham nodded. "Yes, that's where our best High-Containment Continuity Lab is. All our most expert virologists from all over the country flew in last night to get to work on this epidemic." He voice turned very irritated. "But instead of curing the disease, they're sitting in interrogation rooms."

Jam continued her methodical analysis. "Well, your scientists may be stuck there a while. The FBI has landed an army. They even have snipers set up both on the roofs and in the trees along the edge of the campus. I hope you have an idea of how to get your people out because we'd need every peacekeeper in the BrainTrust to make a frontal assault.'

The doctor wiped the sweat from his lip. "I have a plan for getting in and out of the building, but I'll need help getting our best people out of their clutches."

Jam spoke soothingly. "Not a problem if we can sneak through their perimeter."

Wolf brought up a logistical problem. "You do understand we can't escape with everybody. We have two vans, and a submarine off the coast capable of carrying just about as many people as the vans can bring."

Aar continued. "So I'm afraid you have some difficult decisions to make. You have to pick a couple dozen of the people you most want. We may be able to get the others out of the building, but they'll have to find their own way to the BrainTrust."

Ping added, "Or at least to the spaceport ship off the coast of New York. We've gotcha covered from there."

Simon nodded. "I understand." He turned his attention to his tablet and started writing down the names of the people he most wanted. He jerked suddenly to a halt. "Oh, no."

Ping jumped on it first. "What's wrong?"

Simon looked up mournfully. "Velma Highwalker."

Everyone waited to hear the issue.

"She's one of our very best, and she's on vacation this week." He pondered the matter. "She has a getaway cabin up in the Appalachians, close to the Trail. She's probably there."

Aar made the obvious recommendation. "Better call her and warn her to leave before the cops arrive."

Wolf shook his head. "Unless she's using a phone with BrainTrust chips connected to the Starry Night cell system, the call would lead them directly to her. And also to us," he added darkly.

Simon held his hand up in a placating gesture. "I already know that. You would not believe how much trouble Dash and I had establishing a rendezvous point, knowing they could be listening in." He sighed. "The good news, sort of, is that Velma goes completely off-net when she goes to her cabin. We can't reach her, but they can't track her either."

Jam asked, "What are the chances they know where she is?"

Simon brightened. "There's a good chance they have no clue." He grimaced once more. "Of course, there are a couple of people in interrogation right now who can guess as well as I can. Her getaway cabin wasn't a secret. A coupla folks have hiked the Trail with her and stayed at the cabin overnight."

Jam put her hand to her face. "We don't have a lot of time, then. And the longer we wait to get your people out of Roybal, the more entrenched the FBI will be."

Wolf suggested the only solution. "Split forces."

Simon expanded on Wolf's proposal. "If two of you are going to come with me to the CDC, and two go to get Velma, I recommend you two—" he pointed at Jam and Ping— "Go for Velma. She's kind of irritable. Well, she's pretty much a feminazi, hates authority, and has a fierce temper. If she weren't so good at her job..." He pursed his lips. "Anyway, you two have the best chance of talking her into a trip to the BrainTrust."

Ping got the coordinates for the cabin from the doctor and turned to Jam. "Let's go. I've got the van—"

Wolf coughed. "Uh, we're gonna need both vans for the escape from the CDC, don't forget."

An expression of consternation spread over Ping's face.

Jam laughed as she watched Ping. "I guess you know where that leaves us."

Ping whined, "Can't we just go back and get the copters?"

Jam waved her hand at the distance. "Ping, we ditched the copters in the national forest outside Greensboro. Do you really think it would be faster to go back?"

Ping's shoulders slumped. "No. I can't believe what we're gonna do."

* * *

Ping sat morosely in the back seat with her arms crossed. She'd been sitting there for half an hour already. She grumbled again. "I can't believe we're invading America in an Uber car."

Jam stared at her fiercely, jerking her finger at the driver. "Ping, stop talking foolishness. What invasion? We're just going up to visit Velma at her cabin in the woods." She whispered, "Besides, you remember what Wolf said."

Ping waved her hand. "Yeah, yeah." When Aar had started laughing at Ping's downcast recommendation that they use an Uber driver to get Velma, Wolf had pointed out that in WWI, the French had gotten their troops to the front line facing the Germans outside Paris by using fleets of taxis. This had shut Aar up about Ping's Folly eventually, but not soon enough for Ping's taste.

Jam had just shrugged phlegmatically and called for a driver. "Whatever works," was her only comment.

Now they were speeding through a mixed oak-pine forest, having narrowly avoided hitting a white-tail deer a few miles back. They were on their way along the road toward Amicalola Falls, though they would stop before they got that far.

Indeed, minutes after Ping complained about their Uber assault, the driver announced, "We're just about to the rest stop where you said she'd meet you."

Ping bounced in the back. "Great!"

Moments later, Ping waved to the driver as he departed.

Jam was already jogging down the road. "Hurry up," she called with a hint of laughter in her voice. "Or I'll get her myself."

Ping growled and zoomed down the road to pass her.

Less than ten minutes later, they slowed to a halt and

crouched in the thick undergrowth across the street from Velma's house. A black SUV sat outside the wooden shack. Ping whispered, "Too late."

Sounds of a violent confrontation emanated from the house, led by a woman shouting what sounded like a war cry. Several thumps followed, including an agonized male grunt.

Jam whispered, "Sounds like Velma is softening them up for us. Regardless, shouldn't be a problem."

The door swung open, yielding a sequence of three people. First came a button-down FBI agent nursing a growing purple swelling under his left eye. Second came a woman with straight black hair and a reddish-chocolate skin tone that slightly masked the similar swelling of her right eye; her hands remained behind her back, presumably in handcuffs. The woman was followed by another FBI agent, grimacing as he struggled with the woman who kept leaping and twisting in his grasp.

Ping commented in admiration, "Feisty."

Jam replied repressively, "Untrained. And intemperate. She attacked when unable to win. Where's the strategy?"

Ping jumped to her feet and strutted onto the road, responding to Jam with, "Completely correctable." Ping waved at the party approaching the SUV and yelled, "Velma! Who're these people? You need help?" She glared at the FBI agent in the lead.

Jam growled, slid to her feet, and followed Ping. "I'm calling the cops. Let our neighbor go."

The lead agent held his hand out placatingly. "It's OK. Calm down." He reached into his jacket and flipped open his badge. "We're with the FBI."

Ping peered at the badge from a distance, then started trotting. "The other guy too? Show me."

In no time at all, Ping was leaning over in front of the second agent, studying the badge. "Hey, Jam, how do we know these are even real?"

Jam was similarly leaning over the lead agent's badge. "Cameron Ballard. What do you want with Velma?"

Cameron relaxed into his standard patter. "She's a person of interest in an important investigation."

Jam gave him a skeptical look. "Hmph. Ping, there's only one way I know of to be sure these badges are real. Ready?"

Ping answered brightly. "Ready."

Jam sighed. "Now."

Ping, who had been holding herself so taut she practically quivered, jerked up with lightning speed and delivered an uppercut to her opponent so fast he was still trying to figure out what had hit him when he wrote his report the following day.

Jam reached out and touched Cameron's badge with her right hand as if to scrutinize it even more closely. As she rose, dragging the badge, and with it Cameron's right hand, out of the way, she twisted into a left jab that connected with Ballard's unblemished right eye.

Ballard dropped his badge and, swaying slightly but nonetheless gamely, hurled himself forward. Jam stepped sideways and pulled him past, gently pushing his head down to kiss the hood of the car.

Ping stomped on the other agent's stomach to get him to raise his head, then kicked him in the chin to smack his head against the gravel roadway. He groaned and lay still.

Jam rifled Ballard's pockets and tossed the keys for the handcuffs to Ping.

Ping stepped behind the ex-prisoner. "Velma High-walker, I presume? Nice to meet you."

As soon as Velma got free, she leapt away and held up her fists. "Who the hell are you people anyway? Are you with the terrorists releasing the plague? Because you better believe I'm going to find a cure."

Ping eyed the ferocious CDC scientist. "Jam, I see what you mean." She looked down at Ballard, whose right eye was now swelling to catch up with the left. "You gave him a matched set," she offered approvingly.

Jam responded with a small smile of acknowledgment. "Martial arts are supposed to be artistic, after all."

Velma interjected. "I demand you tell me who you are."

Jam looked her in the eye. "Velma, we're from the BrainTrust."

Velma shook her head as if to clear it. "The BrainTrust created the plague? I don't believe you." She took another step back and waved her fists again.

Ping reluctantly put her hands up in a combat stance.

Jam spoke soothingly. "Ping, give her a moment. She's pretty shaken up. She'll figure out we're the good guys in a second." She pulled out her cell phone. "Meanwhile, we have to get out of here. I guess it's time to call another Uber. Wish we could've made the other one wait without seeming suspicious."

Ping turned her attention to Jam. "Uber? Why call Uber?" She pointed behind Jam. "When we have a perfectly nice SUV waiting for us." Her eyes lit up. "I'll bet it even has a siren."

Back in Atlanta, after Jam and Ping had departed in their Uber on their trek to Velma's house, Wolf had turned to Simon Bingham. "You have a plan?"

Aar looked at Simon eagerly. "It would be most excellent if it were a very good plan. Just taking out the snipers as the first step in a frontal assault would be more exciting than wise, and someone could get hurt."

Simon hesitated. "Well, I don't know if my plan is excellent, but it's not bad. There are utility tunnels connecting all the buildings in the complex."

Wolf's eyes glowed. "Very good! Can we get to them without being seen?" He walked over to one of the vans. Aar took the other one.

Simon followed Wolf. "I believe we can. It's a fairly large campus, and I think the FBI put just about everybody in the HCCL."

Half an hour later they ditched the vans a reasonable distance from the campus. They came to the place on the periphery that best blended concealment, distance from the FBI around the HCCL, and nearness to a building with tunnel access.

Aar noted a problem. "I believe Dr. Bingham here represents a small issue for us. The way he's dressed, if anyone happens to look our way, he looks a tad too much like a CDC scientist/terrorist."

Wolf grunted. He turned an appraising eye on Simon. "Good point. Dr. Ballard, if you would be so good as to ditch the tie? And the jacket. And roll up your sleeves like a working man."

Moments later the good doctor looked like the foreman for a furniture-moving crew. Aar gestured elegantly toward the nearest building. "Doctor, please lead the way."

And so the furniture team hustled without running along the sidewalk, into the building, and down into the tunnels.

Upon reaching the tunnels they started to trot, Bingham keeping remarkably good time considering his apparent state of fitness. As they made the final approach to the HCCL building, they slowed down both so Simon could catch his breath, and also so they could watch more carefully for FBI lookouts.

As they rounded a corner, they found themselves confronted by a group of people. Wolf prepared to spring to the attack, but then a woman's voice shouted, "Simon! What are you doing here? I thought you knew, we're under attack. By our own FBI!"

Simon, still out of breath, nevertheless ran to her and hugged her. "So glad to see you all got out of their clutches." He looked at them puzzled. "But...why are you still here?"

Another man answered, "Where else would we go? We're still trying to figure out what to do."

The woman sighed. "We've been talking about just going back in and giving ourselves up. We can't get any work done until they let us back in the lab anyway."

Simon shuddered. "Don't."

Wolf explained. "We have labs all set up for you at the BrainTrust."

The woman lit up. "On board the medical ship, the *Chiron*? I've heard a lot about it. That would be great."

A clamor of conversation followed, from which Simon obtained good intel on locations for the people on his extraction list. Wolf told the others a few strategies for getting to the BrainTrust, assuming they could get off the campus. Aar added a few words of caution with a suggestion. "You might want to stay in the tunnels for a little while. We'll see if we can create a distraction that'll give you all a better chance."

Everyone thought that sounded like a good idea.

Wolf had another idea. He looked at the woman who first hailed them. "Do you happen to have a makeup kit?" He turned to another woman, one with blue lipstick. "And you?"

Both women pulled out their compacts. Wolf asked one more question. "What are your chances, with your red and blue lipsticks, of giving Simon here a makeover? Something that makes it look like he has a black eye?"

Once an appalling black eye had been neatly emplaced, Aar, Wolf, and Simon quietly departed the tunnel for the uppermost basement level of the CCCL building.

Simon looked even more disheveled and battered. "At least it won't be a difficult acting job pretending I've been hunted, beaten, and captured."

They turned a corner and ran headlong into a pair of FBI agents.

Aar waved and unleashed the full power of his British accent. "Chaps, good to see you. Interpol. We've got your missing scientist, Simon Bingham." He pushed Simon forward.

The FBI agents gaped. "Interpol? What're you doing here?"

Wolf poked Simon forward as they rapidly approached the agents. "He was up in the ventilation shafts. Classic. Aar had to go up and get him; I didn't fit." Wolf was approximately large enough to terrorize the bears at the San Diego Zoo.

Wolf and Aar came within arm's length of the agents. Time to finish this.

As the agents focused on Simon in the center, Wolf and Aar moved smoothly in opposite directions, outside the agents, and snapped out their arms as if each were a football tackle clotheslining a charging runner.

On the BrainTrust, peacekeepers rarely carried any weapon other than a baton. They trained relentlessly in techniques for pacifying residents without harming them. Today both Wolf and Aar chose the Rear Naked Chokehold for their adversaries: each wrapped one arm around his respective target's neck so that the windpipe was in the crook of the elbow. With that hand, they then grabbed the bicep of the other arm, and...well, in a few moments, they gently laid the agents on the ground before zip-tying their hands and feet together.

One of the agents was about the same size as Aar, so Aar got to upgrade his clothing to a proper FBI outfit. and Both peacekeepers adorned themselves with FBI headsets.

The rest of the assault went quite smoothly, with Simon leading them from place to place to gather his chosen scientists, stopping to pacify the occasional FBI agent, releasing the occasional cluster of captive CDC employees, learning from them the locations of more of the people on Simon's list.

They had collected all but two of Simon's top priority

people when the FBI comms told them the jig was up and they needed to hightail it out of there. Most of the released workers besides Simon's picks agreed to hang around to keep the FBI confused, while others Simon specified went with them as far as the tunnels to ensure they had the best possible chance of escape if or when the FBI departed.

All the people left behind, whether part of the masquerade or hidden below, were invited to make their way to the BrainTrust however they could, where they were guaranteed an enthusiastic welcome.

And so Wolf and Aar, with two vans packed full of the best and brightest virologists, molecular biologists, and epidemiologists in the world, headed back to the coast and to the sub that awaited them.

The sound of a siren blaring in the distance brought Acting Assistant Director Cameron Ballard slowly to his senses. He groaned, rolled to his side, and sluggishly rose. The gravel cut his hands as he pushed himself up. Next he patted down his pants to get the pressed edges realigned.

He was even more certain now that Ms. Highwalker was responsible for the plague than he had been before the arrest.

Long before joining the CDC—over the objections of the FBI agent who'd done her background check, after a direct intervention on her behalf by Simon Bingham—Velma Highwalker had been a radical. Comfortably supported by her share of the profits from the casinos on Cheyenne land, she'd had plenty of time to protest and riot about causes that caught her interest, most of which involved opposition to the policies proffered by the President for Life.

Most notably, she objected vehemently to the President's ruthless support for racial profiling by law enforcement officers. The President's enthusiasm often went to the point of pardoning those officers who ran afoul of the Constitution's protections from unreasonable search and seizure.

Velma was a hot-tempered troublemaker. Just because she'd turned her passion eventually to virology and gotten a doctorate in short order with extraordinary grades, it didn't change the fact that she was a radical who opposed the presidency.

It was all becoming clearer in Cameron's mind, leaving him gasping over the size of the conspiracy. Clearly Simon Bingham, Velma's defender who had also somehow escaped the raid on the CDC, was involved. And Cameron had overheard one of the terrorists who'd rescued her say something about the BrainTrust.

The BrainTrust? Would they really involve themselves in a direct attack on America, when almost half the residents there were American citizens? Yet it made sense. It was an open secret that the BrainTrust had viciously rejected repeated polite requests from the Chief Advisor for medical assistance. They had it in for the President as much as Velma did.

The shape of the bioterror attack made sense too when integrated with all the information he'd acquired between his first readings about the plague and his arrival at the doorstep of the Roybal complex.

The epidemic had broken out simultaneously in all the major cities along the Pacific coast, as well as all the cities along the northeastern seaboard. Looking at the layout of this attack through the lens of a political map, it had struck directly at all the major Blue strongholds—a clear attempt to frame the President and the Chief Advisor.

And it was very interesting indeed that this pattern also left the CDC headquarters on the southeastern seaboard untouched. The perpetrators had not put themselves in harm's way.

Regardless, the plague had become a media circus at the speed of light. Because the disease expressed symptoms similar to measles, itself caused by the rubeola virus, the newshounds had dubbed the plague Blue Rubola—at once both a riff on the famous Ebola virus while also denoting the political nature of the attack. And the Blue media had wholly bought the idea that the Chief Advisor had released the virus to weaken his opposition. Some of the most extreme Red media had agreed, though they had of course praised the endeavor.

Still a little dizzy, Ballard swayed, caught himself, and turned to help his fellow agent. His partner too had struggled to his feet, and exclaimed in exasperation, "They took our car."

Ballard nodded. He reached into his pocket to grab his cell. "I'll call for backup." A few moments later, he exclaimed in exasperation, "Damn, they took our phones." He looked down the lonely road. "I guess we're walking until we find someone to help us."

An hour later they arrived, dusty and sweaty, at a forlorn mini-market with a lone gas pump outside.

Back in contact with his men, Ballard joined a merry chase, mostly vicariously. A second BrainTrust assault team had appeared mysteriously in the middle of the building housing the High Containment Continuity Lab where the FBI had sequestrated the most likely perpetrators.

Ballard almost swooned as he listened to the growing list of escapees. Could all these people be in on the terrorist bioattack? Why else would they all disappear together?

Then word came of a black SUV with a siren blasting down the roads all through Atlanta. After scaring a couple of children half out of their wits, the SUV had stopped—the driver had shown an FBI badge!—and apologized to the kids and their mother, to whom they gave a ride at full speed to make up for their mistake.

The two FBI agents in the SUV were described as a skinny little Asian and a rather taller more dignified woman of Native American ancestry; the mother figured she was Cherokee or some such. Ballard practically frothed with fury. There hadn't been an Indian FBI agent in decades since they were all security risks. Couldn't the mother have noticed that and called someone? Anyway, the driver had been the Asian, who sounded, according to the kids, like she was from the Midwest. Oh, and the kids had had a blast in the back seat, waving at everyone they raced past with sirens wailing.

Having lost all the best suspects, Ballard abandoned the CDC complex to priority-task most of his agents on getting Velma Highwalker, whom he considered the only certain member of the conspiracy. If his prioritization also helped him get his car back sooner—argh!—that was a fine side benefit.

Twenty-four hours later, Ballard's men found his black SUV. A couple of teenagers making out in the empty bleachers of a high school football stadium had heard a siren roar into the parking lot and then stop. They heard more than saw two black copters land in the field near the fifty-yard line. Some voices of greeting ensued, mostly female, but at least one male with a British accent. Some laughter had followed, then the copters took off again.

Meanwhile, the much smaller team Ballard had set on the trail of the escapees from Roybal managed to track the fugitives to Charleston and onto a handful of small inflatable watercraft bought an hour earlier from Kick's Sporting Goods. The inflatables themselves were found, neatly roped together, drifting a mile offshore, empty and bearing no signs they had ever born passengers.

As the entire FBI contingent zoomed back to the CDC campus to interrogate the remaining low-priority CDC workers who'd not been whisked away by the terrorists, Ballard finally realized he'd been duped. The wailing siren had been meant to draw his men off, and now the whole CDC campus was deserted. Following a hunch, he quickly verified that at least two of these lesser targets had made it onto a ferry out to the SpaceR spaceport ship. They were now beyond his jurisdiction.

But at least Ballard had his car back. He opened it to find the keys in the cup holder and a note on the dashboard. "Thank you for letting us borrow your car," the note said, "Sorry for any inconvenience." A second paragraph offered a warning of sorts. "Oh, and the tank's pretty empty. You'll need to get gas first thing. Ping."

A pair of unhappy local Atlanta police stalked toward him, no doubt planning to yell at him for racing his SUV around town like a maniac and creating a serious road hazard.

But the Acting Assistant Director for the WMD Directorate disregarded them. He stared at the note the terrorists had left him, focusing on the part he didn't understand.

What did pinging have to do with anything?

7

RACE FOR THE CURE

Many scientists are on the autism scale, so technically, autism causes vaccines.
—Anonymous viral Facebook observation, 2019

Amanda stood at the podium of the *Chiron's* auditorium. A hushed crowd of scientists sat waiting for her. She saw her old friend Simon Bingham waiting patiently in the front row. A woman of apparent Native American heritage waited beside him with no patience whatsoever, fidgeting as he repeatedly whispered words meant to calm her down —words that failed dismally. Many of the others waited in a state of mild shock at the sequence of events that had brought them here.

"Welcome aboard, everyone." She scanned the audience, nodding to a number of scattered members of the crowd whom she knew. "Welcome to my home. I know a number of you, and a number of you know me, but for the rest, I am Amanda Copeland, head of BrainTrust medical research and currently Chairman of the Board for the BrainTrust Consortium. So not only do I understand the technical details of the problem we face, but I also understand the tools we have available to address that problem. To put it succinctly, this project has the full resources of the BrainTrust archipelago at its disposal."

Velma yelled, "Do we have labs to work in? When can we see them? If they aren't biosafety level four, we've got squat."

Amanda glared at her. "You can see them when you have a clue how they work. They're rather different from what you're used to." She lifted her eyes from Velma. "But you're quite right; we must get to work. So I'd like to introduce you to Dr. Dyah Ambarawati, whom you all might as well get used to addressing as Dash." Amanda waved to the small Balinese scientist in her signature white lab coat waiting to the side. "Dash, they're all yours."

Dash hurried out and launched without further introduction into the technologies they would work with. She looked directly at the fiery woman in the first row. "To address your concern, since we heard about the epidemic, we've had swarms of bots working 24/7 to bring up a series of room-size Class III biosafety cabinets, the most important component of a level four lab. We're turning the whole Red Planet deck into a level four facility, more or less."

Velma spluttered. "Room-size cabinets? How can we work with those? Gloves won't reach. If it's room-size, it needs to be a protective-suit lab."

Dash paused in the face of this vehemence.

Another woman, tall, lithe, with a skin tone similar to Dash's, rose from a corner seat in the front row. "Hi, everyone. I'm Chance Dixon, Dash's partner. Any time you have a question, you can ask me." She glared at the demanding woman. "Including you. We'll get to work a helluva lot faster without the interruptions. Things are different here, and you'll see why, get calm, and learn something. Bots are the answer you're looking for. The answer that you didn't think of because you're ignorant of the possibilities."

After a moment, Dash answered the question more politely. "We make the cabinets room-size or even larger and work remotely using bots inside the cabinets. We'll have a bot wrangler assigned to each cabinet to operate them according to your instructions until such time as you are trained to wrangle the bots yourselves." She saw the woman in the front row gearing up to speak again. "Who are you, please?"

"I'm Velma Highwalker, and—"

Simon interrupted, "—and she's one of our best when she's working rather than complaining."

Velma glared at them both. "What if the cabinets leak?"

Dash twitched her nose. "We have some standard procedures. For example, the whole deck is now partially sealed and over-pressured outside the cabinets. We also have some nonstandard defenses in place: outside the cabinets, the whole area is now flooded with UV-C radiation."

Velma glared. "UV-C? UV lighting is against regs. What's UV-C?"

Amanda came back out to join Dash. "UV-C is part of our standard isle ship defenses against airborne infections, and you've never heard of it because it never got certified for use for sanitization dirtside. It's a higher-frequency form of ultraviolet than the UV-A and UV-B people worry about when getting suntans."

A twitter of laughter ran through the audience, then stopped as everyone remembered how serious the situation was again.

Amanda continued, "Understand, Dr. Highwalker, the BrainTrust knows a little bit about reducing the risks from infectious diseases. Cruise liners before the advent of isle ships were infamous as breeding grounds for disease, and once a norovirus started up, it quickly swept through the entire ship."

Amanda took a breath. "These outbreaks were always more rare than the news stories would lead you to suspect, but when they occurred, they were acute. We couldn't afford any outbreaks like that since everybody on the BrainTrust has too much work to do, so we added a number of measures to our ships after the first norovirus outbreak fifteen years ago. We circulate air at twice the rate of the old cruise liners, we have bots continuously disinfecting all the public surfaces, we have UV-C irradiating the flow in the air ducts 24/7, and any time a passage or a cabin is unoccupied, we flood the area with UV-A, B, and C light. We still have infectious outbreaks, but they never become acute."

Velma grumbled. "It's still a far cry from a biosafety level-four system."

Chance interceded. "Which is why we've retrofitted the deck where we have the biosafety cabinets with additional precautions. I'll go over it all with you myself. *After* we're done here."

Dash popped the image of a large machine onto the screen behind her for all to see. "This is a CRISPIER."

The room hushed. Everyone had heard of the CRISPIERs. Everyone had wanted to try one out. Amanda had been reluctant to sell one to anybody because they were still too cranky and too hard to operate, though she had yielded to Dash's request to build enough to support a whole floor of rejuvenation patients, for whom the CRISPIERs were required.

Even Velma shut up and listened as Dash dived into the details of what a CRISPIER could do and how it could help them end the plague.

Gina eyed Colin suspiciously. She liked Colin all right, but somehow he always seemed to have an additional plan in mind. It usually worked out for everyone, but…she still eyed him suspiciously.

Colin addressed her and her husband Matt Toscano, Werner Halstead, Alex Turner, and Dawn Rainer with considerable urgency. "So you see, we need all your help to pull this off. If we don't come up with a mass production capability, it'll make no difference whether Dash and her team come up with a vaccine or not."

They were all seated in a conference room on the the *Argus*, the BrainTrust's own manufacturing ship.

Alex raised his hand as if asking permission to speak, then spoke. "Have you talked to Amanda about this?"

Colin nodded. "The Consortium is all in. You're fully

authorized to put the *Argus* to work full-time on the manufacture of CRISPIERs."

Dawn interrupted, "This'll put us behind schedule on getting our new isle ships fully operational, won't it?" She scowled. "I don't like it."

Gina touched Dawn on the shoulder, trying to calm her down.

Alex disregarded all this. "What about the *Hephaestus*?" The *Hephaestus* was an isle ship manned only by robots and anchored far from the main archipelago, where toxic materials were handled. It too was a manufacturing vessel, though rather specialized in its equipment.

Colin looked back and forth at Dawn and Alex, clearly trying to decide which one to answer first. Gina figured Alex had asked the easier question, and sure enough, Colin answered him. "If you can use the *Hephaestus*, by all means, go for it."

Colin turned back to Dawn. "You don't need to complete your ships to get them productive, it turns out. Thank you, by the way, for supplying berths for the CDC scientists on the *Eos*."

The *Eos* was one of the two ships Gina and Dawn were building; it was the one closest to completion. The quarters were incomplete and unadorned, but the beds were comfortable, and far better than sleeping in the passageways of the *Chiron*.

Gina noted with some amusement that many of the scientists were sleeping in the passageways of the *Chiron* anyway, to lose not a minute of working time.

Dawn shrugged. "Renting the *Eos* was hardly an act of

charity. Simon promised to pay us back as soon he could access CDC funds again."

Gina pushed Dawn on the matter. "But let's face it: there's still a lot of risk there. He may never get access to the CDC again. We'll be in pretty bad shape if that happens." At least, Gina would be in bad shape. For Gina, those ships were make or break. For Dawn, it was an amusing side investment.

Dawn acknowledged the problem. "True enough, but we still have an avenue to profitability. What do we have here? Colin, will the Consortium rent our second ship as a place to set up a vaccine-production facility? I think Simon's pretty tapped out, even if he does get back to the CDC."

Colin winced. "Well, actually, we're hoping that you'll buy in for a percentage of the profits."

Matt and Dawn guffawed together. Matt took up the criticism. "So, let's see now. You want me to turn the *Helios* into a CRISPIER manufacturing ship, along with the *Argus* and the *Hephaestus*. Then the CRISPIERs go onto Dawn and Gina's ship and start producing vaccine?"

Colin nodded mutely.

"And how do we make a profit?"

Colin explained. "It'll be a more or less standard manufacturer/distributor/customer business enterprise. The distributors will buy product from us and get reimbursed by the customers."

Dawn responded with pure scorn. "No pharmaceutical chain is going to touch this without an FDA certification. Do you expect to get certified?"

Colin laughed. "Not a chance. We'll have to go a little less traditional." He explained his worst-case plan.

Dawn and Matt joined everyone else in laughing.

Alex brought up another point. "You know, loading a boat with CRISPIERs may work for this one emergency if we can get ahead of this virus before the whole world is infected. But the CRISPIER is not a mass-production device. We need a better solution, and it probably needs to be someplace else. An isle ship is a damned expensive piece of real estate for a factory to produce low-cost pharmaceuticals."

Colin nodded. "Already working on it."

Dawn thumped her fist on the table. "In any event, I'm in." She looked at her business partner. "Assuming Gina is in."

Gina moved her arms in an energetic albeit truncated version of one of the cheers she had led in college. "Let's go!"

Velma highlighted another molecular structure on the wallscreen. "As you can see, this is one of the elements of the protein coat that distinguishes Blue Rubola from the measles rubeola virus." She growled in frustration. "The viruses are so similar, it's incredible that the measles vaccine doesn't work at all. Like, not at all."

Dash studied the image. "It's not that surprising. Antibodies are very specific indeed. This just looks like normal, natural genetic mutation from here." She sounded as if she were still hopeful that Blue Rubola was a natural phenomenon, not an engineered bioweapon.

Chance, with a more negative view of human behavior, squashed any such optimism. "The big differences are in the nuclei. Look at these sections of the RNA transcript." She pointed at several sections. "Somewhere in these segments, there are explanations of why Blue Rubola is so much more infectious and so much more lethal."

Velma waved her hands impatiently. "Yeah, yeah, we need to figure that out someday, but today we need to focus on that protein coat."

Simon entered the room. "I can put a team to work studying the RNA, figuring out what's what."

Velma practically screamed, "We don't have the manpower."

Simon closed his eyes. "We certainly do. Not everyone here specializes in the same thing, Velma. Some of them are experts specifically in molecular simulations, and about half of them will soon be twiddling their thumbs."

Dash changed the subject. "Simon, how is everyone else doing?"

Simon chuckled tiredly. "I've got almost everybody working on something. We have separate teams researching each of the major approaches to creating a vaccine. One team is trying to make an attenuated live virus akin to the one we use for measles, another team is trying to create a dead virus, and a third is focused on manufacturing just enough of the protein coat to stimulate the creation of antibodies."

Chance nodded vigorously at the last. "Manufacturing a

part of the protein coat—that's where the CRISPIER will help. I'll get on it as soon as we're done here."

Velma jumped in. "Then let's be done. More talking isn't going to help."

Dash held up a finger. "Actually, I have an additional idea. It occurs to me that we could use the CRISPIER to directly manufacture the antibodies." Her eyes brightened as she had yet another idea. "Or we could design injectable factories that would manufacture antibodies."

Velma got excited. "If we could inject enough antibodies, it would sort of be a cure, and if it slowed the virus down enough, it would work as a vaccine as well, giving the body enough time to figure out how to make the antibodies on its own." She shivered. "How would these factories work?"

Dash started to explain how the CRISPIER could be used in this fashion, quite different from the way it was used for her normal rejuvenation work, figuring it out as she went along.

Simon whispered to Chance, "Go talk to the team working on the protein coat vaccine. See how you can help."

Amanda came in carrying a tray. "Anyone care for some illegal drugs?"

Velma and Simon looked aghast; Chance and Dash looked puzzled. Dash made the obvious observation. "I didn't think any drugs were illegal here on the BrainTrust."

Amanda chuckled. "Oh, there are actually a couple we frown upon. But you're right, nothing's banned outright. People who get themselves messed up so badly they can't do their jobs and don't respond to therapy are invited to leave." She set the tray down. "What I've got here is Modafinil."

Simon blinked. "Used to prevent narcolepsy, right?"

Amanda nodded. "And one of the most popular drugs abused by college students as a study drug. It'll keep you awake and alert for an extra twelve hours."

Simon replied slowly. "I suppose it's illegal without a prescription, but it's hardly heroin."

Chance injected, "Seems likely we can get prescriptions if we really want them. Is there anybody here who *isn't* authorized to write prescriptions?"

Amanda picked up her pill bottle and started dispensing oblong white pills with L234 printed on the side. "You don't need to take it if you don't want to, but if you find yourself in the middle of a task and you're falling asleep, this will get you through the project." She pursed her lips. "The epidemiologists are estimating almost half a million people are infected already. If the mortality projections hold up, we're looking at fifty thousand deaths."

Simon whispered, "And the day is young."

Maneuvering ever so slowly, flying nearly blind with nothing but the paltry help of night-vision goggles to assist him, Wolf dropped the stealth copter onto the roof of one of the buildings in the University of California San Francisco Helen Diller Medical Center in Parnassus Heights. He'd studied pictures of the place before taking off. The campus featured a forest of randomly sized white skyscrapers packed so densely that, were they alive, they would all be choked to death.

He got out of the copter, found an access door to the roof, broke in ever so quietly, and made his way down to the first floor, clutching a backpack with a handful of small bots.

Wolf could not believe why he was here.

In order to manufacture the antibodies and the antibody factories to make the cure (Dash said it wasn't really a cure, but as nearly as Wolf could figure, it was), Dash needed the existing antibodies from people who were infected. To get the antibodies, she needed blood samples.

But the scientists from the CDC had left Atlanta with barely the shirts on their backs, plus the occasional thumb drive full of data.

And now no one was willing to give them blood samples. When they'd called the CDC, an FBI honcho had answered and offered to send all the materials they wanted as soon as the BrainTrust sent back all the scientists for questioning. Colin called the Chief Advisor and got essentially the same answer. A phone call to the Governor of California got intercepted by the Attorney General, who told them to go to hell.

As Wolf understood it, Chance had been climbing on board a copter to fly to San Francisco to get some goddam samples herself when Simon intercepted her and demanded she get back to work and said there were tasks that needed her skills more, but did she have any ideas about who might be a good choice for this mission?

So Chance had called him, and here he was. He did have some expertise in stealth recon, and it was not all that much different. Well, it was entirely different, but he was happy to volunteer.

The medical systems of all the major California cities were already being overwhelmed. Here in this complex, the dental clinics building, a little separate from the main cluster, and its adjoining parking lot had been turned into a makeshift isolation unit. Wolf pulled on a lab coat—ridiculously tight on him, but he left it unbuttoned so he still had circulation through his arms—and made his way confidently across the campus to the place where, if he were not careful, he'd catch the infection and die.

Fortunately, he did not have to go all the way into the building or screw with a moon suit (as if there were a chance he could find one that fit). He stopped outside, dropped his little robotic friends on the concrete, and guided them through the door he held open for them.

Now all Wolf had to do was play the video game on his bot control console, driving the bots through the wards, having them sneak up on sleeping and unconscious patients, and slurping up a little blood.

Soon the bots were done. They exited through the parking lot that had been cordoned off but not sealed, sprayed each other with short blasts of hot decontamination foam, and made their way back to him.

Suddenly he heard a loud male voice bearing down on him. "Are they insane? They can't just close down the CDC in an emergency like this. Those people need to get back to work!"

Two people in lab coats, a man and a woman, practically ran over him in their haste. The man who had been speaking confronted him. "Who the hell are you?" He looked at the control console in Wolf's hands, heard the soft clacking of the bots running back to him, and pulled out his phone. "You stand right there until someone comes for you."

Wolf's first thought was to knock them both out swiftly before the doctor finished dialing. He could do it, of course.

But even if they placed the call, Wolf was still sure he could get away. So he tried something else. "Let me explain what I'm doing here." He continued to explain as he picked up the bots and put them back in the backpack. In the end, he looked helplessly down at the doctor before him.

The doctor bit his lip. "So, you're here from the Brain-Trust? You need samples? And those imbeciles won't give them to you?" He looked at his companion.

She gave him a half-laugh. "I just can't help thinking that they're on our side."

The doctor nodded grudgingly. "Come inside for a moment."

Wolf followed them into the room separated from the isolation unit by a large window and an airlock. The doctor went into the airlock and pulled on a moonsuit, then disappeared into the main facility.

Half an hour later, he came out and placed a large foam box in Wolf's hands. Opening it briefly, they could see rows of vials, each packed in a separate form-fitting hole in the foam. "They're all labeled. Be damn careful with them, obviously."

As Wolf carefully resealed the box, the doctor pulled out a business card. "I'm Doctor Lancaster. If there's anything else you need, call."

Velma and Ted scrutinized the operation of the bots in Biosafety Cabinet Seven. They were in the main shopping area in the middle of the Red Planet deck, decorated as a relentless Mars-scape of red rock, relieved only in one place where the geodesic dome enclosing the Falcon's Nest colony sank into the red dirt.

At the moment, much of the austere beauty of the Martian surface was obscured by the Class III biosafety cabinets that had supplanted the shops.

Watching as one bot moved swiftly to pour the wrong vial into the wrong Petri dish, Velma jerked her hand up in a helpless gesture. "Stop!"

Ted mashed a button, and all five of the bots in Cabinet Seven froze. "Sorry. This is darn tricky, and we don't have hardly any preprogrammed subtask modules to help." In the days before Ted's copter design and manufacturing business took off, he'd supported himself while taking Accel classes and designing copters by wrangling bots when someone needed extra help.

Five bots were about half what a typical wrangler could manage on a normal job and a quarter of what Ted had often controlled. "I need to take some serious time to upgrade the software on all these bots. We're wasting too much effort." He pointed at the rows of cabinets running off to the left and the right. "All of us are wasting our time."

Velma built up some venom to chew Ted out, but Dash walked up at that moment and intervened. "You're right, of course. Colin talked to Lenora, Chen Ying, and Jun Laquan about helping make these bots more effective." She chuckled. "Though from what I've heard of Jun, he's at least as likely to design a whole new bot for us as to help with the current ones." She looked down at her tablet. "Chen Ying and Jun should be on Matt's Global Express by now." She turned to Velma. "You'll meet them in a couple of hours."

Ted, although working furiously, still had the mental capacity for conversation. "Dr. Dash! I haven't seen you in an age. I hear your family's coming to visit."

Dash smiled. "My aunt and uncle and my cousin will be coming once we have this emergency out of the way." The smile faded. "My uncle is not in very good shape. I've tested him, and he qualifies for rejuvenation."

Velma, still watching the bots as they started up again—more slowly this time—asked distractedly. "I thought your rejuv was still crazy expensive."

Dash sighed. "Somewhat less so than when we started, but yes. I'm paying for my uncle myself." She brightened. "I can't wait to introduce you all to my cousin Astri. She's very outgoing and exuberant, even by American standards, to say nothing of Balinese."

Velma harrumphed. "Unlike you, so grumpy all the time."

They heard a commotion down the passageway as a large number of people approached.

Velma turned to them and demanded, "Who are you? How the hell did you get in here?"

The leader, a young man with the pasty white skin suggesting he was a software engineer, brought the small mob to a halt. "I'm Chad Duncan, and we're your lab rats."

Dash and Velma both looked at him without full comprehension.

"Colin's been talking to people all over the archipelago, identifying volunteers for your first human trials. I understand you're pretty close to having something to try." Chad gulped. "He says, and I agree, that we have to short-circuit the usual testing process here, sort of like you did for rejuv. Except the stakes are higher."

Another one of the new lab rats, a woman about the same age as Chad, augmented this. "We hear almost two hundred thousand people are already projected to die."

Dash looked at them with consternation. "We bypassed almost every tenet of medical testing for the rejuvenation therapy because we could run our tests on people who were already dying. You are not."

Chad waved his hand at the people behind him. "But our families might as well be dying. Most of us are Americans. If we can help protect them, we will."

Dash objected. "We are not going to try this on perfectly healthy people as the first thing. For one thing, when we first test the live attenuated virus, we could actually give you Blue Rubola." But the more she thought about it, the fewer alternative ideas she had.

Velma intervened, delighted with the volunteers, completely blowing Dash off. "Yeah, Dash, sure, it'd be nice to have some people already at risk to experiment with. But how are we going to get test subjects with Blue Rubola out here? That would be dangerous to the whole archipelago. And we sure can't go to them. The Feds would have us in chains in a heartbeat." She held out her hand to Chad. "Velma Highwalker. Overjoyed to meet you."

Dash frowned. "But..." She tried to formulate an objection, then threw up her hands. "I'll need blood samples from all of you. Follow me."

Velma tossed aside the pillow covering her eyes and rose blearily from the cot. She had slept, sort of, in a passage near the Red Planet shopping area where the biosafety cabinets resided. Although she had been assigned a real bed in a real cabin on the *Eos*, she, like many of the others, was hot-bunking by her experiments. She had just finished a quick nap while her experiments were running, between the times of furious activity as they analyzed the results of one experiment and set up the next.

Velma no longer had any idea whether it was night or day outside. In addition to all the other changes, they'd set the lighting to a constant lab-level brilliance for the duration of the emergency.

The BrainTrust had continuously upgraded the equipment as the work progressed. They now had a CRISPIER for every scientist on the deck. Chunks of every data center in the archipelago, from the *GPlex III* to the *BrainTrust University*, had been rented to run billions of simulations.

Hundreds of robotically managed experiments in petri dishes looked for a fragment of Rubola protein coat they could mass-produce that would also properly trigger the B-lymphocytes. Once triggered, these specialized white blood cells would transform into a cluster of plasma cells that poured out antibodies.

Meanwhile, other hundreds of experiments sought

variations of the antibodies from rubola victims that were also mass-producible and effective.

As Velma approached her cabinet, Ted fiddled with the bot controls. Samples from the petri dishes slid into digital microscopes, and a number of videos popped onto Velma's tablet.

A restaurant bot, commandeered into the project, handed her an espresso as she glanced at the results of the latest experiments.

Suddenly she no longer needed the caffeinated coffee to get her blood flowing; an adrenalin rush gave her all the energy she needed. She put her coffee cup on the desk where Ted sat and slaved a part of the promenade's renderable wall to her tablet. With a whoop, she wrapped her arms around an astonished Ted Simpson and kissed him on the cheek. "Everybody, come see!"

On the wall, a video of molecular structures flowed—incomprehensible to any normal person yet easily understood by the scientists of the Red Planet deck. The key element of the video was this: the smaller molecules were clumping around the larger structures and encasing them, almost like foam drowning a car on fire.

The viral particles were being neutralized with speedy dispatch.

A cheer started, and Simon yelled, "Velma, you've done it!"

Everyone crowded around her, congratulating her.

Moments later, Dash and Chance rushed into the promenade with exciting news of their own. They stopped before reaching the packed crowd around Velma.

Dash watched the celebration with a philosophical smile.

Chance muttered grouchily, "Well, it's great that Velma figured out the vaccine. But you just figured out how to inject antibody factories that don't even need to go through the step of stimulating the white blood cells."

Dash shrugged. "My molecular factories get filtered out of the bloodstream after a day or so. They can keep a patient alive for a while, but we need the traditional vaccine as well."

Chance frowned. "But…Velma's merely developed a vaccine. You've made an extraordinary breakthrough! Something new under the sun! You can even save people who are already deep in the grip of the infection!"

Dash answered sternly, "And we'll tell Simon and the others in a little while. After Velma's received all the congratulations she can stand."

She pulled out her phone. "In the meantime, we can tell Amanda to gear up the mass production system. With the two victories we've just achieved, I'm thinking we can start trials on our local volunteers this afternoon, and unless something goes wrong, manufacture our first shipment of vaccine in the morning." She shook her head. "I can't believe I'm saying that. Talk about a truncated test and evaluation process!"

Chance grunted. "Meanwhile, I suppose we should go congratulate her."

Dash frowned. "Why don't we wait a couple of minutes, until the crowd thins out?"

Chance remained grumpy. "Sure. Then she can gloat more."

Dr. Lancaster was rushing down the street to the isolation unit, now bursting to overflowing, trying to figure out where to put the next batch of patients. He was indescribably tired. And defeated. It was getting worse, and he knew nothing that could stop it from getting far worse indeed.

As he rounded a corner, he found the same enormous man standing in the same place where Lancaster had accosted him several days ago, holding a foam box that looked identical to the box Lancaster had given him.

Lancaster raised an eyebrow. "Need more samples?"

The man shook his head, his eyes alight with good humor. "Presents." He carefully opened the box. "This may be both a vaccine and a partial cure."

Lancaster's raised eyebrow rose further. "You apparently don't know it doesn't work like that."

The man's expression turned stubborn. "Dr. Dash said that that wasn't a good way of saying it, but she said there was a grain of truth in it." He pulled out a sheet of paper and handed it over. "This is what Dr. Dash actually says about it."

As Lancaster read the missive, his heart started to beat harder, and he straightened from the slumped, tired, nearly hopeless posture he had fallen into a few days ago. "If this works, you've just saved tens of millions of lives in the United States alone."

The man put a friendly hand on his shoulder. "Let's try it before we get too excited," he said, echoing a passage from Dash's missive.

Lancaster took the precious box, suppressing an urge to

hug it. "How will I contact you to let you know what happens?"

"My name is Wolf, Dr. Lancaster, and you'll find both Dr. Dash and me on speed dial here." He slipped a cell phone into Lancaster's pocket. "This is a BrainTrust phone, so we can talk in private."

Wolf nodded and walked away.

Lancaster hurried into the building, into his moonsuit, and into the part of the isolation unit where the patients with nothing left to hope for except swift death resided.

Twenty-four hours later, he took a deep breath and called Dash. "I injected two dozen patients in the terminal ward. Normally there's a ninety-five mortality rate among them. Today, three-quarters of the patients I injected are showing signs of improvement. It's hardly even a preliminary result, but...please send me as much of your vaccine as you can. *Please.*"

Rodrick Sprague, the recently minted Acting Commissioner of the Food and Drug Administration, sat down in the chair facing the Chief Advisor's desk.

He gripped the leather arms of his chair, firmly suppressing his thrill at being here, called in to give advice to the most important man in the world on the most important assault on the most important country in all the history of the world.

The old commissioner, Horacio Chapin, had in Rodrick's opinion always been a poor one. He'd been a hasty fellow, always talking urgently about new ideas for how to streamline processes, reduce costs, and get solutions into the hands of the health care system ASAP.

Of course, that enthusiasm for innovation had done Horacio little good. The regulators of the FDA had held firm on their standards, and the commissioner had had very few successes—few enough that Rodrick had been expecting Chapin to resign for some time.

Really, the old commissioner had been a borderline loon. It cost millions of dollars in research and analysis to eliminate a regulation. If people had jumped every time Chapin proposed a faster, lower-cost way of getting things done, the FDA would be bankrupt by now. And at least one new drug or medical instrument that slipped through Horacio's streamlined certification process would have killed somebody, leading to a blistering news media assault on the agency.

Worse, Chapin had refused to honor the President for Life with fervent support. Chapin never said anything critical, but often when a staff member praised the President or the Chief Advisor, Rodrick had seen Chapin press his lips together in a thin, disapproving line. Radical ideas proposed by a man like that obviously should be dismissed out of hand.

The country was fortunate that Commissioner Chapin had died in a freak car accident a few weeks earlier. His self-driving car had veered off the Francis Scott Key Bridge into the Potomac for no apparent reason.

Now that control of the FDA had returned to the competent hands of a serious professional, the country was much safer. No matter how much panic roiled across the nation, the FDA would stand firm, a rock of calm competence that would ensure proper procedures were followed properly. Only in this way could the safety of the people be protected in the long term.

The Chief Advisor jumped right to the point. "Got a call from the BrainTrust. They say they have a vaccine for Blue Rubola, and all we need to do to stop the disease is to let them ship it to us." He pursed his lips. "They say it even works for most of the people who already have the disease as long as they aren't too far gone."

Rodrick rolled his eyes. "And this is why you can't trust anybody who's in business just for profit. As any first-year medical student can tell you, that's not possible. Vaccines don't work that way."

The Chief Advisor took a deep breath. "Still, it's the BrainTrust. I don't like those sardines-packed-in-a-can any more than you do. Probably less. But they do create new things—unheard of things—pretty often."

Rodrick's expression turned sour. "Maybe, maybe not. Even if they did develop some fancy new trick, they can't possibly have put it through anything like a proper certification process. For all we know, it would kill even more people than Blue Rubola."

The Chief Advisor blinked. "Really? Because I'm hearing reports that the death rate from the disease is over ten percent."

The acting commissioner waved it away. "Preliminary numbers only. You're getting that from the CDC, right? The second-raters who're left since the top epidemiologists abandoned their posts and snuck off to the BrainTrust?"

The Advisor nodded reluctantly. "Although I suspect

they're talking to and working with the people who went to the BrainTrust."

Sprague leaned forward. "And who among them has a reason to tell the truth? The bigger the crisis appears, the more likely they think we are to panic and pardon them *en masse*."

He leaned back again in his chair. "Besides, I've just heard a report from one of the University of California medical centers. In San Francisco. Apparently the lethality of the disease has dropped off dramatically. It looks like the disease is unstable, and mutating to a more benign form."

The acting commissioner shrugged. "That's a common pattern for diseases, of course, but it seems to be happening with extraordinary speed with this engineered bioweapon. This genetically-edited virus is unnatural, and falling apart as we speak."

The Chief Advisor visibly relaxed. "That's a relief. Still, any idea what the status is for developing a vaccine of our own?"

Rodrick twitched his nose. "I don't really know. I'd imagine it's slow going since we lost so many key personnel." He shook his finger in a sign of commitment. "But rest assured, the moment they have something, we'll give it top priority. We'll cut every legitimate corner to get it out quickly. Six months from the moment they put something legitimate in our hands, we'll release it."

He thought about it for a moment. "Or nine months, to be realistic. Call it nine months."

Colin hung up the phone after talking with the Chief Advisor one last time. A huge roomful of people held their breaths: Matt, Gina, Dawn, Dash, Chance, Simon, and Velma, among others. "No dice. Looks like we're going with Plan B."

Dawn shrugged. "Probably more profitable anyway."

Dash glared. "That is hardly the most important aspect."

Dawn smiled warmly at the woman who had, if only for a day, brought Dawn's mother back to life. "And it'll save millions of lives, too. I'm very excited."

Getting the word out to the people of America that the BrainTrust had a vaccine that could also cure many of the people already infected was easy. The Federal and California governments could not stop the flood of messages from the former CDC scientists that had gone, well, viral.

Having failed to prevent the dissemination of the BrainTrust's information, the governments had tried to bury it with denunciations, labeling the vaccine a child-killer, among other things, and also asserting that Blue Rubola was not actually as dangerous as fearmongers would have you believe. Peculiarly, the more the Red and Blue governments berated the vaccine, the more eagerly people sought to get their hands on it.

Of course, getting the vaccine into those hands was a little trickier.

Trey stood on his corner taking orders and collecting money, watching his business hop. That was literally true. In the old days, when he used to hold the drugs for his father, he had dispensed the purchases directly to the buyers in their cars.

In the modern era, when his little brother held the drugs and did the distribution, over half the deliveries were made by drone copter. One such copter was hopping down by his brother now, having fulfilled an order. Another was hopping up, up, and away on a trip, probably to the suburbs.

The delivery process was not the only thing that had changed in the illegal drug industry. Two key societal and regulatory changes had transformed every aspect of the business.

The first thing that had happened was the country had gone crazy legalizing marijuana, his father's most popular product. Sure, the margins were better on coke, but weed was the staple in his corner of the world.

With pot legalization, times had gotten tough until the government bailed them out by introducing rapidly increasing regulatory hurdles for procuring opioids. Driven by a burst of media frenzy over the opioid death rate, it had taken only a few years to reach the tipping point—the moment at which it became easier to buy pain medication from street dealers than from pharmacies.

After his dad went to jail, Trey had remade himself as one of the entrepreneurs on the forefront in the reborn industry. Soon Vicodin was his top-selling item.

Of course, with the change in products came a change in clientele. Whereas his father had mostly served college kids looking for a score, now a majority of Trey's customers were elderly retirees looking for the relief they needed to get out of bed in the morning.

It was hard for these new customers to get down to his corner in Compton, so taking innovation to the next step, Trey had introduced copter delivery. One thing led to another, and soon he was processing automatic renewals. Now he had a small though lucrative business lending money against future Social Security checks.

Some things hadn't changed, though. Customer cars still stopped on the street to deal at his corner, and the neighborhood was still freaking dangerous. Especially now, when it looked like a turf war was heating up just a block over from his stand.

So when he recognized a battered, antiquated silver Edison all-electric car rolling to a stop beside him, his first words were, "Grandma Jenkins! You shouldn't be here. It's too dangerous." He looked around a little wildly; fortunately, it didn't look like violence was about to break out in the next two minutes. "I just shipped you your monthly order of hydrocodone last week. Did something go wrong?"

The little old lady shook her head. Small, tight curls of silver hair waved in the sunlight. "Got it right on time. But I'm here for a special order." She looked around, eyes wide, as if afraid of being overheard. "We're not on any government vidcams here, are we?"

Trey snorted. "Not a chance, Grandma." The street dealers generally took Monday off, since that was the day the government came around and repaired/replaced all the vidcams. Tuesday morning the younger children practiced their baseball skills by using both their pitching and their batting abilities to knock the vidcams back out.

Grandma Jenkins spoke in quiet desperation. "I need

the BrainTrust vaccine for Blue Rubola. You happen to have any? Or know someone who might? I need the real thing, Trey, absolutely no substitutes."

Well, Trey understood both her caution and her urgency. Trading in the rubola vaccine was a serious offense. Both the Feds and the California government were hot to stop it.

Trey was, of course, one of the first entrepreneurs to take on the forbidden product. BrainTrust wholesale prices were surprisingly low, probably because of their level of automation, so there was room for fat margins in the distribution chain.

He nodded to the grand old lady. "My little brother has trained to make the injections, so he can fix you up right here. Or if you have experience with injections yourself, you can do it on your own."

He rolled up the arm of his t-shirt and pointed to the meat of his shoulder. "And as for the quality of our product, it's straight from the BrainTrust. See that kinda reddish blotch on my skin? It's a characteristic of the real vaccine, and it lasts about a week. If you don't get that, you didn't get the real vaccine." He rolled his sleeve down with a laugh. "The first person my brother practiced injecting was me. Disaster. But he got the hang of it pretty quickly. We've already inoculated everyone in my family, most of my friends' families, and most of their friend's families. Not a sign of Blue Rubola among any of them." The old warning to drug dealers didn't apply to Blue Rubola vaccine, Trey figured "do not use your own product" would be a mistake in this case. He doubted there was a single person in his 'hood who hadn't gotten vaccinated.

Trey changed the subject. "And I should mention that, although we can just sell you the vaccine if you prefer, we do offer the injection and the disposal of the needle as a free service to our regular customers."

Grandma Jenkins frowned. "I don't want just one, Trey. I need enough for my whole family, and their friends."

Trey gave it a moment's thought. "I can give you a great deal on a whole carton. Fourteen hundred doses in dry packets; you just need to follow the instructions and mix with distilled water before injecting." He quoted a price. "You want that much?"

Grandma Jenkins pondered this for a moment, nodded. "That's enough to vaccinate both the whole high school and the elementary school where my grandkids are. I hadn't planned on that, but I think the PTA will reimburse me. Can I get it now?"

Trey tapped out a message to his brother. "Sure can, Grandma. I'll put it on your account."

"You're a good young man. Thank you."

Before she rolled up the window, Trey made one last urgent point. "And if you need more, don't come back down here, you hear me? Message me saying how many blue candies you want, and I'll send it by copter just like always. I don't want you getting hurt just to see me."

Grandma Jenkins smiled, waved, and drove down the street to Trey's younger brother.

Trey stood a little straighter as he watched her depart. He always enjoyed giving good service to his best customers.

Oziegbe stepped off the BrainTrust ferry onto the rocky shore many miles south of Ensenada in Baja California, the Mexican peninsula south of San Diego. Dozens of people and hundreds of bots followed him.

What an odd place this was. He'd experienced this kind of heat before, but nothing this dry. Ciara had warned him to drink even when not thirsty while thrusting into his hands a huge water bottle imprinted with the words, Welcome to the BrainTrust.

Colin—an interesting person, that one—had pressed a tube of lip balm on him. "You'll get chapped lips, something you've probably never experienced before." Colin had shown him how to use the lip balm because he was right—Oziegbe had no idea what he was talking about.

As the first ferry pulled away, the second one slid into place. The bots scurried to haul out the most important items. First of all were the beta batteries, which had to be set up before the bots were all drained of power.

Second were a number of crates of Blue Rubola vaccine.

Colin and the BrainTrust had, Oziegbe knew, paid a remarkable number of bribes to get the permissions to build here so quickly. As Colin had explained it, the bribes came in two forms: cash was, of course, popular with the government in Mexico City, but there was something even more valuable than cash: the ability to ensure that one's family would survive the plague.

At first, the Mexican government had been uninterested in the vaccine. They figured it was an American problem, no matter how patiently the BrainTrusters tried to explain that viruses knew no borders. Mexico would be a hotter plague zone than America all too soon, particularly Mexico City, with its frighteningly dense, shockingly poor slums where proper nutrition was a dream. "No big deal," the politicians had muttered, "The Wall will protect us from the Americans."

Their attitude had undergone a radical revision after the plague had broken out in Puerto Peñasco, a coastal city that had been transformed, decades earlier, into a giant retirement home for Americans on Social Security.

As Blue Rubola spread from that minor local extension of the Yankee empire, the politicians' attitudes had experienced such a remarkable change that soon the clink of SmartCoin was considerably less interesting than the availability of hypodermic syringes filled with pale-blue survival.

The limited amount of SmartCoin needed to seal the deal by that time had already been transferred to the politicians in the capital. They would get their doses of vaccine the moment the factory went online.

The crates of vaccine now offloaded from the ferry were bribes for another key market segment: the local residents in the nearby towns. Ensenada would, if things proceeded according to plan, be immune to the virus within the week.

The first things Oziegbe had to do included vaccinating all the locals, hiring some of those locals, bringing in more BrainTrust bots, getting more locals through basic training with the Accel modules Ciara and Lenora had lured several of their module authors into whipping together, ordering materials to be brought by truck down Route 1 through Ensenada, building a road spur from the factory location to Route 1 in time for the trucks, and getting a helluva lot more bots on site.

Then he had to order all the stuff they hadn't thought of yet that they were going to need in time for it to arrive before they needed it. It was a management nightmare.

Oziegbe rubbed his hands together. "This is going to be great!" he exclaimed to the hot wind that blew through the crisp blue sky above him.

The leader of the epidemiology team stood in front of the auditorium, briefing everyone on the race between the spread of the virus and the spread of the vaccine. "So, as you can see, we're starting to win. Now, that's a lot different from actually winning; it could take years to bring this epidemic to a conclusion since it went international virtually the first day of its release. Some of the PEZ-like dispensers were found in international airports, and they were very effective."

The epidemiologist took a sip of water. "But we've started shipping stocks of vaccine to all the major cities of the world. If an outbreak occurs, almost every nation has agreed to break their regulations, based on our experiences with the United States, and inoculate the at-risk populations."

Dash raised her hand. "This is all wonderful news, but I can't help noticing an anomaly in your numbers." She synced her tablet to the wallscreen and drew lines around several clusters of data. "Am I confused, or did the Blue Rubola hardly affect the people in these impoverished areas? I think you call them 'ghettos?' If so, what was the special characteristic that protected them? Wouldn't we normally expect these densely populated, low-income neighborhoods to suffer disproportionately more, not less?"

The epidemiologist chuckled. "Good catch, Dash. This is indeed a bizarre anomaly, quite the opposite of what we'd normally predict. We're analyzing the phenomenon with all the resources we can afford." He shrugged. "Our best guess at this time is there's something special about their diet that confers a limited immunity, but that's only a hypothesis."

As he shut off the wallscreen, he made a promise. "I'll let you know when we have something concrete. If we ever have something concrete. Sometimes these things just remain a mystery."

8

SEEING RED

The threat of mutual suicide is a very uninspiring concept, no matter how logical it may seem.
—Herman Kahn, *On Thermonuclear War*

Khalid poured over the results of his latest tests and the accompanying extrapolations of the resulting pandemic. The door behind him opened, and Sabaah came in from a short venture into the out of doors to incinerate the bodies of the mice used in the most recent experiments.

Sabaah wore blue jeans as usual since the mice had all been confined in a Class III biosafety cabinet. He'd removed the mice by wrangling a pair of bots to take them up and out of the tunnels. Now he stood on tip-toes to peer over Khalid's shoulder at the death projections. "Am I missing something, or is this one only about as lethal as the last one?"

Khalid shrugged. "If anything, this one is a little less lethal, but not much."

Uwais joined them. "Don't we want higher lethality? I'm confused."

Sabaah piped in, "Yeah, I know you were disappointed with the mortality rates from the last one. What was it? You projected twenty percent, but only got ten."

Uwais continued, "And then they came out with that wretched vaccine. How'd they figure it out so fast, anyway?"

Khalid sighed. "I'm still experimenting." He pointed to a far cabinet filled with test tubes filled with nearly-fluorescent orange powder that practically screamed death. "That one is far more lethal, but I'm holding it for our most critical target."

He pointed at the near cabinet housing the cherry-red cysts of the virus currently under examination. "This one is designed for more effective proliferation. It's even more contagious, and the amount of time when the virus is communicable before becoming symptomatic has been extended."

Sabaah shook his head impatiently. "OK, I guess, but is it really useful to run this test? Can we really achieve our goals with these low death rates?"

Khalid laughed. "Oh, trust me, this one will sow plenty of death." He reached into a cabinet adjacent to the cherry-red virus and pulled out a vial of clear liquid. With quick movements, he loaded hypodermics and injected his compatriots.

Sabaah, who hated needles, grumbled, "And this. Is this

even necessary? We won't be exposed, will we?" He closed his eyes as the needle went in.

Uwais laughed. "Better safe than sorry."

Khalid answered their earlier question indirectly. "Are you two familiar with the inner workings of an H-bomb?"

While Uwais waved his hands in a so-so gesture, Sabaah shrugged. "More or less."

Khalid continued. "Well, it's a two-step process. First you blow a normal atomic bomb, powerful enough to shatter the heart of a city like Hiroshima. But that's merely the trigger. The purpose of the A-bomb is to activate the fusion of hydrogen atoms in its core. That fusion, the second stage, produces the signature H-bomb explosion, which is up to a thousand times more powerful."

He pulled one of the red test tubes from the cabinet. "Our little bioweapon here is stage one. The real carnage will be unleashed by the stage two it activates."

He shifted closer to the computer monitors and pointed at the map where the simulation ran. "You see where we're going to release it? You understand the consequences?"

Uwais and Sabaah studied the map for a moment, then smiled. Uwais answered reverently, "Glorious."

As Dash approached the Red Planet biocabinet area, she heard angry, loud voices. Even before she could make out the words, she could identify the speaker. She sighed. Velma again, undoubtedly fighting with Simon. She wondered who else was involved in this battle. There was always at least one other person involved, the person who'd come up with an idea that needed to be pursued who needed a biosafety cabinet for that pursuit. Or a CRISPIER. Or another specialist who was currently assigned to another experiment.

Even here on the BrainTrust, resources were not unlimited. Even if they had unbound room with unbound equipment, there were not enough people to investigate every avenue of attack.

There weren't even enough people to investigate all the avenues of attack Velma came up with. And Dash had saddled Simon with the management position, i.e., the responsibility for allocating those resources and determining which experiments would live and which would die. She felt not the least bit guilty about giving Simon that duty; it was after all, similar to the job he had held at the CDC. Still, the prioritization and allocation process was wearisome. It needed to be improved upon.

Velma started yelling again.

Dash straightened her shoulders. She hated yelling matches; she hated confrontation of all kinds. No more. Today she would solve this problem.

As she headed in the direction of Velma's voice, she saw that today's third disputant was Chance. Watching them with an eye that had become expert at such assessments, it seemed clear that Chance was giving as good as she got, although in a softer voice.

Dash marched up to them and waited to get a word in edgewise. Chance saw her and held up a hand, not quite shoving it in Velma's face. "Dash needs a word."

Velma turned to accost her. "Yeah?"

Dash smiled pleasantly. "It is time to bring this bickering to an end. I have made it so." She turned to Simon. "If you would gather everyone into the auditorium, I have a new technology with which everyone needs to familiarize themselves."

Velma put her hands on her hips. "What? We're having a very important discussion here."

"After I show you CEREBRUM, you may change your mind. Now if you'll excuse me, I must go prepare."

Fifteen minutes later, everyone reassembled in the auditorium. Dash filled the main wallscreen with a list of predictions for what would happen with all the experiments currently underway. Experiments that had had to be postponed, having been judged less likely to produce valuable results, were also listed.

Dash started her presentation. "This is going to be an interactive demonstration. Please pull out your tablets and get an account link as you see on the screen.

As the audience entered the system, someone muttered too loudly, "It looks like I have a thousand dollars in my account. Is this real money, or is it SmartCoin?"

That got a twitter of laughter from the audience.

Velma continued to study the screen. "So we're starting a betting pool?"

Dash considered the merits of having Chance gag Velma for the duration of the discussion but reluctantly decided against it. "In a word, yes. If more words are allowed, no." She wrinkled her nose as she once again tried to decide where to begin. "Some of you may have heard of a technology known as a prediction market. In such a market, forecasts of future events are presented, and the participants may buy Yes and No positions on each forecast. Research suggests that such prediction markets integrate human knowledge and insight more effectively than any other known approach."

Simon interrupted this time. "So, we're going to run a prediction market to choose which experiments to run next?"

Dash nodded, then shook her head. "Not exactly. To work successfully, a prediction market must have large numbers of participants, what is known as a 'thick market.' Without a thick market, the system is prone to many types of failures, not the least of which is groupthink."

Chance glared at Velma. "No risk of groupthink here, with a group of people who couldn't agree where to go for lunch."

This got another twitter of laughter from the crowd, but Dash shook her head. "You'd be surprised at just how terrible the groupthink can become among people who argue incessantly." She flipped the screen to the view of a questionnaire. "However, back in the '90s, a team of researchers at HP Labs developed an offshoot of the prediction market, the Behaviorally Robust Aggregation of Information in Networks system known as BRAIN. By using a set of psychological analyses to assess each individual participant's relevant personality characteristics, such as appetite for risk, the experimental economists at HP were able to create a market with just a few people—often just a small team of experts—that had the positive properties of a thick market."

Another anonymous voice offered, "So you're going to determine which of us belong in the loony bin and weight the outcome to disregard them?"

Several people responded to this, suggesting that the fellow who asked the question should be the first into the bin.

Dash struggled to regain control of the meeting. "Not exactly, but more or less yes. Lenora and her researchers at the Accel Corporation have developed an enhancement of BRAIN that, among other things, enables conditional predictions: if we do X but not Y, can we still get to Z?"

Velma voiced her skepticism. "I still don't see how this is different from a gambling pool. And I still don't believe it'll work."

Dash was pretty sure that Velma's definition of "working" was, "all Velma's ideas will be the top priority." She sighed. "If you think it's a gambling pool, you're in good company. The American Gaming Control Board outlawed all serious large-scale prediction markets decades ago since they concluded it was a form of gambling."

Chance knew how to get Velma's goat at this point. "So, Velma, do you agree with the government? I know you're always eager to support them."

Velma glared.

Dash shook her head. "As for whether it works or not, HP Labs got some remarkable results from their work. Teams of experts were able, with BRAIN, to make better forecasts than they had made working as a team in the usual fashion. The results saved millions of dollars."

Velma crossed her arms. "What kind of results?"

Dash continued as if she hadn't heard. "Colin was unable to tell me anymore. He regretfully told me it was still confidential even today."

Simon requested confirmation. "So, this is Colin's idea?"

Dash nodded. "Colin's, Lenora's, and mine." She reconsidered. "Really, it was mostly Colin and Lenora."

Dash's main contribution had simply been to ask if there was any way to do the resource allocation so there wouldn't be any more yelling on the deck.

After the meeting, Simon expressed his pleasure with the new system. "I'm so glad to be off the hook."

Dash laughed. "Off the hook? Not hardly. The system will help, but you'll still have work to do. Suppose the highest-rated experiment requires resources needed for both the second and third best choices. CEREBRUM isn't quite smart enough to decide whether to run number one or both numbers two and three unless you carefully strategize and formulate the predictions. That's all up to you."

"I guess I'm glad I'll have you to help me then."

Dash shook her head. "Work with Colin. He knows this stuff better than I do. And besides, I'm going to be gone for a while."

Simon stared at her. "Gone? Where?"

Dash smiled mischievously for a moment before turning sober. "There are even worse things that can happen than a plague, you know."

Simon was going to say, no, he didn't know, but she was already hurrying away.

The first couple of days of the new system created more yelling than the old one when Velma found that some of her proposals did not make the top of the list. And of course most of the researchers, in those first two days, bought For positions mostly on their own work. But some of them lost much of their original thousand dollars—it was real money, Dash had explained, and when the crisis was over everyone got to keep anything they'd won—while others accumulated some serious cash.

By the third day, people were buying For and Against positions with the cold impartiality of financial analyst on the GS *Prime*. Dash even had Keenan give a brief presentation on how this sort of thing worked with commodity futures, which were also similar to CEREBRUM forecasts.

By the fifth day, the predicted outcomes for experiments were aligning more correctly with the actual outcomes of those experiments than anyone had ever seen before. Criticism of the new system faded away as everyone realized they could now pick their projects with more precision and develop the vaccine faster than would have seemed possible before Dash had put them all to work this way.

That same day, as Chance entered a conference room to meet with Simon, she found Velma peering intently at her tablet. Chance, who always moved rather more silently than most, slid sideways to peer over Velma's shoulder. She failed to muffle a gasp of surprise.

Velma looked up at her. "Chance. See anything interesting?"

Chance looked her in the eyes. "Am I confused? Are you buying a For position on a proposal that was made by one of the scientists you call a moron? And you're taking an Against position on one of your own proposals?"

Velma looked away. "Yeah, well. The moron had a good idea. Gotta go with the best ideas, you know, even if they come from morons."

Chance studied Velma for a moment, more charitably than ever before. She decided to offer to do a good deed, understanding that such deeds rarely went unpunished. "While you're in a learning mood, there're some things I'd like to show you if you're interested. Whenever you feel like taking a break. I promise it'll be worth your while."

Velma shrugged, distracted. "Whatever." She returned to the topic that was bugging her. "What I don't understand about the moron's proposal is, it's so obvious. Why didn't I think of it in the first place?"

***

Technically, the small city where Khalid met Uwais and Sabaah was not the closest city to their training camp/laboratory/home, but it was a fitting location. This city housed thousands of ancient documents, and Khalid was personally quite fond of the Ahmed Baba Center for Documentation and Research. It was worth traveling a little farther to get here.

Their home was still far away from this parched desert spot, which was ironic since English dictionaries used this city as a metaphor for the concept of a "faraway place." So his team lived far away from the place considered by western civilization to be far away. How fitting. How well-suited to their needs.

Sabaah and Uwais approached him as he sat in a street-side cafe beneath a table umbrella that kept the worst glare at bay. He smiled at them. "Trouble?"

Sabaah shook his head. "None at all."

Uwais shrugged. "As expected."

They were at the edge of the town. He scanned the whole thing, the endless low mudbrick buildings and their tenants going about their daily lives.

Starting over five years earlier, key elements of the history of this town had been written by himself. Once this city had attracted tourists, but then Islamic jihadists had decided to turn it into a playground for kidnapping and murder.

The last thing Khalid wanted was either the French or the Americans trudging through this desert in search of terrorists, so he and his two brothers-in-arms had used the jihadists as practice. Khalid gave quiet presentations to both the local people and the militants, telling earnest stories of the end of times and how the Western Christians would themselves create the tools that would create the great plague, wiping the world clean. He demonstrated his credentials as a scholar in religious, practical, and scientific matters, and gently suggested he knew how to accelerate the process of preparing the way for the Mahdi. With uncomfortable speed, the townsfolk, like his brothers in arms, started whispering of him as the Herald.

He then suggested he could use their help. He didn't need their money, but he needed their faith and commitment. Many joined him, and passed word to others in distant places to come listen to the Herald. His people grew in numbers.

Many of the jihadists had joined him. The ones who insisted that petty atrocities against tourists offered a more beneficial contribution to the cause ceased to be targets of Khalid's persuasion. They became targets upon which Uwais and Sabaah could practice their skills in assassination.

Eventually the tourism trade returned.

Khalid twisted in his chair to look out beyond the city, over the dunes heaped just beyond the edge of this desperate outpost of civilization. He remembered the despair he had felt coming here the first time.

This desert had been here for several million years, but it had not always been this desolate. Trade routes had run here; this city of antiquity stood as a testament to that flow of commerce.

But in the end, the humans had supplied the straw that broke this camel's back. The rudimentary social institutions long ago had enabled a "tragedy of the commons" in which the grazing land was freely available but the cattle herds were privately owned. The person with the most cattle, who consumed the most of the limited grasses, "won." But all too quickly this led to vast swaths of land stripped bare of vegetation, where the wind could whip up vast storms of sand to pile upon and destroy the places where vegetation yet survived. In the end, as desertification swept the habitable areas, everyone had lost.

He knew how to restore this land. It would take both time and money, but those were easy. He'd already started working on the problem, down closer to home.

But just as important as the need for time and money was the need for a lot fewer humans trampling the process while he worked. That would require…the very holy jihad he was now unleashing. He muttered to himself in wry self-mockery, "Behold, I am become the world's first Islamic jihadi eco-terrorist."

Sabaah looked at him from ordering *alabadjia*, the traditional nomad dish of meat, butter, and rice. "What was that?"

Khalid stretched. "Just considering the past and its impact on the future."

Uwais observed, "Sounds very philosophical."

Sabaah pursed his lips. "Impractical."

Khalid nodded. "All of the above. But also amusing."

In 2019 in eastern Iran, a bus loaded with elite Revolutionary Guard soldiers found itself faced with a swift and brutal ambush. Most of the soldiers died.

The Supreme Leader knew instantly who was behind the attack and denounced with all his vigor the Israelis who had perpetrated the attack and the Americans who had backed them.

It made no difference that the Israelis had never in the past bothered with random attacks on random soldiers. It made no difference that the Israeli *modus operandi* focused solely on high-value targets such as scientists developing nuclear weapons. It made no difference that an action team of zealous Sunnis operated in the region where the assault took place. Any time anything terrible happened, the Supreme Leader, the government, and indeed all the people, knew who was responsible.

The power of this comfortable certainty held firm when the first cases of vaccine-immune measles arrived at the hospitals in Tehran.

When the patients started dying at a startling rate, the doctors turned from the measles diagnosis to Blue Rubola. But the color of the rash was different—a red so light in hue that it was almost pink. Suspicion that this was something entirely new grew to certainty when hastily-imported Blue Rubola vaccine had no more effect than the measles vaccine.

By the time the new disease had received a new popular name, Red Rubola, the Supreme Leader had already achieved certainty as to who had instigated the attack.

Toni Shatski accompanied the Prime Minister of Israel to the meeting with the Iranian ambassador. Toni wore her F35 flight suit, a silent warning to the ambassador that Israel knew whom the Iranians would blame and Israel would defend itself with every resource, including the Prime Minister's own daughter.

The ambassador's demand was simple. "Give us the vaccine for Red Rubola and pay reparations for the dead. Our nuclear missile silos are already on high alert, and if you refuse to meet our demand, we will bring the Holocaust to all your people."

Toni's father tried to be reasonable. "You have our sincerest sympathies, but you have to believe we didn't do this, and we have no more idea how to make a vaccine than you do. Frankly, what we'd like to do is form a joint task-force—all your best medical people and all ours, together—to try to figure what's happened and who's behind this."

The ambassador spluttered with rage. "We know *you're*

behind it! Who else would care this much about destroying us, and who else has the technology base? Surely you're not suggesting the Americans undertook this heinous assault without consulting you!"

Toni took a half-step to stand between her father and the crazed ambassador, then got control of herself. "You can't be serious. Don't you see, the Americans were the first victims. Red Rubola was clearly developed by the same people who developed Blue Rubola." She licked her lips. "Whoever attacked you hates all of us."

The ambassador waved the assertion away. "Bah, no one hates all of us. Either they don't care, or they're committed to one side or the other."

The Prime Minister interrupted with two words. "Saudi Arabia."

The ambassador stood as if struck for a moment; if Israel and Iran disappeared in twin hellfires of plague and nuclear holocaust, the Saudis would achieve supremacy as the leaders across the Arab world.

Finally the ambassador waved it away. "As for the assertion that the Americans suffered first, the attack on the coastal cities was clearly an experimental deployment using the President for Life's enemies as test subjects. Not only did the deaths help the President in the upcoming congressional elections, but it was only half as lethal as the Red Rubola now sweeping my nation. Clearly a test run."

The Prime Minister rolled his eyes. "You must listen to me! If we had a vaccine, we'd give it to you! We don't! If there is any way we can help, we'll help you, but we don't have what you want!"

The ambassador guffawed. "You'd help us? That's ridiculous on its face."

Toni interrupted again despite her father's glare. "Please think about it. This plague, whoever did it, may have started it in Tehran, but it's not going to stay there. Eventually it will spread everywhere, including Israel. The sooner we stop it, the safer everyone is."

The ambassador looked back and forth between them. "So that's your answer?" He sighed and looked at his watch. "I'll give you two hours to reconsider. If you refuse our simple request, you'll have only yourselves to blame for the consequences." With a final slap of the table, he departed.

Toni's father turned to her grimly. "Join your squadron. Looks like the war we've always dreaded is upon us."

Toni gave the Prime Minister a crisp salute. "Yes, sir!"

He took a deep breath. "I know your plane is designed for air-to-ground combat, but I know you've flown air-to-air quite successfully." He smiled. "Even with a medical scientist as your Weapons Officer."

Toni looked at him in puzzlement. "But we'll be attacking ground targets, right? Why not load me up with the weapons my plane is designed for?"

The Prime Minister's face softened; at this moment he was just a father. "Because I don't want you to carry the lifelong burden of knowing you wiped out a whole city with a nuclear bomb," he explained.

***

As Toni hurried to her airbase to oversee the prepping of her plane and made sure her Weapons Officer—an Israeli professional, not a medical scientist this time—would be there when she arrived, she realized they had one last chance of averting war. She called Dash to see if, by some miracle, she already had a vaccine.

Dash answered on the first ring. Her voice sounded urgent. "Toni. I was just about to call you. Colin has a plan. I'm on my way."

Toni shook her head, disoriented. "Colin what? You're where?"

"Colin has a plan. We're going to see if Jam and I can help." Dash paused, and Toni heard a rough noise in the background, like the sound of the wind across the top deck of an isle ship.

Dash continued, "I'm about to board one of Matt's Global Express ships. I'll be landing in the Negev Desert."

There were so many things wrong with this that Toni had trouble deciding where to start. "I thought those ships needed to land on a spaceport isle ship?" She thought back to the previous year. "Though I guess Matt landed one in Baotong, right?"

Dash chuckled. "And he swore he'd never do it again. But when Colin explained the stakes and I offered him a big enough premium, he relented." She hesitated. "I'm going to need you to get a team of engineers together, however, to work the problem of refueling the ship."

Toni responded to this with puzzlement. "Ping got into and out of Baotong without refueling, didn't she?"

She could almost hear Dash nodding. "Yes, but this trip will not be a simple in-and-out. If things go as Colin hopes, the ship will be making another stop. Heavily laden. It will be a little complicated."

When Dash said it would be a little complicated, Toni became sure she didn't want to know.

Toni's car swerved around a pedestrian walking blithely into the street. "Hey, you idiot, we're in the middle of the end of the world here, don't you know? Get out of the way!"

Dash asked softly, "Was that for me?"

Toni laughed. "What else did you want?"

Dash sounded sheepish. "Well, it would be good if you could get me permission to land. I'll be in a standard Global Express ship, so it'll look like an incoming missile on your radar. I'd appreciate it if your military didn't blow me up on re-entry."

Again Toni expressed puzzlement. "I'd have expected you to come in the Black Titan." The Black Titan was a Global Express prototype ship, complete with a stealth coating. The Israeli Missile Command wouldn't know about it until it landed. "Matt's still got that one, doesn't he?"

Dash sighed. "Jam needs that one."

Toni realized there was a much bigger problem than getting landing authorization. "Hold it. You said you'd be here in two hours?"

"About that."

Toni exhaled sharply. "Dash, you must not leave yet. Do not leave until I call you back. You got me? Do not leave yet."

Dash grunted. "The longer it takes me to get there, the more risk that this situation will get out of hand."

"Trust me, girl. If waiting four hours is too late, getting here in two hours will be too early. Please."

After Dash agreed to Toni's terms and hung up, Toni sat back, trembling.

If Dash had landed in two hours, she would have arrived just in time to be killed by the first flight of Iranian missiles.

Over the course of the millennia, the act of combat had evolved into a generally more compressed affair. Wars became shorter, almost in inverse proportion to the number of casualties. Sure, there continued to be engagements euphemistically referred to as Low-Intensity Combat that could go on and on, but the days of the Hundred Years War and the Thirty Years War had been left behind. They had yielded to a brutal future of encounters such as the Six-Day War.

Under many circumstances, nuclear missiles had flight times under twenty minutes. If one's goal was to use a demonstration attack to persuade the enemy to acquiesce to terms, there might be a preliminary demonstration attack followed by an all-out response, then a final full-force counterattack, so one would achieve a new level of compaction. Call it a sixty-minute war.

When the stipulated two-hour period of reflection ended, the Israelis made one last effort to dissuade the Iranians, repeating the offer to work together. Five minutes after the Iranians rejected this plea, satellites from every major nation in the world detected the infrared blooms of three missile signatures from Iranian silos.

Why three? Both American and Israeli analysts found

the number unsurprising. Over the course of decades of testing, in which the Iranians routinely accused the Americans of sabotage (quite possibly correctly), the Iranian long-range Hoveiseh missile still had a sixty-six percent failure rate during testing. They fired three because this was the only way they could be confident of landing one.

Given their goal, it turned out the Iranians had made a wise decision. Israel's infrared satellites detected, seconds after the launch bloom, an additional bloom much larger than any of the launches as one of the missiles exploded over its silo.

Israeli battle management switched from satellites to ground-based radar as the other two missiles ended their boost phase and faded from infrared detection. All too soon, the nuclear warheads showed up on radar, and the Israelis watched helplessly as the warheads ballistically fell back into the atmosphere on a clear and implacable trajectory for Tel Aviv.

Moments later, one of the warheads flickered on the radar screens and disappeared; the capsule holding nuclear destruction had started to tumble and the ablative bottom heat shield spun out of position, thereby exposing the unprotected surfaces of the small craft to the plasma of high-speed re-entry. The capsule disintegrated, taking its payload with it.

The third missile fell straight and true until it came within range of Israel's Iron Dome anti-missile defense.

The Iron Dome, despite numerous enhancements through the years to counter an ever-increasing missile threat, was not really up to dealing with this attack. Taking out a warhead moving at many times the speed of sound with an anti-missile warhead was akin to stopping a bullet by biting it with your teeth.

Remarkably, the Iron Dome had plucked missiles with only moderately less difficult attack profiles from the sky from time to time. It was worth trying.

Three, then four, then five antimissiles shot into the air in a last desperate attempt to save the city.

None of them hit.

But one blew up in close enough proximity to bash in the side of the capsule and dislocate some of the explosive elements needed to create the tremendous implosion needed to compress the plutonium core and light the hellfire.

The explosion diverted the Iranian missile miles off course, to dig a large impact crater in the desert where it landed. The crater was large by the standards of plummeting meteorites but negligible compared to the size of a crater left by a nuclear explosion.

The Israelis drew a shuddering breath. When the Iranians did not follow up, the Israelis concluded the Iranians too were holding their breaths, with no follow-up plan except to hope that the Israelis would reconsider and send them the vaccine.

For just a moment, nobody seemed to want the sixty-minute war that had just begun.

Toni called her dad, then called Dash. "Get your butt over here, and hurry. We may have a chance to fix this, but it won't last long."

As Dash agreed, Toni remembered an extra proviso and said urgently. "Wait one. There's another important thing you need to know."

"Yes?"

"You need to move your landing zone. The place you were planning to come down is no longer as level as it used to be."

"What happened?"

Toni answered reluctantly. "There's a big crater there. It may be radioactive. Best to avoid it."

"Radioactive. Got it. OK, then."

9

WITH BATED BREATH

The only winning move is not to play.
    —WOPR, the supercomputer in charge of NORAD, in the movie *Wargames*

Brilliant fire flashed through the heavens and thunder filled the sky. As the fireball came to Earth, passengers in cars traveling down the Babaei Highway east of Tehran could just make out, in the dawn light, three tall black cylinders above what turned out to be three separate smaller fireballs.

After it settled on the ground, an enormous metal staircase unfolded from the side and a lone figure in a full black burqa gracefully descended halfway down the stairs. If the woman within the burqa felt any of the anxiety appropriate to someone who had just violated Iranian airspace, the garment hid it perfectly.

Soon videos of the ship and the woman went viral

across social media, thereby alerting the Iranian military to the invader's location. Much consternation arose amongst the officers as they realized just how perfectly they had been taken by surprise. Given the last two hours of nail-biting tension, they suddenly understood that had the tech presented by this spaceship been used to deliver a nuclear warhead without warning, the Iranian military could have easily suffered a decapitation strike before the decapitated head realized anything had gone amiss.

The first vehicles to reach the scene were a pair of tank transport trucks dutifully carrying their tanks. Only half the people needed to crew the tanks, however, had managed to scramble aboard before the trucks departed.

Had the woman on the staircase carried one of the BrainTrust's BT-12 PGM autolaunchers, the men knew full well she could have decimated this first combat unit before they even got their armor onto the ground. But if she were so armed (and she could have been, the soldiers familiar with the BT-12 knew it folded into a pack that could easily fit underneath the burqa), she appeared to take no interest in slaughtering her opponents.

More troops arrived, eventually forming a semicircle around the woman, with enough firepower to turn her and her towering vehicle into swiss cheese.

When Colonel Jafar Papkour arrived, he immediately ordered the troops to fall back—a lot. And safety the weapons. He had the terrible suspicion that if they opened fired from their current positions, the fuel and oxygen tanks of the Black Titan would explode and consume them all, the colonel included. He walked with a military stride to the bottom of the staircase.

He extended his hand, palm up. "Ms., ah…"

"Call me Jam," the woman said with a decidedly beautiful lilt to her voice. She descended the rest of the steps to reach him.

The colonel felt oddly apologetic despite his unquestionable duty. "I hereby put you under arrest for espionage."

Her melodious laugh somehow sounded ominous in the context of her capture. "What do you think you have that I could possibly be interested in spying on?"

The woman's burqa shifted about her, and she held out a box with a label on the top. "Think carefully before you do anything hasty."

Even from a distance, the colonel could hear machine guns being prepped to fire. He held out a calming hand to his troops. "What's this?" For a moment his heart leapt with hope.

This woman had clearly come from the BrainTrust. Everyone knew, regardless of what the Americans might say, that the BrainTrust had cured the Blue Rubola. Papkour wondered, could this be… "Is that the vaccine for the Red Rubola?"

The woman sighed. "I'm sorry. Not yet. We're working hard on it. We will fill boxes like this, however, when we do have a cure. For the moment, this box contains nothing but a promise."

The colonel raised an eyebrow.

"There's a homing beacon inside. Put it someplace safe. Not in your home of course—after all, for all you know, this is a homer for a missile attack—but someplace you can get to it easily. When we have a vaccine, we'll send a drone with a carton just like this one. Vaccinate your family and your troops."

The colonel hesitated for a long moment. Should he thank her, accuse her of bribery, or accuse her of trying to plant a targeting system in his barracks? He compromised. "Very well."

The woman turned brisk. "Now, if you please, take me to the Supreme Leader. If you want to save your country from unequaled catastrophe, that is." She laughed again.

He escorted her to his private armored personnel carrier while calling ahead to see if the leadership wanted to greet her, imprison her, or simply execute her. He argued as forcefully as he could for a greeting. Things were bad enough already without killing an envoy from the one place they knew would eventually cure this plague. Either he was quite persuasive, or they saw the wisdom of bringing her in without his help.

Either way, in moments they had departed for the capital. He asked her one more question before they reached Tehran. "Do you have any more of those homing beacons with you? You really can't bring them into the presence of the Supreme Leader."

She laughed once more. "Fear not, Colonel. I am now wholly disarmed."

Hmm... Before they reached the House of Leadership, he'd have a woman check to make sure she wasn't carrying any weapons.

From what he'd heard about women like this on the BrainTrust, he seriously doubted even that would leave her disarmed, however.

Dash's greeting in Israel differed considerably from Jam's greeting in Iran. For one thing, her Titan had no stealth coating, and the Israelis watched it on radar like hawks. Many fingers twitched in itchy urgency on Iron Dome counter-missile buttons. But they did not shoot her down.

For another— "Dash! It's so good to see you!" Toni squealed as she ran up the staircase to meet her before she'd even descended halfway to the ground. Dash found herself in a hug that made breathing difficult.

Dash managed to get out a strangled, "We should probably be going."

"Of course!" Toni practically skipped as she led Dash to her Humvee. "We have a lot to talk about, but I guess it will have to wait."

"I'm sorry." As the Humvee bounced out to the road, Dash was already pouring over new data on her tablet as it reconnected with the scientists on the *Chiron*.

It took some finagling to get the wallscreen in the Prime Minister's conference room to sync with the wallscreen in the House of Leadership. It took even more finagling to persuade the Prime Minister and his top advisers to let Dash do the talking, even though the justification was sensible. "You are all too angry to speak wisely. In Tehran, Jam is making the same demand of Iran's leaders."

When Toni's father argued with increasing heat that Dash was unqualified, Toni whispered in his ear, "See? You're getting angry already." She let him stew on that for a moment before reminding him, "Remember, this is Colin's plan."

Dash fought down mild irritation at that description. Dash had had significant input too.

For over a year, Dash had been building a model of Colin's behavior in her mind. Her first successful use of this small but nonetheless productive simulation had given her the idea to give Jam stealth copters so she could retrieve Gleb's family so they could release Gleb from the brig.

In the current instance, Dash's most important contribution had been suggesting—well, demanding—that she go to Israel rather than Colin.

She had expected him to fight her over it, but contrary to her Colin-simulation's prediction, once she gave her justifications, he just smiled and told her to get ready. Indeed, he reacted as if he had hoped for, and planned for, her forceful recommendation. Her model of his behavior clearly still needed refinement.

Eventually the leadership of Israel, the leadership of Iran, and the comms systems connecting them were properly engaged. When Dash's screen first hooked into Tehran, a woman buried in the shapeless covering of a burqa filled the wallscreen.

Dash smiled brightly. "Jam! I'm so happy they didn't execute you on the spot."

"So am I, though honestly, I think they would have found that more difficult than they appreciate." A hand peeked out of the burqa and waved the matter into the past. "OK," Jam said in a louder voice, meant for both the people behind her and the people with Dash. "Let's get clear on everyone's status. Here in Iran people are dying from a measles-like plague clearly engineered as a bioweapon."

Dash interrupted, "Definitely designed and manufactured by the same people who released the Blue Rubola in America."

The head of the black burqa shifted as if the person inside were nodding. "Supreme Leader and councilors, forgive me for not having introduced my friend already. This is Dr. Dash, who led the BrainTrust team that developed both the vaccine and the cure for Blue Rubola."

She spun and addressed the Supreme Leader's team more directly. "So just to be clear, if you drop a nuke on Tel Aviv at this moment, you'll kill the person most likely to save your people."

Dash turned to the Prime Minister. "And similarly, if you attack Tehran at this time, you will be murdering my friend."

The Prime Minister scowled. "Congratulations. I think you've just extended the current unspoken truce indefinitely. At least until you leave."

Dash projected her voice for everyone. "Neither of us will be leaving until the vaccine is ready."

She spoke more softly for Jam. "So, are the Iranian scientists on their way?"

Jam turned and addressed the Iranian team. She turned back to Dash. "Enough for a quorum, anyway."

"Excellent." Dash turned to the Prime Minister. "Please bring your scientists in as well."

Soon the screen and the room were filled with new people, all a bit bewildered to be there.

Dash spoke comfortingly. "Welcome. I am now going to bring you all up to date on the BrainTrust's progress on Red Rubola." She prayed no one would ask her how the BrainTrust had gotten Red Rubola samples since it had involved the Mossad. "I shall first give you all a summary, which the leadership of both countries may find informative. After that, Prime Minister, Supreme Leader, you may depart. I promise you will not find the rest very interesting. However, after we are done, I do urge you to speak with your scientists. I think you will all find that, above all things, you want to facilitate our efforts on your behalf."

Jam left the conference room, along with the Iranian leadership, the Supreme Leader, and Colonel Papkour. "Again, I urge you, if your scientists come out of this meeting as enthusiastic and hopeful as I expect, to send them to the BrainTrust. We have far superior equipment for dealing with this kind of thing, a staff that now includes all the leading experts from America, and a proven track record. We all believe your people can maximize their effectiveness by working with our people."

The colonel responded with a wry expression. "I presume your Dr. Dash is making the same pitch to the Israelis?"

Jam chuckled. "Of course. Except they should be easy. Toni Shatzki, the Prime Minister's daughter, is a student in our university. I suspect the Israeli scientists will depart for the BrainTrust as soon as Dash has finished the update."

Papkour led her to a lavishly furnished suite. "These will be your rooms as long as you're here." He departed.

Jam pulled off the burqa with a sigh of relief. She spoke for the bugs her hosts had surely planted in her room. "I feel like the proverbial man who just stepped off the roof of a twenty-story building. As he passed the tenth floor, his comment was, 'So far, so good.'"

Dash accepted all the thank yous from the scientists assembled on both sides of the conference with a humble nod of the head. She could see they were all leaving with their heads higher and their voices more excited and full of hope.

Toni brushed past the last of them on her way in. "Cool, girl. Now you have to come with me."

Dash felt the first soft tentacles of exhaustion coiling about her. "What? Where?"

Toni grabbed her shoulder and shook it. "We've got to get you home. Back to the BrainTrust, so you can get back to work."

Dash shook her head. "But I gave my word that—"

"Yes, yes. You're our human shield. But let's face it, you're more important as a scientist than as a hostage."

Dash looked stubborn for a moment, then started to wilt.

Toni exploited the advantage. "Look, eventually my dad will tell the Iranians that in order to speed the development of the vaccine they need, he kicked you out of the country. Think about it for a moment: the Supreme Leader will be *delighted* that we forced you out." She gave Dash a short laugh. "It's true, you know. You don't have a choice. I'll bring in armed guards to drag you out of here if I have to."

That got a laugh out of Dash. "I can't take the Titan. It has to stay here so it can deliver the vaccine."

"Which is why you're going with me. I hope you enjoyed your last flight in my F35, because that's how I'm getting you home, or at least to the Global Express spaceport ship off the coast of France. Hopefully this trip won't be quite as exciting as the last one." Toni wrinkled her nose. "Besides, we don't want another rocket ship landing here now. You have no idea how nerve-wracking it is to watch a missile with people on board come down when you're expecting a missile with a nuke on board to come down at any time."

As Toni hustled her along, Dash offered one more objection. "What if the Iranians find out I'm gone before this is all resolved?"

Toni raised an eyebrow. "Are you planning to tell them?"

They reached the airfield without incident. As Dash pulled on her flight suit, a sudden sharp realization struck her. "This was Colin's doing, wasn't it? He told you to send me back as soon as the Iranians were convinced I would stay."

Toni chuckled. "Who else?"

Dash sighed. Another missed prediction. She clearly had a long way to go before her mental model of Colin was up to snuff.

Several nail-biting weeks later, Captain Levinsky, who had received much ribbing for his bad luck in being the one to engage the Palestinian *First Chance*, was told to expect a ship from the BrainTrust. He checked his watch again, keeping his arm up to block the wind sweeping across his ship's deck and prevent it from burning his eyes.

The BrainTrust ship was supposed to be here now, but his men couldn't see a blasted thing on the radar anywhere as far as his ship could search, meaning the BrainTrusters were going to be execrably late. Very angering, considering that everything he'd heard about these people suggested they were competent and prompt.

It was especially angering to learn their reputation was overblown when promptness was so necessary to the survival of his nation.

His radarman shouted, "I've got something." His voice turned puzzled. "It's really close. How'd it get so close?"

Levinsky, suddenly alarmed, shouted for General Quarters. As his men moved smoothly to battlestations, he looked wildly around in search of the object the radar had detected.

A whale breached the surface a hundred meters from the ship. Except, as the breach continued and the full shape of the breach became evident, Levinsky saw it was no whale at all. It was a blasted submarine.

Well, Levinsky presumed it was a sub. It had no sail, i.e., no large fin on the top. It presumably had some other means not in evidence for maintaining vertical stability.

Levinsky had studied modern submarines. Even disregarding the missing sail, this seemed different: non-cylindrical, almost triangular in its beam. Overall, it seemed narrower than the biggest modern subs, but at least as long, maybe longer.

His radioman interjected, "They're contacting us. It's the BrainTrust ship. They're asking us to come aboard."

By the time his people had secured from General Quarters, they'd come alongside the sub that dwarfed his patrol boat.

He wound up taking the RHIB from his ship to the sub and clambering up a series of ridiculously awkward handholds across the soft, presumably sonar-absorbent, skin.

A lone man waited for him and his inspection team. "Captain Levinsky? I'm Captain Samuels. Welcome aboard the *Alcyone*."

After shaking hands, the captain led him down into the sub. Levinsky looked around, puzzled. "This seems a lot smaller on the inside than it is on the outside."

Samuels chuckled. "Your normal sub is constructed more or less as a single cylinder. On the BrainTrust, the largest cylinder we can manufacture as a single piece is seven meters wide." He patted the curved arch by his shoulder. "The Alcyone has three such cylinders strapped together and interconnected in a triangle. As you can see here." He pointed to one hatch that descended to the right, and another that descended to the left. "We made some different tradeoffs, obviously."

As they clambered down through the port hatch, Levinsky asked the critical question. "I presume all these boxes everywhere are filled with the vaccine?"

Samuels nodded. "We have the boat stuffed to the gills."

Beside them, a crateful of boxes sat on top of a device Levinsky guessed to be a 3D printer. Samuels reached into an open crate and pulled out a smaller box, easily held in one hand. "That's fourteen hundred doses right there."

Levinsky whistled. "How many total?"

"Almost one hundred eighty million. You can vaccinate everyone in Iran and everyone in Israel, and still have over half left over to vaccinate anybody else who needs it." He frowned at Levinsky. "But you have to deliver the vaccine to Iran, or you'll lose more people in a nuclear war than you'd probably lose to the rubola."

Levinsky took a deep breath. "Don't worry, we get it." He waved his hands. "This whole ridiculous dance wherein you deliver it to us so we can deliver it to them—I presume there's some silly political reason for it? Otherwise you would've just sent the vaccine direct."

Captain Samuels gave him a wry smile. "That's the kind of absurdity you get when you let a bunch of game theorists into the negotiation. Don't ask me what the purpose was." He forced the carton he still held into Levinsky's hand. "Take this back to your ship. Make sure everyone gets injected."

In a few minutes, Levinsky's inspection team had done a hasty survey. Levinsky addressed Samuels. "Let's get you on your way. People are dying while we stand around here chatting."

Samuels nodded. "And are your people ready to let a full boatload of Palestinians on board after we've offloaded?"

Some of Levinsky's superiors objected to this free flow of potential terrorists from Gaza, but Levinsky was fine with it. And the members of the leadership who knew just how close a call they'd just had wanted no hiccups. "It should all go smoothly, Captain."

"Thank you."

Levinsky stood by his XO, watching as the sub cruised off towards the shore. The XO observed, "It's a beautiful ship in its own way."

Levinsky nodded. "I've been wondering what it's for. I mean, it's not a military vessel. And while it's big by normal sub standards, it's dinky by isle ship standards."

The XO thought it over. "It seems to be working quite well for hauling sensitive and urgent cargo, presuming it's as much faster than a normal cargo ship as I suspect. But I see your point. That's hardly a compelling reason to build something as expensive as that sub."

Levinsky shivered. "I think I may know why they bothered. It's an oceanic disaster bunker."

The XO looked at him in puzzlement.

Levinsky smiled. "This is the second militarized epidemic in three months. What if one of them succeeds? Unless I miss my guess, they've made that sub capable of building agricultural reefs, manufacturing bots, and remaining totally self-sufficient for years. If things go badly enough, the *Alcyone* could wind up being all that remains of humanity."

The XO stared in the direction in which the sub had disappeared. "And until the sub gets back to the BrainTrust, it'll have no one on board except Palestinians. If the whole world died except the *Alcyone*, would that qualify as a Hamas victory?"

Captain Levinsky grimaced. "I sure hope that vaccine works."

A week after Red Rubola vaccine landed in Tehran, the Empress of Benin found herself pushing her jeep north at a maniacal pace from the Porto Novo Highlands. The surroundings grew ever more dry and ever more desperate. She spoke to her companion in the passenger seat loudly enough to be heard over the wind across the open-top vehicle. "Road trip! Thank you again for taking time out from your busy schedule of negotiating treaties to end nuclear wars." She smiled mischievously. "It's always great adventuring with you."

Jam gave her a wan smile. "I'm glad to be here too, though we both know why I had to come."

Ping's voice took on a sour note. "Joshua talked with you too, I take it." Taking Jam with her any time she went into a situation that might involve violence had been one of the conditions Joshua had laid upon her.

Jam laughed musically. "I'll do it, you know."

Ping already knew the answer but asked anyway. "Do what, exactly?"

"Stop you."

A loud snore arose from the back of the jeep. Ping reached behind and smacked Benin's retired Beloved Advisor for Life on the leg. "Quiet back there."

Jam frowned. "Did we really need to bring him with us?"

Ping's voice turned cheery. "Oh, yes. He's my negotiator."

Jam stared at her. "But—"

Ping shook her head. "You'll see." After a moment, she went back to the earlier conversation. "You won't have to stop me. I'll never do to anyone else what I did to him."

Jam grunted again. "We certainly agree on that."

Ping offered another assurance. "I've got full control of myself now."

Jam raised an eyebrow. "Well, I see we don't agree on everything quite yet."

The drone that had been flying just behind them whirred past to check out what was over the next ridge.

Jam observed, "Looks like we're coming up on our first customers."

As Ping watched the drone go by, her voice turned irritated. "I think we're too well-equipped here. I don't suppose we've lost our entourage yet, have we? I've been trying to ditch them for miles."

Jam twisted to look behind them. She didn't speak until the road curved slightly, letting her get a view far behind them that was clear of their own dust cloud. "Still there, both the full truck and the empty one."

Ping growled. "Argh."

Rubinelle had insisted that a truck of Amazons follow her on this expedition. Actually, Rubinelle had first tried to insist that it was a matter for the Amazons to deal with, but at that Ping had played the empress card. They had compromised. The truckload of troops followed as far behind as possible while still being close enough to assist in an emergency.

So now Ping and Jam led a crazy-quilt expedition into northern Benin to negotiate with the more egregious of the thugs there.

Ping looked once more into the sky. As the jeep tried to swerve off the road without her attention, she muttered, "I still can't see the dirigible."

Jam didn't even bother to look up. "Of course you can't see it, silly. It's too high, and it's sky-blue besides."

Someone from Ping's team from the first incursion into Djeregbe had apparently mentioned to someone else her fantastical story for the local thugs about a dirigible, too high to see, maintaining constant surveillance. That someone had apparently mentioned it to someone else, who'd mentioned it to Ted Simpson.

Ted had concluded it sounded like a good idea, so he had taken the design for the hydrogen dirigibles used by the BrainTrust to deliver hydrogen for power and water generation to San Francisco and upgraded it. He'd powered the new ship with a beta battery, and hooked it up with a dehumidifier to extract water from the air, and then electrolyzed the hydrogen from the water. So even though hydrogen balloons necessarily leaked the energetic little hydrogen molecules from their bags, Ted's new design constantly replenished the hydrogen. The thing would never have to land.

Ping acknowledged grudgingly that for a country like Benin with vast expanses of land where warlords and other thugs could roam, it wasn't a bad idea. But did Ted really have to give her one for her birthday?

Anyway, the dirigible had videoed a number of roadblocks set up by small groups of entrepreneurial bandits to extort money and worse from unwary travelers.

Jam pointed ahead. "There's the first one now."

Half a dozen young men in disheveled military fatigues, casually carrying AK-47s as if they were golf clubs, appeared before them, lounging around a pair of trucks parked sideways across the road. A couple of the hooligans knelt and pointed their guns more or less in the direction of the Jeep.

Ping slammed on the breaks and skidded sideways to a halt. The apparent leader of the bandits, holding only a sidearm, waved them forward. "Come ahead. We won't harm you. You just have to pay the toll."

Ping dialed her phone.

Ciara answered, "Ping. You guys ready?"

Ping answered. "Whenever you say. You getting good data?"

"I and my trusty Dark Alpha 43 were getting good data before you even showed up. Ted's surveillance dirigible is just glorious."

This made Ping grumpy again. "So, is that guy waving us forward the leader?"

"Yes, based on a study of the body language and the facial microexpressions. As I've said before, the microexpressions aren't reliable in this hookup, good as the video is the resolution still isn't perfect for this application. Anyway, he's the boss."

Jam interrupted. "I'm guessing he's not half as nice as his friendly invitation would make it seem. Right?"

Ciara replied approvingly, "Quite right. We'll know

more in a few minutes, but right now, I think a sweeping regime change for this gang of kids is in order."

As this conversation went on, Ping climbed out of the driver's seat and lifted out a piece of equipment sharing the back of the Jeep with the ex-Beloved Advisor. "Clumsy thing, this." She started setting it up behind the Jeep, invisible to the men manning the roadblock.

Meanwhile, the young fellow whose fate was being discussed took a few more steps forward, frowning. "Hey, I said come up here." He stared at Ping as she rose out of the Jeep. The light of recognition shown in his eyes. "Empress Ping?" His frown changed into a wicked smile. "Oh, my. I think the toll just went up a lot."

He barked at his men. "Boys, keep them covered!" He pointed at the ground in front of him. "And you, Empress, get over here now."

Jam murmured, "Now would be a good time, Ping."

Ping grumbled, "Hold on. I'm trying to work a catapult here." She shook her head. "A catapult in the twenty-first century. Ridiculous." She finally got it set up and loaded with a large rough-surfaced ball that hummed like a swarm of buzzing bees.

Jam hopped out her side of the Jeep and yelled at the bandits, "Technical difficulties. We'll be with you in a minute."

The boss was getting increasingly angry. "Hurry it up!"

Ping sighed. "Here goes. Good thing I practiced a lot before we came out here." She flipped a lever, and the ball flew across the intervening space to strike one of the trucks. It broke apart.

The humming the ball had offered earlier grew so loud

they could hear it even at their considerable distance as a small army of hornets arose like a thick cloud from its shattered core.

Ping and Jam had stopped far enough away that only a decent marksman could have reliably hit them. The few shots the bandits let off while being attacked by the hornets were not even pointed in their direction. The gunfire was more of a futile attempt to make the hornets back off than anything else. They managed to shoot two of their own men.

The boss, just far enough away to escape the wave of angry hornets, started running toward the Jeep, waving his gun. "Stop it!" He paused for a moment to point his gun.

Jam pulled out her own gun, muttering, "I probably should have brought a taser." But just as she set up for the shot, the leader slapped at his neck and started dancing around, waving his gun at the hornets. Soon he slumped to the ground, not exactly unconscious but not noticeably connected with reality.

All the bad guys were now laid out on the ground, trying to crawl dizzily in different directions.

Ciara observed through the speakerphone, "Well, that went pretty much the way Shura said it would. The hornets' venom has been genetically engineered so it's just as painful but less toxic. And it's loaded with Rohypnol."

Jam asked, "Rohypnol?"

Ping answered, "A date-rape drug. Ironic much?"

A hornet flew up to Ping to start circling around her head. She waved it away. "Looks like the cream she gave us to keep the hornets off is working too." She looked into the back seat of the Jeep. "You OK, Chief? Anything stung you yet?"

The ex-Beloved Advisor shook his head.

Jam watched the hornets scatter across the landscape. "And Shura swears they'll all die a couple hours after being released?"

Ciara replied decisively, "Oh, yes. That was the first thing we tested."

The Amazons' truck rolled up, and a bright young woman snapped off a salute. "Empress, shall we collect them?"

Ciara answered, "Empress, with your permission, I'd suggest taking the leader into custody."

Ping winced when Ciara called her "Empress" but said nothing. She supposed it was just as well for Ciara to use her ridiculous Benin title when the Amazons were listening, but she knew the real reason Ciara did it was for the entertainment of irritating her. Ping would have to figure out a way to get back at her someday.

Ciara continued, "I'm sending you a picture of the one with the best combination of leadership skills and—just maybe—a decent blend of ethics and integrity. He's the one you should work with."

The Amazon lieutenant had her women throw the ex-leader into the back of the truck that had, until now, been empty.

An hour later, the designated new leader came around enough to have a serious talk with the Empress. All the bandits' guns had been confiscated, and the new leader was strapped spread-eagled across the front of the Jeep with half the Amazons pointing their firearms at him like a firing squad. The other half kept watch on the other bandits, crowded together in a small cluster as they watched their new leader.

Ping spoke to him. "Relax, all the guns are safetied." She raised an eyebrow at the lieutenant, who rolled her eyes before waving to her troops to safety their weapons.

The Empress then walked up to him. "Let me explain the new rules. You and your guys can do anything you want as long as you don't kill, kidnap, rape, steal, threaten, or hurt anybody who lives around here or anybody traveling through the area." She pulled a second phone from her pocket, stuck it into his shirt pocket, and patted it. "You and your guys will study the educational software on this phone, and my people will see if there are any jobs you'd be good at in town or in one of our new factories. Or as one of the members of the new road-blockade-busting police force. It may take a while, but eventually we'll find something for you. Deal?"

The young man nodded vigorously.

Ciara interrupted. "Uh, he's probably convinced, but he may waver after you leave."

Ping smiled at Jam. "You wondered what we brought the Beloved Advisor for?"

Ping walked around to the back of the Jeep. "Time to earn your salary." With uncharacteristic gentleness, she helped the man out of the vehicle and led him around to the fellow strapped to the Jeep.

She spoke with quiet sincerity to the new boss. "This is the old Benin Beloved Chief Advisor for Life. He was the last guy who crossed me. He will now negotiate with you."

The Beloved waved his arms and shouted in inarticulate efforts to express his outrage and give orders.

The boss stared at the Beloved's gesticulating limbs, then stared at his mouth. "His tongue?"

Ping brandished her chura. "Nope." When the new leader looked away, Ping reiterated, "Deal?"

The young man, looking rather older and much more tired, nodded. "Yes, Empress. Deal."

Ciara assessed his new agreement. "And…that's a wrap."

The lieutenant stepped up and saluted. "Empress, forgive me for making a suggestion."

Ping smiled at her. "You're always welcome to make suggestions."

The young woman did not smile back. "Thank you, Empress. I cannot help thinking that if we canvassed the local villages, we would find evidence that the old leader we have in the back of our truck has committed grievous acts of violence worthy of execution." She shrugged. "It would simplify our logistics if we could just bury him here."

Jam turned away, covering her mouth in a failed attempt to muffle a chortle.

Ping's smile stayed affixed to her face, frozen in place. "Thank you, Lieutenant. As I said, recommendations are always welcome. However, this is one recommendation we shall not follow through on. Is that clear?"

The lieutenant saluted again. "Yes, Empress."

As Jam turned back to face her, Ping observed, "You may need to watch over our lieutenant here more than me."

Jam shook her head. "Oh, but Empress, it is so educational to watch you work."

Khalid was packing for his next trip when Uwais and Sabaah came back from theirs and offered him an update on events in Iran and Israel.

Not for the first time, Khalid wished he could put up wallscreens in their home in the caverns, but considerable work would be required to fix the rock walls before they could do so. Both bringing in men to work on the walls and transporting the wallscreen elements would have left too many people in possession of Khalid's laboratory's location. Instead, they made do with a number of large freestanding displays.

Khalid listened to his men's reports while studying the data they'd brought him and finished summarizing the events of the past few weeks. "So, that's where we stand. Any questions?" On his upcoming trip Khalid would be incommunicado, except for a half dozen innocuous code phrases he could post through his FB account. If they had any concerns, he needed to address them now.

Uwais shook his head. "I don't know about you, but it looks like just about every part of the plan failed. I can't believe how quickly those BrainTrusters developed a vaccine."

Sabaah defended Khalid's results. "But this version of the virus really did spread more aggressively. And the mortality rate was about twenty percent, almost twice what the first version got."

Uwais looked at Khalid. "Which brings up an interesting question. You didn't think it would be any more lethal. Any idea why it worked so well?"

Khalid shook his head. "It doesn't surprise me, although I continue to doubt that the virus was actually more lethal. The United States has always been a black hole for infectious diseases, dating all the way back to the SARS outbreak that started in Hong Kong. People did fly to America with the disease, but it snuffed out without any secondary infections at all. If we released Red Rubola in the USA, it probably wouldn't fare any better than Blue Rubola did."

Uwais went back to his original point. "So that didn't go any better either, really."

Khalid just shrugged and gave him a small smile.

Uwais pressed on to the most important hiccup. "And to top it all off, now everybody's going to the BrainTrust. All the top scientists from all over the world. While it's humorous to think about the Iranian and Israeli scientists working shoulder to shoulder—surely one of them is going to kill the other one, praise Allah—with all the best and brightest gathered in one place, their response time to the next epidemic is going to be incredible. They'll have vaccines on the scene before the first person with a rash gets to the hospital. It's a disaster."

Sabaah looked stricken.

Khalid's eyes gleamed. "Ah, yes. How satisfying. All according to plan."

10

CONDITION ZEBRA

Not only strike while the iron is hot, but make it hot by striking.
—Oliver Cromwell

Over the next several weeks, the people on the *Chiron* spent much of their time greeting new arrivals. Everyone wanted, above all things, to meet Dash. Then Colin or Chance or Amanda would show them to their new quarters on the *Eos* before letting them rush into the whirlwind where they learned to use the new tools, wrangle the bots, study the CEREBRUM forecasts, and explore the potentialities of the CRISPIER.

Two of the last to arrive came from the American University in Beirut. Jubair el-Parani, a heavyset man with a defensive edge to his voice, introduced himself. Dash welcomed him with enthusiasm, rattling off a number of his research papers she had read. You could see Jubair's smile grow more proud with every paper Dash mentioned.

Finally Jubair introduced his friend. "And this is Hilaal el-Mousa, my archenemy."

Dash raised an eyebrow at this. Hilaal, a tall, graceful man with a warm smile and a twinkle in his eyes, explained. "Jubair and I competed in college." He looked sideways at his friend. "In the end, he ran me out of town. I decided to join Doctors without Borders rather than have to compete with this one for grants and journal space for papers."

Dash looked a little taken aback. "So *that* was what happened to you. I remember one paper you wrote." She named an obscure article in an obscure journal. "It was exceptional in its clarity and incisiveness. I remember looking forward to great research in the future." Her smile broadened. "I'm utterly delighted to have you here."

Hilaal looked astonished she knew his work; Jubair looked just the littlest bit annoyed.

Chance took over hostess duties from Dash, and as she led them through the ship, the mood was still almost cele-bratory even though the crisis had ended almost a month earlier. They had cured Red Rubola in record time, and while outbreaks continued to occur, stockpiles of vaccine were rushed to the affected areas with the speed of a FedEx delivery.

But a party atmosphere had never quite taken hold. The advent of Red Rubola had demonstrated that the terrorist, whoever and wherever he was, had both the capacity and the determination to launch new plagues virtually at will. The second rubola plague had been twice as lethal as the first, and no one doubted either that there would be another one or that the next one would be even scarier.

However, in one quiet corner of the *Chiron*, in Dash's personal quarters where she had gone after greeting the new arrivals, a quieter kind of happiness had arisen.

Dash had made the mistake of letting her cousin Astri get settled into Dash's cabin while she was off with Jubair and Hilaal. By the time she got back, Astri had, as so often before, raided her closet.

So when Dash returned, she found Astri resplendently decked out in the Tory Burch Evalene Cold Shoulder dress with tassels Daniella had created for her for First Launch.

Astri took her eyes off her own reflection in the mirror, startled by Dash's arrival. But instead of looking embarrassed or apologetic, she boldly arched her back and looked down her nose at the dress's owner. She held out a limp hand with royal elegance. "Come, you may attend me."

Dash started to frown, then broke into laughter. She pulled out her phone and held it up in the classic picture-taking stance. "Hold that pose."

Her cousin Astri held that pose, then moved to another.

Dash observed between snapping photos, "You seem to have memorized every position used by professional fashion models to show off their clothes."

Astri giggled. "Are they showing off the clothes or themselves?"

"Is there a difference?"

Astri switched positions once more. "In this case, we're definitely trying to highlight the clothes. I'm not fashion model enough to be worth showing myself off."

Dash put her phone down. "Nonsense. You are as beautiful as any model I have ever met."

Astri laughed. "And just how many fashion models do you know?"

Dash decided against telling her about Gina, the only fashion model she actually knew, who was drop-dead gorgeous.

Astri looked back into the mirror and wriggled, watching the folds of the Tori Burch work of art shimmer. "It fits like a glove."

Dash offered with gentle humor, "So glad I can be of service, working as a test model for your clothes."

Astri twisted again for the mirror.

Dash had an idea. "You don't happen to have any formal affairs coming up, do you? Any weddings, perhaps? You're welcome to borrow the gown if so."

Astri looked at her with amazed glee, then turned away. "Oh, thank you, Dyah, but I couldn't. This has to be worth thousands of dollars."

Dash decided it would be best not to tell her just how expensive it really was. "Nonsense. Let me know when you need it and I'll ship it to you."

Three days later, Astri had worked her way through Dash's entire wardrobe, and Dash had initiated the rejuv therapy for Astri's father. Dash was explaining the next steps in the process for her aunt, uncle, and cousin when her phone rang with ABBA's *Take a Chance on Me*. "Chance. How can I help you?"

"We've had a little spat down here. It's been taken care of for the moment, but you should probably come down."

Dash closed her eyes. "Velma?"

Chance hesitated. "She's not the one who started it."

Dash found Chance's defense of Velma amusing. The two had fought over everything down to the layout of equipment on a lab bench when Velma first arrived, but something had happened shortly after Dash introduced CEREBRUM. Now the two of them seemed inseparable, even on breaks and after work. Very interesting.

Dash turned to Astri. "Your father is all hooked up and resting comfortably on the Wenara Wana deck. You should go visit." With that, she departed at a half-run.

Dash still couldn't quite grasp the idea of Velma's innocence. As she trotted down the passage, she tried to imagine a spat where Velma didn't fill the role of starting it.

Cameron Ballard went through the metal detectors at the ferry dock to the GS *Prime*. He touched his chest nervously where he normally carried his shoulder holster under his suit. Before departing from San Francisco, he'd held his gun for a long time, trying to figure out a way to carry it, but in the end, he'd acknowledged he'd never get it through the metal detectors. It was all very annoying for the man upon whom the entirety of America now depended to thwart the next bioterror attack, or at least track down the culprit behind the first one.

He already knew who was responsible, of course, though he was uncertain how many accomplices she'd had. Once he got his hands on her, however, he was confident he could sweat her until she delivered on all the members of her conspiracy, all the people in the CDC who worked with her, and all the people on the BrainTrust who backed her.

The artistic theme here on the GS *Prime* grand promenade deck—the deck that had the gangways to adjacent ships that he needed to cross to get to the *Chiron*—was The Midas Touch. Everything that could be gold was gold, but in the GS *Prime* version of the story, Midas could turn the power to transform things into gold on and off at will. Hence the majority of the living things depicted on the rendered walls, and in the small parkland, were still alive... except for one unfortunate tree and an adjacent rose bush that had been turned into lustrously beautiful metal forever.

Cameron just shook his head. It was all crazy but unimportant compared to his mission.

Soon enough he reached the *Chiron* and started asking if anyone knew Velma Highwalker and where she might be. It turned out just about everyone knew Velma, and as he watched their reactions, he was fascinated by the intensity of the mixed emotions her name evoked.

Very smart, people acknowledged. A valuable member of the team, they admitted more reluctantly. Best to avoid crossing her path, they confessed with trepidation.

As Cameron hustled down to the Red Planet deck, he chewed on what he'd learned. Velma the terrorist was respected but not liked. No surprise there. He gingerly touched his eye where she'd clobbered him after taking him by surprise.

Unfortunately, even if they didn't like the woman, if

they thought she was an asset to the research team, they would not support him if he tried to drag her back to America in cuffs. He swallowed bile as he considered more tactful approaches.

The time he had spent trying to figure out how to retrieve the terrorist had left him more and more furious with the existence of the BrainTrust. As a practical matter, it was a simple extension of the United States. Well, OK, over half the people on board were foreigners, but the ships had been built with American money and organized by American companies, and the Board for the BrainTrust Consortium was heavily weighted with Americans. They had no business claiming to be Liberian-flagged cruise liners in international waters. An FBI agent with a warrant should be akin to a god here. Instead, he was powerless.

His only consolation was that he had some confidence that he could lure the hot-headed Ms. Highwalker into giving herself away in public.

So he trudged down to the shopping area of the Red Planet deck and stood not quite on tippy-toes to survey the area lined with biosafety cabinets. Moments later he spotted his target, arguing about something with another tallish, thin woman who was probably of Hispanic descent.

He strode up to them with confidence. "Ms. High-walker. I'm so glad to have finally tracked you down." He nodded to the other woman. "I'm Cameron Ballard with the FBI." He held out his badge—farther out than he had in the past, having learned caution from his last encounter with a BrainTruster.

He had expected the other woman, who spoke like a

native of Arizona, to acknowledge at least some respect for his badge. He pursed his lips as her expression darkened.

Then she smiled. "Chance Dixon. Nice to meet you." She shook his hand.

While still holding his hand, she looked at Velma. "So this is the guy who tried to imprison you back in Atlanta?"

Velma scowled. "That's the one."

Ballard found himself wishing Chance would let go of his hand. Finally she did. He spoke to Chance as if hoping her judgment would support him. "We got off on the wrong foot. I was moving with desperate speed to catch the perpetrator of the bioterror attack on America." He shrugged. "It's no longer so urgent since the epidemic died out."

Velma turned to Chance, also wishing for her support. "Notice that he thinks the epidemic just died out mysteriously. No vaccine involved."

Chance gave Cameron a hard look. "So, all the incredibly long hours and hard work we did here had nothing to do with it?"

Ballard found himself getting warm around the collar. "I'm just telling you what the FDA concluded: the virus had a defect that caused it to mutate into a nonviable state."

Ballard spotted Simon Bingham coming to join them out of the corner of his eye. Chance shouted to him. "Simon! Hey, this FBI guy says the FDA says the epidemic just died out because of a mutation."

Simon raised an eyebrow. "Funny, that should be the CDC's call. And I certainly never said that."

Ballard frowned. "Technically, sir, you're not with the CDC anymore."

Simon ground out, "True enough."

This attempt to have a useful conversation in public had somehow gone sideways. "Regardless, Ms. Highwalker is a person of interest in the case, and I must insist on an opportunity to speak to her about it." His voice sounded strangled as he made his best offer. "Just a few questions over a cup of coffee in a café." He barely had enough breath for the last word. "Please."

Chance frowned. "In case you haven't heard, the terrorists launched another plague in Iran since Velma here escaped your clutches. What was her motive for that?"

Ballard spent a moment being pleased that Chance at least understood Velma's motive for attacking the United States. Still, "I don't care about that, Ms. Dixon. The Blue Rubola plague is an American matter. I still need to talk with Ms. Highwalker here."

Velma put her hands on her hips and jutted out her jaw. "Not in a million years, you moron."

Ballard looked at Simon and Chance in bafflement. "How can you all not understand? The terrorist who unleashed this terrible epidemic had to have means, motive, and opportunity. America is so well sealed from the outside world that the opportunity is far better for American citizens than for anyone else, and no one has the means except scientists who specialize in genetically manipulating viruses. Taking all the scientists into custody was the fastest way we had of ensuring we had removed the guilty party from circulation."

He pointed an accusatory finger at Velma. "And this one has a long record of conflict with our nation's government. She's a perfect fit for the profile." His mind filled with righteous indignation and fury. "I really must speak with her." He reached out and grabbed her wrist.

Velma twisted her arm to break his hold. With a shriek, she took a roundhouse swing at his face the same way she had the last time he'd encountered her.

But this time he was ready. He leaned back, and as she stepped forward for another swing, he blocked her.

At last things were going as he'd hoped. Now everyone could see she was a loose cannon. He thought with smug satisfaction of the vidcams capturing this moment as she lost control.

Alas, she followed up with a sharp jab to the chin which he failed to fully block. She didn't quite break his jaw, but he had to shake off the dizziness. Since no one was doing anything to stop her or help him, he could see he would have to defend himself. He set himself for a counterattack.

Then Chance spoke with authoritative disapproval. "Velma. That is totally unacceptable. You know better."

Velma glared at the woman whom Ballard now suspected was her supervisor. "OK, OK."

Ballard relaxed.

Velma swept around in a graceful flying kick that smacked him in the temple.

He collapsed to his knees, staggering as he struggled to stay upright. He looked helplessly at Chance.

Chance nodded to Velma. "Excellent. See how much better that works? Just like I taught you." She looked back at Ballard. "Discipline and practice, Velma. Discipline and practice."

Velma scowled. "Yeah, yeah, you're right. Happy now?"

Ballard looked one last time at the women, then his eyes lost focus and he thudded on his face, unconscious.

Dash arrived in time to see a man in a suit face-down on the deck with Chance kneeling over him. Four bots came in, lifted him, and carried him away, presumably to a hospital bed. "Is he going to be OK? Who is he, anyway?"

Velma answered one question. "He's the FBI creep who tried to arrest me dirtside. He just tried to arrest me again."

Chance answered the other question. "He may have a mild concussion, certainly nothing more. Velma pulled her punch."

Velma scowled. "I gave him everything I had."

Chance sighed. "I repeat. Discipline and practice."

Dash, alarmed, added, "And care. You really don't want to cause permanent injury." Her alarm grew as Velma showed reluctance to agree.

She pulled out her phone. "Wolf, we need your services. Velma had an encounter with an FBI agent." She listened to him, then asked Velma, "Is this Cameron Ballard?"

When Velma nodded, Dash spoke to Wolf. "Apparently so." More conversation followed, and Dash rubbed her temples. "At the moment, you can't really throw either of them in the brig. Mr. Ballard needs to stay here under medical observation until we can declare him fit for release." She sighed. "And we still need Velma analyzing these viruses. We have to be as ready as possible for the next one." She listened again. "I guess you're right, it's all under control for now. Take your time. Thank you, it would be good if you scheduled a meeting with Mediator Chibuzo."

Dash had barely put her phone away when Chad, the leader of the semi-official Lab Rats, ran up to them. "Come quick! Trina's really sick."

Dash, Chance, and Velma followed him at a dead run to the medical suite where the bots had Trina wired like a piece of stereo equipment. All three donned facemasks as they entered.

They all examined the rash on Trina's neck. Dash finished her assessment first. "See the core of purple?"

Velma drew the conclusion. "New."

Chance followed up. "Moonsuits?"

Dash pondered the question. "In a moment."

The bots had already loaded blood samples for molecular analysis. They left Trina's bedside and went into a nearby lab to look at the preliminary results. The massed power of data centers all over the BrainTrust poured through the data, guided by Dark Alpha 43, to identify striking and unusual structures.

Something caught Dash's eye, and she gasped. Before either of the other women could even ask what she'd seen, she was running full speed down the passageway.

In an earlier generation, dirtside buildings had been reliably equipped with glass cabinets that sat flush to the wall, containing either red axes or, with later more relevant technology, fire extinguishers. While these items supplied the occasional convenient prop in horror movies, the most interesting thing about them was just how uninteresting they were. These cabinets, which had given rise to the popular phrase, "In the event of emergency, break glass," were in fact quite invisible to the casual passerby.

On ocean-going ships, similar needs were met with similar equipment. On a ship, however, such gear was more important because of the risk that a disaster could cause the loss of the entire vessel and everyone aboard. The BrainTrust isle ships had similar needs, though the technology was quite different. For example, out-of-control fires were much less likely simply because a swarm of bots could be called in moments to fight the flames. On an isle ship, one didn't need equipment on hand. One simply needed a comm connection that bypassed every conceivable intermediary.

On board the *Chiron*, therefore, the glass with the fire extinguisher had been replaced by a smaller transparent plastic cover, still recessed into the wall, with a palm-size bright-red button behind it. It was still invisible to the casual passerby, unless and until one ceased to be casual.

Dash ran to the nearest such emergency station, slapped the glass up, and smashed the button. She tore her face mask away. "Condition Zebra!" she said as loudly as a gentle Balinese woman could bring herself to shout. "Get tight!"

The Condition Red alarms wailed just as they had wailed on Assault Night, although the emergency was quite different.

Chance and Velma caught up with her. Velma looked wildly around as automated doors started to slide closed and bots rolled up to manual doors and dogged them shut by hand.

Chance asked the obvious question, although she

suspected she knew the answer. "Condition Zebra? What's that, exactly?"

Dash answered distractedly as she dialed her phone. "It's a long-standing nomenclature used aboard ships to alert everyone of a hull breach, and all the waterproof hatches must be sealed to delay or prevent the ship from sinking."

Velma still looked disoriented. "Is the ship sinking?"

Chance understood now. "No, girl, but the watertight seals will also slow the spread of an airborne infection." She turned to Dash. "Right?"

Dash disregarded this as her phone connected. "Amanda. We need to set the whole archipelago to Condition Zebra immediately. We're under attack from a new bioweapon, designed and engineered specifically to target the BrainTrust." Dash paused. "If we're very lucky, no one will die except all of us on the *Chiron*."

They collected air samples to confirm Dash's hypothesis. She pointed at a captured virion on the wallscreen of the lab. "Look at that protein coat."

Velma and Chance both scrutinized the molecular layout. Velma, who specialized in virology, whistled. "That's the most complex set of capsomeres I've ever seen." The capsomeres were the building blocks that self-assembled to create the coat. They were typically simple since a virus had only enough RNA or DNA to manufacture a few proteins.

Dash nodded. "Even the most complex natural viruses

are able to produce less than two hundred proteins. I estimate these are able to produce almost three hundred, and many of them are involved in that coat."

Chance asked the obvious question. "Why? What's so special about this capsid?"

Dash highlighted a chunk of protein forming an outer layer on the outer layer, then waited for a moment, hoping someone would spot the significance. When no one responded, she explained. "This capsomere can totally block ultraviolet radiation. UV-A, UV-B, and also—" she paused dramatically—"UV-C."

Chance balled her hands into fists. "So it's immune to our most important sterilization system?"

Dash gave her a smile of approval. "Precisely." She drew carefully on the screen, highlighting the whole outer coat. "It's almost like a separate shell. When the virion escapes the cell into the blood, the plasma starts to break it down so it can infect the next cell. But if it gets expelled from the body, it enters the outside world virtually invulnerable."

Chad came running into the room, his eyes glistening with unshed tears. "Trina's dead."

And they all found themselves running again, to stand quietly for a moment beside the bed of the once-beautiful young woman, The rash that had earlier grown at an incredible pace to cover her body had, in the last moments of the disease's progress, started to fade. She looked at peace.

Velma started to scream in horror, then as quickly stopped. She looked at Chad. "Did she have any special medical conditions? I don't understand how she could have died so quickly."

Chad shook his head in bewilderment. "I can't understand it at all. She was a marathon runner; you could see her moving at an incredible speed all over the archipelago. She once told me she hadn't been sick once since she was twelve years old. That was one of the reasons she volunteered: she figured if anyone could survive a test that went wrong, she could."

Dash exhaled in a shuddering breath. "Of course. That's what's going on." She whipped out her phone once again and started giving orders for bots to bring her a long list of chemicals. She could see from their expressions that Chance and Velma had no clue what she had planned.

It made no difference. Unless she was completely off-base, every minute that now passed without action would cost lives. Dash called Amanda again, putting her on speakerphone. "Any chance we called Zebra in time to protect the rest of the ship outside the Red Planet deck? I'm sure that's where it originated."

Amanda's answer from the Command Information Center, her duty station during a Condition Red emergency, was grim. "About half the decks are reporting infections. There's no particular pattern to the decks reporting the disease. I'm almost certain the whole ship has been exposed, there are just some parts of the ship where no one has gone symptomatic yet."

Dash nodded. "Can you partially repeal the Condition Zebra? I need all the air ventilation systems and the doors and hatches open if I'm to spread my, ah, solution."

Chance asked hopefully, "You have a cure? Already?"

Dash frowned. "I have something to mitigate the side

effects of the disease, and hopefully save most of the people on the ship."

Amanda answered the earlier question. "I've put out the orders to unseal all the interior compartments." Even as she spoke, they could hear the automated doors gently whine as they slid back. Bots ran once again to open the doors they had previously closed.

Chance asked, "So what's the plan?"

Dash gave her a wry smile. "I'm going to sabotage all our immune systems to make things easier for the virus."

Velma started laughing. "Of course. I get it now."

Dash started shifting back and forth on her feet. "I should really explain the plan, but we have no time." She turned and started running again.

Velma yelled at her departing form, "Go. I presume you're planning to pump an aerosol into the ventilation system. I'll explain to everyone."

As Dash ran down the corridor toward the down ramp, bots with equipment and chemicals emerged from the side passages and assembled behind her like a line of ducklings behind their mother.

Chance smiled as Dash disappeared. "She took the phone we were talking to Amanda on." She pulled out her own cell. "Poor Amanda. It has got to be tough being in charge when you have so little control."

Amanda's face appeared on the small screen. "OK, everyone, I believe I have been reasonably patient and accommodating. Would someone please tell me what the hell is going on?"

Velma took a deep breath. "Now that Dash is doing what can be done, we might as well get comfortable for a moment." She hustled into the nearest conference room and slipped into a chair while Chance brought Amanda up on the wallscreen.

Amanda appeared to be ready to tear out her hair. "Remember my patience earlier? It's all gone."

Velma started with a story from the past. "Dash realized why Trina died so quickly. It's like the 1918 Spanish flu."

Chance squinted at her. "The Spanish flu? I know it was the most lethal flu pandemic in history, but this rubola is derived from measles. I don't see the connection."

Velma grimaced. "Neither did I, embarrassingly enough." Some internal dialog held her entranced for a moment. "One of the striking characteristics of that flu was that the onset and death could be unbelievably sudden. There's one well-documented case of a man getting on a trolley in downtown New York with no symptoms at all and dying before they reached his stop on the outskirts of town."

Amanda nodded. "Like Trina."

Velma leaned forward. "Precisely. They didn't know it at the time, but closely related to this extraordinary speed was the demographic pattern of the disease's lethality. The flu slaughtered healthy young adults while leaving the elderly and the children sick but still able to recover."

Chance looked away thoughtfully. "So it struck the people with the best immune systems hardest."

Amanda added, "Again, like Trina."

Velma leapt up, apparently unable to relax although she was the one who had insisted on getting more comfortable. "The disease didn't kill them. The virus didn't have enough time during a ride on the trolley to kill anyone. The patient's own immune system killed him as it reacted violently to contain the virus."

Amanda concluded, "So Dash has dumped something into our air to weaken us, so our own immune systems don't destroy us."

Dash ran up to the door of the conference room, saw everyone gathered there, and slumped against the door frame. "It's done." She looked at Velma. "Did you explain?"

Velma nodded. "Spanish flu. Immune system over-reaction."

Dash seemed to slump farther. "Almost everyone will get violently ill, but I expect most people will now survive." She straightened up sluggishly, her voice turning grim. "But as is all too often the case, there are side effects. Having released the spray into the ventilation system, I not only weakened the immune reactions of the healthy people but also of all the people whose immune systems are already weak."

Velma stopped pacing. "The elderly."

Chance gasped. "All the rejuv patients. They're almost all already compromised. This could wind up killing every last one of them."

Dash took a breath. "Hopefully not that bad. We do already have them all hooked up to the best care they can get. But it will be bad." She looked away. "I don't see how my uncle will be able to survive." She turned to go.

Chance leapt up to follow her. "Let me check on most

of our patients. You go be with your family."

Amanda looked at something off-screen. "No!"

Everyone turned to look at her.

She looked horrified. "Oh, no, no, no." She looked at Velma. "Since Dash and Chance have to go see the rejuv patients, you have an additional assignment. I'm sending another patient down to you." She choked back a sob. "Colin Wheeler has gone symptomatic."

Ping and Jam had been traveling north clearing toll blockades for several days.

Jam looked over her shoulder again. "Congratulations, you finally lost them."

Ping dodged another crater in the road. "Ha! Free at last!" She looked around, essentially daring the landscape to wreck the Jeep while she was distracted. "Looks like we lost the drone, too."

Jam shrugged. "I think it went back up to the dirigible to recharge. I wouldn't count on having lost Ciara if I were you."

Ping growled but said nothing.

They crested a hill, and Ping squinted into the distance. "Is that a solar power farm up there?"

Jam squinted as well. "Can't think what else it could be." She switched back to an earlier subject. "So how's the cybernetic limb factory coming? Any idea how long it will be before we can fix up the Beloved Advisor?"

Ping answered brightly. "Excellent news. The factory is operational. Not ready to run at full capacity yet, but we got the first production run yesterday. Shura's scheduled to get her hands first, and I think she goes in for surgery tomorrow." Her voice turned grim. "As for the Advisor here, there's a long line in front of him."

Jam clapped. "I'm glad Shura is first. She certainly deserves it." She raised an eyebrow at Ping. "Even if she did trick you into being empress."

Ping scowled. "I half-expect her to take the hands off again. She's so facile with that clamp-thing, I can't help thinking a normal hand may be a step backward."

Jam grunted. "She better keep at least one hand. Everybody is going to feel safer once we've removed that Stylus of Death she has on the other arm."

Ping grudgingly conceded the point. "There's that, too."

Jam pointed forward. "Looks like our fleeing criminals have given up the escape." Up ahead, a battered brown truck bounced to the side of the road and two young men jumped out with their handy-dandy assault rifles.

At the last toll booth/roadblock, two of the bandits had managed to dodge the hornets long enough to start a truck and charge away. Ping and Jam, after making sure the main group of thugs was quiet enough for collection by the Amazons, had torn after them.

It had been a long chase, the driver of the truck being every bit as insane as Ping. She'd even complimented him a couple of times as the pursuit continued long beyond expectations.

Once again, Ping slid the Jeep sideways to a stop.

The men lit up the landscape with their guns for a few seconds until they'd shot their magazines dry. Both Jam and Ping winced as a handful of rounds hit the Jeep.

Jam took careful aim and fired three times. With nothing but a pistol the range should have been too great even for Jam, but she managed to take out a tire nonetheless.

The men ran around behind the truck. Ping hopped onto the hood of the Jeep and yelled at them, "Hey, guys, do I really have to send you another batch of hornets? Throw out your guns and come out here with your hands up."

Ping waited with moderate patience while a barely recognizable argument went on behind the truck. "OK, I haven't got all day. I'm going to load up the hornets now. Last chance."

Two AK-47s thumped on the dirt in front of the truck, and the men stepped out with their hands up.

Jam ran over while Ping covered her, quickly stripping the rifles and pocketing the firing pins. "Hands behind your backs."

As Ping sauntered up, she asked, "So, why'd you stop here, anyway?"

The driver ground out, "Ran out of gas."

Ping nodded. "Important safety tip: fill up before running for your lives."

Jam threw her a doubtful look. "Since when have you been into that kind of long-range planning?"

The prisoners now quiescent, Ping looked to the north. "Let's go check out that solar panel field. Who's up here, anyway?"

Jam pointed at the men. "What about these two?"

Ping shrugged. "Either the troops pick them up, or they escape on foot." She waved her hand around the empty landscape. "Either way, I'm happy with it."

"Fair enough." Jam looked north at the solar farm. "You sure you want to keep going? Not only did we leave the troops behind, but I'm also pretty sure we left the country behind."

Ping chuckled. "I'm pretty sure we had already left the country behind even before that last roadblock." She shrugged. "Easy enough to check." The GPS showed they'd crossed most of Niger and were on the verge of entering Mali. "So, outside my jurisdiction."

"At last, I don't have to call you empress any more. Still want to go north and see the solar panels, even if you're not head honcho?"

Ping grinned. "Road trip."

The solar farm that had looked so close at hand took over an hour to reach. Even Ping was tired.

As they slowed to a halt, Jam looked around disapprovingly. "Honestly, I'm tired of wandering around parts of the planet that have turned to desert. First northern China, now this." She swept her hand across the landscape. "According to the history books, the Sahel didn't used to come this far south."

Ping hopped out and walked toward the solar field. "Everything changes."

A young man stepped out from under the shade of the panels. "Good afternoon. My name is Quraish. And you are?"

Ping pointed to her partner. "This is Jam, and I'm Ping."

The fellow nodded politely to them both, then swiveled his head sharply back to Ping. "I think I may have heard of you. Are you the Empress of Benin?"

Ping buried her face in her hands.

Jam coughed to hide her laugh. "She certainly is. I don't suppose you'd care for the job?"

Quraish looked at her in puzzlement.

Ping answered, "This is Mali, right? I'm not the empress here. Call me Ping."

Quraish nodded. "As you wish. May I ask why you are here?"

Ping shrugged. "We were chasing bandits, and during the hot pursuit, we wound up just south of you."

Quraish's expression turned grave. "Ah, bandits. It used to be worse than that here, you know. Boko Haram came, intent on slaughter, but then several years ago, our benefactor arrived and drove them away."

Ping clapped. "Marvelous. Glad I'm not the only person around here snuffing out terrorists. I guess I don't have to worry about your people, then." She glanced around. "Really, you're kinda outside my jurisdiction anyway, so I'm doubly glad you've got someone to look out for you."

Jam listened intently. "Your benefactor?"

Quraish smiled dreamily as if contemplating a scene of peace and serenity. "Shortly after arriving, he also started building our solar power field."

Ping homed in on the original question that brought her here. "Exactly what are you doing with this solar farm, anyway? There aren't any cross-country power lines to take the power to the cities, are there?"

Quraish shook his head. "We use the power locally to the extent we can. In the afternoon on most days we get enough power to do many things, like running an arc welder to repair the bicycles, but the rest of the day, it's almost useless. Many of us think it's more trouble than it's worth, but not me." He pointed at himself. "I come out every day to check on the wiring and clean the panels."

Ping frowned in frustration. "So if it's not that useful, why did your benefactor put them here in the first place?"

Now puzzlement filled Quraish's face. "Our benefactor says they will bring back the rain. He explained how, but honestly, I didn't understand it."

Jam asked with bemusement. "So this fellow drove off the terrorists, built a solar farm, and plans to make the desert bloom. I'm almost afraid to ask: what else does he do?"

Quraish's dreamy expression returned. "He teaches from the Quran." He winced. "And more recently, he brought us vaccine, and made us all take shots lest we suffer if the plague in America reached us."

Ping muttered to Jam. "Quite the jack of all trades."

Jam smiled back mischievously. "Remind you of anyone?"

Ping looked dazed, as if she had been struck in the face. Together, Ping and Jam said in chorus, "Dash."

Ping wrinkled her nose. "But only sort of. I mean, he's not a techno-geek, he's just into a lot of different good things for people."

Jam nodded acknowledgment.

Quraish took them on a brief tour of the facility. "Sorry there's not more of interest, Empress." He looked away. "I mean, Ping."

A loud squalling came from the Jeep. Jam put her hand to her lips. "We forgot about the Chief." She smiled warmly at Quraish. "It was very nice meeting you." She turned to

Ping. "I'll see you back at the Jeep." She jogged off to attend the unhappy ex-Advisor.

Ping turned to Quraish. "It's been delightful spending this time with you. Thank you."

Quraish shook her hand. "I'll tell our benefactor you visited. He'll be sorry he missed you."

Ping chuckled. She was about to ask the name of this benefactor, contemplating the creation of an alliance between their two forces of civilization, when her phone played *Another Brick in Wall* by Pink Floyd. "Ciara, what's up?"

The answer sent her running headlong back to the Jeep with barely a wave of thanks and goodbye.

Uwais nestled another ceramic shuriken in his belt. He was clothed in loose-fitting black pants, a similarly loose black shirt, and black sneakers, looking for all the world like a ninja, if ninjas were made in XXL sizes. "It sounds like everything is going according to plan."

Sabaah grunted. "I'm a little surprised that they opened the internal compartments so soon. Shucks, I'm surprised they declared Condition Zebra so quickly."

Uwais twisted back and forth, stretching. "Yeah, they pushed up our timetable all right. Fortunately, we're ready." He thought about it for a moment. "It's probably that Dr. Dash Khalid's been so crazy about."

Sabaah secured the last of his ceramic throwing knives and grabbed his plastic paintball gun. "Well, that's what we're here to take care of. Ready?"

Uwais snapped the magazine into his own paintball gun. "Let's go."

They programmed their small yacht to surge forward for a few minutes, then stepped onto the roof where they had their sky-blue powered hang gliders strapped down. One after the other, they strapped the gliders to themselves and lifted into the freshening wind.

Each had an earbud with which to talk to the other. Sabaah, of course, had some issues with the strategy they had undertaken. "Let me guess, you're delighted at this opportunity to learn all about hang gliding."

Uwais answered in a bellow. "Why not? And think how much fun it would be someday to hang glide to the top of a mountain with skis and come back down."

Sabaah shook his head. "So much trouble just to get to the blasted ship."

Uwais answered phlegmatically, "Hey, if we went through the security checkpoints like we did the last time, the AIs would do facial recognition and sound every alarm on the deck. 'Aha! There're the guys who stole our CRISPIER.'"

As they rose higher and flew eastward, eventually they spotted the archipelago in the distance—the towering white superstructures of most of the isle ships, plus the dazzling multi-color delight of the *Elysian Fields*. At this point they dropped their engines and batteries, the only parts of the glider with significant amounts of metal. They were now, for all intents and purposes, invisible to radar, and infrared, and visual detection.

They landed on the *Chiron* helipad and trotted down the ramps to the Red Planet deck. As they arrived there, they started firing paintballs to splatter all the vidcams as they charged through. This surely alerted the peacekeepers, but now it was too late for them to intervene effectively.

Coming into the biosafety cabinet area, they slowed to a halt. More than one person turned to stare at them. An older balding guy walked up to them. "This is a biohazard containment area. What are you doing here?"

Uwais stepped up to tower over him. "Where is Dr. Dash?"

The man blinked. "Dash? I have no idea. Presumably dealing with the bioterror attack. You know this ship is infected and quarantined, right?"

Sabaah ribbed his partner. "He's right. The safest place in this ship is probably *inside* the cabinets where they keep the dangerous diseases." He chuckled at his own joke.

Uwais rolled his eyes. He looked at the older man, who stood very straight and very indignant. Uwais chopped him in the throat. As the gagging man fell to the floor, Uwais pushed him down to pound his head on the deck surface.

That surface was a kind of hard rubber, so it did not kill the fellow. But it put him out of commission for the foreseeable future.

Sabaah studied the unconscious body for a moment. "I think that was Simon, the head of the CDC."

Uwais shrugged. He pulled out his phone. "Showtime." He pushed a button.

All over the *Chiron*, the lights dimmed. The doors and hatches between the decks whirred closed once more, trapping any peacekeepers who might have been coming their way on whichever deck they happened to be. The shipwide broadcasting system fired up.

Uwais spoke softly. "Good evening. This is Uwais al-Nassif, your new captain. Your old captain on the bridge and your old Chairman in her sterile little Command Information Center, have been removed from the network. Do not doubt that I am in charge."

Sabaah chortled. He said, loudly enough to be heard throughout the ship, "We control the vertical. We control the—"

Uwais pushed him away. "And that was Sabaah, my partner on this holy quest to cleanse the world. In case you haven't heard, you've all been infected with a new virus. Most of you will die soon enough, but some of you may die prematurely nonetheless." He chuckled. "Or not. I have but one demand you must fulfill, and I shall leave you to whatever may remain of your pitiful heathen lives."

A commotion at the opposite end of the open area caught his eye. "But more on that in a moment. Right now I have to put down an attempted coup." He nodded to one of the two tall women running through the assembled scientists, parting them much as Allah had parted the waters for Moses. "Dr. Chance Dixon, nice to meet you. Shall we dance?"

Uwais reached for a shuriken, but Sabaah whispered, "Better save those."

Uwais nodded. "Good point. These two should be easy. I'll take Chance."

Sabaah agreed. "I'll take the other heathen, whoever she is."

Chance slowed to a dancing rhythm and launched a flurry of strikes: a fist to the face, a kick to the abdomen, the other fist to the other side of the face.

Uwais saw each strike before it started and blocked them all. He then leaned into his opponent and struck.

Sabaah laughed as the other woman just came up, no defense, no tactics, just charged until she was in range and threw a high, twisting kick to the head. He ducked underneath and struck her face with his fists, left-right-left.

She fell without a sound.

Chance blocked Uwais' first blow, but the power he unleashed was incredible. Even blocked, the strike knocked her back. Then he was on her.

She danced back, trying to regain her balance.

But by then Sabaah had finished with the other one. He came from the side and kicked her with the same head strike she had used so successfully on others.

She also fell to the deck.

Uwais rolled his shoulders in a stretching motion. "I guess all that training paid off after all. I think six months ago she would've given me a tough go."

Sabaah grumped. "Whoever the other one is, she's a beginner. I think we spent too much time training, myself."

Uwais shrugged. "With luck, we'll finish here and be gone before we find out."

Sabaah shook his head. "Spoilsport. What's the point of training against these Jam and Ping people if we never even meet them?"

11

SHATTERED

Never confuse a single defeat with a final defeat.
    —F. Scott Fitzgerald

As Jam hurtled the Jeep down the road, Ping asked Ciara to repeat what she'd just said.

Ciara sounded on the verge of hysteria. "It's Dash. And it's the whole *Chiron*. Someone released a new plague on board. They're locked down, but some kind of terrorists were already inside. Now the comm is down. Amanda is writing messages on the windows of the bridge to communicate with the outside world, but she doesn't know much at this point either."

Ping reacted fastest. "Can you drop a Global Express ship here in the middle of the desert? Like you did in Iran and Baotong?"

Ciara spoke in frustration. "The Black Titan is back at

the BrainTrust. If we send it, it won't have enough fuel to make it back there."

Jam jumped in. "So, send a regular Titan from the Prometheus archipelago or from Europe, whichever's available. Can we make it to the BrainTrust with one of those?"

Ciara sighed. "A regular Global Express ship will light up all the radars on the continent."

Ping waved an arm wildly across the empty landscape. "There's nothing here, and not a government closer than you with an Air Force worthy of the name. Just send it."

Ciara paused. "As you wish."

They stopped beside a vast, reasonably flat chunk of desert. Within the hour, a Kestrel Titan, with its gloriously colorful exterior surface, fell from the sky and landed with the grace of an eagle.

Jam observed, "You know, I suspect Matt is making a fortune off all these emergency ship flights for just a couple of people. I wonder if the BrainTrust should maybe buy a few Titans for itself."

Ping grumbled. "For the moment, I suspect I'm paying for this one out of my empress fund. You better believe I'm gonna make Amanda reimburse me, though." She had a thought. "You think I should buy a Titan for Benin? I could use my own spaceship."

"I don't think you should buy one unless you're planning an endless series of kidnappings, nuclear emergencies, and attacks on the *Chiron*. Are you?"

Ping sighed. "Well, truthfully, my people can't afford it anyway. I've got all this money, but I've got to plow it back into the country. Still, it was worth a thought."

Two hours later, they ran out of the space capsule onto the deck of the *Heinlein* and jumped into the copter awaiting them. They left the Benin Beloved Advisor, whom they'd brought along because they couldn't figure out what else to do, behind to wait for the trip back to the Prometheus archipelago.

As Ping pushed the throttle until it was pegged at max, Jam looked around the ocean near the main BrainTrust archipelago. "Oh, no."

Ping blew out an exasperated breath. "Now what?"

"All the warships that usually hang out to the east watching each other, the Chinese, Russians, Americans, and Californians, they're all moving to form a circle around the archipelago." She smiled ruefully. "I'd guess Amanda arranged for somebody outside the *Chiron* to broadcast a general warning to the world about the attack. She probably ordered a full quarantine. And now everybody is going to enforce the quarantine with a blockade."

Ping dived the copter until it was just barely missing the waves. "Are they close to us yet? Did they see us?"

Jam stared around. "I don't think so." She frowned. "We're probably the last people going in or out, though."

Ping sighed. "A plague, terrorists, and now a blockade. Couldn't we just start the day over again?"

Jam answered grimly. "Honestly, the terrorists are the ones who concern me most. They've had three hours to roam free. I just hope we're not too late. What've they been up to?"

After zip-tying the unconscious Chance and her fighting companion, Uwais got back on the shipwide speaker system. "Dr. Dash. We have Dr. Dixon here, and she'd like to say something to you."

Sabaah chortled, and said loudly enough for the speaker system, "Except she's unconscious. But if she were conscious, she'd say, 'Dash, they have a knife at my throat. Please do what they say.'"

Uwais just shook his head. "And there you have it. Surrender yourself to me, wherever you are, or Chance dies. You have thirty seconds. And remember. I have plenty more people I can kill here while we're waiting for you."

Less than ten seconds later a voice with a Balinese accent came back on the broadcast system. "I will wait for you at the aft elevator entrance to the Wenara Wana deck. If you don't know, that's the deck just above you."

The last thing Uwais wanted to risk was having someone fry the circuits for the elevator while he was halfway between floors. "At the starboard ramp, not the elevator."

"As you wish."

Having memorized almost every square foot of this ship, Uwais and Sabaah jogged directly to the ramp without a pause. Uwais tapped on his phone as he ran, opening the automated sealed doors separating Red Planet from Wenara Wana, leaving the rest of the seals between decks closed.

Sabaah, as usual, complained. "You should have made her come to us."

Uwais shrugged. "She wanted to get us away from the scientists we were promising to kill. It was easier to just agree."

Sabaah persisted, "But what if she lied?"

Uwais shook his head. "Worst case, we can just start killing her patients. She knows that."

Uwais had his own bone to pick. "And it would have been better if you'd threatened anybody but Dr. Dixon back there. If Dash proves too resistant, she's our backup interrogation partner."

Sabaah choked on laughter. "A little Balinese girl, timid and shy, resisting? Oh, come on."

As they ran up the ramp, they saw the little Balinese girl in her signature white lab coat and her distinctive glasses standing against the backdrop of the Wenara Wana tropical jungle motif. She looked so frail, and her lip trembled ever so slightly.

Sabaah murmured, "Oh, this is going to be so easy."

They stopped before her. Uwais explained the situation. "This can be easy or hard. We have a few questions we need—Aagh!"

The trembling, frail scientist leapt at him and bit him on the neck.

Sabaah whipped forward and threw her against the wall.

The scientist slumped, dazed.

Uwais rubbed his neck, then looked at his hand. "She drew blood," he said with a mixture of surprise, bafflement, and a certain grudging respect.

Sabaah hoisted her up and trotted to the nearest conference room. "Hard way it is, then."

Uwais stood outside the conference room, watching to make sure nothing went wrong as Sabaah zip-tied her to a chair. He stepped away as Sabaah started asking the list of questions Khalid had given them that he wanted answered about the CRISPIER. When noises started coming from the room that did not sound like answers, he stepped farther away.

Ping and Jam wound up having the same argument with Wolf and Aar they'd had on the phone while they were in zero-G on the Global Express, but this time they reached a conclusion.

Ping held up a hand to count off the points. "Allow me to sum up. Amanda has signaled for us to wait for her to get more information. Which she has failed to do. So we're ignoring the top boss."

Wolf nodded suspiciously. "So far we agree."

Ping counted off another finger. "We can't go in without a moonsuit or the virus will kill us." Her next finger went up. "We can't go in *with* a moonsuit or we'll be so handicapped the terrorists will kill us."

Wolf looked down at her with as much of a twinkle in his eye as he could muster under the circumstances. "I think you've described the fundamental pickle right there."

Ping used the non-counting hand to hold up a "wait one" finger. "We also can't use the smart guns developed by those guys in the GS Gun Club." The terrorists had knocked out the vid feeds the guns needed to accurately bounce bullets off the walls and hit targets. "And we can't use normal guns because the ricochets will kill the people we're trying to save. And mess up the equipment, and poke holes in the biosafety cabinets."

Aar interjected, "That's a pretty good pickle too."

Jam spoke at last. "So the answer is obvious."

Wolf and Aar just stared at her.

Ping grinned at Jam in appreciation. "We'll blow out a window on the Red Planet deck. Jam and I will go in. Without moonsuits. You'll wait out here with the reinforcements." She looked over the assembled team of peacekeepers, every last one from every last ship in the archipelago, watching the debate with grim determination.

Aar got out the stiff words even before Wolf. "We're going with you."

Jam spoke with the quiet authority she'd developed on her journey to Baotong. "On this first foray, we will risk a minimum number of people. Two will do. If two cannot succeed, we need everyone. If we do not contact you in an hour, breach multiple windows." Nobody even suggested just breaching the main gangways, figuring that those obvious infiltration points would be booby-trapped.

Wolf glared. "If it's gonna be just two people—"

Ping poked him in the chest, which required raising her hand above her head. "You remember what happened the last time you and I sparred?"

Wolf kept glaring down at her. Ping glared back.

Aar broke the standoff with the obvious objection. "But without the moonsuits, the virus will kill you."

Ping grinned, waving the problem away. "We'll save Dash, then Dash will cure it and save us all."

Jam and Ping ran like the wind of vengeance through the passages of the Red Planet deck as a team of bots put a plate over the blown window through which they'd entered. In moments, they reached the main area to find a host of scientists barely recovered from a daze. Many of them were now holding odd scientific implements as if they were weapons.

Velma stood unsteadily before them describing a plan of attack.

Jubair lead a team kneeling over Simon; Hilaal had a team working on Chance.

Jam and Ping came up on either side of Velma. Jam whispered urgently. "Stand down, girl. The Marines have landed."

Velma looked at her with a bit of wildness still in her eyes. She then looked at Jam with an expression that flickered between relief and determination. "We're coming with you."

Jam continued, "You'd get in the way. You know it. Tell us about the enemy."

Ping chimed in. "And for heaven's sake, keep your voice down. They knocked out all our vidcams, but they may still have a way of listening in."

Velma blew out a breath and told them about the attackers.

Jam relaxed. "Just two of them?"

Velma glared at her. "They knocked out Chance and me in a heartbeat."

Neither Jam nor Ping paid any attention to this. Ping

looked at Jam. "Just run up the same ramp?"

Jam frowned. "Let's not attack uphill if we can avoid it."

Velma offered, "We can go up the ramp, offer a distraction, and outflank them."

Ping smiled at her. "Thank you for your help. Please keep your people ready, but don't go up there. In an hour the entire peacekeeping force of the BrainTrust is gonna bust in. Wait for them if at all possible."

Ping and Jam trotted to the other ramp. Ping pulled out her chura. "Never leave home without it."

Jam similarly pulled out her K-Bar. "Another thing we agree upon."

They were hurtling down a passage filled with patient compartments when Jam saw a man collapsed against the wall, struggling to move their way. Jam practically cried when she heard him whisper her name.

Ping saw the man and whispered back in a strangled shout. "Colin!"

Colin collapsed into Jam's arms, and she settled him gently on the deck.

Both women knelt over him. He turned to Jam, held his mouth up to her ear, and started speaking in a voice so weak even Jam could barely make it out.

Ping tried to lean in to hear as well, but Colin, either intentionally or just struggling to hold himself up, pushed her out of range. He continued to whisper.

Jam shook her head vigorously, but Colin's grip on her neck held fast, with the desperate strength of a dying man with a last desperate message. Jam shook her head again and again until she finally sagged into him.

He released her and thumped unconscious to the deck.

Ping couldn't contain herself. "What was that all about?"

Jam looked at her with eyes wide and filled with horror.

Ping continued, "You look like you just lost your best friend."

Jam stared at her in dismay for one more moment. Then she blinked, her eyes refocused, and her mouth set in a thin line of implacable determination. She rose with balletic grace to her feet. "Hurry."

They left Colin lying there and ran once more to save Dash.

Shortly thereafter, they came hurtling around a corner into the passage where the terrorists had last been seen.

Standing outside a conference room was the big one, Uwais.

Uwais sang out pleasantly, "Sabaah, the company we've been expecting has arrived." Uwais dug into his belt, and with shocking speed, started throwing shurikens.

Dodging the flying blades slowed Ping and Jam enough that Sabaah joined the party before they could team up on Uwais.

And then the battle began in earnest.

Ping found herself matched with Sabaah. He had pulled a throwing knife from his belt but jammed it back when he found they were too close and swung with his fighting knife, a Gerber Mark II with its double-edged, wasp-waisted blade. Ping twisted while still charging and swung with her chura.

Jam, instead of flying into action as Ping did with her incredible speed, danced to the side, hoping to swing Uwais around off-balance.

The maneuver failed, and Uwais snaked forward with a slashing strike.

Jam foresaw it, blocked his arm with her free hand, and thrust with her own knife.

Uwais foresaw it, slid out of the way, and struck again.

She foresaw it and moved once more to parry and riposte.

He foresaw it.

And so it continued for an impossibly long time.

But an impossibly long time in a knife fight is a very short time indeed. It ended when Ping sliced at Sabaah's neck. He bent backward just in time to evade, then twisted forward and cut her side.

Ping gasped just loud enough for Jam to hear and know what had happened.

For just a moment, Jam moved with Ping's speed, not her own, and leapt to Ping's side.

She then drove her knife into and through Ping's abdomen just beneath her ribcage, just beneath her heart.

Ping stared at Jam in helpless astonishment as she slid off the blade.

Uwais and Sabaah stood in open-mouthed astonishment.

The tableaux held for barely a second. Jam turned to them. "I hope you're done with whatever you're doing here. Any minute now every peacekeeper in this fleet is going to charge through breaches all over the ship. Skilled as you are, you'll still be dead in a heartbeat."

They looked down at Ping, unconscious, lying in a rapidly growing pool of her own blood.

Jam put her hands on her hips. "You think you're the

only ones who dream of the end times, the coming of the Mahdi? You doubt my faith? We must go *now*."

Uwais and Sabaah both shook themselves.

Uwais spoke. "She's right. Let's go."

Sabaah argued briefly, pointing at the conference room. "But Dash didn't answer even one question." He threw his hands in the air. "Last thing." He stepped to the door.

Jam started to speak. "Just leave her—"

Sabaah whipped the throwing knife from his belt and threw it into the room. "Task completed."

Uwais turned to watch Jam's reaction to this final bit of brutality, but she had already turned away.

A few moments later Jam spoke as if nothing had happened. "You better have a copter on this ship. Preferably two, and a remarkable plan for getting out of here."

They followed her to the ramp leading up to the top of the ship.

Chance finally came around and looked up to see Hilaal and Velma hovering over her. "What's happening?"

Velma told her about how Hilaal had brought her around and coaxed the scientists into arming themselves. Then she told her about the brief arrival and departure of Jam and Ping. She huffed as she told Chance that Jam and Ping had told her not to help in the counterattack.

Looking around the crowd of scientists grimly clutching diverse medical instruments with clear intent to bash anyone who challenged them, Chance shook her head. "Well, Ping and Jam were right, you know. Charging up that ramp with a bunch of scientists armed with scalpels would get a lot of good people killed. People we need."

Velma stamped her foot. "We have to do something."

Hilaal spoke softly. "Velma, it sounds like Chance has a plan."

Chance rose to her feet, shook her head, then rocked back and forth to loosen up. "Sort of. It's not that *we* have to do something. *I* have to do something." She led all the scientists over to the bottom of the ramp and turned to Velma. "I'm going up. Come when I call."

Velma growled, then remembered what had happened the last time, and nodded.

Chance ran lightly up the ramp. Neither the terrorists nor Jam were anywhere to be seen. Ping lay in a pool of blood. Chance shouted down the ramp, "Drop the weapons. We need a crash cart stat, and a gurney!"

Before kneeling over Ping, Chance walked over to the conference room to glance inside. As her eyes roamed to the back of the room, to a corner not easily seen until you reached the doorway, she stopped. She blinked in horror, then stood transfixed for what seemed an eternity. A look of implacable defiance crossed her face and disappeared.

Finally, respectfully and ever so gently, she pulled the door closed.

Everyone came running up the ramp, a crash cart and a gurney in the lead. As soon as Chance had shot FoamClot into both Ping's wounds, the minor one on the right, the terrible one on the left, they hoisted her onto the gurney and wheeled her toward the nearest operating room.

Chance was not done giving orders. "Simon!"

He turned from watching the gurney roll away.

Chance spoke more gently. "Simon, put a couple of people in front of this conference room. Don't let anyone in, do you understand? No one."

Simon raised an eyebrow. "What's in the room?"

Chance took a deep breath. "Nothing we can do anything about." She put a hand on his cheek. "Please trust me in this. We'll deal with it later. Let no one in. Don't even look yourself."

Simon frowned, then nodded.

The lighting brightened, and automated hatches opened all over the ship.

Chance blinked away tears. "It's all going to be all right. Somehow, it will all be OK."

Before leaving the deck full of bed-ridden patients, Jam slipped into one of the rooms, grabbed a sheet, and pulled it over her head. A few quick slashes with her K-Bar left a slit through which she could see. After tying a few knots and making a few tucks, she had a crude but serviceable burqa.

Sabaah murmured. "So very modest so suddenly."

Jam answered, "It's good to be properly dressed again. I had the opportunity while in Tehran recently. You probably know more about that than I do, of course. But it was relaxing to be able to wear the burqa once more."

They reached the deck with the copters. Uwais admitted apologetically. "We don't actually have a copter. Sabaah was planning to hotwire one."

Jam just grunted. "BrainTrust copters are reasonably pretty hard to steal."

Sabaah defended himself. "Hey, I specialize in vehicle automation. You have a machine that flies or drives, I can make it sing and dance. Two'll be as easy as one."

Soon they had the copters spinning up. Uwais insisted Jam sit in the passenger seat with him. Jam gave him an exasperated sound, then acquiesced. "Like I could go anywhere or do anything except join you at this point."

Uwais grinned. "Safety first." He flew out, with Sabaah in the copter behind them.

Jam changed the subject. "You'll need to fly low. The Americans are putting up a blockade around the archipelago to enforce a quarantine."

"Ah." Uwais dropped the copter down to ocean level. "I see what you mean."

The blockading fleet had already completed the encirclement of the BrainTrust. But the copters were flying into the west, and the only ships that had come all the way around to that side were the California Coastal Patrol, barely modified yachts that had no anti-aircraft weaponry. The two copters surged through unmolested.

Uwais offered an apology. "It's just as well you made yourself a burqa. We're going to be in very close quarters very shortly. Very close quarters."

Jam pointed ahead, where a small yacht rose and fell gently in the waves. "Is that our getaway ship? It doesn't look so cramped to me."

Uwais chuckled. "That's our getaway yacht. It is not, however, our getaway ship." He chuckled again. "You'll see."

Ping rolled her head and opened her eyes.

Chance smiled at her. "Welcome back."

Ping winced. "What happened?"

Chance turned sober. "You were stabbed. Twice."

Ping's wince turned into a grimace. "Oh, right."

"One of the knife wounds, the one that almost killed you, was made by a wider blade. Like Jam's K-Bar."

Ping closed her eyes. "Yeah."

A commotion in the hall made them both turn their heads.

Cameron Ballard, with half his face covered in a purple bruise, charged into the room. "Tell me everything you know about this traitor, Jam."

Both women pursed their lips and a lengthy pause ensued, as if both were trying to decide how to respond.

Ping answered first. "She stabbed me with her K-Bar." She turned her head away. "I worked with her for a long time. We've saved each other's lives. I never would have believed it."

Ballard nodded gravely. "She was deep undercover. That's how they work." He touched his eye where she'd hit him when they first met in Georgia—gingerly, since now that whole side of his face was swollen. "Now you see what she's really like."

Chance added, "If Jam had stabbed Ping like that anywhere but right here in the middle of a top-notch hospital, Ping would've died."

Ping switched topics. "When you find her, call me. I'll kill her for you." An expression suggesting she had just bitten into a lemon crossed her face before she concluded, "Sorry about the way we roughed you up the last time we met. Most unfortunate."

Ballard acknowledged the apology with a smile. "Glad we're on the same team now."

Chance finished up, "Now, Mr. Ballard, you have to leave. I need time with my patient. We'll talk later."

After his footsteps disappeared down the passage, Chance stepped lightly to the door and looked both ways. She came back and whispered, "He's gone."

Ping exhaled a huge sigh. "Hallelujah."

Chance leaned forward. "So you don't think Jam betrayed us?"

Ping shook her head so vigorously that she winced from the pain. "Not a chance, Chance. In retrospect, it's obvious. She's gone off with them to find the mastermind, the man who's creating all these plagues. She'll let us know when she finds him."

Chance took up the position of Devil's Advocate. "Ping, that really was a fatal knife wound. I told Ballard the truth: anyplace else except here, you would've died."

Ping restrained herself from offering the chuckle she knew would hurt too much. "Exactly, but we *were* here. In the one place where it would not be fatal. She knew it all along."

Chance's expression turned exquisitely sorrowful, as if she were about to tell Ping something horrific, but Ping was still ruminating on the fight. "At least I got a piece of that guy I faced off with. Not as big a piece as he got of me, but still something."

Chance looked at her quizzically.

Ping glanced around. "Is my chura here somewhere?"

Chance reached toward a table close at hand, having known that Ping would want her weapon near. But she had placed the table far enough away so Ping couldn't, in her current condition, reach it without help, also knowing that Ping would need to lash out when she heard the rest of the news awaiting her.

Chance carefully handed the knife to her.

Ping examined the keen edge. "Ha! Just as I thought." She pointed to a barely visible thin red line. "His blood."

Chance blinked, then carefully took the blade from Ping to inspect it. "You're sure?"

"Chance, I am maniacal about cleaning my weapons. It couldn't be anything else. Fact is, I should probably clean it right now."

Chance jumped away, holding the knife with both hands as if it were the world's greatest treasure. She continued to stare at the blood. "Ping, you just saved a whole lot of people."

Ping raised an eyebrow. "Really? I mean, of course. Uh, how?"

Chance smiled, a dark smile full of determination. "I was dreading having to develop a vaccine from scratch against this hairball of a virus, but now we don't have to." She tapped the blade. "This guy was surely vaccinated before he came aboard. I can almost certainly find traces of it here."

She danced like a martial artist hanging just out of reach of an opponent, seeking the moment to strike. "With this, we don't have to start from scratch to make a vaccine. We can just reverse-engineer it."

Ping lay back, eyes closing as she fell suddenly asleep. "Glad I could help."

BESIEGED

Never yield to the apparently overwhelming might of the enemy.
—Churchill

When Ping awoke again, Chance was just sitting down. Ping blinked her eyes clear and asked for the inevitable sitrep. "So, what's been happening while I've been out?"

Chance gave her a quick rundown.

Dash's ad hoc solution to the epidemic that raged through the *Chiron* seemed to be working. People were coming down with the new UVR Rubola at an alarming rate, and everyone was resigned to getting the disease eventually, including Chance. But she was oddly upbeat about it because deaths so far were few, and mostly confined to the elderly.

When the controls and comms systems for the ship had come back to life, Amanda ordered the massed peacekeepers preparing to breach to stand down. Just in time, as it turned out; they'd already set charges on over a dozen windows. Instead of breaching, they all stayed safely outside with no risk from the plague.

A handful of people on the other ships did have the disease, but the Condition Zebra had locked them into sealed compartments in time. Everyone in the compartments with them was becoming sick, but using Dash's treatment, once again few were dying.

Some of the near-deaths, however, lingered. Colin Wheeler in particular remained in a coma. No one was sure if he would ever come out of it.

Ping looked at her in dismay. "Oh, wow. So I guess that explains why Colin hasn't come by." She looked around curiously. "Which begs the question, why hasn't our heroine of the day wandered through? Where's Dash?"

Chance looked like she'd been struck with a baseball bat. "That's what I've been waiting to tell you." She took Ping's hand in hers.

Ping grasped Chance's hand in both of hers, a fierce grip that was almost threatening. "No. Don't tell me that."

Chance hung her head. "Dash is gone. The little Bali girl with the white coat and glasses is dead."

Ping screamed and jerked upright, ripping half her stitches, then collapsed back again. "I don't believe it. I need to see her." She tried to rise again.

Chance put her hand—the one Ping didn't have clenched in hers—on Ping's shoulder and pushed her down. "No." Her voice turned commanding. "Let me tell you exactly what you are going to do. You are going to lay in that bed until I tell you you can get up. Then you're going to exercise, and you're going to train with me."

Ping's nostrils flared, and the fire once again entered her eyes.

Chance continued, "And you're going to get so good that you can beat that guy who stabbed you with one hand tied behind your back. And then we'll get them."

Ping's muscles flexed as if ready to jump straight to part two of the plan, then relaxed again. She turned pensive. "I don't understand it."

Chance frowned. "What?"

"How could Jam have allowed it? Even if it meant losing the chance to find the big bad boss guy, she would've saved Dash above all else."

Chance sighed. "I've wondered about that myself. I don't think she had a choice."

"But—"

"They probably did it suddenly, the last thing. Jam didn't know until it was too late."

Ping slumped. "That would explain it."

After a long pause, Ping made an unusual confession. "It's a good thing Jam was the one who had to go, you know."

Chance looked at her quizzically. "You mean, instead of you?"

Ping nodded slightly. "If it'd been me, I wouldn't have been able to control myself. I would've wound up killing them before we ever found the real bad guy." She sighed. "I guess she really is the stronger one, after all."

Admiral Edwin Beck listened patiently as the Chief Advisor spoke at length. Finally, he interrupted, "But, sir, if we destroy their reef, they'll all die of starvation."

The Advisor's voice was implacable. "All they have to do is cure the disease, then we can ship them all the food they want. They're supposed to be the smartest people on the planet, Admiral. Meanwhile, if they send bots to harvest the fish from the reef, and the bots carry the virus to the reef, somebody could pick up the disease a month from now and carry it home. That must not happen."

Admiral Beck pressed his thumb and middle fingers to his temples. "Yes, sir."

"Excellent. Let me know when it's done."

"Yes, sir." Beck hung up the line and turned to his adjutant. "So, Lieutenant, any idea what we use these days to destroy an agricultural reef? I don't think it's ever been done before. Would Agent Orange do the trick?"

Lieutenant Lambert grimaced. "I don't know, Admiral. It certainly works in the wetness of a jungle, but a reef of kelp and algae seems like another whole class of problem. Let me investigate."

Beck nodded, then turned back to the main display in the Combat Information Center of his flagship, the aircraft carrier *John F. Kennedy*. He frowned at the disposition of forces. He had a problem.

Basically, he didn't trust the Russians and the Chinese to hold any of the key parts of the blockade for a moment. He shot out orders. "Tell the *Vella Cruz* to stay on station on the southeast channel that allows ships through the reef. Our task force will take the northern channel." He peered at a ship on the display to the southwest. "The *Heinlein*. Is that the SpaceR spaceport ship?"

One of the radar operators answered. "Yes, sir. The BrainTrusters routinely fly copters with passengers out there. Of course, they also send ferries, but the ferries have to go through the channel. The copters, though, go straight across."

Beck sighed. "And I'm told a pair of copters flew directly west to a small yacht while we were still underway to get here?"

One of his intelligence officers answered that one. "Yes, sir. A number of peacekeeper copters later flew out there to detain the escapees, but they had vanished. The Brain-Trust peacekeepers flew back home. Word is the yacht was empty, and the escapees were nowhere to be found."

Beck grimaced. "So people who are potentially infected landed on that yacht and disappeared?"

The intelligence officer winced. "Yes, sir."

This virus sounded terrifyingly deadly. A certain level of aggressiveness that would normally be considered far excessive seemed appropriate. "Get the *John Paul Jones* out there to check that yacht." The *John Paul Jones* was an Arleigh-Burke class destroyer, immense overkill for the next orders. "Make sure there's no one aboard, then destroy it."

"Aye aye, sir."

"And if another yacht comes within copter range, I want to know about it an hour earlier."

He frowned at the *Heinlein*. He thought about destroying it as well. But that would create more problems than it solved, not the least of which was that lots of Americans took ferries out to the *Heinlein* to travel all over the world.

Technically the ship was not part of the quarantine; his job was best interpreted as ensuring it did not *become* part of the quarantine. "Position the cruiser *Port Royal* in the lane between the archipelago and the *Heinlein*. If any copters try to fly between them, shoot them down. No warnings, no discussion. Just kill them." If someone wanted to argue with him about rules of engagement, they could do so after the risk of a devastating pandemic was over.

One last thing. "And someone please get me a line to whoever's in charge on the BrainTrust. Amanda Copeland, as I recall." It would only be polite to warn her that any attempt to reach the *Heinlein* would be met with deadly force.

It would also be polite to mention he was going to destroy her food supply.

Not for the first time, Mediator Joshua found himself cursing his fate. He just could not disentangle himself from these crazy events aboard the BrainTrust.

Over a year ago he'd turned mediation duties for the *Chiron* over to Mediator Chibuzo, moving to the much more suitable dispute resolutions afforded by the billionaires aboard the *Haven*.

Normally, a mediator had a cabin aboard the ship where he mediated. But the *Haven* had no room for a lowly mediator. It hadn't really bothered him, since he was quite content with his cabin on the *Chiron* and he enjoyed the walk between the ships to get to and from work.

But he'd been at home, sipping tea, when the alarms had wailed and the hatches had slammed shut all over the ship. He'd missed the action as the terrorists came and went, but the virus had not missed him.

And of course, as he finally started to recover from the UVR Rubola, a secondary infection set in. The flu, of course—the current one spreading from Southeast Asia.

So he lay in the hospital bed having feverish but happy dreams of just dying. Oh, he wanted to die.

Fate demanded more from him, however. It seemed he would be required to pass through Hell before he could get to the dying.

An enormous cavalcade rolled through the door to his bedside. Amanda spoke apologetically. "Joshua, we need a mediation."

He couldn't believe his ears. "Chibuzo," he coughed out.

Chance shook her head. "He was on board the *Elysian Fields* when we locked down the ship."

A man he didn't recognize, who looked the worse for wear with a greenish-yellow bruise covering one side of his face, said with a slurred urgency, "We need you to put this terrorist in the brig." He pointed at a woman, one of the CDC scientists Joshua had seen hurrying around the ship.

The accused terrorist pointed back. "And he needs to be put in the brig for assault."

A wheelchair pushed by a bot rolled in quietly. A wan-looking Ping smiled at him. "Perhaps you should put them both in the brig, in adjacent cells."

Chance one-upped her. "Or perhaps you should put them both in the same cell and let the survivor go free."

Ping quickly endorsed Chance's proposal. "Trial by combat."

Amanda looked to the skies. "Please, we're here for a mediation."

Ping wouldn't let go. "Still, there's something to be said for the classics."

Joshua took as deep a breath as he could without coughing. Mediating another dispute with Ping involved. Now that was a classic.

The fellow with the bruise held up a badge. "I'm FBI Agent Cameron Ballard, Acting Assistant Director of the Directorate on Weapons of Mass Destruction."

In the typical Ping case, the most battered person in the room was typically the assailant. He couldn't help making a prediction. "Let me guess. I will shortly hear that you assaulted this person—"

"Velma Highwalker, your Honor." The woman nodded relatively crisply considering that she was covered in the rubola rash.

Joshua continued, "Thank you. You assaulted her, and..." he looked at the bruising carefully, "Chance over here struck you in the head with one of her signature MMA moves."

Chance smiled broadly but shook her head. "Velma did it all herself. A well-executed strike for someone who only began training recently."

It looked like Velma and Chance were going to high-five each other. Joshua realized he had neither his usual block of wood nor a suitable desk for striking with it to call for order.

He interrupted the looks of satisfaction. "Ms. High-walker, exactly how did Mr. Ballard assault you?"

Velma's look of outrage was peculiarly distorted by the rash. "He said he was taking me into custody. Taking me back to America to be thrown in jail for the rest of my life." She turned to give Ballard an arch look. "When I refused, he grabbed me by the wrist." She held up the offended hand.

Ballard growled, "She still needs to come back to the States with me. I'm quite certain she's one of the terrorists unleashing these plagues."

Joshua turned to ask Amanda about this just as Amanda rolled her eyes. He decided she'd just answered his question.

He looked at Ballard and Highwalker. "So let me get this straight. He grabbed your wrist, and you knocked him out with a kick to the head?"

Velma looked a little sheepish but nonetheless stubborn. "Yes, Your Honor."

For no good reason, Joshua looked at Ping. "Couldn't you people, just once, under-react for a change?"

The women in the room responded with a moment of stricken silence.

Joshua sighed. It occurred to him that he was already in the middle of this mediation, and it still wasn't clear who the perpetrator was. Or what the crime was. There was supposed to be one alleged perpetrator and one alleged crime. A normal court of law would go berserk with this.

But Joshua was a Mediator on the BrainTrust. He rose to the occasion. He would postpone dying a little while longer.

"On the charge of assault, perpetrated by one Cameron Ballard against one Velma Highwalker, no compensation is granted, the perpetrator having already received adequate punishment at the hands of the victim." OK, one down.

Joshua banged his hand against the rail of his bed in a pathetic attempt to duplicate the sound of a gavel. "Now let's discuss this terrorism accusation."

Agent Ballard presented his evidence. "We all know the three key parts of identifying a guilty party, Your Honor."

Joshua thought about interrupting since he normally corrected people when they called him "Your Honor," but he just didn't have the strength. He was still hoping to die, he reminded himself. It put things in perspective.

Ballard explained his theory of means, motive, and opportunity: only virologists had the means, everyone had the opportunity, but Velma uniquely had the motive. "This doesn't prove she's guilty," he admitted, although the expression on his face clearly suggested he thought it did. "But it puts her high on the list. Plus, her multiple escapes from the hands of the law are also suggestive, as well as illegal on their own. We must take her back to the States for questioning."

Amanda interrupted, "Not likely, with the blockade in place. And the doors to the *Chiron* sealed, for that matter."

Ballard nodded. "Which is why she needs to be kept in

the brig until we can depart. I can't afford to lose her again."

Chance threw up her hands in exasperation. "This is crazy. Velma is one of the most productive and helpful members of the team."

Ballard gave her a penetrating stare. "Are you sure she's not sabotaging you? Giving you recommendations that sound good but in fact, lead you away from the answer?"

Chance pulled out her tablet. "Quite the contrary. She's one of our most reliable predictors of what experiments will succeed and which will fail. Take a look."

She threw the results on her tablet up on the one display screen that was not hooked up for medical diagnostics and explained the CEREBRUM prediction market. Velma was ranked second, having won the second-largest pot of cash for the accuracy of her forecasts.

Ballard's eyes gleamed. "Clearly, to rank so well, she has to have insider knowledge. Only a member of the terrorist team could do that well."

Chance blew a raspberry. "Then a week ago you would have accused me." She showed them the historical trace: Chance and Velma had traded rankings in the intervening days.

Joshua intervened. "I think, Agent Ballard, your analytical strategy leaves much to be desired. Or do you insist I put Dr. Dixon in the brig as well?"

Ballard looked distracted; his mind had clearly wandered. "Actually, you may be right. But who is this person who is ranked first by a huge margin? *That* looks like a terrorist team member, and that's clearly a pseudonym." He turned to Chance with an accusatory stare. "Who is Florence Nightingale?"

Chance's faced twisted. She sobbed.

Joshua knew his brain wasn't firing on all cylinders, and he was pretty sure he was about to embarrass himself, but the mediation called for him to ask, "Chance? Agent Ballard has a legitimate question. Who is Florence Nightingale?"

Chance looked away from everyone. "It was a secret. Of course, everyone knew, but she wanted it to be a secret. I should have removed her from the board, but…"

She shook herself and turned back to Joshua. Her voice steadied. "Joshua, look at the list. Who is missing? Who would you have expected to be at the top?"

Joshua studied the list. Yup, his mind was definitely not up to par. So who would he have expected to be at the top of the list? He didn't know any medical researchers, except of course for Chance and…his heart sank. "Dash?"

Chance nodded.

Ballard rubbed his hands together. "Another suspect."

Joshua struggled to get out of the bed to wrap his hands around Ballard's neck. No use. "Agent Ballard, you really are an imbecile."

Amanda stepped forward and carefully explained to the agent why Dash was the most outrageous proposed perp he'd picked yet. "And on top of all that, she was murdered by the terrorists when they boarded the ship." She blinked as a moment of realization shook her. "Of course. They had special instructions to kill her. They knew that, above all things, they had to kill her to stop her from foiling their plans."

Ballard looked around the faces in the room, then started looking as if he wanted to escape. With a momentary burst of something like empathy, he said the only legitimate thing. "I'm so sorry."

Joshua closed his eyes; it was surprising how much better he felt without the glare of the lights. "Agent Ballard, you have repeatedly made rash accusations against the people on this ship, each accusation being more ridiculous than the last. I am trying very hard to figure out why I should not put you in the brig until the quarantine is lifted and we can kick you back to America."

Ballard's stubbornness returned. "I'm still sure the real perp is here on the BrainTrust."

Joshua was still crafting a choice set of crucifying words when Amanda spoke ever so softly. "Don't put him in the brig, Joshua."

Joshua stared at her in amazement.

Amanda continued. "He's right about the fact that the perp has to be a virologist. A world-class virologist." She waved a hand. "Now, when Agent Ballard tried to lock up the whole CDC, he was out of his mind. There are plenty of world-class virologists elsewhere."

Her voice lowered. "But we've brought them all here, Joshua. People from all over the world, from Europe and Russia to South America, have answered our invitation to come and fight this existential battle. We know who all the world-class virologists are, and they're almost all here." She slumped. "And there's another thing. Have any of you wondered, why Uwais and Sabaah didn't bring guns?"

Chance thought out loud, working toward an answer.

"We couldn't use guns for fear..." Her voice faded as she saw where this was going.

Amanda continued, "For fear the ricochets would hurt our own people."

Chance straightened her shoulders, acknowledging the deduction. "But they would not have feared ricochets. Not unless one of theirs was here too."

Amanda finished grimly. "So, Joshua, it might be helpful if Agent Ballard continued his investigation because there's a very good chance that, at this point, he's right."

***

The days faded, one into the other. The epidemic rose and fell in its own rhythm, related yet distinct, as the world watched from afar. Most found the attack on the Brain-Trust horrifying. Most outside of Iran and America found it scarier than either of those earlier attacks because they understood it was a direct assault on those most likely to cure the next epidemic.

Of course, in some places, the BrainTrust assault was viewed as an opportunity.

Pascha rocked lazily on the lap of the Premier of the Russian Union, nuzzling his neck.

The Premier knew why she was so attentive, of course. He was even a little sad he would deny her.

Pascha asked in a little-girl voice, "Please could I speak with my sister?"

The Premier cleared his throat and pushed her mechanically off his lap. "You know you can't. This is a one-way connection."

She snuggled against him. "Could I at least stay while she brings you up to date?" Her whole body melded to his. "I promise I will make it worth your while."

He took a deep breath. "And that is why you can't stay." He ran his fingers through her hair. "You are far too much of a distraction."

The alarm on his cell went off. He spoke a little harshly. "Go now."

Pascha went, rocking her hips to remind him of what he was losing.

His wallscreen lit up with a view of Pascha's sister, Tascha. Except neither he nor anyone else had called her Tascha for many long years. She was now Trixie, the administrative assistant of the American Chief Advisor.

The Premier watched as Trixie casually tossed aside the dress she was wearing and started applying lipstick while nude.

The Premier did so love these conversations, even if they were one-way.

Trixie spoke with clipped haste. "I have to meet him in the Oval Office in five minutes, so this has to be quick. Basically, Chiefy has decided to keep the BrainTrust blockade in place even after they declare the epidemic over. Even after they develop a cure. Since he destroyed their food supply, he figures he can starve them into delivering Dr. Dash."

She lifted an eyelid to start applying liner. "I reminded him she was thought to be dead. He said, 'Oh, right. We'll demand Dr. Dixon instead.' You may remember, Chance Dixon was Dash's intern, and she is now the only person on Earth who knows how to rejuvenate the President for

Life enough to keep him alive so Chiefy can continue to boss everyone around."

She grimaced into her mirror, checking her teeth. "That's the big news. I presume you want to support him in extending the blockade for blackmail purposes." She stood quite still for a moment, looking at herself in the mirror and carefully erasing the lines of intelligence from her face until she achieved her usual presentation as a perfect blond bimbo.

She stepped back from the mirror and wriggled, a sensuous move that belonged in a dance club. She blew him a ditzy kiss. "Give my love to my sister."

She touched the screen, and it went dark.

A butler-bot assigned by Mediator Joshua followed Agent Ballard as he led his newest guest, Hilaal el-Mousa, through the Red Planet deck to a conference room that was now dedicated to his investigation.

He pursed his lips as he thought about the rest of that mediation after Amanda had supported him. First of all, Mediator Joshua had needed a lot of convincing that Ballard would be an asset, even though he agreed investigation was necessary. Much against Ballard's normal instincts, he decided to share some information. He pulled up the artist's renditions of the terrorists made by combining all the scientists' descriptions, plus some poor but interesting images of the terrorists taken surreptitiously with cell phones during their time on the Red Planet deck. He showed them how the integrated image compared to a pair of Middle Eastern-looking men caught on cameras in the various places where the Blue Rubola-carrying PEZ dispensers had been placed along the coasts of America.

Chance had studied the pictures for a while, then a light had dawned. She called BrainTrust security and got the video of the men seen stealing a CRISPIER. Those men had also done an excellent job of concealing their faces, but in the end, everyone agreed that these were all the same people.

Once this continuity of enemies was established, they realized this afforded an explanation of how Uwais and Sabaah had gained such smooth control of the *Chiron's* systems. They could have investigated and physically manhandled her computers while on board to snatch the CRISPIER. Review of videos of the time suggested that the maintenance bots in charge of the command, control, and computer systems had done significant unscheduled maintenance; a hunt for indications that the thieves might have tampered with the bots and subverted them to tamper with the network was still underway.

Ballard himself figured the other terrorist, the one still hiding in plain sight under his nose on the *Chiron*, was the one who had prepped the ship's systems for takeover by Uwais, but he kept this assessment to himself.

After much discussion of the pros and cons of letting the FBI agent roam free, Joshua granted him the right to investigate. Then the mediator had collapsed in his bed and shooed them all away so he could die in peace.

But Joshua had not dismissed Ballard without a remarkable number of carefully detailed instructions. He had not only required Ballard to let this bot follow him around, practically touching him, he'd also required that Ballard under no circumstances touch anyone else. If someone refused to answer civil questions, Joshua himself would review the justification for the interrogation and make a case-by-case assessment. The bar for imposing a forced interrogation, Joshua had made clear, would be quite high.

Joshua had also forced Ballard to recant his conviction that Velma was involved. Ballard conceded she had no motive for either fomenting nuclear war in the Mideast or infecting the *Chiron*—and herself—with rubola. If he wanted Velma to answer any more questions, he would forward those questions to Chance.

Ah, yes...Chance. He half-suspected her. Not only had she been neck and neck with Velma on the CEREBRUM rankings before, but since the mediation, her forecasting had improved markedly. Florence Nightingale was gone from the boards, but Chance now bid fair to establish a similar lead.

The logic he had used to conclude that the highest-ranking forecasters were more likely to be terrorist insiders had not changed. It was a real possibility. So at one point he'd brought Chance into this small conference room and asked her a few questions. In the midst of the questions, he'd complimented her on her remarkable march up the CEREBRUM board.

She'd rubbed her ear and winced. "Yeah, I've really upped my game." She looked away in dismay. "You know, one of Dash's last undertakings was learning how to think like Colin. I didn't think anything about it at the time, but

I've now come to realize that while she was studying to be Colin, I was studying to be Dash."

She touched her forehead. "She's here with me now, you know." She blinked away tears. "I used to make my predictions for CEREBRUM as myself. As Chance. But now I'm trying very hard to make predictions for Dash. As Dash. What would Dash think?" She looked back at Ballard. "Did that make any sense? I'd guess not."

Ballard had assured her it did, although she was correct that it did not. Regardless, no amount of digging, and no amount of contact with his people back home in the Bureau could find a wisp of a motive for Chance. He gave it up.

He'd interviewed a lot of people, most of whom he did not suspect before he interviewed them and most of whom he suspected even less after he finished. He wanted to make sure that the real culprit understood that everyone except Velma was assisting him, no big deal.

His current number one prime suspect in this swirling international stew of virologists was Jubair el-Parani. Ballard was more or less sneaking up on that interview sideways, which was why he was interviewing Jubair's friend Hilaal first.

Ballard had radically altered the conference room for his goals. The walls had been set to stark blank white, and the temperature had been lowered until it was as chilly as it could be without being too obvious. Only three chairs remained, all bare of padding and offering no armrests.

Back at FBI headquarters, when they did real interrogations, the interrogators' chairs were comfortable, but here in these friendly question-and-answer engagements, Ballard was as uncomfortable as his suspect.

The whole idea was to make the suspect want to get out of the room as soon as he reasonably could by answering questions hastily, without the careful thought that might enable better concealment of the truth.

Part of the usual technique involved having an interrogator who looked like, sounded like, and shared many beliefs with, the target. Ballard had tried to recruit the peacekeeper Aar as his second chair, but Aar had just laughed. "Trust me, the last person you want in that room when interviewing a Muslim is a Sikh unless you can persuade them that torture is a real possibility. Then my presence would enhance your credibility."

So for this interrogation, the third chair was empty.

Ballard started, as per standard technique, with questions to put the suspect at ease while he watched for gesture baselines that might later give something away. Flicking the eyes to the right often indicated reaching for a memory, while a flicker up to the left might indicate the creative thinking associated with a lie.

Ballard really wanted to use the nine-step Reid technique on everyone here, but he was certain Joshua would brig him for it before he made any progress, so he stuck to the earlier steps in questioning a suspect/witness.

He kept his nose in his tablet, to ease the pressure on Hilaal. Of course, his tablet was hooked to the vidcam on the wall, so Ballard was studying a crisp image of Hilaal's face and posture as he asked his questions.

As they chatted, Hilaal became increasingly more comfortable despite the harsh light and spine-crunching chairs. When he smiled, warmly and sincerely, Ballard too felt ever more comfortable. He reminded himself to sit more erect.

Finally Ballard delivered an obvious question. "You're a Sunni, right? How do you feel about Iranians? They're Shiites, if I understand correctly."

Hilaal looked worn and tired. "Radical factions on both sides have been trying to kill everyone for centuries. Ever since the death of the Prophet Muhammad."

Ballard persisted. "Still, it would have been a boon to you if the Iranians and Israelis killed each other."

Hilaal frowned. "Such massive death is a boon only to murderers and radicals, Agent Ballard. I've often wished everyone would stop killing each other. There's a long distance between that and wanting to wipe everyone out."

Ballard changed topics. "I understand Jubair el-Parani is the one who invited you to come here."

Hilaal nodded. "We were friends in college, at the American University in Beirut. We competed, more or less, to see who could get the best grades while taking the most classes and graduating soonest. Truth is, he's the smart one. In the end, he won, as you can see from the CERE-BRUM scores. I think he's currently ranked third behind Chance and Velma."

He shook his head. "We met after the Israelis obliter-ated a Hezbollah action team, a missile strike on the edge of the campus." He shook his head. "A lot of good people died that day." His somber eyes filled with sorrow. "'Collat-eral damage,' of course."

"How upset did that Israeli strike make Jubair?"

Hilaal turned pensive. "I think we were all pretty upset

at the time." He looked down and clenched his hands. "I hate to say it, but he never really recovered from that attack. He buried himself in his lab."

"How well is his lab equipped? Do you think he could have developed these plagues?"

Hilaal shrugged. "Maybe. It seems unlikely. The terrorist has developed three different viruses in a very short time. I don't think you could do that without a CRISPIER unless you developed those viruses over a much longer period of time and had them sitting on the shelf, waiting to be used."

"Does he have a CRISPIER in his lab?"

Hilaal blinked in surprise. "I haven't seen his lab recently, so I wouldn't know. But I didn't think anybody had a CRISPIER outside the BrainTrust."

"So you think the viruses had to be developed here?"

Hilaal frowned. "I hadn't really thought about it that way. Now that you've forced me to think about it, I suppose that whoever did it had to have spent years developing these viruses, and is merely launching them in quick succession." He rubbed one of the rashes from the UVR Rubola that had not quite faded.

Ballard switched topics. "I see you've mostly recovered from the rubola."

Hilaal smiled. "The whole ship was lucky that Dr. Dash figured out how to ameliorate the disease before…"

Ballard waved it away. "Does it strike you as a surprising coincidence that Jubair never developed the disease? That he was immune?"

"He wasn't the only one. Maybe ten percent came through the epidemic untouched. I think there were a dozen or so on this deck alone who had no symptoms, like Jubair." He frowned as he thought about the probable deduction and said, "I suppose if the perpetrator were here on board the *Chiron*, he would be one of the ones who was immune. Certainly that makes sense to investigate."

Finally Ballard held out photorealistic renditions of the two terrorists who had boarded the *Chiron*. "Do you know who these men are?"

Hilaal glanced and answered. "Oh, yes. These are the attackers who came for Dash."

"Had you ever seen them before this?"

Hilaal squinted, closed his eyes, and held his hands over his face. "I've tried to remember if I've ever seen them before. I don't think so."

"What about Jubair? Did he know them?"

Hilaal put his hands back down and shrugged. "Not that he's said to me."

Chance finished her report for the interested movers and shakers of the BrainTrust. She and Amanda were in the same conference room together, but the others attended by wallscreen since they were outside the *Chiron* quarantine. "We've started producing the cure for UVR Rubola here locally, and I expect in forty-eight hours we'll have everyone on the BrainTrust vaccinated. Both our pharmaceutical factories in Benin and Mexico will create small stockpiles, but honestly, I doubt they'll be needed. There's no hint the terrorists deployed it anywhere but here."

Ben Wilson sighed with relief. "At least that's taken care of."

Dawn pressed on to the next critical item. "So how long after everyone's vaccinated can we get the blockade lifted?"

Amanda scowled as she rose from her chair. "And therein lies a major problem. I just got off the phone with the Chief Advisor. He said in no uncertain terms that the blockade would continue until we met an additional requirement."

Dmitri, the BrainTrust's Russian arms dealer, put his face in his hands and groaned. "Let me guess. He won't lift the blockade until we give him Dash."

Matt leaned forward. "Doesn't he know Dash is dead?"

Amanda shook her head. "I informed him. I don't think he believes it, but he agreed to a compromise. He'll acknowledge the epidemic has ended, terminate the quarantine, and lift the blockade...after we give him Chance."

Everyone looked at Chance, whose eyes widened. "Whoa. News to me." She glanced at Amanda. "So, it's the same old demand, really. Rejuvenate the President for Life or face the consequences."

Dawn's mouth puckered into a thin line. "Would it work to trade Chance? Chance, are you OK with this?"

Chance gave her a wan smile. "Honestly, I'd rather not. A new lease on life for that creep?" She shuddered. "I'd pass if we had another choice."

Dmitri added, "And you can bet that the Russians will back this play, and part of the deal will be that Chance will have to rejuvenate the Premier as well."

Ben noted, "I can see where this ends up. If Chance goes, she'll never be allowed to come back, will she?"

Amanda's expression grew even grimmer. "Unlikely."

Matt, who spent more time on logistics than the others, brought them back to the major problem with keeping Chance. "So, Amanda, how much food do we have in the archipelago? How long can we last? Long enough to do any good?"

Amanda took a deep breath. "We maintain only a thirty-day supply of food. We've already used up over a week of that."

Ben's eyes bulged. "Thirty days? That's it?"

Amanda's shoulders slumped. "Colin insisted we wouldn't need more. He assured the Consortium in the early days that 'the stochastic genius of the BrainTrust would feed everyone in the event of an emergency.' Nobody quite understood what that meant, but storage space on our ships was so dear, everyone agreed to follow his advice. The question never came up again, until now."

Chance tilted her head to the side and banged her ear; as she had explained apologetically to everyone, the UVR Rubola had left her with a lingering ear infection, and it bothered her at random times. She gurgled a laugh. "Colin's in a coma, he may never recover, and he's still the one running the game plan."

Dawn joined her laughter. "Looks like it." She shook her head. "Well, one thing is certain. We aren't handing Chance over to that bastard."

Chance looked doubtful. "It may come to the point where we have no choice." She winced and banged her ear again. "But I'm perfectly happy to see how Colin's plan unfolds first."

Matt concurred. "By all means, let the Chief Advisor do

battle with Colin. Even in a coma, my money's on our guy." He turned grim. "Though it's never a bad idea to have a backup plan. I'll investigate ways of breaking the blockade with the Black Titan."

Amanda interrupted the long pause that ensued. "That's it, then? Shall we meet again, say, when we have forty-eight hours of food left?"

Everyone assented, and the wallscreen images blinked out until only Matt was left. "Chance, if it comes down to it, I can get you off the archipelago."

Chance considered it, then shook her head. "Wouldn't make any difference. He could still insist on my surrendering myself. If it meant the survival of the BrainTrust, I'd go."

Matt acquiesced. "I still don't think it will come to that."

Chance's expression turned thoughtful. "Nor do I, Matt. In truth, I think we'll figure something out, and it will all be fine."

When Ballard told Jubair he had a few questions, Jubair tapped his tablet and asked irritably, "Do we really need to do this? I have experiments in process."

Ballard gently insisted, and Jubair threw up his hands and followed him, although he kept up a continuous stream of criticisms of anything that pulled him away from his work. By the time Ballard waved Jubair to the table in the conference/interrogation room, he was considering committing murder himself.

Jubair frowned as he sat, squirming to find a comfortable position. "Where did you find these awful chairs?"

Ballard grimaced as he sat down. "Trust me, I hate them at least as much as you do." He'd spent so many hours in these torture devices, he wanted to confess to the crime himself.

Ballard tried to continue in this vein to establish a rapport with mutual sympathy, but to no avail.

Jubair squirmed around in his chair and leaned forward to bring his anger and distrust into the open. "Forget all this good cop stuff. We all know what you did to the people in the CDC. Straight from your old playbook, isn't it? Steven Hatfill and Bruce Ivins."

The agent winced. In 2001, a series of letters with anthrax had been mailed around the country, killing five people and endangering many more. For years, the FBI had pursued Steven Hatfill with sufficient vigor that Hatfill had won a multi-million-dollar harassment award. Eventually the FBI stopped targeting this man who was most probably innocent and turned their attention to Bruce Ivins. Under the FBI scrutiny, Ivins committed suicide. The FBI closed the case, effectively declaring it a success.

Cameron Ballard had indeed been following this playbook when he launched his assault on the CDC: harass the small numbers of people with the means to conduct the attack until one of them cracked. It had seemed so sensible when he started. He wasn't quite sure how he'd wound up here.

Jubair wasn't finished. "So now you're dead certain that the man behind the attack is me or Hilaal, two Sunnis with world-class credentials who, if we follow your stereotypes, want to see Iran, Israel, and the United States all dead. You're as certain that it's one of us now as you were a little while ago that it was Velma."

Ballard decided the better part of valor was to avoid responding to this outburst. Instead, he sidled up to the questions he wanted to ask. "Speaking of Velma, I see you're number three in the CEREBRUM rankings, just behind her."

Jubair sat back and smiled. "I hope to pass her now that I've gotten the hang of it."

Ballard smiled back. "Are you surprised Hilaal is just ninth?"

Jubair frowned. "I am." He leaned forward conspiratorially. "I think he hasn't quite gotten the hang of how CERE-BRUM works. It's not just a matter of which prediction you think is right, it's a matter of how confident you are and what the odds are at any given moment." He shook his head. "You know, there are days when he shows flashes of being every bit as good as I am."

Jubair's eyes sparked with anger. "But it's even more ridiculous to think Hilaal is the culprit than to think it's me. He may be the most compassionate man I know." He thought about it for a moment. "Besides, as a Doctor Without Borders, where could he have a lab?"

Ballard pulled out the renditions of the shipboard attackers. "Know who these people are?"

Jubair glanced at them. "The people who attacked us."

"Ever seen them before they came here?"

Jubair rolled his eyes. "No. And no."

In the end, Ballard released Jubair to hustle back to his experiments. The agent reconnected his tablet to the general wifi and discovered a message from his team back in the Hoover building in D.C. He smiled. At last, they had a break.

Ballard practically ran down the passages as he called Joshua and Amanda. "We've got him," he crowed.

Joshua still lay in the hospital bed, though his mood had improved considerably when his fever and chills finally broke. "Show me."

Ballard explained as he connected his tablet to the free monitor. "I've had my people searching for connections between anyone here and those two men who attacked the *Chiron*. They finally found something."

On the screen everyone watched a nightmare scene unfold. Sirens were blaring, smoke coiled from the wreck of a building in the background, and all the people running to and fro were smudged with soot. The camera tilted and twisted to focus on a wild-eyed Jubair. He turned to speak to someone off-camera, and the camera turned once again to bring the other participant into focus.

Sabaah.

Ballard commented. "I just finished interviewing Jubair. He said he'd never met the attackers before."

On-screen, Jubair shouted something at Sabaah. Sabaah nodded and ran off camera one way while Jubair went the other.

Amanda watched and muttered, "It was a disaster scene. He might not remember."

Ballard clenched his fists to keep from screaming. "He lied to us! He's in on it!"

Joshua looked back and forth between the two of them. "Amanda may be right."

Ballard's eyes bulged. "Your Honor, you can't just disregard this."

Joshua sighed. "But while Amanda may or may not be correct, Agent Ballard is certainly correct."

Ballard blurted, "Yes!"

Joshua disregarded this and turned to Amanda. "Do we have any peacekeepers under quarantine with us?"

Amanda sighed. "Still recovering from rubola."

Joshua shrugged. "Very well. Have Chance and Velma escort Jubair to the brig."

He pondered the matter for a moment. "We'll try to deal with this more definitively after we're clear of this current quarantine, but for now, we'll hold Jubair in custody."

13

STOCHASTIC GENIUS

No great discovery was ever made without a bold guess.
 —Isaac Newton

The stochastic genius of the BrainTrust started slow. First Amanda did a fleet-wide broadcast announcing that the blockade would continue indefinitely even though they had the vaccine, and food would be rationed.

Forty-eight hours later, after everyone in the archipelago had received the vaccine, Amanda lifted quarantine of the *Chiron* and reopened the internship gangways. Coincident with this enabling support for collaboration and cooperation, fruit- and vegetable-filled plant containers started showing up in the passages, in the promenades, and in the parks. As people saw other people carrying pots with beans and zucchini and tomatoes, ever more people started copying the idea.

Soon the *Helios* and the *Argus* had shifted their production processes to accommodate the demand for PVC pots, and all the nuclear reactors started processing the brine that was the main byproduct of fresh water production/magnesium extraction into a reasonable facsimile of mud. Seeds and seedlings came from the greenhouse decks to go into the new pots with the fresh dirt.

Merrilee Winston, a former GPlex employee now running a startup on the *Dreams*, led a programming team that included her thirteen-year-old son Charlie and created a new app to wrangle the general purpose bots to take care of the plants. The chip foundry on the *Warenhaus* switched to manufacturing red and green LEDs to maximize the chlorophyll-powering light, giving the passages a faint yellow hue as people walked through them. And the decks' themes vanished as all the lights on all the ships were brought to max power and held there 24/7. The ventilation systems were modified to increase the density of CO2 in the air—not enough to harm the people, but enough to encourage the plants.

Soon the ships looked like they'd all been overrun by a very domesticated jungle.

Three more days passed before the next stochastic event occurred.

Gina sat down with Dawn in one of the main *Haven* cafeterias to discuss the difficulties of signing up home buyers in the middle of a quarantine. Gina already knew it would be an unpleasant conversation; she had no idea that the food would contribute.

By this time the menu throughout the BrainTrust had gone pretty much vegetarian since fresh fruit and vegetables were the crops grown in the two agricultural decks on each isle ship. There had been a brief effort early in the history of the BrainTrust to bring egg production in-house as well, but that had proven abortively cost-ineffective.

So when the human waiter brought the menus with three vegetarian entrees, Gina was surprised when he said, "We also have a special today, an experimental dish we're offering to everyone as a sampler."

Dawn looked at him skeptically. "I'm afraid to ask what it is."

The waiter visibly steeled himself. "A fine ratatouille with a delicate mealworm sauce."

Gina did not drop her jaw. "Mealworms?"

The waiter answered with hard-won enthusiasm, "Got them from a professor with a biology lab on the *BrainTrust University*. Very high in protein. And mealworms grow very quickly indeed, with very little overhead." He spread his arms. "You lace a disc of dirt with mealworms, then lay more and more unlaced discs on top until you have a cylinder, then let the mealworms multiply. It's best if the dirt is saturated with, well, human waste for rapid growth."

The waiter's eyes glowed with the eagerness of a true advocate; Gina found herself thinking he was wasted as a waiter and decided that after this crisis was over, she'd offer him a job in real estate. He continued, "As the mealworms multiply, they migrate up through the cylinder. Then you can slice off the bottom, extract the mealworms, and grind them for the sauce."

Dawn held up her napkin to hide the expression on her face. "Sounds captivating."

The waiter smiled. "Shall I bring you each a sample?"

Gina maintained a fixed smile on her face. "Sure, why not?"

Gina and Dawn agreed, after going over the finances for their isle ships, which after all were making real revenues from rentals for both scientist cabins and manufacturing laboratories, that the numbers for their venture were mighty fine compared to the flavor of mealworm ratatouille.

Years later, gastronomic historians came to agree that the most important breakthrough came a couple days after the introduction of mealworms into the BrainTrust diet. In a demonstration of heroic willingness to put competitive differences aside in the midst of desperate crisis, the five-star chef on the *Haven* collaborated with the five-star chef on the *GPlex I.* They created a series of dishes whose names did not include the word "mealworm" but whose contents most certainly did.

The new dishes got rave reviews and continued to be served long after the blockade ended, noted throughout the civilized world as the finest examples of the next generation of *nouveau BrainTrust* cuisine.

UVR Rubola had been wiped from the archipelago, and the threat of famine had been averted. With the development of protein-rich rapid-growth mealworm-augmented fine cuisine, the BrainTrust could endure the blockade indefinitely. Still, the blockade was a nuisance.

Then the weather turned miraculously balmy. This inspired Chance to lead the first counterattack a few days later, starting as soon as the sun rose high enough to illuminate the battlespace. She bounced up onto the top deck of the *Chiron* wearing nothing but a red, white, and blue G-string, displaying her arm covered with a bioorganic tattoo sleeve, her opposing leg with biomechanical, and her back covered with her best work. A couple dozen women similarly clad followed her up the ramp. Chance whirled an arm over her head and shouted into the empty air, "OK, guys, crank us up!"

All the isle ships in the archipelago answered her call, blaring Beyonce's *Single Ladies* to the blockading fleet. The girls started dancing, some of them awkwardly at first, but as the music swept over them and the general party atmosphere washed across them and the rhythm took them, even the shyest ones upped their game with ever more sinuous motions.

By early afternoon, word had reached the Chief Advisor that something untoward was happening with the blockade. He clicked open a window on one of the recommended livestreams airing from the BrainTrust with a closeup of the festivities. At first he thought he was looking at some sort of stripper club, then realized the floor upon which the girls danced was actually a helipad, and this was the roof of an isle ship. "What the hell are they doing?" he demanded.

Trixie, snuggled up close to him and touching him constantly for signs of arousal, frowned in surprise at his failure to respond to the scene of nubile women in his usual fashion. She gave the obvious answer. "They're dancing, Baby." Giving up on her usual job, Trixie looked at the video more intently and pointed with her free hand, "Isn't that Doctor Dixon? The one you talk about needing?"

The dizzying gyrations of the bikini-clad bodies had kept him confused. Now that Trixie pointed her out, he gasped. "Dammit!" The direction of his thoughts changed. "Fantastic! Now we've got her." Pushing Trixie away, he tapped his cell phone.

The Advisor had groomed a Seal lieutenant for the mission of kidnapping a doctor from the BrainTrust well over a year earlier. Not coincidentally, that lieutenant and his team were a part of the blockading fleet. When the Advisor's call had gone through, he was met with the lieutenant's enthusiastic "Yes, sir!"

The Advisor spoke quickly. "You know the doctor I wanted you to take is dead, right?"

The lieutenant answered cautiously. "That's what our best intel says, Sir, but not with a lot of confidence."

The Advisor snapped his hand in a dismissive motion. "Regardless. Take a look at this." He juggled his phone and his computer until he was sharing his main display with the Seal. "See that woman with the tattoos?" The Advisor stopped talking for a moment as Chance spun in place and the tattoos on her back came into view. Wow.

Get a grip, the Advisor told himself. "She's Doctor Dash's replacement. Chance Dixon."

The lieutenant pondered the scene for a moment. "So, she's dancing in a crowd of other women on the roof of an isle ship?"

"Yes, exactly! You can just copter over, jump onto the

roof, grab her, and bring her back. But you have to go now, before she leaves!"

Puzzled concern entered the lieutenant's voice. "But, sir, that's a plague ship. How many of the people she's dancing with are infected? Is Doctor Dixon infected?"

The Chief Advisor clamped his jaw tight before he could yell, "There's no plague! It's all gone! Just go get her!" Leaking that information, even to a Seal, would be bad.

The lieutenant gulped loud enough to be heard as he offered the next words. "We couldn't really wear hazmat suits for this operation. Too slow. She might actually get away." He paused, steeling himself. "We can go without the hazmat, Sir, but it wouldn't be just my team and me at risk. When we got back to our ship, we'd be placing the whole crew in danger."

The Chief Advisor buried his face in his hands. "Stay with me. I'll get the admiral, and the three of us will see if we can work something out."

More women wandered up onto the deck to join the party as others wandered off to take a break, although Chance continued to dance full steam. The men of the BrainTrust, having heard about the party secondhand or seen parts of it on the numerous now-viral videos, started showing up, forming a ring around the impromptu dance floor three deep.

A new crew of women, uniformly curvaceous and buxom beyond the norm, led by a vixen with honey-gold hair laced with streaks of blue joined in—and could they dance!

A team of enterprising mechanical engineers went to work in support of the ladies' efforts, installing a number of stripper poles for those interested. The blond vixen spoke to them, giving encouragement and thanking them, and they walked away straighter and prouder.

The new women went directly to work on the poles. By mysterious means, despite the need to avoid damaging the integrity of the helipad, the engineers had anchored the poles so robustly that they stood rigid no matter how the girls whirled through their presentations.

Chance found the fluid motions of the women mesmerizing. She spun and swirled across the deck to dance with their leader. "Chance Dixon," she introduced herself. "Who are you guys?" she asked at a changeover in the music. "Where'd you all learn to dance like that?"

The blond spun lithely around Chance and answered in a long slow drawl, "Sonia Manning. And honey, if you can't guess who we are, I can't tell you. It would burn your ears."

Chance frowned. "Just about everybody on this ship is in the top one percent in some field of research."

The blond spun around her once more, so close a sheet of paper could not have fit in the gap. The blond whispered in her ear, "Oh, honey, trust me, we're in the top one percent in our field, all right."

<hr>

Admiral Beck stared at the Chief Advisor on his wallscreen, aghast. "You want to kidnap this woman from a plague ship?" He somehow managed not to scream in addition, "Are you totally insane?"

Clearly the Advisor heard the unspoken rebuke, and he ground out, "She is incredibly important to the survival of the State. Trust me on this, Admiral."

Beck looked down, masking his face with his hand. He ground his teeth. "Very well, sir. We can surely rig some sort of quarantine here on the deck of the *Kennedy*." The *Kennedy* was a Ford-class carrier, the most advanced class of naval platforms on Earth, populated by more people than some cities and powerful enough to wipe out the entire Japanese Navy from WWII all by itself.

The US Navy had done quarantines before on aircraft carriers with far less equipment and tech than this one had, but never after intentionally exposing a Seal team to a plague that allegedly produced over fifty percent casualties.

Beck was steeling himself to ask whether he should really give the orders to launch this mission when the Seal lieutenant interrupted, "Ah, sirs, there's another reason this may be a mistake."

Both his superiors glared at him through their respective wallscreens, but he was a Seal and not easily intimidated. "Look here. And here and here." He drew virtual circles on the shared view around three well-muscled, extremely fit young women gyrating through the crowd on the *Chiron* wearing yellow bikinis.

The Chief Advisor looked, then barked, "So? All I see is three more BrainTrust dancing skanks."

The Seal nodded. "That was my first thought too. But those bikinis are the same shade of yellow as the shirts worn by the peacekeepers. That specific swimsuit is one of the peacekeeper uniforms authorized for beach patrol."

This pronouncement was greeted by a long pause. The admiral, who really wanted to put the kibosh on this mission anyway, set aside his desire for sanity and reluctantly complained, "Surely your team can take out a couple of peacekeepers along the way." *Especially half-naked ones—they are clearly unarmed*, he did not add.

The lieutenant shrugged. "History shows that every assault team that has ever discounted BrainTrust peacekeepers has reliably been destroyed by them." He started making more marks on the video. "But it gets worse." He zoomed the shared view to a man wearing some sort of Muslim turban. The fellow was watching the girls, clapping to the rhythm of the music and clearly enjoying the show. "This man is a Khalsa, an elite warrior of the Sikh. We have a dossier on him. He has almost as many medals as I do."

He panned the zoom and froze on an immense man with short blond hair. "Major Wolf Griffin, Marine." The lieutenant did not call him an ex-Marine; there was no such thing. "He definitely has *more* medals than I do." Wolf Griffin was not watching the girls; he was glaring out over the water in the direction of the admiral's flagship as if he knew he were personally under scrutiny.

The Chief Advisor tried to take up the admiral's complaint. "OK, so, they're, uh..."

Admiral Beck interrupted. "Formidable."

The lieutenant visibly relaxed as the admiral supported him. "Yes, sir. Even discounting the peacekeepers in bikinis and the mixed martial arts skills of Dr. Dixon, which I'm now reading are legendary on the BrainTrust, this would be a hard fight."

The Advisor persisted, nearly pleading. "But still, can't you take them? All we need is the one girl."

The lieutenant turned grim. "I haven't gotten to the worst part." He panned to a gray backpack lying casually, tucked out of the way near Major Griffin. "I'm almost certain that that pack contains a folded-up BT12 PGM autolauncher, known informally as 'Ping's Big Gun.' Intel thinks they may have used this to knock down as many as a dozen Chinese stealth fighters."

The admiral stated the obvious conclusion. "This is a trap."

The lieutenant shook his head uncertainly. "I don't know, sir. If it were really a trap, they could have concealed it better."

The admiral looked puzzled. "A warning? A taunt? Awfully subtle."

The Chief Advisor smashed his fist on his desk. "I thought that bastard Colin Wheeler was in a coma!"

The admiral, who had studied Colin Wheeler as he would an opposing admiral, answered cautiously, "So either our intel is just bad, or we've been deceived, or he just recovered." Another thought struck him. "Or…there's someone else over there who thinks like him."

The Chief Advisor just groaned. "I still don't get the point. What are they trying to accomplish?"

As twilight fell, the electrical engineers did their best to outshine the mechanical engineers. Literally. They strung lights and hung mirrors to work the Autonomy Day lasers and flood the deck with a brilliance comparable to sunshine…if sunshine strobed and shimmered like a scintillating continuum of disco balls.

Gina Toscano came onto the deck with a couple of other women who, like Gina, looked like they had stepped from the pages of Vogue. Gina wore a string bikini that matched the cherry-red color of her husband's copter, which in turn matched the suit of armor in the reception area of the *Helios*.

By this time Sonia Manning had organized a series of dancing lessons. Newbies under the tutelage of her girls were working the poles, learning body waves and knee hooks; one talented beginner was showing off a Venus spin.

Gina and Sonia fell into conversation like old friends, and soon the strippers and the models were exchanging secrets. The worlds of exotic dancing and high-fashion modeling would never be the same, demonstrating once again the fundamental principle of the BrainTrust, namely, that if you brought together the top people in divergent fields of endeavor, the creative mixing of disciplines inevitably led to new technology, deep insights, and, well, high art.

In the Omega conference room of the Blue Lagoon deck of the *Chiron*, SpaceR CEO Matt Toscano, venture capitalist

Ben Wilson, and BrainTrust Chairman Amanda Copeland sat back after a long discussion of their joint undertakings. Matt flipped the wallscreen to a livestream of the festivities taking place above them. He breathed out in wonder, "Isn't she lovely?"

Neither of his companions asked to which of the lovely women he referred since Gina was in the middle of the frame. As they watched, Chance came dancing up to Gina, no doubt to discuss tactics.

Amanda sighed. "Chance asked me to come up and dance for the brave men and women of the American Navy as well."

Ben looked her up and down appraisingly. "You should go."

Amanda sighed again. "She even gave me a present for the party, a one-piece Speedo." She pursed her lips. "If I were just ten years younger…"

Ben persisted. "You should still go." His eyes acquired a wicked gleam. "I promise I'll have eyes only for you."

Amanda raised an eyebrow. "You're a delightful if poor liar, Ben." She glared, then slumped. "I've never before felt any desire to enter Dash's rejuv program." Even though they had lost Dash, sometimes people still talked about her in present tense, as if she would walk into the room at any moment. "Maybe next year."

Throughout the blockading fleet, enlisted sailors unanimously agreed they needed to do serious intel on the enemy. Those on watch duty turned binoculars and sensor suites to the *Chiron's* top deck. Mess halls on every ship turned their wallscreens to the livestream of the BrainTrust dancers. A great deal of cheering, clapping, and whistling accompanied the careful analytical study of OpFor tactics. As the analysis went on, different variants of one question kept arising.

One enthusiastic youth aboard the flagship *Kennedy* voiced the problem succinctly. "Where's the plague? Does that look like a plague ship?"

One mate added, "I've never seen a bunch of people who looked so, uh, healthy. Are we really sure there's a plague? Looks like bad intel to me."

Another added dreamily, "Who cares? I'll risk it. Let me lead the first boarding party."

A room full of amens greeted this hard-won assessment.

The news media picked up the viral video and ran with it. The Blue media gleefully observed that the Reds couldn't even distinguish between a dead zombie and a, uh, vigorous young woman. The Red media did not pass judgment on the Red government, of course, but ran the video anyway lest they lose their audience. They didn't need to comment, however: their viewers drew the conclusion easily enough without the assistance of a talking head.

Long before lunchtime, both the admiral's senior officers and his adjutant Lieutenant Lambert were gently asking whether they were engaged in a sham of massive proportions. The admiral reminded them that they had orders, and they would damn well obey those orders. He started daydreaming about transfer opportunities.

The next day, around noon East Coast Time, the Chief Advisor felt the onset of a major headache. Leaders of the wheat lobby and the cattle lobby showed up, first demanding an audience, then demanding that he lift the ridiculous blockade so they could get back to shipping wheat and beef to the BrainTrust. The Chief Advisor begged off for fifteen minutes to deal with an emergency.

He withdrew from the Oval Office and pressed the wall panel that opened a secret door. The panel, the door, and the staircase to which it led had been built in 1987 for President Reagan in the event of a terrorist attack.

The staircase led to a closet near his private elevator, thence to many places including the Presidential Emergency Operations Center under the East Wing. The Chief Advisor looked yearningly down the steps to the closet, but he did not really consider using it.

The staircase had another feature that attracted him now: it was virtually soundproof. He screamed over and over until he felt better.

Chance saw Hilaal sitting quietly, alone, at a table in the cafeteria. He had just sat down with a tray loaded with biryani, a rare treat amidst the usual menu of mealworm/vegetable/somethings. She slid into the seat opposite him.

He smiled warmly at her; as usual, when Hilaal smiled, it was like the clouds had parted, the sun shone through, and there was nothing you could not achieve. "I persuaded them to use some of the rationed supplies to make one of my mother's favorites. Would you like to try some?"

Chance looked yearningly at the dish, but she was sure it meant more to Hilaal than to her. She shook her head. "I have to run, but I thought I'd let you know what's happening with Jubair. I know you were very upset when we put him in the brig."

Sorrow filled his face. "I still don't believe it. I'm sorry I was so vociferous about it when you announced it."

Chance shrugged. "Understandable. Anyway, as I pointed out at the time, we're all worried we have an innocent man in jail. I wanted to tell you, we're doing a double-check."

Hilaal raised an eyebrow.

Chance continued. "The BrainTrust happens to have the world's foremost authority on facial microexpressions, Lenora Thornhill. She's the Mission Commander for the Fuxing archipelago, so it's hard to get hold of her, but she's agreed to come here and interview Jubair. We're hoping she can either clear him or make his guilt more definitive."

Hilaal's eyebrows rose in astonishment. "She's coming here in the middle of the blockade? How is that possible?"

Chance chuckled. "We have our ways."

Hilaal looked forlorn. "I'm very skeptical of such things." He shrugged. "Still, if there's a chance of setting him free, I'm happy." He dug his fork into his biryani. Suddenly he froze, staring off into space.

Chance knitted her eyebrows together. "Hilaal? Are you OK?"

Hilaal blinked. "Sorry. I get these kinds of flashbacks once in a while." He looked at his fork. "Sometimes I wonder if I have a mild case of PTSD."

Having entered the *Dreams Come True*, where many of the startup companies had their offices, Chance wandered down the passages of the Dr. Doolittle deck, with walls rendered as scenes from the fictional Victorian town of Puddleby-on-the-Marsh. On her way to her destination, she passed a tree where the parrot Polynesia and the owl Too-Too discoursed in frustration about the inability of humans to speak any recognizable language.

Eventually Chance came to the door to Replacements, Inc. As she stepped inside, she started to address the person standing there waiting for her, then stopped, stunned.

Sonia Manning gave her a brilliant smile. "Honey, so good to see you again."

Chance looked her over from top to bottom and back again. She was dressed in a perfectly form-fitting lab coat and had her hair tied tightly back in a bun. "Sonia?" Chance had meant to say it as a statement, but it came out as a question.

Sonia chuckled. "Amanda wanted us to show you what

we've been working on. She called it 'the next generation of stochastic genius.'"

Before Chance could embarrass herself by just gaping, Sonia swiveled on her pumps and walked deeper into the facility. She began explaining. "You probably don't even know what Replacements, Inc. is about, do you?"

They stopped at the edge of a remarkably large lab. Enormous, considering the cost of real estate on the *Dreams*. A number of people, a couple of whom Chance recognized as stripper-pole dancers and teachers from their day entertaining the US Navy, moved among numerous benches that held beakers and test tubes. Computers were hooked to an amazing diversity of gadgets, some of which Chance recognized. "Organic chemistry of some sort," she surmised.

Sonia smiled warmly. "Ever so correct." She pointed at a large glass cylinder with tubes running into it on the bench beside her.

Chance shook her head as she stared into the cylinder. Under any other circumstances, this would have caught her eye above all else. "A human liver?"

Sonia rolled one hip out, put one hand on it, and gestured with the other hand like a presenter on a game show. "Ta-da. An honest-to-God human liver, grown in this vat from scratch. Welcome to the second most important application of the CRISPIER, right behind your own rejuv."

Chance stepped closer and scrutinized the liquids circulating through the organ. "It's not quite right. Is it actually alive?"

Sonia uttered a sound of disgust. "So far we are unable

to keep them operational for more than forty-eight hours. Very annoying." She regained her good cheer. "But a month ago they lived less than twenty-four hours, so it's improving."

Chance looked back at Sonia in excitement. "This is amazing. Anything I can do to help?" She thought about it, then partially retracted the offer. "After we've dealt with these bio-terrorists, that is."

Sonia nodded. "Quite possibly. We had some questions for Dr. Dash, but..." She shrugged.

Time to move on. Chance switched topics. "So, this is potentially marvelous sometime in the future, but Amanda sounded like there was something urgent and relevant to the blockade."

Sonia stood straighter and gestured to a far corner of the lab. "And so there is." As they walked, Sonia continued, "Our organs don't live as long as they should, but they are otherwise pretty indistinguishable from the real thing. It turns out that there are applications even for short-lived organs, notably muscle tissue."

As they came closer to their destination, Chance caught the first whiffs of an extraordinary aroma. Like Pavlov's dog, she found herself swallowing her saliva.

They came to a bench that had been cleaned of apparatus. There was a bag of plastic forks, a steak knife, and a plate with chunks of a partially-cut-up prime rib.

Sonia grabbed a plastic fork, speared a chunk of meat from which juices still flowed, and held it up to Chance's lips. "Say 'Aah.'" She popped it into Chance's open mouth.

Chance's eyes rolled back in her head in ecstasy. She

chewed slowly, luxuriating in the flavor. "Oh, wow. I'd pretty much forgotten what that tasted like."

A crowd had gathered around them by this time. Everyone was smiling as they watched Chance's reaction.

Sonia spoke for everyone. "Amanda wanted you to double-check our results to make sure our steak-in-a-test-tube was actually nutritious and not poisonous."

Chance laughed. "If it's poisonous, it's fine, because it's to die for."

This was greeted with some clapping and a number of cheers.

Chance pointed at the plate. "I'll need that for experimental purposes."

This got a number of catcalls.

Chance laughed along with them. "Unbelievably, I'm serious. Amanda's right; we need to make sure it is…" she tried to find the right phrase, "everything it tastes like."

As one of the researchers wrapped the test prime rib, Chance frowned at Sonia. "You gave me the impression that you did something else for a living. Something more, ah, artistic."

Sonia gave her an easy laugh and drawled, "Oh, honey, I *do* do something more artistic. And frankly, the art pays a lot more than this does at the moment." She swiveled her shoulders sensuously. "But if we ever get that liver working, that'll change overnight."

Chance smacked her lips. "I imagine the BrainTrust will pay you pretty well just for the prime rib, at least for the duration of the blockade." Chance reviewed their conversations. "So, when you said you were in the top one percent in your field, was this the field you were talking about?"

Sonia laughed once more. "Why, honey, can't a girl be a one-percenter in two different fields at the same time?"

Chance winced and rubbed her ear. "Don't ever doubt it."

———

The sonarman on board the submarine USS *North Carolina* muttered to his captain, "I'm getting it again, sir."

The captain rolled his eyes. "The jet ski?"

The sonarman nodded. "Just for a moment or two, in the middle of that pod of dolphins."

The captain asked, "How close is it to the *Port Royal* in the *Heinlein* lane?"

"Very close, sir. Almost adjacent to them. At the moment, there are dolphins all around the cruiser."

The captain considered that. "Isn't this the time of day the pod swims over to the reef, away from the *Heinlein*?"

"Yes, Sir. I concur that it seems unlikely a jet ski would be going *into* the quarantine area."

The captain closed his eyes. "You've heard this now, how many times? Three times?"

"Four times, sir." The sonarman hesitated. "It could just be an odd reflection off a thermal eddy from the jet skis that are zooming around inside the reef all the time, but four times is a lot."

The captain sighed. "Very well. The next time we break comm silence, I'll let them know to stay alert for a jet ski frisking with the dolphins as the pod swims by. Hopefully the *Port Royal* will spot it before it rams them."

Lenora felt the little submarine tap gently against the dock. Wolf threw the hatch back, and as they climbed out, Lenora shook her head. "I'm still amazed they aren't picking you up on sonar."

Wolf shrugged. "The dolphins, which we've trained to go back and forth between the *Heinlein* and the BrainTrust once every day, seem to mask our sounds. Certainly, while our subs are pretty quiet, they're nowhere near as silent as a US Navy sub." His eyes shone mischievously. "But if they do hear us, they probably get confused. The sub uses a variant of a pump-jet. To the extent it sounds like anything, it sounds like one of those." He pointed out into the water between the *Elysian Fields* and the reef, where numerous personal watercraft bounced about.

Lenora smiled. "Ah, yes. Confusion unto our enemies."

She made her way through the ship to talk to Amanda, who led her down to the brig. They released Jubair, and Lenora led him into a conference room that had been transformed in the opposite direction from Ballard's interrogation center. Whereas Ballard's room was designed to make one uncomfortable, this was virtually a living room.

Jubair sank into a cushioned recliner with a sigh of relief. "This is the first time I've been comfortable since, well, it seems like forever."

Lenora smiled sympathetically. "Just so you know, I'll

be taking you back to the brig after this interview, but perhaps not for very long. We'll see."

Jubair nodded, and the interrogation began.

Three hours later, Lenora led Jubair back to his cell, grabbed a bottle of water, and took the elevator to brief Joshua and Amanda on her results.

Amanda and Joshua sat patiently while Lenora rubbed her throbbing temples. "There's not the least hint that he has lied to us, nor any hint that he's a terrorist." She drank another slug of water. "I'd say let him go, but…"

Joshua prompted her. "But?"

Lenora pursed her lips. "The real culprit, as I understand it, has to be one of the world's greatest geniuses. Am I correct?"

Amanda blew out a breath. "He seems to have figured out how to use the CRISPIER on his own. Even Dash had Byron to work with." Her voice became even grimmer. "And these viruses he has designed, especially this last one? I don't know if even Dash could have developed it."

Lenora nodded. "As I questioned Jubair, I found myself wondering how this would go if Dash were the terrorist. Could she compartmentalize her thoughts so that the part answering the questions would be living in an alternate reality constructed by the rest of her mind? If so, when she said she was innocent, she'd be telling the truth, even though it was a lie."

Joshua pushed for a conclusion. "So we shouldn't let him go?"

Lenora slumped. "Not yet. I have to give this some thought." She brightened. "You have all the tapes from all the other interviews, correct? Let me take a look at those while I stew on Jubair."

Chance skipped into the Command Information Center. "I have an idea."

Amanda had her head down on her crossed arms on the main conference table, her eyes closed. "I am trying to take a nap."

Chance poked her in the shoulder. "Get up, sleepyhead." Chance knew, like everyone else, that Amanda had hardly left the center since the plague had struck and the blockade had moved into position. "If this works, you can go back to your cabin and get some real sleep."

Amanda struggled upright. "Well, you have my attention."

"Good. Now close your eyes."

Amanda growled. "My eyes were closed just a moment ago before you decided to interrupt me."

Chance's good cheer was irrepressible. "Sorry. But trust me, it'll be worth it. Now close your eyes and open your mouth."

Amanda did as she was told. A moment later a rich, beefy flavor she hadn't tasted in weeks filled her mouth. She chewed luxuriously, keeping her eyes closed. "I take it Sonia came through."

"Like, oh, wow, yeah."

Amanda opened her eyes. "So, between one thing and another, I'd guess our food supply problem has come to an end." She frowned. "I'd call the Chief Advisor and tell him his blockade is now pointless, but first off he wouldn't believe me, and second, he probably wouldn't care."

Chance's eyes gleamed. "Which is why we have to tell him so much more authoritatively." She explained her plan.

Now Amanda's eyes gleamed back. "Oh, that is so very crafty, so very…" Her eyes grew sharp. "So very Colin. Has he come out of his coma?"

Chance's eyes lost their gleam and a haunted look entered them. "You know, I've been telling people that I've been trying my best to do what Dash would do." She pursed her lips. "Well, at the end there, I think you know that Dash was trying to understand Colin's thinking patterns." She shrugged. "I guess that in my efforts to mimic Dash, I've succeeded a little bit in mimicking her as she mimicked Colin."

Amanda eyed her speculatively. "Ah, yes. You've certainly done a remarkable job, replacing her as well as you have."

Chance rubbed her ear. "Just doing what's necessary."

Amanda cleared her throat. "So, you're still going with that explanation?"

Chance's eyes widened. "What do you mean?"

Amanda shook her head wearily. "Never mind. Just the fantasy wishes of a very tired woman."

A long pause ensued. Chance raised her eyebrow. "So?"

Amanda's smile looked suspiciously like a grin. "Well, I think your proposal has tremendous merit. You prep the package, I'll prep the call." She muttered, "The Chief Advisor will never know what hit him."

The Chief Advisor sat behind his immense, forbidding desk and reiterated his stance. "Just because there are a small number of young men and women with no signs of infection doesn't mean there's no infection. I will not sign off on new food shipments until they have a completely clean bill of health. Until they have a proven, certified vaccine."

The wheat lobbyist and the beef lobbyist had been joined today by the dairy lobbyist. And the corn lobbyist. The pack was growing, and growing hungrier.

Mr. Wheat complained next. "But it could take them years to get their vaccine certified!"

Mr. Beef, the biggest loser in the blockade—and recipient of the largest emergency subsidies against the loss—amplified the point. "Our whole market could be dead by then. They're starving!"

The Chief Advisor manfully refrained from observing that the Decktop Danceathon dancers had not only looked clean of infection but well-fed as well. He was curious about that, actually. In the opening days of the blockade, the CIA's informants on the BrainTrust had said they should run out of food in less than a month, meaning that now they should be out in a couple more days, though later reports had suggested they'd figured out ways to extend the food supply. It shouldn't make any difference; he could wait, within reason. *Just a little longer*, he reminded himself, closing his hands into fists beneath his desk. *Just a little longer. We can rejuv the President, I can remain in charge, and all will be well.*

Right on time, Trixie stuck her head in the door. "My

apologies, Chief Advisor, but you have a national emergency to attend to."

The Advisor rose and shook their hands apologetically. "I'll see what I can do to speed this up. I have some ideas."

They grumbled but promised their support. After all, he *was* the only game in town.

Trixie sashayed in carrying a box roughly the size and shape of a frozen dinner. She displayed it for him, stroking the edges and licking her lips. "It looks really yummy on the cover."

The label on the box promised The BrainTrust's Own Beef Wellington. The accompanying photo looked so luscious, even the Chief Advisor found his mouth watering.

He grasped the package to rip it open, but it was a BrainTrust box, and when he grasped the Open Here tab, the box opened like a morning glory in the dawn light.

Inside the promised dish, sliced through the middle so the juicy center could be seen through the transparent film on top, resided adjacent to a cell phone. The Chief Advisor sighed. It was a BrainTrust phone.

Trixie rubbed his shoulders. "Shall I stay? Would you like me to taste-test the Beef Wellington for you?"

He patted her hand. "You'd better leave me alone with whatever this is."

Trixie bent over and inspected the pastry-covered meat. "I don't know, Baby. Sometimes you really *can* tell a book by its cover."

"Not when the BrainTrust is involved." He slapped her on her derriere. "I'll save some for you."

Trixie left, pretending to be in a huff. He picked up the phone and connected to the number on speed dial.

Amanda Copeland's voice came through. "Chief Advisor," she said far too cheerily for a person with over a hundred thousand people dying of starvation. "You'll want to see what we've got for you. Vidscreen us."

He slaved a wallscreen to the phone. Amanda sat in a room surrounded by wallscreens, desk screens, and a screen built into the tabletop.

A tall, lithe young woman of Hispanic complexion stood beside her, smiling. The last time he'd seen her, she'd been wearing a bikini on the deck of an isle ship. Today she wore a white lab coat. "Chief Advisor, so nice to meet you." She spread her arms in greeting. "I'm Chance Dixon."

The Advisor smiled back, delighted. Ha! He'd known they'd have to cave!

Chance gushed on. "I'm so looking forward to meeting you someday!" Her expression turned skeptical. "But not anytime soon." She pointed at a Beef Wellington on the table before her. "Before we make our counterproposal, let's have a bite, shall we? Set the mood."

The Advisor had a feeling that somehow he'd lost the initiative. However, the beautiful steak before him had been calling to him for some time, so he did not object.

She showed him the button he needed to push to bring the Wellington to its heated, mouth-watering best. The transparent top peeled back of its own accord—the Advisor had to confess, the BrainTrust never did things halfway—and Chance showed him how to open the hidden compartment with a knife and fork.

It was the best steak he'd ever had in his life.

Chance savored his reaction. "I thought you'd like it. As it happens, this is what you're forcing us to eat every day."

The Advisor stared at her as the delicious steak turned to a cold lump in his mouth. He swallowed it half-chewed.

Chance was not done. "Let me introduce you to Sonia Manning, the leader of the team that developed your meal."

Another woman stepped into view. She was impossibly curved, and her lab coat fitted her like a second skin. He was quite sure she too had danced on that top deck.

Her smile curved as deliciously as her hips. "Chief Advisor. So glad to meet you. Please let me tell you a little about our research at Replacements, Inc. I hope it will excite you as much as it excites me."

She spoke briefly of their plan to grow new livers, kidneys, and hearts in vitro, and of how the blockade and the impending famine had persuaded them to travel in a new direction. Then she showed him the production-scale vats they had hoped to use to grow life-saving organs, now filled with top sirloin and filet mignon.

Chance took over the explanation. She picked up her compatriot's cheery tone. "Isn't that marvelous? Who needs cattle anymore?" Her face and her voice turned grim. "We can mass-produce Sonia's equipment and ship it to people all over the United States. Within a year, there won't be a market for cattle-based beef. We can do the same thing with every other agricultural product. Visualize the American economy when the entire farm sector is wiped out."

The Chief Advisor could see the consequences so clearly that for a moment he was blind to everything else.

Chance continued, relentless and angry, "In forty-eight

hours, you will lift the blockade and we will go back to importing food from you, or the first batch of beef-culturing gear will ship from the Fuxing archipelago to the United States."

Amanda chimed in with her indomitable will, "Do not doubt us on this."

With that, Chance leaned forward, beaming her brightest smile. "Like I said, good to meet you, sir." She blew a kiss to him and shut down the connection.

The Chief Advisor just hated those people.

Twenty-four hours later Chance, Sonia, and Amanda gathered in a small cozy conference room with couches and padded chairs to drink a toast. The American cruiser had just left the lane between the archipelago and the *Heinlein*, and the aircraft carrier and its escort ships had turned around, headed for wherever such task forces sailed when not engaged in a blockade.

Sonia spoke a cautionary tale. "It was a great bluff, Chance, but just so you know, with our current tech, it costs about three times as much to produce steak in a vat as it does to breed cattle."

Amanda beat Chance to the punch. "But was it really a bluff? You're going back to work on your transplantable liver now, correct?"

Sonia nodded.

"Suppose instead you spent the next couple of years refining your system for manufacturing beef. How expensive would it be then?"

Sonia thought about it, and a mischievous smile spread slowly over her features. "You know the old political promise of putting a chicken in every pot? Given a couple of years of streamlining, I think we could put a solar plate that grows sirloin on every rooftop."

14

DARKNESS

During my eighty-seven years, I have witnessed a whole succession of technological revolutions. But none of them has done away with the need for character in the individual or the ability to think.
   —Bernard M. Baruch

White is the color of mourning for a Balinese funeral. Black is forbidden.

The procession started on the *Chiron*. Most isle ships, the *Chiron* included, had one deck that was two decks high for those social activities that required a more sweeping sense of grandeur. The movie theaters resided on this deck, as did the theatrical stage and the auditorium through which most residents passed when arriving on the BrainTrust for a brief intro to the workings of the ships.

Upon this deck also resided the houses of worship for religious groups, as diverse as the people on that particular ship. The *Chiron* had a handful of different Christian churches, a Jewish synagogue, a Muslim mosque, and modest versions of both Hindu and Buddhist temples.

Dash's funeral did not start in the Hindu temple. Due to the size of the gathering, and the necessity to make some accommodations between tradition and the physical reality of the BrainTrust's unique strengths and weaknesses, the procession started in the auditorium.

In the typical Balinese funeral, as Ping understood it, the body was placed in a white shroud. They had done that here too, but they had augmented it with more white: the deceased wore her lab coat, with her name crisply stitched into the shirt pocket. It fit her in death as it had in life.

She lay surrounded by brilliant Balinese flowers, brought from the botanical garden on the top deck of the FB *Alpha*.

The shroud that covered her face bothered Ping. She wanted—she *needed*—to see her friend one last time to make a solemn vow. Completely oblivious to the demands of convention, she reached for the white covering to pull it aside.

A pale white hand stretching from another white lab coat caught Ping's hand as it reached. Amanda spoke softly. "No, Ping. Let her lie."

Ping turned angrily to Amanda, but the woman stood her ground. Ping slumped. "I have to see her face again."

Amanda released her hand. "You need to focus your anger. Build it. Prepare it. Because one day not far in the future, we will find the people who did this, and you'll have to be your best."

Ping looked away.

Amanda changed the subject, seemingly. "You know, in Dash's own religion, this is a happy time. Her spirit is about to be cleansed and purified. They believe the spirit is reborn into another member of the family."

Amanda leaned over and whispered in her ear, "But I think reincarnation is a bit more complicated than that. I wouldn't be surprised if Dash has already been reborn."

Ping stepped back and stared at her. "Where?"

Amanda pointed through the crowd to where she could just barely see Chance standing alone, rubbing her ear and talking to herself. "I think she's sharing mindspace with our own Ms. Dixon."

Ping finally smiled. "I suddenly find myself believing in reincarnation." She stepped backward away from the body and straight into an elderly Balinese couple.

Ping jumped in place and spun to acknowledge them. "My apologies." She eyed the pair. "Are you Dash's aunt and uncle by any chance?"

The two nodded their heads graciously. The wife said humorously, "No poking the body. We're watching you."

Ping looked away sheepishly.

The husband, clearly struggling to maintain a bright mood, looked past Ping at the body. "Dyah saved my life, you know. Rejuvenation therapy." He laughed. "They tell me I'll soon be fifteen years younger." He lost the smile. "I've never felt so old."

Ping helped hoist the body into a very Balinese sarcophagus, a *Singa Mangaraja*—an orange lion with two wings. Normally the lion would have been atop a tall tower, but this was an isle ship; it had to fit into the elevator. The tower would come later.

In another break from tradition, women, including Ping, helped carry the coffin into the elevator and up to the dock, where all the ferries of the BrainTrust waited in polite lines to collect and carry the people on the next step of the procession. Almost half the people wore white lab coats, enabling them to follow both Balinese and Brain-Trust traditions at the same time.

The ritual required that the procession follow a meandering path to confuse the bad spirits, so the line of ferries circled the BrainTrust just inside the reef, then passed out through the southwest channel.

Cremation was the next step. The whole winged lion would be set afire. Throughout most of the BrainTrust, however, setting large fires was strictly forbidden. Fortunately there was a place where fires, far hotter than any funeral pyre, were accepted as a routine undertaking.

So once the ferries exited the channel, they turned toward the *Heinlein*. Soon enough they arrived next to the VATT, the immense titanium skeleton that served as the spaceship transport tower. Normally it lifted rocket boosters up the side of the ship and carried them to the launch pad, a pad invented by Dash herself, covered in graphene-reinforced carbon tiles and capable of withstanding the very flames of Hell.

Today the VATT lifted a winged lion to the height of a SpaceR Kestrel Titan and carried it to its final resting place.

The fire was lovely in the setting sun. Once it burned out, Ping knew, they'd toss the ashes into the sea to purify the departed with both fire and water.

But for now, the fire burned its brightest, throwing wave after wave of heat into the chill air.

Ping whispered her promise. "Burn, baby, burn. The men who did this to you will follow oh so soon."

Matt sat in his office on the *Helios* looking contentedly at the numbers, schedules, and budgets on his tablet. The assault on the *Chiron*, the virus specifically designed to target the Brain-Trust, the blockade—all of it had had relatively little effect on SpaceR's operations. The *Helios* was behind schedule manufacturing the next Titan, and there'd been a slump in Global Express passenger traffic between the main BrainTrust and the rest of the world, but these were mere blips.

He sipped his hot chocolate, luxuriating in the flavor that had been unavailable in the later stages of the blockade. Officially, the archipelago still didn't have any chocolate, not even on the *Haven*. The Coke and coffee lobbies had gotten their shipments prioritized first.

But Matt had had his people slip a few kilos of cocoa onto the first Global Express rocket from the Prometheus archipelago carrying passengers for the BrainTrust, so he was sitting pretty, even if everyone else had to wait.

It was good for everything to be back to normal.

His receptionist chirped on his tablet, "FBI Agent Cameron Ballard is here to see you."

Matt's expression turned sour. Some things were not yet normal.

Ballard entered briskly, trailed by his bot minder, to

stand on the far side of Matt's desk. "Good morning." He tapped on his own tablet, and a soft though irritating tone on Matt's tablet announced the arrival of a message from someone not important enough for Matt to have assigned a ringtone.

Ballard continued, "I have a National Security Letter for you. You are hereby requested and required to run a Top Secret tap on every communication through your Starry Night cell satellite network that comes here to the main BrainTrust fleet."

Well, wasn't that a wonderful addition to Matt's heretofore excellent morning? He popped open the message he'd just received. Sure enough, there it was—a National Security Letter requiring he engage in a massive wiretap. The fact that he was doing the wiretap was also classified, so he could tell no one.

Ballard stood before his desk with a triumphant look on his face.

Matt looked up at him wearily. "Why are you doing this?"

Ballard clenched his fists and leaned them on the desk. "Because this peacekeeper, Jam, who was a sleeper agent for the terrorists until just recently, is surely working with someone here on the BrainTrust."

Matt put his tablet down. "I'm not even convinced Jam really is a terrorist."

Ballard glared in amazement. "She stabbed her supposed best friend Ping."

Matt really didn't have much to say to that. It was pretty damning, actually, except somehow he still didn't believe it. "So who do you suspect she's working with?"

Ballard shook his head. "I have no idea, which is why we need all the comm for the whole archipelago."

Matt sat back in his chair. "You do realize, all the comm using BrainTrust phones is encrypted end to end? I couldn't give you the transcripts of those calls even if I wanted to."

Ballard shrugged it aside. "I don't really believe that, but the BrainTrust seems to have convinced everyone, even our own crypto people, that it's true, so I'll settle for the traffic analysis. Who's talking to who? Where are the people doing the talking?" Ballard stepped away from the desk and waved his hands placating. "Don't you see, Jam is our best connection to the mastermind. If we find Jam, we'll find the leader of the terrorists." His eyes glowed. "No matter where they are, I can have a strike team on the ground in twelve hours."

Matt considered pointing out that the BrainTrust could probably have a team in place in three, but he thought better of it. Matt leaned forward and spoke sadly. "Privacy is one of the most important selling points of the Starry Night system. People all over the world depend on our discretion to talk with one another about topics their governments would kill them for discussing."

Ballard's expression turned smug. "I don't give a rat's ass about those people, and I don't care about your reputation or your profits. This is all about saving American lives."

"Except you don't actually know it will save any American lives. You don't seem to have a lick of proof of your allegation that someone here is working for them."

Ballard thumped the desk. "I don't need proof! I don't

care if it's not true! You must comply!" He calmed down again. "Or the next time you go to your spaceport in Texas, you'll go to jail forever for collaborating with terrorists."

After a pause, Matt made a call.

Ballard growled, "Tell anyone about this, and I'll arrest you right now."

Matt chuckled. "That kind of threat hasn't worked very well for you lately, has it?"

The tablet awoke, and Joshua's voice came on the line. "Matt, how can I help you?"

Ballard closed his eyes in rage.

"Hey, Joshua. If, hypothetically, Agent Ballard charged into my office with a National Security Letter demanding access to all the traffic into and out of the BrainTrust, what should I do?"

Joshua's voice darkened. "Oh, my. Hello, Agent Ballard."

Ballard growled.

Joshua continued. "The first thing is, if he hands you such a letter, do not tell me."

Matt answered wryly, "I've got that covered."

"Second, let me investigate. I'm pretty sure you can talk to a lawyer about a legal challenge. I'm also sure Keenan Stull's company gets these things all the time. I predict he'll be glad to help."

"Thanks, Joshua." Matt hung up, then rose and faced Ballard as if planning to charge through him as he would have in his college days on a football field. "I promise you I shall handle this request of yours appropriately. Now you will please get the hell out of my office."

Amanda set a cup of coffee on the conference table in front of Lenora. "Do not spill a drop," she abjured. She pointed to the pot in her hand. "When this is gone, that's the last of it, at least until the cargo ship from South America arrives two days from now."

Lenora sipped it ever so carefully. "No coffee! And so the blockade finally achieves its goal of forcing the Brain-Trust to surrender." She gave a sly smile to Chance. "Too late, of course. Congratulations on having slipped past that bullet."

Joshua muttered, "Clearly our logistics people need to be retrained. How could they have failed to schedule the delivery of coffee as the first thing? Productivity all around the archipelago is going to suffer."

Chance snorted. "Actually, there was an even more important shipment that did get priority service. The energy drinks and sodas arrived in the nick of time to prevent a total creativity crash." She looked away. "Dash would be so happy that the Coke made the first shipment."

After a moment, Lenora rasped out, "Let's get back to business."

Everyone became attentive as Lenora popped a video on the wallscreen. "Now, even with the high-resolution cameras we use, microexpression analysis is weaker with a recording than when it's done in person, which is one reason I insisted on coming in person. But of all the recordings of all the scientists, this is the one that disturbs me the most."

Hilaal's face, suffused with a warm smile, filled the screen.

Chance smiled at the screen. "He's rather handsome, isn't he?"

Amanda chuckled. "And utterly charming."

Lenora nodded. "Exactly. He's a charismatic leader, one of the most dangerous kinds of individuals on earth."

Joshua objected, "They aren't all dangerous. We've had more than one here on the BrainTrust."

Lenora smiled at him warmly. "Quite right, I misspoke in my characterization. Charisma is like a loaded gun. Whether it is used for good or ill depends on the moral character of the one who wields it." She played the tape forward a little bit. "The problem here is that he has managed to charm Cameron Ballard."

Chance listened for a moment, puzzled. "Really? It's not obvious."

Lenora responded dryly, "If you've listened to Ballard interrogate as many people as I have, the gentleness of the tone of his voice is a dead giveaway."

Amanda frowned. "What difference does it make?"

Lenora shrugged. "Perhaps not much." She took a deep breath. "And yet I keep coming back to this recording. There's no moment when I can definitely say he's lying, but there are few markers at all, almost as if he'd taken a Xanax before the interview to diminish his reactions."

Chance shook her head. "Seems unlikely, but it's true he's pretty calm, especially in a crisis." She smiled at a memory. "Like when the terrorists came through. He was the one who rushed to our aid when they knocked Velma and me out, and he orchestrated the scientists in arming themselves after Uwais and Sabaah had gone up to Wenara Wana."

Lenora skipped the recording to a bookmark near the end. "And here, when Ballard asks him if he knew Uwais and Sabaah? See how Hilaal covers his face with his hands? If he knew this was the most dangerous question, if he felt fear of giving himself away, this is how he would respond."

Joshua grunted. "Maybe we need to put Hilaal in the brig next to Jubair."

Amanda objected. "Or more tactfully, have Lenora interview him."

Chance saw a risk. "If he's trained for combat the way his lieutenants are, let me take the second interrogator chair."

Amanda added, "And we'll get Aar to stand outside."

Lenora continued as if she hadn't heard. She flipped to another bookmark in the vid. "But this is the thing I find most disturbing." She played the part where Hilaal said, "I didn't think anybody had a CRISPIER outside the BrainTrust."

Lenora paused the recording and spoke slowly. "There's a hint of a gesture here, almost as if he knew that a CRISPIER had been stolen."

Chance shrugged. "He could have found out about it easily enough. We haven't broadcast the news, but it's a pretty open secret."

Lenora winced. "But why pretend he didn't know? Why not just say so?"

Joshua sat up very straight. "We need to get him into interrogation immediately."

Amanda tapped her phone. "Aar, we need you ASAP."

But when they looked for Hilaal, he was nowhere to be found. A couple of hours of searching showed he had rented a CopterLyft. The copter pilot, a teenager working for Ted Simpson, had been the last person to see him. "He brought a bunch of scuba gear and wanted to go out to the reef. I pointed out that the reef was mostly dead still, not much to see, but he said the solitude of the underwater world allowed him to think difficult thoughts more clearly."

They sent out search copters in all directions, but he had disappeared.

Khalid laid down on the recliner in the back, closer to the engines. The recliner was made of light webbing with no padding; he could already tell sleeping was going to be nearly impossible. "Sabaah, you were right. I needed to make this a bit bigger." His voice echoed oddly off the bare titanium walls of the cylinder within which they were now enclosed.

Khalid had encountered a rumor that the BrainTrust now had a small fleet of titanium submarines almost seven meters in diameter that could dive to two hundred meters, and they were covered with some sort of acoustic tile that felt a lot like dolphin skin. It was just like the BrainTrust to overbuild.

Khalid's sub was considerably more modest. Just two meters in diameter, it was small enough that it had attracted no real attention when he'd printed its snap-together parts, all of which had been easily carted off by bots and robovans from the 3D printer rooms. He'd been pleasantly surprised when the rude, crude little sub had dived to ten meters before it started to leak.

The important part of the sub was of course the beta battery that powered the jet ski electric pump-jet. With the beta battery, which burned no fuel and consumed no oxygen, the rest of building a basic sub was easy. As long as you didn't mind surfacing every night to blow out the stale air.

But now both he and Sabaah would pay the price for being a bit too austere.

Sabaah, settling into the forward recliner with the controls, chuckled at Khalid's acknowledgment of the sub's cramped spaces. "You should have seen Uwais bent over like the hunchback of Notre Dame when he got on board. Then visualize us with a third person—a woman no less."

Khalid shook his head. "Sometimes I really don't treat you two very well. I apologize. And more, I promise that I will do better next time."

After a pause, Sabaah changed the subject. "So, do you have a plan for this Jam person? Should we have just killed her? Do you want to meet her?"

Khalid was, he confessed to himself, fascinated by this legendary warrior who now seemed to be one of his followers. He knew that from time to time Sabaah and Uwais muttered about how he needed another wife. He was not ready; he still mourned Anjum and their dead child. But perhaps someday... Regardless, today was a time of battle. Muhammad had had the woman warrior Nusaybah, who fought by his side and saved his life in the Battle of Uhud. Would it not make sense that he deserved a Jameela to stand by him in a similar fashion? "I think her resolve needs a bit of testing, and I couldn't meet her now even if I wanted to. I have to get back to work on the next virus." He closed his eyes. "I've learned enough, Sabaah. My experiments are complete. This next one will be the one that transforms the world. Let our people in America know. It shall truly be the scythe that reaps the people and clears the path for tomorrow."

***

Weeks had passed since the much-discussed disappearance of Hilaal, and once again it felt as if things were returning a little bit toward normal.

Arriving on the *Helios* after a meeting with Keenan, Matt stepped onto the High Flight deck. This was currently his favorite deck theme aboard the ship, though Elisabeth, who had done the Babylon deck theme for the GS *Prime*, had graciously allowed him to commission one from her just recently. He expected it to surpass this one.

Here on the High Flight deck, as he walked down the passage, sun-split clouds danced the skies on each side, tumbling mirthfully in the sunlit silence.

Far down, the rendering below his feet showed eagles flying with easy grace as high as they dared.

Sunward, rendered on the ceiling, the untrespassed sanctity of space stared back at him through footless halls of air.

Passing the orbital systems control room, he heard cheering. What was going on? Normally, that room was almost stifling in its silence as the operators monitored their screens, punched in adjustments for the guidance systems of the overhead satellites, or occasionally muttered new instructions for an actual in-orbit shipboard pilot.

Cheering was way outside normal parameters. Matt had a few minutes before his next appointment, so he let his legs carry him into the room.

Someone had cranked the dim lights to full brilliance. Brandy sat at one of the control stations, one hand on the joystick for gimballing a satellite thruster while the other danced lightly over the sliders controlling burn intensity. All other workstations in the control room lay abandoned; if an alien starship started shooting SpaceR ships out of the sky, no one would notice.

Another cheer rose from the crowd as they leaned on desks, sat in chairs, and knelt close to the action. Brandy sat back and explained like a professor delving into a subtle and difficult topic, "See how it's done? Now we just have to reel them in."

Matt cleared his throat. "Could someone tell me what is going on here?"

Everyone leapt to their feet guiltily except Brandy. She uncoiled from her seat with an easy grace. "Aaron, why don't you take a shot at piloting it? We're almost there." She turned to her CEO. "Matt! Sorry we didn't call you earlier. We got sorta wrapped up in the game."

Matt raised an eyebrow.

Brandy was the boss of the launch control team. Matt tended to give her a lot of leeway, both because she was so good at her job and because she had played a crucial role in acquiring the equipment SpaceR needed when the California government had tried to destroy the company. But this? "Brandy, what're you doing here? I thought you ran the launches, not the orbital operations."

Brandy gave him a lazy smile. "Yeah, but they called me in for the emergency since I'm also the best pilot we've got here on the *Helios*."

Matt shook his head. "Emergency?"

Aaron, still hunched over the control panel, answered. "Yes, Mr. Toscano. They're trying to break into our Starry Night satellite system!"

Matt knew he was staring at everyone as if he were an idiot. "A break-in?"

Brandy picked up the narrative. "There's a ship trying to rendezvous with one of our cluster routers. I'm thinking it's the FBI, trying to hijack our global cell network." She pointed to one of the display screens. To Matt's trained eye, the pattern of white shapes and pitch-black shadows denoted a lifting-body-style spacecraft along the lines of the *Dream Chaser* designs on the approach.

Matt pondered the matter. "So this is Ballard's next move. Maybe. What's he think he's doing? If Jam really is a traitor and she really was working with someone here, it would have been Hilaal. Right?" He frowned. "Why are you sure it's the FBI? Just about every major power on Earth would like to tap Starry Night."

Brandy punched a few buttons on another console while most of the people in the room relaxed back into whatever position they'd been in before Matt's arrival, although they held quiet now. Brandy's fingers stopped flying, and video of a launch from SpaceR's Boca Chica spaceport rolled. Atop the booster, where normally a capsule sat, a *Dream Chaser*-like craft rested. "I'm pretty sure that that spaceship up there is this spaceship we launched yesterday. It belongs to the US government, it's classified, and some of my friends in the Air Force were complaining about a bunch of FBI guys hovering over their shoulders."

Matt clenched his fists. Apparently, Ballard was assuming there was yet another traitor on board. Visions danced in his head of packing Ballard into the Black Titan, then dropping it at full speed on the Hoover Building, the FBI headquarters in Washington D.C. He concluded reluctantly that that would probably be an overreaction. "So, you're telling me they used *our* boosters to launch a ship planning to sabotage *our* satellites?"

Brandy shrugged. "Hey, they pay, we launch. The Kestrel is just a truck to space. Right?"

Matt stood incoherent for a moment.

Aaron crooned, "I think I've got 'em."

Brandy leaned over his shoulder. "OK, now just before they latch on, pull her away. You want him partially attached before you goose the juice and flip her into a spin."

The mating adapter on the satellite closed with the adapter on the spacecraft and Brandy yelled, "Now!"

Aaron pushed the sliders and twisted the joystick. The view from the docking camera spun dizzily. "Ugh, can't get loose."

Brandy nudged him out of the chair. "Allow me." The spinning accelerated, then twisted, and moments later a gap appeared between the two vehicles. As Brandy kept the thrust at max, the satellite leapt away from its attacker.

"Good thing we've got those oversize fuel tanks on the Starry Night sats. That was a smart call, Matt."

Matt grunted. "Colin insisted." He wondered if this were the actual reason Colin had insisted. The man was definitely scary, the way he planned for unanticipated futures.

"Well, it was a good call, regardless."

Aaron was studying another screen full of graphs and numbers. "And that's it, folks. The FBI ship is tumbling in an eccentric orbit. They have enough fuel to stabilize, but not enough to maneuver for re-entry."

Brandy gave more explanation. "We've been playing a game of keep-away with them for a couple of hours, letting them get closer at an ever slower rate and using the station-keeping ion drives to put on just enough acceleration to keep them burning fuel until they were pretty close to bingo. We only used the real thrusters there for the surprise finale." She pointed at another display with numbers that looked like a bookmaker's odds: Matt's team had set up a betting pool on how long it would take to trick the attackers into a dead spacer's orbit. "OK, folks, time to pay up."

Matt gave her a forlorn look. "So they're trapped up there?" He pursed his lips. "Prep one of the emergency boosters. We're going to rescue them." He glared at everyone. "Is that clear?"

Everybody in the room chuckled with a stumbling chorus of "natch," "yeah" and "of course." Brandy answered, "Already prepped, Boss." She pulled out her phone. "Aar, you ready? Good. Launch control—that's me—says all clear, as soon as I get there." She flipped the monitor to a view of another Kestrel standing ready on the *Heinlein* with a standard crew capsule attached. She turned to depart.

Matt relaxed, seeing his people had already anticipated his instructions. "Who's Aar? And where're you going?"

Brandy smiled as she headed for the door. "Aar's a peacekeeper, and he volunteered to go with me to take custody of the, uh, saboteurs. Normally I'd also take his partner Wolf, but apparently Wolf is on some secret assignment."

Once more, Matt was confused. "Aar is going with you? Why do you need to go? Why not just send him?"

Brandy looked at him like he was a dunce once more. "Of course I need to go. While Aar collects the FBI agents, I'm going to collect their spaceship." She grinned. "Think of it as a war prize." She turned grim. "Or salvage. Or cleaning up the orbital junk."

As she departed, Matt started laughing.

Ping knocked lightly on the door to the single-bed hospital room. Realizing it had been a foolish gesture, she threw the door open—another foolish gesture since the door had a hydraulic limiter to prevent the door from snapping into someone's face.

She walked softly to the side of the bed opposite where a bot stood on constant alert.

He looked so peaceful there. The lines of his face had smoothed out. She couldn't remember a time when Colin's face wasn't ever so slightly wrinkled with worry.

This rest would probably do him good. If he survived it.

There wasn't much else to see. Except, behind the bot was another door. Taped to the door was a sign in red: No Admittance. Keep Out.

The sign was slightly askew. It had clearly been added recently and in haste.

Ping turned her eyes away from it, but they had a will of their own and they kept drifting back. Exasperated, Ping threw her hands in the air. "What could possibly need to be kept secret from me? Surely that sign is meant for random visitors. Is there anything random about me? Not hardly."

She opened the door and went through.

The room beyond was larger than she'd expected. Cages with mice lined three of the walls, and a wallscreen with dozens of windows open on different displays covered the fourth. Lab tables loaded with apparatus occupied much of the floor space. A bot was quietly cleaning one of the cages.

By the wallscreen, a small cot rested, about the right size for Ping to sleep on. She went over to examine the screen.

Chance's voice raged at her. "What are you doing here? Can't you read? The sign says Keep Out. That means you, too, Ping."

Ping spun in place. She winced. "Sorry."

Chance, hands on hips, just glared.

Ping waved her hand at the contents of the room. "Just what is this place, anyway?"

Chance dropped her arms to her sides and came over to point at the wallscreen. "If you must know, I'm continuing another of Dash's lines of research."

Ping's eyes glowed. "And yet something else new and marvelous. What is it?"

Chance sighed. "Hyperhealing."

Ping blinked.

"She started working on this a few days before the assault. Using a variant of the rejuv therapy—a fairly wild variant, hardly recognizable—she hoped to create a therapy that caused an order-of-magnitude leap in cell repair and replacement."

Ping pondered this. "So if you get hit by a truck or you're shot full of bullets, or—"

Chance interrupted with the relevant example, "—or shot full of virus and damaged so badly you're in a coma—"

Ping smiled. "Colin."

Chance nodded. "He'd certainly be my first patient if we had it working."

Ping looked once more around the room with a deeper appreciation. "I take it you still have some distance to go."

Chance shook her head. "I'm not even sure it's possible. Well, it is, but…early in the experimentation, we had one mouse exhibit hyperhealing. We thought we were close." She sighed. "But since then I've experimented with almost two thousand more mice, and not a single positive result."

Ping grimaced. "Sounds as if the one mouse was an anomaly."

Chance chuckled. "Sometimes I have to go back and watch the vid of that one successful mouse just to remind myself that it really did happen."

Ping clapped her on the shoulder. "You'll get it," she offered with more confidence than she actually felt.

"Thank you." Chance pointed to the door. "And now it's time to go. Get out. And this time, keep out."

Ping skipped out, laughing merrily.

Acting Director Cameron Ballard waited politely in the reception bot's area outside Amanda's office. Eventually he was granted an audience and went inside.

Amanda raised an eyebrow at him. "Acting Director Ballard. I commend you on your remarkable display of tact, waiting for me to finish my last appointment. How can I help you?"

Ballard pursed his lips in irritation, then let it slide away. "Once again it's about how we can help each other, but since our enemies have slipped through our grasp, at this point, there's no hurry."

He flicked a set of photos from his tablet to the screen embedded in her desktop. "We have finally figured out who Hilaal really is. His name is Khalid ibn Tariq al-Tabari. When he was a teenager, he was a top-echelon finance manager for ISIS."

The photos did indeed show a teenager, in different levels of graininess, that Amanda could dimly imagine being Hilaal in his youth. "You're sure?"

"Quite sure now. We got a break with a tentative match between a regressed computer extrapolation of Hilaal's face and the face of an ISIS financier long known to be dead. We then tracked back to Khalid's mother, retrieved a DNA sample from her corpse, and matched it to Hilaal's DNA, which was almost as difficult to get as his mother's."

He shrugged. "It was incredibly difficult and time-consuming to get here, but once the FBI gets a thread to pull on, we can unravel any cloth."

Amanda looked at the photos thoughtfully. "Khalid. A teenage-genius terrorist. Well, that explains at least some of this."

Orbital mechanics dramatically changes the nature of combat. A noteworthy alteration in space-based warfare, compared to old fashioned aerial combat, is the way you approach an enemy you hope to take by surprise.

In the air, one desires to fly to a greater altitude than the target, then come down from behind while pouring on the afterburners to scream onto the enemy's tail.

In near-Earth space, accelerating down from behind is strongly contra-indicated. First of all, it burns too much fuel, which is precious beyond the Earth's atmosphere in a way that is barely imaginable to an aircraft pilot.

Secondly, you're starting your acceleration from a position where you're actually going slower than your opponent since lower orbits are faster orbits, so you're burning even more precious fuel just to catch up.

Finally, there is no handy atmosphere supplying friction against which you can brake. An object in motion tends to remain in motion, which means that moments after you get into position behind the enemy, you zoom onward and downward in an elliptical path that soon puts the enemy on your own tail unless you burn even more precious fuel.

Fortunately Brandy had never been a fighter pilot, else she would have had much to unlearn. Instead, she snapped her gum between her teeth and brought her space capsule gently up from behind and below the FBI spacecraft. She took a position directly behind him with an identical velocity from which she could easily deal with any action her opponent might undertake.

Of course, the enemy was unlikely to do anything since they were pretty much out of fuel anyway.

Brandy turned to her companion. "Aar, you ready to rock?"

Aar looked a bit green around the gills from the weightlessness but answered gamely, "Good enough. Before we do this again, though, I think some special training in zero-g peacekeeping might be desirable."

Brandy clapped him lightly on the shoulder. "Good thinking. Fortunately, I think the FBI agents may be equally untrained."

She flipped on the comm system. "Hey, guys, you there? You want us to rescue you, or you want to die over there?"

A grumpy male voice came back. "Come ahead."

"Cool." Brandy maneuvered over and coupled the docking connectors together.

Aar muttered, "This is being too easy."

Brandy nodded. "Good point. They probably figure they can take us." She guided Aar's hand to a button on the console. "If I call out or something bad happens, punch this button. It's pre-programmed."

Aar eyed the button suspiciously. "Then what happens?"

"Then you probably want to grab one of those motion sickness bags."

Aar smiled. "Aha. Perhaps I should grab the motion sickness bag *before* I press the button."

Brandy smirked. "Perhaps." She opened the docking hatch on her side and floated through.

As she reached the other craft's hatch, it opened, and a neatly attired man stuck a gun through and pointed it at her. "We are hereby commandeering your vessel for the FBI."

Brandy grabbed a handle by the hatch and swung herself through. "Really? You're going to shoot a gun at me in a spaceship with paper-thin walls? Are you insane?"

She spun lazily across the enemy cabin and caught herself at the far end. "Even if by some miracle you hit me, it'll go through, blow a hole in the ship, and kill your sorry asses. Give me a break." She pointed at the one with the gun. "For heaven's sake, safety that thing before you accidentally kill us all."

One of the other two FBI agents muttered, "She's right, Sam. Better put it away."

Sam put the gun away but continued the verbal assault. "We're still commandeering your vehicle. There are three of us and one of you."

Brandy chuckled. "Aar, now!"

They could dimly hear thrusters firing as the ship began to tumble. Brandy pushed gently away from the wall and let the ship spin around her. The FBI agents clung desperately to whatever they could reach that seemed solid.

Early in the course of the American space program, it was discovered that most people become disoriented and upset when the room wherein they floated went "upside down." A few, however, found it just as comfortable to have the chairs above them as below and the ceiling lights below rather than above.

The FBI agents were not among those few who naturally felt comfortable in an upside-down ship, but Brandy was.

So she had little trouble separating one agent from the pack and tossing him through the coupling to Aar. "Incoming!" she shouted before following the agent.

Aar was in little better shape than the agent, but at this point, the agent was the one who was outnumbered. Aar zip-tied his hands and strapped him into a couch.

Taking some zip-ties for herself, Brandy returned to the FBI ship and wrestled them, one at a time, across to Aar after first getting their hands behind their backs.

Finally Brandy took the controls in her own space capsule and quickly brought an end to the tumbling.

Next Brandy broke out a spacesuit from a locker.

Sam, the lead agent, snapped, "Now what're you doing?"

Brandy responded cheerfully as she pulled on the suit. "I'm going to refuel your bird over there so I can take it home."

Sam's eyes bulged. "No! You can't do that!"

Aar chuckled. "Is there anything around here she *can't* do?"

Soon enough, Brandy had the ship ready to roll. Before she set Aar's ship on autopilot to land on the *Heinlein,* she realized she had overlooked a minor detail and called SpaceR.

"Matt Toscano here."

"Hey, Matt, I've got the FBI guys, and I've got their ship, but I just realized I've got a problem."

Matt asked suspiciously, "And what might that be?"

"This ship really is a Dream-Chaser style lifting body. It can't land vertically. I need a runway. We happen to have any runways?" The BrainTrust isle ships, of course, did not.

Matt chuckled. "That's quite a pickle you've got yourself. Let's see what I can find."

Brandy hung on the line, not quite able to hear what was happening as Matt made additional phone calls on other comm lines.

Eventually he came back to her. "You're in luck. Not long ago I would have had to say abandon it, but there's now a country that's more than happy to accommodate us."

Brandy pushed him onward. "Yeah? What country?"

"Benin. You know, the country run by Empress Ping?"

Brandy barked a laugh. "They have an airstrip?"

"A beautiful airstrip that's hardly used at all. The Tourou International Airport in the northern part of the country. We'll have a bitch of a time getting it back to the BrainTrust, but you can land there. They'll be expecting you."

"Yeah!"

She disconnected the two spacecraft and sent Aar on his way back to the *Heinlein*. Then she started her own descent.

She'd flown craft like this in simulators but never for real. Fortunately, the computers did most of the work; the thousands of micro-adjustments to the control surfaces of the lifting body needed to avoid having the ship tear itself apart were all automated. She pointed the nose and went.

Soon she came within visual range of the airport. No one else was around, which was just as well.

She was coming in too hot and high. She forced it down, lifted the nose, and tried to bleed the excess speed, but she still hit the ground far in from the edge of the runway. The other end of the strip came at her at a terrible clip.

Moments before running out of runway, the ship finally started slowing faster than it moved forward and Brandy knew she'd make it. "Yahoo! I'm still alive!"

She'd have to try that again someday. After a little more simulator time, possibly.

15

THE WALL AND THE MIRACLE

You can depend upon the Americans to do the right thing. But only after they have exhausted every other possibility.
—Generally attributed to Winston Churchill, original variant probably by Abba Eban

Dr. Lancaster was now famous throughout the medical profession of the United States for having helped develop and promulgate the vaccine for Blue Rubola. Fortunately, however, he had not yet become famous in government circles. He occasionally awoke in a cold sweat in the middle of the night, expecting someone to spill the beans on the role he'd played. Expecting some SWAT team to break down his door and take him to a cell with neither windows nor legal protections.

On the days when he didn't expect the FBI or someone worse to drag him away, he expected instead to be informed that the next Rubola variant had landed. So he was not surprised when a friend from L.A. called him. Dr. Lancaster was on a plane to L.A. an hour later.

As he stood over Patient Zero wearing his moonsuit, his friend explained. "See the little black dot in the middle of the individual rash? I didn't expect the Blue Rubola vaccine to help, and I was right. It didn't. This one is new. Or is it the one released on the BrainTrust? The UVR Rubola?"

Lancaster shook his head as he grimly examined the young woman. "This is new, and probably just as lethal as the UVR Rubola, which they concluded probably would have been eighty percent lethal had they not been able to counter it so quickly." His heart leapt in his throat. "There must already be millions of people infected, and in the course of the next couple days, the whole nation will be swamped with outbreaks."

The other doctor shook his head. "I don't think so. You're right that there are probably millions infected and they're infecting others as we speak, but our patient here has a severely impaired immune system. I think she's gone symptomatic much more quickly than a normal person."

Lancaster straightened up as he felt a spark of hope. "So we could have a week or even more before most of those infected go symptomatic? They'll spend that week infecting others, but if we hurry..." He phoned Wolf. Wolf was not on the BrainTrust at the moment, but he knew who to call.

A BrainTrust copter that had just landed in Silicon Valley flew directly to L.A. It took Dr. Lancaster and his blood samples from Patient Zero directly to the BrainTrust.

By the time he landed, Patient Zero had already died.

The arrival of Dr. Lancaster on the *Chiron* initiated a tsunami of activity. To the outside observer, it would have looked like pure chaos, but everyone had known this day would come, and Simon had spent the quiet time since the end of the UVR Rubola threat pre-organizing everyone on the ship for this moment. They had rehearsed their rapid response to this situation over and over again.

Within minutes of the copter touchdown, blood samples were being distributed amongst the biosafety cabinets. Some samples went into cultures to manufacture more virus particles for later experiments. In other cabinets, the virus was separated, poked, prodded, and molecularly mapped. Simulations running on immense banks of computers now augmented with a whole new data center on the *Chiron* that had supplanted two whole floors of medical tourism beds started cranking, all configured and guided by Dark Alpha 43 with oversight provided by Chance.

Chance herself went into an impossible, fevered overdrive. She was everywhere, throwing down new suggestions and insights as fast as she could talk. Somehow, in addition, she simultaneously participated in the CEREBRUM forecasts and concurrently ran a batch of experiments of her own, with an eerie rate of success.

Never before in the history of science had the process of variation and selection moved so rapidly. Never before had such a variety of alternatives spawned so swiftly.

Never before had the best selections been extracted so precisely.

Ten days later, reports of Black Rubola started coming in from all over the United States. This time the terrorists hadn't just attacked the big Blue coastal cities. This time they'd hit almost every city of reasonable size from coast to coast, heedless of the politics of Red and Blue.

Four days after that, the scientists gathered once more in the auditorium. Amanda and Simon stood on the podium. Amanda gave the introduction. "As you have heard by now, the terrorists have already disseminated Black Rubola throughout America. The hospitals are filling up, and we expect them to be driven beyond capacity within another week. As we had feared, the virus incurs a mortality rate of eighty percent." Into the following silence, Amanda described the consequences. "Barring a miracle, two hundred and fifty million people will die in the States alone. There will hardly be enough survivors to bury the dead."

With that as a preface, she continued, "Which brings us to the miracle. I'll let Dr. Dixon bring you the results since, as you all know, she has contributed the most to the near-miracle we have to announce."

Much cheering greeted Chance's arrival on stage. Her hair was a mess, and despite her naturally dark skin, she looked pallid. She went to the microphone but did not speak.

Instead, she held up a vial filled with translucent green fluid, the gentle green that spoke of pine forests and the resilience of Nature. "Vaccine," she said quietly.

The vial, even more than Chance, inspired wild cheering.

Chance let it go on for a moment, then motioned for quiet. "It's not really ready. This Rubola is so ferocious that the vaccine has to be more aggressive than anything we've ever done before. Make no mistake; this vaccine will kill some people." She took a deep breath. "In a more ideal world, we would continue to evolve it until it was safe."

She finished in a tone of pure determination. "But time has run out. We will go ahead with this. We will save America, and no one will stop us."

Someone yelled from the audience, "Can we manufacture it fast enough? How will we get it into the country?"

At this Amanda took the mike. "Manufacturing has already started. How will we get it into the country?" She smiled wickedly. "With unprecedented speed and authority."

Just as the scientists had prepared for this moment, so had the managers and planners of the BrainTrust. Tendrils had reached across the globe, luring, coaxing, and sometimes compelling assistance. Rooks and knights had been moved into position to protect and maneuver pawns into locations where they could be queened at a moment's notice.

Consequently, long before Dr. Lancaster reported on Patient Zero, Amanda had ordered Major Wolf Griffin to take a paid leave of absence to visit an old friend.

Wolf stood next to Major Drew Moreno, who leaned

against his white four-wheel SUV with a set of red and blue Border Patrol flashers mounted across the roof.

Wolf took a sip of his beer. "You know, I've never been down here before." He gestured to the south. "Quite a sight."

Before him stretched, mile after mile for as far as the eye could see, The Wall: an immense canvass of rust-red steel slats.

Drew looked at it with an expression of awe. "It's remarkable, all right. Big and beautiful, just like he promised."

Wolf changed the subject. "So, how'd you and your family do in the Blue Rubola epidemic?"

A flash of rage crossed Drew's face. "My aunt died, as did my wife's niece." He looked away. "Of course, they were both living in big cities, on the front line. We were luckier, living out here."

Wolf looked at him sharply. "You did get vaccinated, right? Like I told you?"

Drew's expression turned sheepish. "Yeah, sort of. Eventually the epidemic made it to us, and when Molly came down with it, I got us all vaccinated."

Wolf glared. "You waited until your wife caught it? Are you crazy? What did I tell you, blast it?"

Drew nodded. "I screwed up bad. I should have believed you." He looked at his feet. "I should not have believed the jerks in the media or the people in Washington."

Wolf turned earnest. "Listen to me. You know that plague was a bioterror attack, right?"

Drew shook his head from side to side. "Not everyone agrees."

Wolf grabbed him by the shoulders and shook him. "*You know, right?*"

Drew twisted out of his grasp. "Yeah, right."

"Well, the terrorist hasn't been caught yet, and he's going to do it again, but worse this time. A lot worse. That was just a trial run." He told Drew about the attack on the BrainTrust.

Drew turned conciliatory. "Wow. I had no idea. I knew there was a quarantine and a blockade, but the news—"

"—the news *you* listen to, not *all* the news—"

"—never went into detail."

Wolf leaned back against the SUV, getting calm. "It was real dicey there for a while. We lost some of our best people." He held back a sob. "So the next time an epidemic hits our country, you have to listen to me. You have to do what I tell you to do."

Drew scowled. "Like what?"

Wolf told him what he should do, and why he would have to do it.

Drew leaned away from his old friend. "I should probably arrest you just for suggesting that. But there's no way it will come to that. No way."

Wolf figured he'd done enough for one day. He drained his beer and clinked the empty bottle against Drew's. "Looks like you're empty. I am too. Can I get you another one?"

The voice on the phone sounded enraged and on the verge of hysteria. The Chief Advisor could hardly believe that

Amanda Copeland, that infinitely prim, prudish school-marm, could be so close to breaking down. "Chief Advisor, you have to believe me. Unless you change your policy, you won't be the boss of a great nation anymore. You'll be the boss of the largest graveyard in history."

For just a moment, the Chief Advisor felt a chill roll down his spine. Prim and prudish she might be, but had Amanda ever lied? About anything? Or had she been saving it up for today, for one big lie? He shrugged. "I'll take your concerns under advisement. Thank you for the update on what you think is happening."

As she spluttered, he hung up and turned to Rodrick Sprague. "So, is there any truth in what she's saying?" His heart leapt briefly into his throat. "One thing she didn't say, but it lines up. There's not a hospital in the country that isn't overwhelmed."

The Acting Commissioner of the FDA shook his head. "Only the most hysterical media sources are saying that, sir. The hospitals are filling to capacity, but we're a long way from being overwhelmed."

Sprague sat back in his chair. "We do have an epidemic, but an epidemic capable of such death rates? It's simply not possible. No virus in the history of the world has ever achieved an eighty percent lethality rate. Human genetic variation is too great, and viruses are too specialized."

The Chief Advisor wasn't quite on board with this glib analysis. "Still, the Blue Ebola really was killing ten percent of its victims, right?"

Rodrick did not quite correct the Advisor. "More or less, before the plague burned itself out the way I said it would."

The Chief Advisor felt himself catching an edge of the hysteria Amanda had projected through the phone. "Don't you think the bioterrorist who created Blue Ebola could have improved it? Made it more deadly and maybe a little more stable?"

Sprague closed his eyes and took a deep breath. "I understand your concerns, Mr. Advisor, but they are groundless."

When the Advisor's expression remained unchanged, he continued, "Let's suppose for a moment that just a bit of what she's saying is true. Maybe it's a little more lethal and has a little more staying power." He leaned forward in his chair more aggressively then he had ever done before. "But by their own admission, the BrainTrust's *vaccine* is a killer! A one-percent death rate just for taking the cure! Millions would die! That's insane, Mr. Advisor."

Sprague leapt from his chair, heedless of protocol. "This is the kind of lunacy the FDA was built to stop! Imagine the media headlines if we allowed this poison into the country!"

The Chief Advisor blinked. "Media headlines?"

The FDA Commissioner stopped pacing and straightened his necktie as he regained control. "Of course. Understand that if someone dies because of the plague, it's the bioterrorist's fault. But if someone dies of the vaccine, it is *our* fault. We'd get crucified."

The Chief Advisor nodded. "Still, if only a few die of the vaccine and it saves a lot of lives, wouldn't that be better?"

Sprague shook his head. "Not in the long term. The harm it would do to our reputations would make it more difficult in the future to act wisely on rash medical inventions." He sat back down again. "Let's take a look at an example from history: beta blockers."

The Chief Advisor shook his head. "What's a beta blocker?"

Sprague waved a hand dismissively. "It's a heart medication from the twentieth century. Quite good, actually. The European Union moved swiftly to certify it, but we insisted on being more thorough. We took our time."

He continued with satisfaction. "So ten years later, when we eventually certified it, the FDA announced it to the world with all due pride: the beta blockers we'd just allowed the industry to bring to us would save ten thousand lives a year."

The Chief Advisor nodded. "Sounds like a good thing."

Rodrick leaned forward again. "Exactly." His expression turned sour and his voice aggrieved. "But a handful of those crazy anarchists and libertarians complained that, during the extra ten years of investigation, a hundred thousand people died who could have been saved if we'd just certified the drugs right away. They blamed us."

The Advisor nodded slowly. "I see. Sort of."

The Commissioner finished with satisfaction. "Anyway, the claim that those deaths were our fault didn't stick. Five years later, all anyone remembered was the good job we'd done of protecting America from the overeager acceptance of potentially dangerous drugs. It will turn out the same way here."

The Chief Advisor sighed. "So, stay the course? No emergency certifications?"

Sprague smiled. "Trust me. It'll all work out in the end."

Outside the pharmaceutical factory on the west coast of Mexico, Oziegbe stood before his team. And what a team it was.

Ted Simpson had come from the BrainTrust with a dozen copters. Jun Laquan and Chen Ying had come from the Fuxing archipelago to tweak the bots and help him streamline the production lines. And Shura had come from the Prometheus archipelago with boxes of goodies.

"Chance has sent us the process for manufacturing the Black Rubola vaccine. This is it. Take no prisoners. And get those production lines rolling!"

Everybody ran off in different directions except Ted. "Do you want me to take you up so you can see who's coming and who's going?"

Oziegbe looked into the distance. "I can see what I need to see for today." He pointed at the clouds of dust heading their way. "Here comes the cavalry."

Ted shook his head. "That's just the cavalcade arriving. The cavalry is what you'll need to leave again." Ted smiled wickedly. "Let me know when."

<hr>

The Attorney General of California shook his head vigorously. "No, I'm not agreeing with the Chief Advisor."

The Governor responded jovially. "It certainly sounds like it. I'll be amused to hear how it's different."

The AG laughed, embarrassed. "OK, maybe I don't

entirely disagree. But the guy I'm actually agreeing with is the Commissioner of the FDA."

The Governor shook his head. "So all our hospitals are filling up, and you're telling me to do nothing?"

The AG growled. "Of course not. Go out and walk among the people. Seize some warehouses and office buildings to house the sick. Just don't go overboard and let that BrainTrust vaccine into the state." He threw up his hands. "A one-percent death rate from the vaccine? Are you kidding me? There'd be half a million deaths among your voters."

He pointed an accusatory finger at the Governor. "And it would be your fault."

The Governor pursed his lips. "Well, we'll stick with that for now. But if things get worse, we'll have to reconsider."

As the Attorney General left, the Governor unbuttoned the top button on his shirt. The office felt unusually warm. His joints felt a little achy. Just to be on the safe side, he popped a couple of aspirin. While he chugged another couple of gulps of water, he rubbed at an itchy spot on his neck.

Was he coming down with a fever? Just his luck, to come down with the flu in the midst of this emergency.

Drew was letting Wolf drive the SUV, bouncing and plunging, across the desert paths when Drew's phone came to life.

Wolf slowed down a little bit so Drew didn't break his

teeth on the phone as they jounced along. Drew spoke in horror. "He's where? Oh, my God. And there's nothing they can do?" He listened. "Very well. Keep me in the loop. Thanks."

Wolf had a dark suspicion he knew what was coming. "What's happened?"

Drew held his head in his hands. "It's my brother. He's got Black Ebola. They don't think he has much of a chance." He looked up, staring straight ahead. "His wife's just gone symptomatic." A wild look entered his eyes. "And the kids! What'll happen to the kids?"

Wolf stopped the car. "How can I help?"

Drew looked at him furiously. "You were right, goddammit. This is out of control." He looked south; in the distance, they could see The Wall. "I just don't see what else to do."

Wolf stayed glued to Drew's side all that night and the following day to help him stay calm, to help him stay focused, and to protect him if someone showed up intending to disagree with the plan using extreme prejudice.

The sun was sinking as the last report came in from near the Texas border. Wolf asked, "Trouble?"

Drew shrugged. "A little. But we—you, rather—have been warming them up for this for a while, and just about everybody knows someone who knows someone in the hospital. When your FB account is drowning in people talking about their sick relatives, you know you've got a problem on your hands."

Drew looked for a last time at The Wall, so beautifully radiant in the reddish-yellow sunset. "OK, then." He set his phone to broadcast the activation code.

Distant though they were from The Wall, the ground underneath their feet still shook with the immense power of the endless chain of explosions that ran off farther than the eye could see.

All along the Mexican border, from the westernmost point of Arizona to the easternmost point of New Mexico, the light and sound of C-4 going off filled the air.

America's Wall, far vaster in scope than the Berlin Wall of the Soviet Union and even longer than the Maginot Line of France, fell with sinuous grace.

Wolf popped off a text to Oziegbe, then put his hand on Drew's shoulder. "Nothing lasts forever. What is beautiful must be transient, else it would not shine so brightly."

Drew responded with a more proper Marine perspective. "Whatever works."

Oziegbe paced back and forth before the immense gaggle of vehicles sitting outside the pharmaceutical plant.

Ted leaned against his favorite copter; he'd finally figured out how to use paint over the stealth coating of graphene without losing the radar absorbent stealth properties. His newest creation was sky-blue on the bottom and camo on the top, so when flying, whether viewed from above or below it was quite difficult to see even in broad daylight. It would be fun to fly today.

Ted spoke to the weary but eager manager. "Relax. I'm sure Wolf has it all under control." He looked to the far north. There one could barely make out, in the distance, another gaggle of vehicles every bit as seemingly random as the gaggle here in the parking lot. His voice turned dark while remaining cheerful. "And soon enough, *I'll* have it under control."

Soon enough, indeed, before the sun had touched the ocean, Oziegbe's phone blared the words, *From the halls of Montezuma.*

Even before Oziegbe could read the message, Ted had spun and yelled to his teenage pilots, "Go, go, go!" A dozen young men and women leapt into their copters.

Shura skipped up to Oziegbe as he watched the takeoff. "You worry too much."

Oziegbe growled. "I'm the boss. Worrying is my job." He looked down at her. "You're sure this will work?"

Shura touched a plastic and metal hand to his arm. "Yes, boss. You worry too much." She turned and waved to the men by the vehicles. "Give the order, boss."

Oziegbe marveled once more at the commanding presence of the girl. There was just something wrong about being ordered to give orders. He complied nonetheless. He raised his voice, projecting from the diaphragm. "Everybody mount up."

The vehicles in the parking lot came in many shapes and sizes, but they all had two things in common: they were all trucks, and they were all stuffed, packed, and stacked as high as rope could hold in place, with crates and crates of Black Rubola vaccine.

Most were pickup trucks, and of those, many were dualies. Of these vehicles with open beds and netting, all were four-wheel drive. The four-wheel drive had been a requirement to be allowed to take the job.

Some of the vehicles were larger. A surprising number were tractor-trailer rigs, though they bore only the short twenty foot trailers rather than the full sized forty-foot ones. Even at half-size, though, such a vehicle could carry three million doses of vaccine.

Another thing all the vehicles shared was drivers who were familiar with the terrain, the roads, and the official ports of entry in Arizona and New Mexico. A couple of the tractor-trailer drivers thought they'd made good connections with the guards at the official access points and would go through there. Everyone else was quite confident that they knew a couple of ways across the border that their specific vehicles could wangle through.

At this point, Oziegbe lost control. The drivers, with confidence bordering on arrogance because of their numbers, decided it was time to go. With some humorous jockeying for position, they rolled out of the lot and headed down the road toward the first deployment of opposing forces.

While the street operators selling drugs in the United States had survived the transformation of marijuana into a legal industry more or less satisfactorily, the Mexican drug cartels had suffered great pain. Cocaine and heroin continued to make money, but large chunks of their network had to be shut down without the revenues from pot.

The rise of the opioid black market did little to help them. Organizations geared for the rather simple process of transforming grass into weed or cooking out the active ingredients in a flower were simply not suited to the production of high-quality pharmaceuticals.

So the cartels had hungered and raged at the misfortune of drug legalization for years.

And then one day, behold! Someone built a pharmaceutical plant, an enormous facility capable of churning out millions and millions of doses of incomparably valuable medicines right under their noses in one of the most remote regions of Mexico, where the law only applied when the cartels allowed it.

Early in the project, the Tijuana Cartel had sent an emissary to the plant to explain the cartel's role in the factory's well-being. The boss of the project, a black imbecile from the far side of the planet, had listened to the cartel's pitch with patience, then said, "But what do you give us in return? Where's the value?"

The emissary had lowered his voice as his anger rose and explained, "You get to stay alive."

Oziegbe had raised his eyebrows in disbelief. "You do know this is a BrainTrust factory, don't you?" He escorted the emissary off the premises personally. When the emissary offered one last dire threat, Oziegbe had rolled his eyeballs. "Knock yourself out."

Oziegbe himself rarely left the factory except via the

ferry to the BrainTrust, so while the cartel worked up an assassination plan to bring in a more accommodating manager, a second team of emissaries attempted to conduct a brute force demonstration of the merits of working with the local authorities. Four technicals roared into the plant parking lot. Four explosions later a swarm of bots wrangled the remains of the technicals into the open desert. Later investigation suggested the plant's security personnel carried several devices referred to as Ping's Big Guns.

A number of cartel members tried to get hired for the opportunity to conduct sabotage and fulfill the plan of assassinating the boss, but the plant used something called an Accel testing system for new employees. The employment office rejected most of the cartel operatives.

Ironically, the few cartel members to survive the interviewing process were the most vicious and deadly psychopaths of the organization. The day they reported for work they went in gleefully, visions of mayhem and murder in their heads and their hearts.

They were not seen again. A number of ordinary employees, not cartel members, were overheard the next day muttering that Oziegbe had spent the day chattering about having performed a "public service."

The other cartels had laughed at the Tijuana Cartel. Having suffered such a loss of respect, it was not surprising that the other cartels decided to eliminate the weak player. So they'd formed a meta-cartel, muscled the Tijuana folks who survived the resulting war into submission, and watched for an opportunity.

At last, the opportunity was upon them. When the

Black Rubola erupted, they knew that the factory would respond with vaccine, millions of doses. At first, they figured the vaccine would ship out on ferries, but then the plant boss had advertised for truckers to carry the loads. The cartels prepped for engagement even as they wondered exactly where the BrainTrust expected the trucks to go. Did they really think the American Border Patrol would let them in?

Regardless, if they were going to move by truck across Mexican roads, the cartels had them. A couple hundred million doses of vaccine held hostage for the dying would make for quite a payday.

So they too had assembled a fleet of vehicles. Those vehicles, dozens of them with over a hundred armed men, now sat astride the road, waiting.

Both sides had prepared extensively for the confrontation, but of all the forces arrayed on that desolate road for this desperate battle, none had prepared more than Ted Simpson and his cadre of copter pilots.

Ted yelled into his mike, "Higher! Get those copters higher! The first one of you who gets a bullet in his ass because he came in too low will be the last one to see a medic!" He paused. "We do not need a precision drop here, people. The payloads are smart enough."

One of the girls grumbled, "It would still be better if we hit the trucks right on target."

A murmur of assent arose through the channel.

Ted rolled his eyes.

The grumbling teen zoomed passed him low and fast. Ted muttered to himself, "Which way did my people go? I must find them. I am their leader."

Then he screamed, "And slow down! This is not a race!"

Now a chorus arose, "Beat you there!"

The girl in the lead pointed out the obvious. "Yahoo! *Now* it's a race!" Her copter zoomed lower, and flashes of machine gun fire from the trucks sparkled all over the ground.

She dropped her payload, and because they had practiced this maneuver so many times, Ted was not surprised that the half dozen hornet's nests broadsided the lead truck quite nicely.

Then she screamed angrily, "Ach! I'm hit!" Black smoke trailed from her copter, but it kept flying.

Ted examined the wounded vehicle with an expert eye. "I don't think you can make it back to base. Veer west, and get as close to the ocean as you can. I'll cover you." He licked his lips. "At least it's only the copter that got hit."

She slewed her copter sideways. "What do you mean? You dummy, when I said I was hit, I didn't mean the copter! I meant, *I'm* hit!"

Ted's eyes widened in alarm. "How bad?"

Now the girl's voice filled with irritation. "What do you think? I think I've got a chunk of the copter in my butt."

Meanwhile, other events proceeded too rapidly for Ted to track, much less organize. The main flock of copters arrived, now going lower and faster than planned, helplessly vulnerable to another fusillade. It was too late for the pilots to pull up; they were committed.

However, the cartel thugs on the ground had erred as

well. They'd become fixated on the lead copter and continued to fire at it well after it dropped its load, right up to the moment when another distraction intervened in their lives.

The first hornets hummed outward in all directions from the first truck, hungry for vengeance, and found them.

As had happened in Benin, the men responded to the hornets by swinging their rifles in wild arcs before running for their lives. The cartel members, however, were better trained than the road blockaders in Benin, or at least were more practiced. They managed to avoid shooting each other, and when they ran, they took their guns.

A force of Roman infantry with iron will and unyielding discipline might have seen what would happen next and might have made an attempt to prevent it, but this was not Roman infantry. Their failure to stand together and focus on the succeeding waves of copters led to the inevitable result: unimpeded by gunfire, the next copters released their payloads unmolested and plastered the area with dozens of nests.

The buzzing grew so loud that no one could hear the screams.

Now most of the men dropped their rifles to run, then dropped in their tracks as the stingers injected the Rohypnol that made further running impossible.

Meanwhile, the truck convoy, hurtling down the road with pedals to the metal, trying if possible to out-speed the copters, approached. Ted tried to persuade them to try something sane. "Hey, whoever's driving the lead truck!

Slow it down! The guys with the guns are all gone, but there's a roadblock up ahead."

The driver of the lead tractor trailer responded with sarcasm in his voice. "Idiots. I can ram through a couple of puny SUVs without even noticing."

"No you can't," Ted snapped. "That roadblock has five pairs of SUVs stacked up. Try to ram through that, and your truck'll jack-knife, and it'll take us all night to clean up the mess so someone can get through."

As the truck driver grumbled and slowed down, another voice came up. "Don't sweat it, my boys and I have got this."

Four dualies, each with a thick steel grill on the front end, peeled out of the convoy into the lane of oncoming traffic...though of course there was no oncoming traffic; the way was clear.

They roared passed all the other vehicles and slid back into the right side of the road, then barreled forward, letting a little distance into their spacing so each had some room to maneuver.

The first dualie crashed into the first pair of SUVs, spun them off the road, and spun off the road himself.

The next three dualies each took out another part of the barricade in a similar fashion.

One of the cartel members had reacted with remarkable insight and dispatch when the hornets billowed around him; he had dodged into the nearest SUV with the windows closed and awaited events. When the dualies pushed his SUV aside, he knew it was now or never. So he machine-gunned his windshield and started hosing down the offending vehicles and their drivers.

However, by the time he'd emptied his first clip, futilely because the swirling mass of the insects distracted him, the hornets had become aware of his presence. His truck cab filled with angry stingers. He threw open his door and took two heroic steps before falling to his knees and succumbing.

Once the dualies had cleared the first four barriers, the tractor-trailer driver saw that, as Ted had explained, only one pair of SUVs remained. He gunned his engine and proved he'd been telling the truth all along by plowing through them with no perceptible loss of speed.

In the darkening twilight, as Ted drove his copter toward the place where his wounded pilot had touched down, he saw one more pair of cartel thugs. They were moving in the same direction he was, survivors with clear intent to take home some sort of trophy.

Ted had been brooding for the last few moments that he'd never even had a chance to drop his payload. He waggled his copter blades for the folks below, who fired pointlessly at his copter, much higher in the air than his first overeager pilot. The payload fell away, the hornets buzzed up, and the thugs collapsed on the ground.

He landed beside the wounded copter and its wounded pilot. As he helped her into the passenger's seat on his own machine, she muttered, "So, are you really gonna make me be the last person to get medical attention?"

Ted responded cheerfully. "Oh, absolutely. Of course, since you're the only person to take a hit, you'll also be first."

The convoy roared off to the border as the horizon swallowed the sun.

16

TUMBLING DOWN

I am not afraid of an army of lions led by a sheep; I am afraid of an army of sheep led by a lion.
—Alexander the Great

In the town of Roma, Texas, a problem had festered for over twenty years. The fishermen could not fish, and the children could not swim in the traditional community swimming pool.

Roma lay on the north side of the Rio Grande River, adjacent to the town of Ciudad Miguel Aleman on the south side.

In the days before the building of The Wall, fishermen on both sides of the river caught fish and children from both sides of the river went swimming in the Rio Grande, which at that point was shallow enough and slow enough to work effectively as a miles-long community pool. With neither fencing nor border guards, trade flourished. The people of Ciudad Miguel Aleman came north to purchase tools from the local hardware store, and the people of Roma went south for the excellent fish tacos.

On neither side of the border did anyone pay the legally required thirty-five percent tax on imports, and national statisticians failed to notice the impact on either the trade deficit or the unemployment rate.

The people of Roma used a curious epithet for the people to the south, an epithet that revealed a shocking lack of Texan political correctness: the Romas called the southerners "neighbors." Curiously, the northerners never noticed any hordes of thugs, murderers, plague carriers, or drug runners pouring through the town on their way to invade America and destroy its culture, but the town was clearly one of the most vulnerable places on the border.

So Roma was one of the first towns to receive the blessings of an invigorated national defense determined to protect them from the perils of intermingled communities. The President for Life bulldozed all the homes too close to the border and put up some of the first sections of The Wall to protect those who still had places to live. Soon the children of Roma found themselves looking mournfully through the steel slats protecting them from their most excellent swimming hole.

When the Border Patrol blew down vast swaths of The Wall to the west, the Roma town council recognized the opportunity it afforded, so they called their southern neighbors and urged them to get the children and the fishermen away from the river while the northerners undertook an important project.

Forty-eight hours later, after the expenditure of inordinate quantities of dynamite (because, as Jake, the owner of the hardware store liked to say, if one stick of dynamite is good, two is better) accompanied by the consumption of comparably inordinate quantities of beer, the Great Barrier separating Roma from its neighbors and the Rio Grande had fallen.

While Jake led a team that roped large numbers of fifty gallon plastic water barrels together over the river, and slapped steel plates down on top of them to make a crude but serviceable pontoon bridge, several wives sent messages through diverse social media to let the truckers carrying vaccine know that another south-north route had opened, and drivers would be welcome if just one of them would stop to sell them enough vaccine for all the inhabitants of the two townships.

Twelve hours after that, the first trucks rolled across.

Now that the southerners had a bridge to cross on and no Wall stood vigilant to keep the northerners safe, the people of Ciudad Miguel Aleman invaded America. To assure swift victory, they brought their heaviest weapons: plates stacked to the point of toppling with fish tacos. The Texans engaged in a full-scale defense with an enormous wall of beer kegs.

By mid-afternoon, most of the men from both towns were a little wasted, all the children were once more splashing in their most excellent community pool, and everyone was stuffed with good food.

Both sides declared the invasion a draw and accepted the final truce.

Dennis Gordon had once been a truck driver. An independent driver, hauling cargo from all over the country into California, he had enjoyed the road.

But fate had intervened in the form of the California governor and a truckload of computer chips for SpaceR. The California Agricultural Department goons who manned the checkpoints between Arizona and California had confiscated his truck.

He'd wound up, after almost dying on the road he'd once enjoyed, getting a series of gigs through his newfound benefactor, Lindsey Postrel of Cogent News. Much to his astonishment, he'd been transformed into a motivational speaker.

The gigs paid well. Much better than independent trucking, actually, but he still missed the road.

So when Lindsey told him in a mysterious whisper (very odd, they were talking on BrainTrust cell phones, after all) to hightail it down to southern Arizona, he complied.

Then the Wall came tumbling down, and trucks of all sorts came rumbling through.

He was not surprised when Lindsey called him again. "Get over to Tucson ASAP. One of the drivers seems to have come down with food poisoning. He needs a replacement driver."

Dennis's heart leapt in his throat. "You mean, I get to drive again?"

"A tractor-trailer. It's not as good as yours was, but still, yeah, you get to drive."

Now, many hours later, he was approaching the California border on Route 10 while the truck's owner lay in the back trying not to throw up.

Dennis saw the checkpoint looming ahead, a wide line of concrete barriers with narrow passages. His heart leapt in his throat again, but this time it was with fear.

Fortunately, he had instructions not to challenge the barricades. He slowed to a stop on the shoulder of the road before reaching California.

A goon strolled on over to him, waving. Palms sweating, Dennis rolled down the window. Dennis blurted, "You can't confiscate my truck. I'm still in Arizona."

The cop waved it aside. "Stay cool. No one's here to hurt you. Quite the opposite." He looked back at the trailer. "You're carrying Black Rubola vaccine?"

Dennis's heart leapt in fear once more, but he forced his reaction aside. "Yes, sir. Three million doses. Minus one; I got injected when I took over the truck."

The cop nodded. "Smart thinking." He waved to the checkpoint.

A truck wove through the barriers. "When your partner recovers, he should take this truck to Louisiana. It's full of Blue Rubola vaccine, and there's been an outbreak."

As Dennis nodded, another truck escaped the boundaries of the barrier. He could hardly believe his eyes.

The cop smiled broadly. "And that's another truck full of Blue Ebola vaccine. Headed for Minneapolis. You up for taking it?"

Dennis's eyes glowed. He gulped and nodded.

Miraculously, it was his old truck.

Dennis choked out, "Thank you."

The cop shrugged. "Thank a woman named Postrel. She insisted that if you were gonna save millions of Californian lives, we damn well better give you your truck back."

The cop shook his head. "We're bending the law back on itself doing this, but I'm thinkin' it's the right thing to do."

Dennis spent a few minutes caressing his beautiful rig: the tires, the fenders, the doors.

Then he was on the road again.

Admiral Beck looked up as his adjutant came in with news. After a quick salute, Lieutenant Lambert reported, "Another ferry has left the BrainTrust stacked with crates, presumably carrying the illegal vaccine for Black Rubola."

"Excellent." Beck strode swiftly into his operations room and issued an order. "Get me the captain of the *Vella Gulf*."

The captain reported their status. "Sir, the ferry is approaching one of the California Coastal Patrol boats. I expect them to start transferring cargo in about ten minutes."

Transferring the cargo at sea seemed idiotic, but as Beck understood the situation, the cargoes of vaccine were getting confiscated and dumped by the Customs officials in the San Francisco harbor when delivered on the ferries. The Coastal Patrol boats, on the other hand, came and went pretty much as they pleased, particularly when they docked south of San Francisco in Half Moon Bay.

Beck issued his next order in his most commanding

voice. "Very well, Captain. I want you to move in and confiscate that shipment. Every last crate."

"Aye aye, sir." The captain hesitated. "Sir, if we start confiscating these shipments, how will the people of California get the vaccine?"

Lieutenant Lambert interrupted, "They'll hardly notice the loss of a single shipment. Besides, all these shipments together are not enough to save California. The bulk will have to come up from Mexico through The Wall."

Or through what was left of The Wall, Beck thought. He glowered at his adjutant, then growled for the captain. "Just get the vaccine, then vaccinate everyone on your ship. I'll send the *Port Royal* to relieve you, and you'll bring the rest of the shipment here so we can vaccinate everyone in the fleet." It was all very well for the government to follow the dogma of the day and outlaw the vaccine, but Beck had a fleet filled with personnel to keep operational at all costs, even if it dented the warped reality of the politicians and bureaucrats.

When the captain hesitated, Beck continued, "And give the captain of the ferry a P.O. number. We'll reimburse them for the confiscated materials."

The captain sounded ever so slightly relieved. "Aye aye, sir." He cleared his throat. "Uh, sir, the BrainTrust has told everyone that this vaccine is dangerous. They estimate one percent of the vaccine recipients will die of the inoculation. I'll almost certainly lose a few people."

Admiral Beck replied grimly, "I understand, Captain. The Navy is a dangerous place when we're at war."

The captain responded with puzzlement. "But, sir, we're not at war."

Beck looked into the distance. "If this is not a war, Captain, why does it feel so much like one?"

A figure in a black burqa entered the dingy office attached to the dingy warehouse outside Cairo.

The proprietor rose from his chair and brought his hands together. "How may I help you?"

The voice that came to him from beneath the burqa had a beautiful lilt. "I understand you made a deal with Khalid, then charged him full price for a half-shipment."

The proprietor took a step back. "As I explained, there was a sudden shortage. I couldn't get my hands on the rest of the chemicals. And in the midst of the shortage, the price was fair." He licked his lips. "Tell Khalid I'm sorry, and the next time he will get a much better price and a full load. I'll cut him a deal." His eyes gleamed. "Let's face it. We both know why he wants that stuff. It's not like he could go down the street and buy from just anybody. He's lucky to have someone willing to deal without calling the police."

A hand holding an immense blade thrust out from the burqa. "I will cut a deal for you." She moved forward with lithe grace, and the cutting began.

Uwais waited impatiently across the street for a while, then meandered over to stand outside the office. Within he heard a woman's voice, almost singing in a melodious delirium. Puzzled, he stepped through the door.

Blood splattered the walls and the floor. The figure in the burqa straightened and turned. The burqa was soaked in red.

Uwais stared around in stupefaction.

Jam growled, less melodiously, "You said to leave a message."

Uwais shook his head, amazed. "I guess I did."

Jam spoke succinctly. "No one will send Khalid a half-shipment ever again."

Uwais acknowledged it. "I guess they won't."

———

Dennis happily rolled north on I-35, having just passed Des Moines, while *Rocky Mountain High* played on his stereo. He glanced back in his mirrors from time to time to ensure that Mateo, another tractor-trailer driver he'd hooked up with making the same trip, was lined up in his wind shadow, drafting to make the most of their fuel. He whistled off-key with the stereo for a moment before realizing he'd offended the gods with his poor musical performance. A police siren wailed, and the bubble lights of a cruiser blinked in his external mirror. With a few moments of maneuvering, the cop made it clear that both trucks needed to pull over.

Dennis started sweating as the cop waved him and Mateo out of their cabs. No, not again! He'd just gotten his truck back!

The cop motioned the two men back, all the way off the shoulder between the two trucks. He shook his head cheerfully. "You two are in such deep shit. I'm surprised you can breathe." He tapped his baton on Mateo's chest. "Now, why do I doubt very much that you have a Real ID?"

The cop was still talking. "I'll wager a week's pay you

don't have a visa and passport, either, do you?" He chortled. "Go ahead. Show me."

Mateo, whose English was scanty at the best of times and who generally used the translator app on his phone, just mumbled an apology.

The cop continued, "Let me guess. You're one of the invaders who just blew up our beautiful Wall."

He turned to Dennis. Glaring, he spat in Dennis's face. "And you, traitor. Harboring an illegal. Treason." He licked his lips. "I'd just as soon shoot you where you stand, but my boss would object, more's the pity."

He looked back at the trucks. "Whatcha carryin'?"

Dennis brightened. Perhaps, just maybe, the man could be persuaded to let a shipment of vaccine through. He didn't really believe it, but he had to try. "It's vaccine. Two vaccines, really, one for the Blue Rubola, one for the new Black Rubola."

The cop spat again. "Poison, then. I've heard about this stuff. Kills half the people who take it."

Dennis objected. "We've both taken both shots, sir, and I've seen dozens of people injected. No one's died so far." That was a little stretch. He knew people died from the Black Rubola vaccination since he'd read the bright warning on the packets, and on the boxes that contained the packets. He'd been lucky not to see anyone die yet.

The cop's eyes gleamed. "So you say it works, huh?" He turned thoughtful. "Might have some value then." He finally said the words Dennis had been dreading. "I'm confiscating the whole lot."

Just then another siren blared once and quieted.

The cop standing next to Dennis muttered, "Shit."

Another cop car rolled to a stop. The policeman driving it stared for a moment, then muttered, "Shit."

Soon the newly arrived, much agitated police officer joined them. He glared at Dennis and Mateo, then glared at the arresting cop. "Jason, just exactly what're you doing with these folks?"

Jason glared back. "Just doing my duty, Sheriff. This one," he pointed at Mateo, "is an illegal. And this one," he prepared to spit again but didn't, "is a traitor."

The sheriff eyed the two truckers again. "I see." He closed his eyes for a moment. "Good work, Jason. I'll take it from here."

Jason seemed reluctant to leave. "Don't you want backup, sir? There's two of 'em, after all."

The sheriff shook his head. "Donny and Bob'll be here any minute. I don't think our desperadoes are going to be doing any escaping in their trucks."

Jason looked like he might object again, then grunted and went back to his car. With a screech of hot rubber, he took off down the highway.

The sheriff shook his head. "Jason is as corrupt as the day is long, but he's got an incredible gift for nosing out criminals. Here you two were, obeying all the laws, just innocent truckers rolling down the road, but damn! He sniffed you out anyway. Remarkable."

The sheriff sighed. "So, where're you two boys heading, anyway?"

Dennis answered, "Minneapolis, sir. Our folks heard there's a bad outbreak of rubola there. The trucks are full of vaccine. Both kinds, black and blue."

The sheriff was writing furiously on his tablet. "Both kinds, huh?"

As Dennis assented, two more police cruisers braked into locations before and behind the trucks. For one moment, when the sheriff had waved Jason away, Dennis had had a moment's hope. Idiotic, in retrospect.

"Well, Jason's right about one thing. Your shipments are hereby confiscated."

Dennis felt a glimmer of hope when the cop said he'd take the shipments: might that mean Dennis could keep his truck? He decided to make an offer to test the waters. "Could Mateo and I, uh, take your containers somewhere for you? Drop them off?"

For the first time the sheriff smiled, a thin grudging line of humor soon wiped away. "I was hoping you'd offer. We need to deliver them ASAP, and it's a pretty long drive."

Dennis just watched as the sheriff grew grim. "We'll be impounding the cargoes in Minneapolis." The sheriff paused to let that sink in. "Donny and Bob'll escort you to the Minnesota border so there aren't any more mix-ups. There should be a coupla Minnesota officers there to escort you to the impound location by the hospital."

Dennis blinked. "So we'll have an Iowa police escort here and a Minnesota police escort the rest of the way?"

The sheriff nodded. "Sorta like a game of basketball with a zone defense." He handed Dennis and Mateo business cards. "If you have any trouble coming back this way, give me a buzz." He scowled. "Now get the hell out of here."

Moments later they got the hell out of there, with sirens wailing fore and aft, gunning the trucks to speeds suitable for a racetrack.

Dennis started whistling off-key once more. Life was grand.

Many people who defend the validity of science in the face of non-scientific opposition argue that science reflects our best understanding of reality, and thou shalt disregard it at thy peril.

This is not as true as it sounds. In the philosophy of science, it is understood that science is not about reality at all. Rather, it is about the construction of ever more sophisticated models to explain experiential observables. These models are not reality themselves. Any claim that they are real depends solely on Occam's Razor, which on its best day is still only a heuristic that lies outside the bounds of science, so the models might or might not be true.

Nevertheless, these models enable the making of predictions. The important feature of these models and their predictions is that they are required, through rigorous scrutiny and ruthless rejection via the scientific method, to produce ever more accurate predictions of real outcomes when certain events occur.

The power of these models for creating correct predictions is quite remarkable, especially for well-established fields of investigation. Epidemiology is such a field.

Selena Herron scratched idly at her neck as she walked her guests through a series of questions on her weekly talk show. The scratching did not stop the itching; if anything, the scratching made it worse. By wrap-up time, the itch was driving her mildly crazy, and she had to squeeze her hand tight and hold it down with the other hand to avoid any further undignified scratching while on air.

Finally she asked her guests Robert De Hiro and Hubert Kennedy for closing remarks. Hubert led. "At least when the so-called Blue Rubola form of measles broke out, the government finally admitted that their vaccines don't work. And now for this latest Rubola outbreak, even the vaccine manufacturers admit their cure's a killer. These admissions are great steps forward, but we still have a long way to go before the government will give us full disclosure on just how many and how big the lies about vaccination have been throughout our lives."

Robert, oozing his signature rugged sincerity, answered, "You just can't say it any better than Mahatma Gandhi: 'Vaccination is a barbarous practice, and it is one of the most fatal of all the delusions current in our time.'"

Selena clapped along with her in-house audience. "Thank you for joining us. And that brings us to a close for this week's episode of *The Whole Truth*."

After thanking her guests once more, Selena stepped offstage to join ten of her closest friends, all members of her vidcast team. They planned a quick review of the show, to be followed by drinks at the bar next door.

At last she was free to scratch, and she did so vigorously. She twisted her neck so her friends could see. "Is there a bite or something on my neck? It's driving me insane."

Betsy bent nearer, then stepped away suddenly, holding her hand up to her mouth, then as suddenly pulling her hand away as if afraid her hand were covered with poison.

"It's a rash. A red rash but darker, with a black spot in the middle."

Another friend scrutinized the rash, a tricky feat since the scrutiny occurred as she stepped farther away. "It's not Blue Rubola, and I've seen pictures of Red Rubola from the Middle East. It's not that either. It's…something else."

Just then Selena's cell phone beeped. Her baby sitter wept hysterically. "Mrs. Herron, your daughter has this terrible rash all over her face. Oh my God, Mrs. Herron, the ambulance came, and the paramedics were wearing those white suits like they were on the moon!" The girl moaned. "I feel feverish. Am I going to die?"

Selena snapped her phone off and raced to the hospital, leaving her friends—anti-vaxxers all—with some difficult decisions to make. Of the ten friends, five decided to abandon their principles and delved as deeply as necessary into the world of illegal drugs to get vaccinated. The other five held steadfast to their convictions.

The scientific models that made predictions about the outcomes for these ten people experienced no hiccups. They made a number of extrapolations, all of which came true:

One of the ladies who rushed for a vaccination, who already had a rash breaking out on the back of her neck that had been concealed by her long black hair, was in too advanced a state of infection when she got her shot. She did not survive.

The other four who got vaccinated lived. While one in a hundred would die of the vaccine, four was too small a number for that statistic to have a significant chance of impact, and it did not.

Of the five stalwart anti-vaxxers, all got infected since the protections supplied by the epidemiological phenomenon known as "herd immunity" do not apply when the whole herd is anti-vax and the bioweapon has been derived from a virus that is notoriously infectious. Four died, aligning with the eighty percent death rate Khalid had planned.

The lone unvaccinated survivor took over operation of *The Whole Truth* vidcasting, but not for long. Upon announcement of Selena's tragic demise, half the audience lost enthusiasm for her particular brand of truth while waiting in line for their vaccinations. For the rest, Black Rubola mowed through the anti-vax communities like a wheat combine at harvest time.

The ten percent of the listeners who remained after that did not constitute an audience large enough to merit a show.

In this fashion, *The Whole Truth* brought America a poignant reminder of an important truth: Though scientific models are not reality, nevertheless thou shalt disregard them at thy peril.

The Chief Advisor held his head in his hands, elbows resting on his desk. "Let me guess. You think we should stay the course."

Rodrick Sprague looked at him with sublime confidence. "Of course. The virus should start breaking down any day now."

"And the mortality rate?"

Sprague licked his lips. "It is higher than expected." A moment of honesty intruded on his well-being. "Considerably higher, actually."

The Advisor clenched his fists and glared back at him. "Very well. But we will take some measures just in case it takes a little longer."

The Acting Commissioner of the FDA frowned. "What, exactly?"

"Yesterday the first case of Black Rubola was officially diagnosed here in D.C." It was a puzzle, actually, why it had taken so long. Every city in the country had been targeted for simultaneous release of the virus except D.C. Why would the attackers leave untouched the one city with the power and leadership to craft a suitable emergency response?

The Advisor continued, "To ensure the continuing operation of the government in the off chance this becomes a crisis, I hereby require all personnel who come in contact with the President for Life and myself to get vaccinated."

The commissioner's frown deepened. "This will send exactly the wrong signal to the people."

"It will also send the wrong signal if the most critical assets of the nation die."

The commissioner could see he would not win this battle. "I understand."

The Advisor pointed a finger at him. "This means you."

An electric chill ran down Sprague's spine. "But...but... that vaccine's a killer!"

"And if it kills you, you will have made a courageous sacrifice for your country."

The commissioner pressed his lips together. "Where will we get the vaccine? From some street drug dealer?"

Darren, the man who ran the Advisor's strict interrogation team, had already gotten all his people vaccinated, and when the Advisor had asked, he'd been quick with an answer. "Exactly. There's a dealer on the corner of Fourteenth Street and Constitution Avenue next to the Department of Commerce. I want you to go down there and buy a carton of vaccine packets." He thought about it. "Better get a full crate." He glared the commissioner into submission. "Do you understand?"

The commissioner gritted his teeth and obeyed the Advisor's commands. He also forced himself not to scream in outrage as the White House doctor drove the needle into his arm.

For days he expected to die suddenly of the vaccine, to show the world and the Advisor how right he'd been, but after a week, a curious thing happened.

He felt relieved, knowing he wouldn't be getting Black Rubola.

Khalid was standing at the main entrance to their home when Sabaah arrived. Sabaah shook his head. "It's pretty crazy out there. Almost as if the Black Rubola had worked."

Khalid grunted and accepted the package Sabaah had brought him. "How's Uwais doing with Jam?"

Sabaah grinned. "Oh, just fine. You know I had my doubts about her in the beginning, but man! She is something else with that knife. I've never seen a burqa so covered with blood."

Khalid pulled apart the box and extracted a small packet labeled Black Rubola Vaccine. Warning: This vaccine will cause severe side effects, including death, in up to one percent of recipients. For instructions on reconstituting this powder for injection, see the other side.

Once he'd transferred the contents of the packet to various devices, tubes, and vials, he finally responded to Sabaah's update. "I'm delighted she's doing well. I look forward to meeting her."

Sabaah's smile turned a little mischievous. "She's beautiful, too. Of course, you already knew that from the vids and sims we have of her."

"Uh-huh." Khalid pointed at the simple metal table that served many purposes, one of which was being a dining table. "Sandwiches there. Take a couple. Let me get this started."

Sabaah grabbed a sandwich and opened his tablet to glance at the news. For a while all was quiet.

Eventually Khalid moved some preliminary results onto his tablet and sat down across from Sabaah. He idly munched on a sandwich while studying the new information.

Sabaah took Khalid's partial break for lunch as a signal he could speak. "It all looked like it was going so well. How could they have possibly pulled together a vaccine so fast? I don't get it."

Khalid rubbed his face. "Sabaah, you're absolutely sure you killed her?"

Sabaah knew who he meant. "Absolutely, positively.

When I threw the knife, it went into the throat just underneath the jaw. I severed her spinal cord. Not even the BrainTrust can fix that." He gave Khalid a suspicious glance. "Why do you ask?"

"Because I've been studying the vaccine's molecular antibody factories." Khalid sat back and looked at Sabaah for the first time. "You're a programmer. You know that every programmer has a signature, a distinctive style of writing code?"

Sabaah nodded. "Of course. Programming is almost as much art as it is engineering."

Khalid took a deep breath. "Well, the same is true of people who design these molecular factories. I recognize the style of these DNA strands. I can draw only one necessary conclusion."

He finished in a voice filled with both irritation and admiration. "Dash is alive."

17

REINCARNATION

Distrust all in whom the impulse to punish is powerful
 —Nietzsche

Once upon a time, she remembered, she had had dreams. Many different kinds of dreams, some flying, some laughing, some…happy.

For some time now she had had primarily nightmares. She'd stopped trying to escape them. Tonight, as usual, was Astri's night.

The voice of a man, harsh and brutal, blared through the shipwide intercom. "Surrender yourself to me, wherever you are, or Chance dies. You have thirty seconds. And remember, I have plenty more people I can kill here while we're waiting for you."

She hooked into the broadcast system and replied after a moment's thought. "I will wait for you at the aft elevator entrance to the Wenara Wana deck." She wouldn't go down to them, she would make them come to her. She would force them to leave all the scientists behind where they would be, if not safe, then at least not in as much danger as they were now.

Her eyes swept the room: her uncle on the bed, her aunt standing beside him, and her cousin Astri close enough to touch. "I have to go."

Astri's eyes bulged. "Are you kidding me? They're going to kill you." Her eyes grew even wider. "Or torture you and make you answer questions."

Dash was about to object. What kinds of questions could they possibly want to ask her? But she bit down on the response. She knew the answer: the bioterrorists would want answers about the CRISPIER. There were still things she alone in the world knew about its operation.

She tried a different tack. "They have a whole deck full of scientists they can execute one after another until I go."

She turned to depart, but Astri jumped in front of her. "No way."

Dash looked at her wearily.

A light came into Astri's eyes. "I'll go."

Now Dash's eyes bulged. "Are you insane? You could get killed!"

Astri was already pushing her toward the bed. "Mom, help me. Don't let her go."

Her mother tried to object. "But darling, this is crazy."

Astri responded grimly, "No crazier than everything else that's happening."

When she knew she was right, Astri could be a bulldozer—a short Balinese bulldozer. She slid Dash's lab coat from her shoulders and slipped it on, then whirled, looking down at herself. "Fits like a glove," she announced, "Just like the dress."

Dash reached out to take the coat back, but now her uncle

reached up and ever so gently grabbed her arm. "Astri's right, you know. You can't give them what they want."

Dash turned her head to him. "This is very improper. Very... unBalinese." She struggled harder to get out of his hold, but the harder she struggled, the more fiercely her aunt and uncle both held her.

Astri giggled. "You've been telling us to break the Balinese mold for ages, Dyah." She grabbed Dash's glasses off her face and put them on. "Ugh. How can you see through these things?" She ran into the bathroom and peeked over the top of the glasses at her reflection.

Then, in a voice that bore an uncanny resemblance to Dash's own, Astri announced, "Still, I am satisfied. I do not believe this can be improved upon."

She came out of the bathroom and put her hands on her hips. "Gotta go." Her lip trembled.

Dash tried one last time. "You can't. I can't let you."

Astri hugged her. "Hey. Right now, I'm going to save you." She looked at her father. "Then you're going to save everyone else."

She turned and rushed out the door.

As usual, at that point in the nightmare, Dash awoke with a start and jerked to sit upright on her small cot. She looked around the room at all the mice in all the cages and whispered, "Never again. I shall not be so helpless the next time."

Khalid ached in every bone. How had this happened? All that planning, all the brilliant preparation, all the radical new viral tech decades ahead of its time—a failure.

Sabaah punched him in the shoulder. "Hey, grumpy, get it together." He led his nominal boss out of the room with all the computers into a smaller room with a couple of comfortable if battered chairs and a long couch. He forced Khalid to lie down.

He then told Khalid things he already knew. "Every plan that sets out to transform the world faces setbacks. It was all going too smoothly before. I am confident that when we pass this Test, we shall find the Way." He watched as Khalid finally closed his eyes.

Khalid let his thoughts drift, loose and uncoupled from the path that had led him here.

He had studied his enemies until he understood them better than they understood themselves, and still the Americans had surprised him.

One of the aspects of America he had studied had been their history. The story of the Red Ball Express had particularly fascinated him.

In WWII, as part of the invasion at Normandy, the Allies had bombed the French railroads out of existence to deprive the Germans of supplies. Consequently, as the Allies pushed forward, the enormous mountains of supplies they needed had to be delivered by truck. It was a Herculean undertaking.

The Germans, highly organized and methodical, had uniformly convoyed their trucks in long lines that made brilliant targets for Allied air power.

The Allies too had ordered their truckers to haul their

loads in convoys, to stick to the main road, and to drive at a reasonable speed lest they cause a wreck that would block the following convoys and cause delays with fatal consequences for the troops on the front lines.

But the Red Ball Express drivers quickly developed the lamentable tendency to remove the governors from their engines and, the moment their truck received its load, they pelted down the road hellbent-for-leather, breaching all military doctrine, all orders from their leadership, and all rules of common sense while pressing the laws of physics until they bent beyond recognition. Thousands of individuals, acting independently, achieved a victory far beyond the grasp or understanding of their nominal superiors.

Since that time, the Americans had encased themselves in rules and regulations. The spirit of the Red Ball Express had been left far behind.

But Khalid had, irritatingly enough, reminded them of who they were. For one brief moment, the common people had risen to their former glory.

Khalid confessed it had a certain irony to it all. It was the common people of the world whom he most wanted to help, to protect them from all stripes of madmen who would kill them or leave them to be killed by other madmen.

Confronting himself with the truth, he acknowledged that he had always been a little dissatisfied with his plan of simply killing eighty percent of the people on the planet. Oh, it would have accomplished the goal, destroyed the corrupt and vicious world order, and left a populace eager to find a new and better way forward. But it was so wasteful.

Allah, in the end, had frowned upon his plan. Khalid sympathized. He muttered, "Blessed are the meek, for they shall inherit the earth."

Black Rubola would have left a world for the meek to inherit, but what good is an inheritance if you have to die to receive it?

Could he do better? He knew so much more now than he had known when he first developed the plan. What had changed since that first plan? What new insight might offer a better way? Could he develop a more sophisticated virus, one that would…

And it all became clear in his head. He could already see the proteins to be programmed with the CRISPIER to achieve it. He whispered, "Allahu Akbar."

Sabaah caught the words. "So, did you figure it out? Do we have a new plan?"

Khalid rose from the couch and embraced him. "We'll have to send Uwais' engineering plans to our people all over the world. I had hoped not to expose our followers like this, but with Dash leading the scientists of the Brain-Trust, their cycle time to cure is too swift. We have no choice. We must achieve hyperspeed dispersion."

His voice choked up. "Sabaah, it will be beautiful. We shall truly make the mountains sing and make the angels cry."

———

As often happened, Simon, Chance, and Velma occupied the central location surrounded by the biosafety cabinets. As usual, as the tempers flared and the voices rose, the scientists and bot wranglers working with the cabinets moved out of the way and focused on other aspects of their projects. CEREBRUM, while it had indeed reduced the conflict among the scientists, had not entirely eradicated it.

Chance was nearly nose to nose with Velma when something flickered in the corner of her eye. She bit off a thought in mid-sentence and stared. Velma and Simon followed her gaze.

A diminutive figure in a black burqa moved deliberately toward them.

Chance jumped in front of her. "You can't be here," she hissed. "Stop. Go away."

The woman stopped but did not go away. In a voice that was achingly familiar to those who heard it, she spoke. "Our ploy has served as well as it might. I believe we surprised him with our response to Black Rubola."

The woman started lifting the burqa; she wore a white lab coat underneath. "But the ruse can work no longer. By now he has examined the vaccine, so he knows. Everyone else might as well know too." She pulled the burqa over her head.

Velma gasped first. "Dash!"

A chorus of voices rose, exclaiming her name. Dash looked around the room. She spoke with surprising strength, projecting her voice with a clarity that reached every corner of the considerable space. "I am sorry Chance and I deceived you for so long, but I believed it was necessary."

She licked her lips. "Khalid has been two steps ahead of us every step of the way, ever since he launched his first attack. When he thought he had removed me from the equation, we saw an opportunity to get ahead of him, if only for a moment." Dash shifted to stand rigidly erect and look every person in the area in the eye. "We took that opportunity."

She explained about how Astri had switched places with her, and the sacrifice Astri had made. Dash's face was wet with tears, and her words were stumbling by the time she finished.

A numb silence followed. It clung to the assembly like a mournful fog, oppressive in its weight.

Eventually, after a proper interlude of grieving, Chance decided to lighten the mood. "Well, at least there's one good thing about this." She bent sideways, tossing her head as she thrust her fingers deep into her ear. After a struggle, she eventually pulled free a tiny earbud. "At last I can get you out of my head."

Minutes later Ping came running onto the deck. Wordlessly, she ran to Dash, grabbed her, and threw her in the air. "You're real!"

Dash, upon being returned to her feet, straightened her lab coat carefully. "Of course." She then hugged Ping as Ping had taught her.

Ping danced around her until she caught sight of Chance. "You!" She ran at Chance with a series of fist strikes. "You knew all along!"

Chance was not taken entirely off-guard and countered with a series of blocks, leaps, and twists to avoid the fury of the assault.

Ping continued to pursue her. "How dare you not tell me!"

Dash stepped into the middle of the attack and Ping froze midway through a heel strike, nearly flipping herself onto the deck to avoid hitting the wrong person. Dash caught her. "She didn't tell you because I told her not to. I told her not to tell anyone. If the brilliant mind behind these bioweapons was aboard—which he was—and if he were as intuitive and insightful as seemed likely—which he is—we dared not let anyone know. Even having Chance out in public, knowing, was a risk."

Ping glared, then gave her a smile with the power to launch a Titan. She whispered, "I'm so glad you're alive."

Amanda quietly joined them at that moment. She gazed at Dash. "About time you decided to rejoin us."

Ping stared at her. "You knew too?" She launched herself at Amanda, then froze when Amanda just stood there staring at her stolidly, and it became clear that Amanda would tolerate none of Ping's shenanigans.

Amanda glanced at Chance. "I didn't know, I suspected. I hoped. Chance more or less managed to fend me off."

Ping shook her head as if to clear it. Apparently making a decision, she whirled and hugged Dash one more time, then muttered. "We'll celebrate later. Right now I have to go hit something." Another whirl took her streaking into the distance.

Chance took Ping's place in the discussion. "Well, that was about as exciting as I'd feared it would be."

Dash offered, with admiration, "At least you held your own with her. That's good, isn't it?"

Chance winced as she touched a tender rib. "Held my

own? I'm lucky she's still recovering from that knife wound." She frowned. "And I'm *very* lucky she wasn't really trying, or else at this point, I'd look like a splattered jar of spaghetti sauce."

Uwais kept the motor idling as he sat outside the bazaar, watching the packed marketplace.

The crowds parted in dramatic horror as a blood-drenched burqa glided through with graceful haste. The burqa plopped into the passenger's seat, and Uwais frowned as he gunned the engine and headed into the desert. "It takes forever to get the blood off these seats," he complained. "And it never really comes out all the way."

Jam growled. "Not a problem. I won't do this again."

Uwais was not surprised. The last time he'd spoken to Khalid, the man had predicted this. "Why not?"

Jam's voice sounded tired. "Because he was innocent, Uwais."

Uwais acted affronted. "He refused to do business with us."

He suspected Jam was rolling her eyes underneath the burqa. "Surprise, surprise. I wouldn't do business with you either."

He pushed onward. "And he was going to inform on us."

Now the voice from the burqa filled with rage. "No. He was not. You let your paranoia take control of your planning. You wasted a good person." Her voice fell. "Never again. Not on my watch."

Uwais decided the time had come to move on to the next step. "Congratulations. You pass."

The burqa greeted this with a moment's silence. "I pass?"

"You're not a blind, unthinking believer. You bring more than just a deadly knife to the mission. Surely you knew you were being tested." Though he doubted she knew all the tests she had been given, the most intriguing one having been Khalid's instructions on how to watch her when Uwais told her that Dash was alive.

Often Uwais had wondered if Jam wore the burqa at least as much to hide her reactions as to behave properly. He wished he could see her face as he told her, but in this case, it had proven unnecessary.

Jam had given him a shuddering sob as if delighted to hear that the heathen who'd once been her BFF were still in the game. Uwais was all set to try to kill her when she sobbed again. "Next time you want to kill that bitch, leave her to me. I can't believe Sabaah screwed it up."

Uwais had been tempted to observe that Jam had done no better when she'd tried to kill Ping, but thought better of it. She was already pretty testy.

That all lay in the past. A brighter future beckoned. "We're off to see Khalid. Just one more stop to make, then we'll bring you to your new home."

18

CHARITY GALA

"If not you, then who? If not now, then when?"
— Hillel, first-century Jewish scholar

Matt found himself hosting Dash's meeting in a conference room on the High Flight deck of the *Helios*. He arrived as the meeting was supposed to start.

Gina sat at the head of the table. Other than her, the room was empty.

Matt looked at her in puzzlement. "So it's just you and me, and presumably Dash? What's the topic for our meeting, anyway?"

Gina shook her head. "Dash said she might not be able to make it. Said to start without her."

Matt nodded. "OK. Ahem. I still don't know what we're meeting about."

Gina slaved the monitor embedded in the table to her tablet. 3D diagrams rotated slowly beneath her finger. "She wants to talk about this—a new fleet of custom-built cargo capsules. And a bunch of satellites like this one. And a few more boosters."

Matt looked at the CAD models. "OK, I can see how each of these would work, but I don't understand why."

Gina explained Dash's prediction for how the next attack would occur and her plan for stopping it.

Matt shook his head. "We don't know that that's how the next attack will go. We don't even know there'll *be* another attack."

Gina just stared at him, the way she always stared at him when he was being stupid.

Matt grumbled, "OK, there'll be another attack. And it makes sense that the attack will be like this." He waved his hand across the models of the new systems. He sounded forlorn. "Honey, SpaceR can't afford this. My God, it would set us back years! The charges against the company, the board—they'd throw me out in a heartbeat."

Gina scowled. "The next attack will probably succeed in doing what the Black Rubola almost did: it will kill eighty percent of the people on Earth. If eighty percent of your customers die, how exactly is that going to impact your bottom line?"

Matt bit his lip. "Even so, if I started a crash development effort on this, I'd be thrown out before the first capsules and satellites came off the line. Nothing would see deployment."

Gina smiled. "But you'd do it if you could, right? And for the sake of keeping its customers alive, the board would agree to taking a hit, right?"

Matt rolled his eyes; he always knew when Gina was about to spring a trap. "I suppose so."

Gina kissed him hard. "I love you so much." She tapped on her phone. "Amanda, come on in."

Amanda Copeland, clearly wearing her title of Chairman of the Board of the BrainTrust Consortium, entered briskly. Gina explained the plan. Amanda took a deep breath. "The Consortium has gotten used to this kind of problematic outlay of funds on behalf of our customers in defense of our long term profits, at least sort of. We can pay for part of this."

Gina pulled out her phone and dialed the next victim.

Dawn Rainer stopped at the doorway when she saw the people Gina had with her. She raised an eyebrow. "Why do I suspect we're meeting about something bigger than the status of our isle ship manufacturing business?"

Gina blushed. "I'm so sorry to blindside you like this, but it's pretty important."

Dawn looked at Matt and Amanda again, then surmised, "This is about the bioterrorist, isn't it? Khalid. Nobody wants to lose eighty percent of their customer base. Or the vendors we buy from, for that matter."

It didn't take long to get Dawn on board. Her family owned a controlling interest in their business, so Dawn had no worries she'd be kicked out. She did offer one dry observation. "Just so we're all clear, there's no way at all of getting our money back on this. We don't dare try to negotiate with outsiders before we deploy lest Khalid find out, and there'll be nobody we can coerce into paying afterward since it's a one-off." She frowned in disapproval. "We'll be supplying a public service."

Gina didn't lie. "Afterwards, when we distribute the actual vaccine, we'll be able to recoup some of the losses. But yeah, let's face it: we're doing this because someone must, and only we can."

Lenora Thornhill, Qi Ru, Chen Ying, and Fan Hui teleconferenced in from the Fuxing archipelago representing Oceanic Mining Unlimited, the first major corporation founded on the Fuxing. Things went smoothly until Fan Hui objected, "This is all very well, but we shall require a few concessions to agree to it."

At that point, Lenora dragged Fan Hui off camera. Everyone could hear the occasional phrase as an argument raged, passages such as, "your family," "your people," "the people of China," "iterative gaming," and "seat at the table."

Qi Ru raised an eyebrow at the offscreen battle.

Chen Ying folded his arms on his chest. "We're in."

Qi Ru shrugged. "Yeah, good to go."

When Ben Wilson came in, he looked at the plan, got up and paced back and forth, growled, paced some more, and sat back down. He turned mostly cheerful. "Well, at least I'm in good company."

Matt found some amusement in the various rationalizations offered by the different billionaires for doing the right thing, but Dmitri Mikhailov topped them all. "I am the world's premier arms dealer, and here this terrorist is giving away weapons of mass destruction *for free*. I shall do whatever it takes to destroy this lowlife undercutting competitor." He opened his arms majestically. "Isn't that what capitalism is all about?"

The last person to enter was Keenan Stull. He appeared

in an immaculate three-piece pinstripe suit with a sky-blue tie covered with SpaceR Titan rockets, each alive with the signature whirl of rich colors that was the Titan trademark.

Gina started her pitch, but Keenan waved it away. "Dash gave me a quick brief before she departed." He frowned. "Before I tell you our offer, I should probably give you some background. Back in the days before the Great Depression, there were periodic panics that threatened to bring the economy down the same way the Depression did. Each time such a panic started, a consortium of bankers led by JP Morgan intervened to prevent the collapse."

He pursed his lips. "But when the 1929 crash started, the consortium fell apart and refused to act. The Depression pounded them, and the bankers never recovered the glory they'd once had." His expression turned speculative. "One Nobel Prize-winning economist thought they could have made all the difference. In failing, they destroyed both the global economy and themselves."

Keenan shrugged. "Old news. We'll help, but it'll be a little different."

Ben, Matt, and Dawn groaned in chorus. Ben spoke for them. "Exactly what are you going to do to us?"

Keenan chuckled. "We're offering you loans to cover the costs." As looks of disgust and dismay flooded the room, he held up a finger. "The interest rate will be *minus* two percent for the duration of the loan."

Amanda squinted at him. "So, for the duration of the loan, *you* will be paying *us*."

Dawn jumped in. "And you'll be taking a loss."

Keenan nodded. "Yes, our losses will be comparable to yours for this charity gala."

Matt, speaking from his background as a football player with a more or less head-on approach to life, slapped the table. "Why don't you just pitch in some cash like the rest of us?"

In retrospect, Matt realized it was an odd thing to say, since SpaceR, more anyone else, was pitching in materials and services. Matt thought sourly about how, when there was a rush job, the vendor was supposed to make a premium profit.

These undertakings with the BrainTrust almost never worked out the way they were supposed to.

Keenan shook his head at Matt's proposal to just throw a chunk of SmartCoin on the table. "Oh, come on now. We specialize in exotic financial instruments. You couldn't expect us to do it the easy way, could you? Our customers will look at what we did, and while they'll see just as clearly as you do that we took a loss, they'll figure it was a clever strategy that allowed us to take a huge profit off-book somehow."

His eyes turned shiny. "Besides, we'll show you all how to write this off over multiple years. No reason to take a big charge in the next quarter."

The last bit sold everyone on Keenan's offer. Matt perked up a bit as he realized he might not lose his job after all.

Even before the meeting broke up, all the manufacturing ships in all the archipelagos, from SpaceR's *Helios* to the Prometheus' *Archimedes*, turned their attention to the crash-priority manufacture of satellites and cargo capsules.

As they finished, while Matt stood and stretched to get out the kinks from such a long meeting, he remembered a disturbing absence. "Wasn't Dash supposed to be here?" He turned to Keenan, who'd mentioned she'd contacted him. "Did she say anything to you?"

A look of dismay crossed Keenan's face. "I don't have any more of an idea than you do."

Ben voiced the obvious question. "What could she possibly be doing that is more important than this?"

***

Normally, Ping would have fidgeted in Dash's lab until she found an excuse to leave Dash to her toys, but these days she hung out even in the lab, as if afraid that if she left Dash alone too long, she would cease to exist. Or more likely, she feared that if she left for a moment, Dash would get killed by another of Khalid's assassins.

Ping did depart from time to time to engage in a new round of frenzied rehabilitation, not merely to regain her former skills, but to go beyond her previous best. During these times she always took either Wolf or Aar along as her practice target, leaving the other behind to stand guard over her friend.

Ping was determined to be ready when the time came to act. In the meantime, she prepared.

Dash also prepared in ways very different from Ping's, ways that mystified even the most dedicated onlooker. She prepared for battles such an onlooker could not even imagine.

Unsurprisingly, this frustrated Ping more than a little,

leading to a nearly constant stream of questions, most of which Dash answered happily if a bit obscurely.

At this moment, Dash was working with three test tubes whose contents looked identical. Ping blurted, "So what's in the tubes?"

Dash answered the way she answered most questions these days: in a grim tone. "Three different DNA samples. One each from Khalid, Sabaah, and Uwais."

Ping gave this some thought, then scratched her head. "OK, so you got Sabaah's DNA from the blood on my blade. Where'd the others come from?"

Dash poured one tube into another tube with a brand new fluid straight from the CRISPIER. She pulled on a pair of goggles and looked at the result. "Excellent."

As she worked with the second DNA sample with another vial of a different fluid, she answered Ping's original question. "Khalid's DNA was remarkably difficult to track down, considering how long he lived among us, but with a little behind-the-scenes help, Agent Ballard was able to retrieve a sample from the sewage system underneath his shower."

Ping waited a moment for more, then prompted, "And Uwais?"

Dash stood frozen for a moment, then whispered in a much darker tone, "All unwittingly, Astri got a sample for me."

Ping decided not to push for more data on that one.

Long before digging into work with the test tubes, Dash had called in a team of rocket scientists—real rocket scientists, from SpaceR, from the *BrainTrust University*, and from the *Dreams Come True*. They were almost as mystified by

Dash's requests as Ping was, but they set to work, and CAD images and simulations of new hardware came to life. They stopped by from time to time to work out kinks as the evolution of the new vehicles and systems moved forward.

She put another team of molecular chemists to work on yet something else. Her explanation was almost as obscure as the directions. "The next epidemic will be delivered at hyperspeed. We must be able to counter it without even knowing its makeup."

Ping guessed, "A general-purpose virus-killer?"

Dash shook her head. "Don't I wish. We must rather exploit the greatest invulnerability that Khalid's viruses now share."

Ping shook her head. "Didn't you mean, 'the greatest *vulnerability?*'"

"If I'd meant that, would I not have said it?"

Another time Dash sat in her office making obscure phone calls while Ping played with her jade Ganesha statue. She called SpaceR and told them to hold the Stealth Titan, and explained she would pay the fee to keep it permanently on hot standby "until events require its launch." She called the Geology department and had an even more impenetrable discussion that involved subterranean shock waves.

Ping couldn't contain herself. "I'm afraid to ask what you're doing."

Dash closed her eyes and smiled. "One thing Chance said while I was in hiding was true. I *had* been working to understand how Colin Wheeler thinks." She frowned. "Khalid's skills in anticipating and preparing for the future are terrifying. Ever since we discovered his true identity, I've been working to perceive his deepest nature, to anticipate him even as he anticipates us. I am doing my best in hopes that it will be enough." Her shoulders shuddered. "If we had Colin with us, this would be much easier, but that part of Khalid's plan came off as intended. We must step up our game." She licked her lips. "Step up or perish."

Diab, surrounded by friends and family, waved to the latest mini-isle ship to sail from the *Archimedes* manufacturing ship. The *Aceso*, named for the goddess of healing, was a pharmaceutical production ship headed for Europe. It would take station with the SpaceR port ship until it was needed.

No one doubted it would be needed.

He looked around the ocean at the other half-dozen mini-isle ships to come off the assembly line, most filled with additional Palestinian refugees, friends of friends of friends. Having watched the departure of the *Aceso*, they would all now head back to their agricultural reef to continue the harvesting.

The mini-isle ships in Diab's archipelago southwest of the Prometheus fleet were no longer just residential. Diverse businesses had sprung up, as Ciara had predicted. The most successful by far was the cell phone factory. They had leased the rights from the *WarenHaus* to manufacture older Intel chip designs, a right that the *Warenhaus* had leased from Intel.

In the wake of the repeated epidemics, in order to quell

popular discontent, the autocrats of Africa had once more taken refuge in an old trick they had started using in 2018 in response to Ebola: they had shut down the Internet and cell phone infrastructures so people could not tell each other the truth about what was happening and complain about the government's incompetence in responding. This did not reduce the people's anger. In fact, it increased their anger. But angry people in isolation do not overthrow their beloved dictators.

So throughout Africa, people seized eagerly on the new cell phones from Diab's offshoot of the BrainTrust, desiring both to use the unblockable Starry Night cell system and to avoid using a phone that governments could eavesdrop on. Via Starry Night, popular communications about the plagues and about many other things adversely affecting the government's preferences flourished.

Indeed, the African autocrats discovered that, having shut off all forms of digital communication in their nations, the people now had far better communication with each other than the government did with its armies and other enforcement organizations. The armies hastened to procure phones from Diab's archipelago as well.

Meanwhile, Lenora on the Fuxing fleet had licensed the plans from which the Aceso had been built. He understood that their progress had been remarkable—their ship could already produce pharmaceuticals, though no one had taken the time yet to hook up the engines.

So Diab's people were doing well. And when the next plague hit, all over the world at once if the predictions from the BrainTrust experts were true, his people, through the manufacturing abilities of the *Aceso,* would do their part to prevent the slaughter as soon as the *Chiron* delivered the next vaccine. Who knew, they might even make a profit—doing well by doing good.

Uwais' and Jam's journey was long and dusty. Perhaps the pinnacle was the encounter with a sandstorm, which half-buried their truck.

At last they arrived at…well, Jam wasn't quite sure where. It should have been the Town on the Edge of Nowhere, except she'd already been to the Town on the Edge of Nowhere in northern China. Could there really be two? Or more? She had trouble grasping it.

They rolled to a stop outside a bazaar, Unlike the last bazaar where she had killed someone, this one seemed filled with tourists. She girded herself to refuse to slaughter all these carefree, laughing, ridiculous travelers.

As she watched the bazaar over Uwais' shoulder, someone tapped on her own passenger-side window. She snapped around, knife in hand.

Sabaah stood there, laughing as gaily as the tourists. "Let's get something to eat, then be on our way home."

Jam hid the knife. "Home?"

Uwais leaned over. "I told you, we're going to see Khalid." He pursed his lips sadly. "I don't suppose you would consider getting rid of the burqa, would you? I understand you took it to impress us, but Khalid is not like that. You have such a pretty face. Khalid deserves some beauty in his life. Please believe me."

Jam considered the request. "May I go into the bazaar and buy a suitable scarf?"

Matt was sound asleep next to Gina when the buzzing of his phone was accompanied by a ferocious pounding on his door. The two of them leapt up as one person, pulled on robes, and charged into the foyer.

Opening the door, they found Dash standing patiently as Ping prepared to batter the barrier until it broke free of its hinges.

Dash led them to the bar, where they all stood around as Dash pulled out a phone.

The phone was on an active call, but all they could hear was muffled voices as if the phone were wrapped in cotton.

Dash pointed at the phone. "Colin's."

Matt once again found himself falling behind the understanding curve. "Colin's phone? What are you doing with it?"

Dash looked away, out the giant window in the living room to the open sea. "Colin prepared for this—for the day he might not be available. When his computers realized he was gone, they unlocked his phone and gave me his library of contacts. All the people all over the world who might be willing to do him a favor." She paused. "I'm still digesting all this information, what it all means." Her nose twitched. "This number does not belong to anyone in Colin's lists of contacts."

Gina peered closely at the screen. "A BrainTrust phone.

So we can't even figure out where they are, much less who they are."

Ping answered with absolute confidence. "It's from Jam. She's sending us a message. She's found Khalid."

Dash continued for Gina, "And you're right, neither Ping nor I can find these people." She stared at Matt. "But the CEO of SpaceR can."

Matt backed away from the bar waving his hands. "Oh, no. I've already spent a considerable amount of time and energy fighting off Agent Cameron Ballard. The privacy of our customers is sacrosanct."

Gina went to him and took his hand in hers. "Just one customer. Who, if they were here, would tell you to violate their privacy just a little bit if it meant saving their lives, their families, and their whole communities."

Matt closed his eyes and sighed heavily. "Don't make me regret this." He called a number, described the situation, and waited.

Finally he turned to his audience. "The phone's anonymous, so even I can't tell you who's there. But I know *where* they are." He shook his head in amazement. "They're in Timbuktu."

Minutes later the Black Titan roared into the sky. It departed on a well-publicized course to take it suborbitally to the SpaceR spaceport ship off the coast of Europe, but unbeknownst to anyone trying to watch the behavior of the stealth craft, it dropped its cargo into a steep descent over Western Africa on its way.

The cargo screamed through the atmosphere on a collision course toward Timbuktu before unceremoniously exploding, spewing its contents into a vast circle around the ancient city. A fine mist, essentially invisible and undetectable without special equipment, descended to the ground.

After ordering the launch of the rocket, Dash stood for a moment in Matt's home, her head back, her uplifted eyes flicking back and forth across the ceiling as she mapped out possible futures. At last her eyes fell to focus once more on Matt. "You have another Titan ready to launch?"

Matt frowned. "There's only one Black Titan."

"A regular Titan will do."

Matt nodded crisply. "Gotcha covered."

Gina and Matt coptered Ping and Dash out to the *Heinlein*. As they watched the two blast off for the Prometheus archipelago, Gina hugged Matt tightly. "Can you think of anything else we can do?"

Matt hugged her back, then pulled out his phone once more. "We can send backup. I can't help believing they'll need it."

Ping kept the pedal to the metal on her favorite stealth copter as they flew north from the topmost tip of Benin, where they'd stopped for gas at a tiny village with gasoline sold in liter-sized glass jars from the store that also sold off-brand cola and counterfeit gummy bears.

Dash pulled out the goggles she'd fiddled with when she was working with DNA from Uwais, Sabaah, and Khalid.

She strapped them over her face and started twiddling dials.

Ping glanced at her with irritated bemusement; she was tired of Dash acting as mysterious as if she were, well, Colin. "Hey, girl, what's with the goggles?"

Wonder of wonders, Dash attempted to give her a straight answer. "I'm looking for the fluorescent signatures of the men we're following."

Well, that was not quite as straight an answer as Ping had hoped for. "They have fluorescent signatures?" She felt a moment of alarm. "Do we all have fluorescent signatures? What does that even mean?"

Dash gave her a relaxed laugh. "I'm so sorry. I'm trying very hard to keep my head full of Khalid and Colin. Forgive me if I seem a bit disconnected."

Ping gripped her shoulder, still enjoying the firm sense that Dash was alive, if not altogether here. "Don't sweat it."

Dash amplified on her explanation. "Anyway, one of the things I've done with their DNA is create molecular factories that can detect and identify their unique DNA fingerprints." Her head lolled back as if visualizing the factories in operation "When they detect the DNA, they start reproducing, and at the same time, they start throwing off molecules that will fluoresce at a specific frequency."

Ping thought she saw part of where this was going. "Let me guess. That pod you blew up over Timbuktu was full of these factories for detecting and fluorescing."

Dash nodded. "Even if they're zooming away in a car with the windows rolled up, I believe that enough skin and hair will be thrown out to cause a glimmer of the light. Our best chance of detecting it will be at twilight and in the hour or so thereafter when the background light is low but the fluorescence hasn't started to fade."

Ping looked out the window at the setting sun. "So it's pretty much now, or wait until tomorrow evening."

"Very much so." Dash tapped her goggles, then sat up very straight as she stared off to the starboard side. She banged the goggles in a sort of helpless attempt to fix them.

Ping watched this with concern. "What's wrong?"

Dash pointed down. "I think there's something wrong with the goggles. I'm picking up the frequencies for Uwais, Sabaah, and Jam down there."

Ping didn't even ask about Jam's inclusion in the DNA sampling; Dash had probably gotten it from Ciara, who no doubt had raided Jam's cabin and taken it from a hairbrush.

Instead, Ping peered in the direction where Dash said she could see a trace. Ping gasped.

Before the sun disappeared, she saw long, neat rows of solar panels.

She heeled the copter over and headed for the power array.

Dash asked with alarm, "What are you doing? Where are you going?"

Ping answered grimly. "There's nothing wrong with your goggles. I just figured out who Khalid is. Some bene-factor indeed."

Ping landed using her own goggles: infrared night vision goggles, the best the BrainTrust had to offer. The panels showed up faintly as they cooled rapidly in the first moments of near-darkness. She was not surprised to see one human outline coming toward them.

She pulled off the NVGs, popped the hatch, and yelled, "Quraish!"

Moments later Ping was introducing the keeper of the panels to Dash.

Quraish bowed ever so slightly. "Even here, we've heard of you. You cured the Blue Rubola, correct?"

Dash sounded embarrassed. "We had a large team of very smart people working together on it."

Quraish nodded gravely. "Of course. Still, you make a most fitting companion for the empress." He coughed, then hurriedly corrected himself. "I mean, Ping."

Ping gave him a short laugh. "It's fine, Quraish. I'm not here to harm anyone." Then, realizing, she was indeed here to harm someone, she went to the point. "I need to see your benefactor. I'm thinking his name is Khalid. Is that right?"

The moon was bright enough that Ping could see Quraish's eyes widen in surprise. "It is indeed."

Dash put her hand to her lips. "Oh, my."

Ping figured she'd investigate a claim from the last time she'd seen the young man. "Dash, according to Quraish, these solar panels are not here for power, although his people do use the power to the extent possible."

Dash scanned the solar field. Her eyes widened. "Of course. He's planning to bring back the rain."

Quraish's eyes seemed to grow even larger. "How did you know?"

Dash pointed between the panels and the sky. "Once a desert landscape sets in, the sands in the harsh light of day heat the air, which rises and dissolves the clouds. So once the rains are gone, rain cannot come back again." She sighed. "Back in 2018, they ran the first simulations that showed that, if you planted a vast enough field of solar panels, the panels would soak up enough energy to disrupt the heating of the air, so clouds can once again form and deliver rain."

She pointed to the area. "The field is not yet large enough, however."

Quraish gasped. "That's just what Khalid said." He looked down at his feet. "Not that I understood it any better this time than last."

Ping grasped his shoulder. "I don't understand Dash half the time either, so don't sweat it."

As she squeezed Quraish's shoulder, she became concerned. She looked him up and down, sharply. "Have you lost a lot of weight? I remember you were a skinny thing, but now—"

Dash was also scrutinizing him at this point. "Early-stage malnutrition. Have your crops failed?"

Quraish stepped back, waving his hand and shaking his head. "No, nothing like that. Our fields are richer this year than last."

He swept his hands in a world-girdling gesture. "Our benefactor—Khalid—has prophesied that the next terrible wave of devastation to sweep the land shall be survived only by the devout, who must have demonstrated their faith by intense fasting. He has given us very strict dietary rules to follow until the devastation passes over us. We are storing all the grain we are not using, and look forward to the feast after we have been saved."

Ping looked quizzically at Dash. "Any idea what that means?"

Dash's shoulders sagged ever so briefly before they straightened once more. "I have no clue. Try as I might, he is still ahead of me."

Ping changed the subject. "Quraish, where does Khalid live?"

Quraish took another step back. "He told us never to follow him, and to tell no one if we found out."

Dash spoke urgently. "For the sake of all humanity, we must see him."

Quraish nodded. "Of course. The coming of the end times, one of his favorite topics when he teaches the Quran."

Ping could just bet that that was one of his favorite topics. She stifled the roar of rage she felt. "Quraish, as empress I must see him. I must see him before the end times begin."

Quraish wavered, but in the end, he yielded to the empress card. He pointed to the north, and a little east. "I do not know where, but his home is in that direction."

Dash nodded. "It lines up with the fluorescence."

Ping now grabbed Quraish by both shoulders. "Thank you. The whole world owes you a debt of gratitude."

Ping and Dash leapt back into the copter and soared toward their new destination.

Dash looked back at the solar field and spoke as if in a dream. "He's right, you know."

Ping asked in exasperation, "Who? Quraish?"

Dash shook her head. "Khalid. It's so like him. He was working to bring life back to this place even as he was working to bring death everywhere else." She sighed. "After we deal with him, we must finish this project of his. The Sahel shall be made to bloom again."

Ping rolled her eyes. "And just how are you going to pay for it?"

Dash frowned, then smiled. "I'll ask Ben for ideas. One way or another, we'll finish this. It will make a fitting legacy for a man who cared so passionately about humanity's future."

At least, Ping thought, Dash was referring to Khalid in the past tense, even if Ping couldn't for the life of her understand the rest of Dash's perspective on the bastard.

Ping flew as Dash gave directions, changing course ever so slightly back and forth as the fluorescence guided them.

All too soon Dash started muttering, "We're losing the fluorescence. If we don't find them in the next few minutes, we'll have to wait till tomorrow evening."

Ping bounced back and forth in her seat, trying to make the copter go faster.

Suddenly Dash pointed, "There! I see Khalid's signature as well. He must have come out to greet them!"

Ping veered in the new direction.

Dash gasped. "Cell tower! Land the copter! Land it now!"

Ping growled as she obeyed Dash's command to hit the deck. "Why do we care about a blasted cell tower?"

"He can use the cell tower to detect us."

Ping spluttered, "What are you talking about? This is a stealth ship. You can't see it at all."

Dash chuckled. "Exactly. When we fly between towers, we create a shadow and the signal drops. It's like a black plane on a clear night occluding the stars."

Ping growled. "So he knows we're here?"

Dash replied, oddly cheerful, "Oh, yes."

***

A low warning tone echoed off the walls of all the rooms in Khalid's compound.

Sabaah pricked up his ears. "That can't be her, can it?"

Uwais brought up a display of their sensors. "Whoever it is came in a stealth copter. Can't see for sure that they're heading to us, but…"

Jam, whose face was now uncovered but who had been looking away when the alarm went off, turned to them. "Let me get my knife."

Khalid shook his head. "All in good time." He looked dreamily at a blank wall. "It is she, but she will not come directly here." He frowned, puzzled. "But she wouldn't have come yet if she didn't already have a plan for…"

He sighed. "I don't know what she's planning. Try as I might, she is ahead of me."

***

Dash hopped out of the copter and opened the storage compartment. She pulled out Ping's batpack and handed it to her. "Ping, your pack feels light." Last time Ping had carried it, she'd had a parachute, among other things. "What all have you got this time?"

Ping shrugged. "It's mostly empty this time. I've only got my standard gear. You know, rope, baling wire, duct tape."

Dash had pulled out her own lumpy backpack while Ping was talking and strapped it on.

Ping was about to ask what all Dash had in her pack when Dash reached into the compartment again. "Two for you and two for me," she said as she handed Ping a pair of the metal rods she'd brought from the geology department on the *BTU*.

Ping was about to ask Dash what they were going to do with the sticks when Dash drove one into the ground a short distance from the copter. She pressed a button, and the tip she'd just driven in started spinning and digging deeper.

Ping decided to ask the question anyway. "What're these for, anyway?"

Dash gave her a wide grin in the nearly full moonlight. "Geology experiment."

Dash's gaze turned dreamy as she stood, pondering and planning. Then she walked into the distance, talking on her phone.

Ping caught up with her as she finished. Dash snapped the phone shut.

The metal rods had straps; Dash put her remaining one across her body, the strap running from her left shoulder to her right hip. Ping loaded her pair off opposite shoulders, giving her some symmetry.

Dash turned north, then stopped. She stared at the stars.

Ping whispered, "What's wrong?"

"This is our last chance to think deeply. We must defeat Khalid before we arrive. If we try to defeat him in the heat of the moment, we shall surely lose, for then he will have outplanned us."

The moment passed, and Dash started trotting. "Let's go."

Ping caught up with her. For a while they ran along in silence. Finally Ping had to observe, "You're holding up better on the running than I would have expected."

Dash whispered between breaths, "I've been secretly training with Colin, running through the archipelago four times a week."

Ping gurgled with laughter. "Secretly? You think the two smartest people in the archipelago can go running through all the ships without someone noticing?"

Dash objected, "But we've been avoiding the main promenades."

Ping continued to laugh for a long time as they trotted along.

***

They had planted the second stick and trotted a fair way when Dash spasmed to a stop.

Ping backpedaled and came next to her, ready to grab her if she fell.

Dash shuddered. "I know his next plan."

Ping put a hand on her shoulder to try to comfort her.

"He's going to tie the virus to fat cells. People suffering from malnutrition will barely experience the symptoms of the disease, although they will become carriers. But the wealthy parts of the world will suffer the effects of a virulence that makes even Black Rubola look like a pale imitation."

Ping whispered in horrified awe, "Blessed are the meek, for they shall inherit the earth."

Dash slowly straightened up. "It's brilliant in its own way. Even in the nations that stand forever on the brink of starvation, this will wipe out the elite—the corrupt and vile politicians, dictators, and oligarchs. And of course, it will leave the nations Khalid hates the most, from America to Israel, effectively wiped clean of human life. Western civilization will cease to exist." She closed her eyes for a moment, then leaned forward into a run.

Khalid stopped pacing for a moment and gazed unseeing at the ceiling in wonderment. "I know her plan. She's going to play my people off against each other." He laughed. "Clever girl."

Jam had already traded her usual clothes for a set of black tights. She swung her blade. "Not as clever as this is sharp."

Khalid's tone now matched Jam's. "This is going to be more difficult than I'd planned, but we will prevail."

All four of them chorused, "Allahu Akbar."

19

FIRE AND BRIMSTONE

And there Rained a Ghastly Dew from the Nations' Airy
Navies Grappling in the Central Blue
— Alfred Tennyson, *Locksley Hall,* 1835

They were planting the third stick when Dash's phone rang. She answered, "Chief Hart? Why are you calling? I'm in the middle of something here and must not be interrupted."

Chief Hart choked on laughter. "I'll bet you are. Vasily and I just landed on the European spaceport ship and took a copter down to Africa. We're heading for Timbuktu as fast as we can go." He explained proudly, "We're your backup."

At that moment, Dash's phone rang with a second call. With a sound of exasperation, Dash apologized to Hart and put him on hold.

Wolf was on the other line. "Dash, Aar and I took the

next Global Express out after you left. We're south of Timbuktu, heading your way. We're your backup."

Ping's phone added to the chorus. She rolled her eyes. "I have such a bad feeling about this," she said as she put the phone on speaker for Dash.

Rubinelle's voice came through crisp and enthusiastic. "Empress, I have a battalion of my best women with me, and we are making haste as our trucks permit. We've crossed the border into Mali. Please hold your assault until we get there. We're your backup."

Dash put her hand to forehead and squeezed her temples. "Let's get you all on a conference call."

Moments later all the voices were talking at the same time. Dash overrode them. "Halt. Listen. We are now far from Timbuktu. We are at Khalid's hideout." She gave the coordinates. "Now listen carefully. I need you all to stop an hour's distance from here."

Wolf complained, "But we can help."

Hart, seeing where this was going, tried a different tack. "Ping, please tell Dash to let us help."

Rubinelle came from yet another direction. "Empress, you cannot deny us our part in this heroic battle."

Ping just looked at Dash and shrugged.

Dash shook her head. "You must listen to me. Understand that Khalid can kill all of you with a flick of his finger."

Wolf objected. "You don't know that."

Dash's voice turned cold. "I know that because if it were me, I could kill you all with a flick of *my* finger."

For the first time, true silence reigned.

Dash continued, "If a larger ground assault can help, I

will call you." Her voice cracked. "But I cannot protect you all. I will be hard-pressed to protect just Ping and myself."

Vasily interrupted, "And Jam."

Dash smiled. "Of course." Her voice became distant. "Besides, I have already called for support."

Rubinelle objected, "What can someone else offer that we cannot?"

Dash's voice remained distant, although now the air of detachment had a terrifying edge. "I have called for the Inferno. We are to be joined by Hell on Earth."

⁕

Toni wove her entire squadron of Israeli F35 fighters through the briar patch of Egypt's numerous radar systems. It took time and patience, and an annoying amount of paying attention to the instructions of her weapons officer in the back cockpit of her F35 Adir.

Toni just wanted to throw her engines to max power and plow through while screaming, "Leave us alone! We're not here for you!"

But threading this needle made vastly more sense, and Dash had given her enough advance warning that she could take her time.

Really, there was no point in hurrying anyway, because as of yet Dash had no precise target coordinates, only the general location where her bombing run would take place.

She had just breathed a sigh of relief, having cleared the obstacle path, when a warning tone told her an acquisition radar had nailed her.

Dammit! Now she'd have to tell half her people to drop

their external fuel tanks and fight a rear engagement to give her a chance to reach the real target.

For just a moment, she wished there was a way to talk to the Egyptians cruising up her tailpipe and make them listen to reason.

Then a familiar voice intruded on her headphones on a private channel—an Egyptian voice from years before. "Hey, Stormfront. Guess who's on your tail?"

Toni ran her tongue over her teeth. "Hi, Jetstream."

Toni sat at a small table in a cafeteria on the *BrainTrust University*, scraping a teaspoon across the surface of her raspberry ice cream. She then drove the teaspoon through her lemon cake and put the blended confection in her mouth. She licked the teaspoon luxuriously as she stared across the table at her wingman, whom she would probably have to kill someday.

Decades before Toni Shatzki, call sign Stormfront, met Rabi el-Hasan, call sign Jetstream, America had periodically hosted pilots from all over its far-flung network of Cold War allies for its Red Flag exercises outside Nellis AFB. Since allied status was an inconstant and fluctuating matter of political vagary, the formation of these polyglot international teams occasionally yielded peculiar results, such as when the Israeli and Egyptian fighter pilots flew on joint missions into mock combat.

As America withdrew from the world, it looked likely that this remarkable confluence of usual enemies would come to a sad demise.

But Colin Wheeler had stepped in to offer a neutral place where such people could come together and get to know one another, all in the course of brutal shared combat.

The BrainTrust, of course, had no airfields. They could not duplicate the marvels of Nellis and Red Flag. But they did have the best simulators on the planet. It was enough. Generations of pilots from all over the world, including Egypt and Israel, learned strategy and tactics from one another in a place devoid of national politics.

In this fashion, just like their fathers before them, Captain Toni Shatzki and Captain Rabi el-Hasan had met.

Rabi watched Toni linger over her raspberry ice cream and lemon cake, then took a thick scoop of his lemon ice cream and combined it with his raspberry cake. "Mine's better," he asserted.

Toni chuckled. "After you mash them together, they're probably the same."

Rabi swallowed his spoonful of dessert. "We were great today." They'd wiped the floor with their opponents, a team of American and British flyers. "Of course, we'll be even better tomorrow when you're the wingman and I'm the lead."

Toni pointed her spoon at him. "Fat chance. Though I'll still be able to compensate for your mistakes."

Rabi sighed. "You know, someday we may meet in the air. For real."

Toni twitched her nose. "I sure hope not. I'd hate to have to shoot you down."

Rabi laughed. "Not a chance. I hear they're sticking you

in one of those slugs with a second cockpit. You won't be able to shoot anybody except the grunts on the ground."

A glint appeared in Toni's eye. "Won't matter what kind of plane I've got. If we meet in the sky, I'll leave you kissing the flames from my afterburners."

Rabi leaned forward. "I certainly hope so. How else am I going to get a missile shot straight up your tailpipe?" A moment of honesty made him blurt, "You know, it would really be interesting to find out which one of us is actually better."

So here they were on the battlefield together for real at last.

Toni shook her head. "Jetstream, we're just about out of here. I don't suppose you could cut us a little slack and let us go?"

Jetstream chuckled. "Is there any Egyptian airspace you *didn't* violate to get here? I'm thinking you've done a powerful lot of corkscrewing between one thing and another."

Toni figured a little trash talk wouldn't hurt. "So, you're finally getting to look up my skirt. Like the view?"

Jetstream chuckled. "Love the view. You should eject now, or I'll kill your sorry ass."

Toni chuckled in reply. "Funny, I was going to say the same thing." She asked, ever so casually, "By the by, how did you find this channel for talking with me, anyway?"

Rabi dropped the trash talk and answered with puzzlement, "Some girl called me on *my* private channel. Told me Colin Wheeler needed a favor."

Toni smiled. "That would be Dash. Dr. Dash to you. Or perhaps just Dash; I'll introduce you sometime. She's taken over for Colin while he's in a coma."

"Ah. Well, that explains some of it."

Toni took a deep breath. "Dare I ask what favor she requested of you?"

Toni could almost hear him shaking his head the way he used to do when she was flying as his wingman. "She told me to tell you to tell me the absolute truth. She told me that I should then believe you."

At this, Toni shook her head the way she used to do when he was flying as her wingman. "Sounds like Dash. I'm going to tell you the truth." She paused. "And Jetstream, for the sake of all of us, you better believe me."

Silence filled the channel for a moment. "Stormfront, I have never known you to lie."

So Stormfront told Jetstream the truth about the man named Khalid who had set out to destroy the world, and the plagues he had released, and the plagues he had planned, and how, if Rabi survived, he would regret it because he would have to bury everyone in his family. But there was no need to worry, because Stormfront was carrying a thermobaric bomb, a weapon specifically designed to pour hellfire through complex cavern and tunnel systems. That bomb had Khalid's name on it.

More silence answered Toni's explanations. At last, Rabi replied, "So I guess we'll have to wait until another day to find out who's really the best."

The tension in Toni's shoulders had started to leak away when a new set of threat alarms went off.

Rabi heard them over the comm. "What's that?"

Toni groaned. "Libyans."

Rabi responded, "Where?"

Toni gave him the heading and the distance.

Rabi swore using a language Toni did not understand and her translator could not translate. "How did you find them?"

Toni laughed. "Oh, Jetstream, do you really expect me to answer that?" She paused. "So, decide. Get off my tail, or I'll have to take you out before I take on those idiots."

Jetstream's laugh came from deep in his gut. "You go deal with Khalid. I've got the Libyans."

They set up a comm channel shared by all the Israeli and Egyptian fighter pilots. The Egyptians peeled off as Rabi explained to his people that they were under new orders, and, unbelievable as it might seem, they were working with the Israelis. There was a modicum of grumbling, but the chance to shoot down some Libyans seemed to mollify most of them.

The battle was as short as it was ferocious. At one point an Israeli pilot with his far superior integrated sensor network told an Egyptian pilot how to maneuver to avoid getting a missile in his engine flare. The Egyptian followed the recommendation and survived.

Rabi came back on the line. "OK, Stormfront, that's it. We're all bingo fuel here. Furthermore, I have to hurry to help set up my own court-martial for helping you. Clear skies."

As the Egyptians departed, all the Israeli fighter pilots

broadcast compliments for the Egyptians on their skill and bravery. Almost half of those compliments were even sincere.

While Ping planted the fourth and final metal rod, Dash pulled a pair of boxes out of her backpack and fiddled with a phone app that controlled them. Both devices whirred so softly they could barely be heard in the night that was silent save the sound of the digging tip of the rod.

Ping looked up from her labors. "Dare I ask what your boxes are?"

Dash answered without taking her eyes from her work. "These are miniaturized, simplified CRISPIERs. We're using these to manufacture the vaccines at our pharmaceutical factories."

One of the boxes went silent, and Dash attached a glass sphere encased in metal lacework to the box. A fine dust, a powder of particles so microscopic they danced even in the still air of the sphere, poured across.

Having finished with the rod, Ping leaned over and peered at the powder. "Pink? It's hard to tell with just moonlight."

Dash confirmed. "Pink it is." The other box finished, and Dash attached a second glass sphere.

Ping watched this one as well. "Black."

Dash's voice fell. "Oh, yes."

Ping stood up suddenly. "So, this little box can produce the cure, but it can also produce the virus."

Dash disconnected the boxes and returned them to her

backpack. She hefted the spheres, one in each hand. "A classic double-edged sword, is it not?"

Ping had a thought. "So, could you, like, cure the common cold with these things?"

Dash looked at her with startled eyes. "Why, of course."

Ping pushed. "So you could make like, a trillion dollars with this?"

Dash frowned. "I suppose. But would it be as important as rejuvenation?"

Ping shrugged. "If it only took you a few days…"

Dash sighed. "I could get another intern and set her to work on it." She grumbled, "I really do have to learn to delegate more."

Ping looked around. "What next?"

Dash waved a hand with a sphere in it. "The entrance to Khalid's cavern system is over there."

They started to run again. Ping asked, "You want me to carry your spheres?"

Dash answered with surprising abruptness, "These are mine."

***

Sabaah stared in amazement at the feeds from outside. "How could she possibly know where our main entrance is?" He scowled, and pointed at Jam. "How did you tell her?"

Jam chuckled. "You've been watching me like a hawk since we left Timbuktu. How did you miss it, whatever I did?" A bemused expression came to her. "As for how she figured it out…"

At this point, both Khalid and Jam shrugged their shoulders and in unison said, "It's Dash."

They watched as Dash and Ping paused for a moment, deciphering the doorway. It hardly slowed them down. Uwais offered, "I presume you want her to come in. Otherwise, you'd have locked it from the inside."

Khalid nodded. "And she knew I'd leave it unlocked, which is why she didn't bring explosives. She thinks she can defeat us here in our home."

Sabaah asked the obvious question. "Can she? Defeat us here?"

Dash answered Ping, "Not a chance. We cannot defeat them here. But I hope they can be persuaded."

Ping asked the obvious question. "Can they? Be persuaded?"

Khalid answered Sabaah, "Not a chance. I will fail to persuade her, but…"

Dash answered Ping, "The world's future would be so much brighter. I have to try."

Khalid answered Sabaah, "The world's future would be so much brighter. I have to try."

Ping pressed the issue. "That's all very well, but what will we do if you can't persuade them?"

Dash slowed to a stop in the long tunnel which, as she'd already explained to Ping, was long enough and deep enough so bombs could not reach the heart of Khalid's bunker. She reiterated the question. "What if we can't persuade them?"

Ping watched as Dash's eyes lost focus—as she turned inward and looked at all the horror around the world, the horrors that Khalid had already unleashed and would repeat if given the chance. Ping shivered as she realized that Dash, of all the people of Earth, could visualize that vast sweep of calamity more clearly than any person could bear.

The little girl ran her fingers over the cold gray tombstone.

Her new mother looked at her tablet. "This is your great-aunt, Louise Hall Goldstein, just where you told us she'd be." She watched as Willa shifted her hands to run them over the next tombstone. "And this is where your mom is."

Willa's new father added, "And your dad is right next to

her."

In a little while, Willa finished touching the markers. "Can I run some in the park?"

Willa's new mom and dad looked at each other forlornly. As the Black Rubola epidemic ended, the number of dead parents and dead children had grown to the point where a new online matchmaking service had arisen.

Willa's parents were gone, and her new parents had themselves lost their little girl, so the service had brought them together. Technically the match was illegal; no long, costly vetting process by the government had endorsed the new family, but at least for the moment, no one was paying much attention.

The father figured out how to answer Willa's request to run in the park. He turned to his wife. "You stand here. Willa, you'll start from Mom, then, when I shout, you'll run to me, OK?"

Willa smiled brightly. "OK!"

They started with a short distance, then the parents moved farther and farther apart, shouting for her. Willa laughed as she ran between them. "I think the park is even bigger than it used to be."

Neither parent answered.

Eventually Willa stumbled. The mom called a halt. "That's enough."

Each parent grabbed one of Willa's hands and swung her into the air. "Whee!"

Before they walked back to the car, her mom caressed Willa's cheek, rough with thick scars from the rubola rash.

Most little girls would have been upset if they had suffered such severe damage to their faces. Willa didn't care for the same reason she thought the cemetery still had wide open spaces even though the land was actually packed end to end with graves and tombstones.

She was blind.

———

Dash's eyes refocused with grim intent. "If we cannot persuade him, if we must instead stop him, then…" Her breathing became irregular, and she whispered, "Then I will kill him."

Her voice acquired a core of steel. "You must leave him to me. I shall decide his fate. He is mine."

They came to the inner door. A blast door, for all intents and purposes.

Dash stepped close to the barrier and inspected it. She handed one of the spheres to Ping so she could run a finger across the door and tap it ever so gently. "Titanium, microscopic honeycomb. Like the Titan but much thicker." Her finger ran down a perfectly smooth section in a straight line. "Manufactured in pieces, each of which is small enough to be carried by two people. See the seam?"

Ping blinked. As far as she could tell, the surface was perfect.

Dash breathed a last comment. "Just as I would have done it."

She reached down and pulled a tab on her sphere. A thin sheet of plastic slid out from between the metal lattice and the inner glass sphere. Ping could see tiny metal spikes in contact with the glass: throwing the sphere, or dropping the sphere, or even just closing your hand convulsively on the sphere, would shatter it and propel the contents to every point of the compass.

Dash gingerly removed the tab from the sphere Ping held, then took the sphere very gingerly back.

Ping took a deep breath. "This is it, then. Ready?"

Dash stood calmly, waiting.

Ping pressed the button to slide the thick titanium barrier out of the way.

———

Khalid watched them slow down as they reached the blast door. "This is it, then." He pulled out his phone and broadcast a final message to all of his people all over the world, then looked at his compatriots. "Ready."

———

All over the world, the believers in the Herald of the Mahdi received The Word.

They had finished their work with their leased 3D printers long before, then waited. Finally, the last part they needed had arrived: large translucent cylinders labeled Grape CoolAde. They handled the cylinders ever so carefully, for if the extremely fine purple powder ever got out, the surprise would be ruined and the end times would not come.

CoolAde loaded, they had waited some more, knowing that patience would be rewarded.

Then Khalid's final broadcast reached them, and they embarked on their final mission.

Around the world, medium-range missiles built to Uwais' specs took to the air. They flew from boats, from ghettos, and from isolated mountains and forests. These missiles were not as elegant or refined or reliable as the rockets of SpaceR, but they didn't have to be. Like the rockets of the Palestinians in the 90s, they were barely good enough to do a job, and that was good enough.

Not all the missiles were launched by followers of the Herald. Diverse groups of radicals, disaffected or disenfranchised, participated with varying levels of understanding of the consequences.

In southern America, most of the neo-Nazis were happy with the policies of the President for Life. However, one group of Neo-Nazi survivalists, impatient for the Apocalypse, took part. They were unaware that a few of their compatriots farther north were Muslims who had been isolated and ghettoized by the very policies the Neo-Nazis had championed.

In Europe, a small band of maniacal Basque separatists unknowingly had a common cause with a splinter group descended from the defunct Irish Republican Army. And the Russia Union had the Chechens, the Chinese had the Uighurs, and so on and so forth, around the world.

All these insanely angry pockets of fury fired their missiles at the major cities of their enemies.

Primary targets in Western Europe included the German cities of Berlin and Bonn, the French capital of Paris, and of course the European Union's premier financial powerhouse, Edinburgh, the capital of the Republic of Scotland.

In America, they reached for all the same cities that had

once served as dispensing points for Blue Rubola, with the addition of others, including Atlanta and Miami and Houston.

In the Russian Union, they launched from Chechnya for Moscow as the number one target, with as many other major cities as they could reach.

All told, as the plan unfolded across every continent, it became clear to anyone with a surveillance satellite that almost a billion people would be infected within the hour.

———

Matt paced back and forth in the deathly quiet of the orbital systems control room. All the operators from all three shifts were there at their stations; they had been there for a while, and would continue to be there for as long as Matt deemed appropriate.

Brandy, who this time was there for no good reason at all, snapped her gum at him. "Relax, Boss. Either it'll happen or it won't."

Matt answered himself as much as he answered her. "Wouldn't it be wonderful if after all this preparation, it turned out to be unnecessary?" He stopped pacing for a moment to contemplate this marvelous future. "Of course, if it turns out to be unnecessary, the profits we've thrown away will compel the board to toss me out on my ass." He took a deep breath. "But I'd make that trade in a heartbeat."

Soft warning tones filled the silence.

Brandy summarized the good news. "Cheer up, Boss. Looks like you're gonna keep your job after all."

Matt stopped in his tracks. "Deploy," he commanded.

Buttons were pressed, toggles were thrown, and they could see the results from the vidcams in orbit.

All around the Earth, satellites rotated, and spindly legs, miles in length, unfolded. The Mylar sails attached to the legs snapped majestically open.

Raw, undiluted solar power bounced from those sails to focus unparalleled energy upon Stirling engines that trailed miles of graphene radiators to offer a heat sink that would drive the engines to unparalleled efficiency.

The power poured into graphene supercapacitors, to wait eagerly to surge forth into bank after bank of free-electron lasers.

Matt spoke again. "All interceptor pods free. Fire at will."

His people had been training for this ever since the programmers had completed the simulators for the new equipment, so everyone knew what to do. They performed with the smooth coordination that comes of doing once more the things they had done a hundred times before.

As each of Khalid's rockets heeled over to fall gracefully toward its designated city and the altitude of optimal dispersion, a precision-guided pod from one of the custom cargo capsules overhead detached and headed for the same point in space.

There was no attempt to intercept the missile before it exploded to disperse the fine powder of its payload, no attempt to catch a bullet with one's teeth. Rather, the pods arrived in the same general area within a minute of the missile's explosion. The pod then exploded to release its own fine aerosol spray.

Each droplet of the spray contained, in its purest form,

a brew of those molecular components of human blood that dissolved the outermost protein coat of the virus, the coat that made the virus immune to all frequencies of ultraviolet radiation.

Then the power in the supercapacitors of the satellites surged into the lasers, flooding the area with UV-A, B, and C.

Trillions of viral particles, stripped of their defenses, were torn apart by the blasts of radiation.

Not all the viral particles were touched by the plasma droplets, and not all the particles touched by the droplets were blasted by the UV. But a cloud of death that should have infected ninety percent or more of the city achieved a mere fraction of that.

Until a vaccine was developed people would still die, but because the initial infection rate was low, if the city engaged in a sufficiently militant enforcement of quarantines, the great majority of its citizens would live.

Matt watched tensely as Khalid's missile assault reached its peak, then fell away to its end.

Brandy snapped her gum. "That's it, then."

Matt frowned. "Is it? Are we sure?"

One of the cargo-capsule operators made an observation. "You know, we had to bring the capsules down into the fringe of the atmosphere to reduce our pod interception times. The capsules' orbits are starting to degrade, and we don't have enough fuel to re-orbit them. If we don't retrieve them now, they'll all burn up."

Matt sighed. "Bring them home. At least most of them. But leave a few." Anticipating the objection, he continued, "Yes, the ones we leave will burn up. I'll live with the loss."

20

LEAP OF FAITH

In order to achieve victory you must place yourself in your opponent's skin
    —Tsutomu Oshima

Ping danced through the blast door, barely touching the ground with the balls of her feet, ready to jump in any direction. Her chura glinted in the harsh fluorescent light.

She became aware that Dash had entered behind her.

To the sides stood rack after rack of computers, punctuated here and there by monitors and the occasional table of equipment Dash surely recognized.

Before her, her opponents faced her, similarly poised for sudden movement. Sabaah stood to the right, Uwais to the left. In the center, well in front of the others, stood Jam, her knife glittering in time with Ping's movements.

Sabaah spoke to Jam with bright malice. "Now finish what you began back on the BrainTrust."

Ping pointed her knife at Sabaah. "You're next after I finish with this bitch."

Jam stepped forward. "You should not have come here. You will not survive a second time."

Then Ping ran at her, her arms spread wide, offering herself as a helpless target to her former friend. Into the air she leapt, and flew forward.

Jam threw her knife with unerring accuracy at Ping's heart.

At this, Ping's heart sang. In all the time since Jam had left her, she had known that Jam was merely playing a part...except that sometimes, when Ping was exhausted by training, a dark doubt would creep into her thoughts. Now, as the knife hurtled toward her chest, her doubts fell away.

Ping twisted as she flew and snatched Jam's knife from the air.

Jam crouched and flipped into a backward somersault, planting her feet firmly in Ping's stomach and launching her with all her strength into a higher, faster arc. Had there been an Olympic event in pairs martial arts gymnastics, they would have surely earned a perfect ten.

Ping flipped and rotated until she flew feet first and face-down between Uwais and Sabaah, sweeping with her knives in both directions to cut them both across the abdomen.

Ping had aimed for killing blows, but although her opponents had been taken completely by surprise, their rigorously trained nearly-autonomous reflexes saved them. They twisted away, and although each suffered a bleeding gash to the side, neither died.

Ping landed and rolled backward, almost hitting Khalid. She swung her knives, but Khalid blocked with casual speed, foreseeing every move Ping might make even though he was clearly distracted. He never took his eyes from Dash.

Ping followed Dash's instructions to leave Khalid alone. She slid sideways, bounced to her feet, and dashed into the space behind the racks of computers.

Sabaah grimaced with pain, then followed after her.

Uwais barely winced from Ping's knife slash before turning his attention to Jam.

Jam finished her backward somersault, leapt up, and spun to face Uwais.

Jam barely spent a moment marveling at how perfectly Ping had responded to her thrown knife. It had been beautiful, but now it was ancient history. She threw her first strike at Uwais, who blocked with deft anticipatory speed.

Jam had of course been sparring with Uwais since her departure from the BrainTrust, or at least since their release from the ludicrous submarine.

Her knowledge had grown unceasingly. Uwais, big as he was, should have been slower than she was, but he was instead faster.

And she knew that he saw her next move, and her move after that, with the same clarity she saw his.

She had worked relentlessly to up her game. She was confident she had done so, although it might not matter. As in fencing and chess and many other competitions where strategy counted, the best way to get better was to pit yourself against someone better than you.

So just as Jam had learned much, so had Uwais. As she looked into the future of their battle, she saw that Uwais was at a disadvantage: the knife he held would slow him down, while Jam, having given her own weapon to Ping, was free to move at full speed.

Uwais tossed his knife aside.

The two of them moved swiftly beyond the foolishness of their first encounter with its endless strikes, blocks, and counterstrikes. Now they only started the motions, saw the beginnings of the opposing response, and shifted tactics.

The started motions became shorter and shorter and the sequences of never-completed strikes became longer and longer, until finally they stood virtually motionless. Only gestures such as the twitch of a finger, the glance of an eye, or a minuscule shift in balance denoted readiness to commit to action.

She realized she had finally achieved the state her teacher long ago had demanded of her, the state that she could never quite reach. She now watched "everything and nothing" in a highly attentive yet at the same time unfocused hyper-awareness. She knew, just as Uwais surely knew, the next time one of them moved, one of them would die.

Jam hoped she was doing her part to keep Uwais occupied. She dimly heard a crash against some wall as Ping did something and Sabaah did something else.

Silence reigned for a moment. Then Jam heard Khalid and Dash whispering to each other, thus beginning the primary battle that would unfold in whatever exotic form such a battle between two such people would take.

Jam stayed focused on Uwais, forlornly wishing that someone could give her a clue what was going on.

Dash watched Khalid raise his hand in a beckoning offer. "Dash."

Dash made no beckoning gesture since her hands were filled with pink and black death. "Khalid."

Khalid smiled. The power of his warm, caring personality blazed through the cavern. "You've learned my name."

Dash could not help smiling back. "I've learned many things."

He twitched his hand, insistently inviting her to join him. "Come with me, and we shall destroy all that is evil."

Dash beckoned with her eyes. "Come with me, and we shall nourish all that is good."

Khalid shook his head sadly. He began to whisper descriptions of molecular structures; this first one Dash recognized as a drug similar to phenytoin, an aggression suppressor.

He continued with a sequence of nucleotides, spliceable genes, and Dash struggled with them until she dimly grasped that these sequences could lead to the manufacture of the phenytoin molecule. Her ability to comprehend, she peripherally realized, was beyond anything she had ever experienced before.

The DNA strands Khalid was proposing were mere skeletal prototypes. To truly build them correctly and safely would require the two of them working together for decades. But the outline was enough since the result was clear.

If a virus that edited the genome in this way infected the world, how would it affect the people and their societies? For Dash the answer was now obvious: they would become unalterably peaceful.

Even before Khalid had finished mapping it out, Dash started seeing other possibilities.

Dash realized what was happening. As in fencing and chess and many other competitions where strategy counted, the best way to get better was to pit yourself against someone better than you.

Here they were, the two greatest minds of their age in unbridled conflict. Necessarily they were learning from each other, bootstrapping together to an unparalleled realm of understanding.

Dash began to whisper another sequence of DNA patterns for Khalid. With her sequences, the neurons would tighten and fire faster. Dash proposed to make people smarter.

Khalid countered, and Dash responded to his response.

Now new visions took shape in the space between them, visions of the different societies that would emerge based on the genetic variations they imposed on the people forming them. Dash knew that what she saw, Khalid also would see. The insignificant details might vary, but the crucial details would be identical.

There was no telepathy involved. If you sent messages to two high school students at opposite ends of the Earth, asking each to compute the sum of two plus two, both students would say four with no mysterious means of communication.

It was the same way two people with sufficient insight and knowledge would look at a field of solar panels in the desert, see the changing air currents, and perceive the resulting rain that would bring life to the parched land. No mystical intervention was required.

So Dash and Khalid shared visions of the fruits of their genomic labors. Whole civilizations rose and fell in the empty space between them, coalescing out of the nothingness.

A city of graceful glittering spires rose, where the people lived in perfect repose. Where even the labor of opening a door was performed by robots.

In another vision, the machinery and technology merged and disappeared into the surroundings as the bots split into two categories. One type became microscopic, too small to be seen. The others labored underground, too deep to be heard. The people wandered, carefree, through hushed woods or gathered for banquets on long swards of manicured grass.

In each of Khalid's futures, the people of Earth achieved an easy serenity, the kind of happiness one feels when coming home from a turbulent journey. It was the kind of future that Dash, a pacifist by nature, would appreciate in a way Khalid never could.

In each of Dash's futures, war was rare but competition and confrontation ran rife as people drove one another forward with boisterous ebullience to greater heights, different from yet similar to what Khalid and Dash were doing now. It was a world in which Khalid, even more than Dash, would thrive.

But another feature distinguished the two sets of visions, an inevitable outgrowth of the first difference. In each of Khalid's worlds, the viewpoint was always from ground level—the ground of Earth.

In Dash's visions, the viewpoint always came from beyond, from the habitats orbiting planets and the *munditos* of the asteroids. Always a few people were hollowing out small moons, strapping on immense engines, and setting out on adventures vast enough to span the stars.

The similarities and differences became repetitive and dreary. Dash broke the trance. "Your people are marionettes," she whispered. "Marionettes acting on a stage built and scripted by others. Vast wealth, yet not a single dream."

The noise of Ping bouncing along the walls chased by Sabaah crashed in on them. Khalid and Dash returned to normal space.

Khalid lunged forward to grasp the sphere holding the black powder.

Dash swiveled to keep the glass out of his reach. Whether she or Khalid moved more swiftly, no one could ever say: Ping launched herself from behind the computers and knocked Khalid to the ground.

Sabaah leapt upon Jam, disrupting her one-on-one contest of future moves with Uwais. Uwais struck, and the sickening *thunk* of a human joint twisted beyond its capacity filled the air. Jam fell away to crash down on Khalid moments after Ping lunged away from him.

Dash hurled the pink sphere across the room, intending to strike the wall.

Uwais jumped desperately to catch the spinning container, and miraculously, succeeded.

But to maintain his hold, he grasped it too tightly. The metal needles of the latticework punctured the fragile glass.

The sphere shattered, and the pink powdered erupted across the room.

Dash spoke in an altered voice, a full octave deeper and a full megawatt more commanding. "Ping. Jam. Out now."

Ping and Jam ran for the door. Dash backed out more slowly, the black sphere clutched firmly in her hand.

Khalid touched each of his men on the shoulder. "Let them go."

Dash stepped beyond the blast door.

Ping slammed the button that slid it shut behind them.

Dash hurled the remaining sphere against the titanium barrier. The black powder erupted, covering them all.

Ping coughed, waving futilely at the clinging dust. "Really? In the midst of escaping, you had to cover us in soot? Are you kidding me?"

Dash led them at a trot through the caverns.

Ping could not get past the black powder. "So let me get this straight: the pink powder is composed of viruses specifically targeted to Uwais', Sabaah's, and Khalid's DNA."

Dash answered while continuing to urgently check her

phone for the moment when they came close enough to the surface to have service. "Correct. It's a slow virus; they have about two weeks before they become symptomatic and die."

Ping continued, "And the black powder is also tuned to their DNA, but it would kill them in less than a day."

Dash barely nodded.

"So you popped the black powder to make sure they wouldn't follow us."

Dash acknowledged this. "They'd still kill me if they could."

"So why didn't they open the door and run straight into the powder?"

Dash sighed. "Because Khalid knew I'd leave the powder outside the door."

Ping pounced, triumphant. "So if you knew that Khalid knew, you didn't have to pop the container after all. You didn't have to cover us in soot."

Jam took the next step. "But Khalid would know that she knew, so he would know he could open the door safely."

Dash laughed for the first time in what seemed forever. "Just so. I didn't release the black powder to stop Khalid. I released it to stop the infinite deductive recursion."

Dash came to a sudden halt. "Signal!" She studied a flying series of numbers and maps that flicked across the screen, then started madly typing a message.

As she worked, she answered a question Ping had asked long ago. "You were wondering what the metal sticks were for."

Ping grinned. "At last. A secret about to be revealed."

"They're seismographic sound generators and sensors. Think of them as radar for the ground."

Jam prompted her. "So, you were mapping these caverns?"

Dash smashed her finger on the Send button and began trotting once more. "I was looking for the caverns and tunnels forming the secret back entrance to Khalid's head-quarters."

Ping shook her head. "How'd you even know he'd have one?"

Dash looked back at her with eyes that were wide and unseeing; or rather, they saw something that was not here in the tunnel. "I knew he had a back door because if it had been me, I would have had a back door."

Dash ran faster as the exit appeared, a patch of soft red light from a sun that had not yet risen over the horizon. They ran out, and Dash turned and pointed north.

A squadron of fighters roared near, and a muffled flash arose as if a bomb had gone off underground and only a fraction of the light reached the surface. The ground vibrated beneath their feet.

Dash spoke with satisfaction. "So much for the back door." She turned once more and started to run yet again. Her voice filled with urgency, she said, "Now we must depart this place before they do the same thing here."

Minutes later the explosion repeated, closer this time. The ground shook so hard it nearly threw them off their feet.

The planes zoomed over them, and Ping, Jam, and Dash waved to them. The planes waggled their wings in a synchronous acknowledgment, then wheeled to return the way they had come.

Ping slapped at her clothes. "At least that blast shook off some of the dust."

Jam looked at the place where the entrance had been moments ago. "So, is that it? Did those blasts kill him?"

Dash laughed. "Behind those blast doors? Of course not." Her eyes once more looked off into a distance where no one else could go. "Nor could he have escaped through the back door before Toni's fighters arrived. He had to stay because only in his own lab could he cure the pink virus in the time he has remaining." She thought some more. "It's obvious what he's doing right now."

Ping asked, "What?"

Khalid sat down next to his main monitor and keyboard. Best to get cracking on the cure for the pink virus while he was still in a state of elevated clarity.

It was amazing how much he'd learned in such a short time. He already missed her terribly. It was a shame he hadn't managed to kill her.

As he brought his machines to life, he learned yet another new thing. He began to laugh, first with admiration, then with a contorted, wracking pain.

With the transcendent vision he had achieved, he finally saw a basic truth. He had never been fighting just Dash, one on one in a battle of two minds. No, he had always been fighting—

"—a great civilization," Colin Wheeler explained in a voice that had finally gotten stronger than a whisper. "I know we haven't heard back from them yet, but we know the outcome. Khalid had no more chance than Hannibal."

He took a sip of the warm chicken broth Amanda had placed beside him. "Hannibal of Carthage was the greatest general of his time. He won battle after battle, but could not, no matter how many his victories, win the war against Rome. Even when he took Rome itself and sacked it, he could not win." Colin tapped his temple. "By the time Hannibal arrived, Rome was no longer a city, no longer a place. It was a set of beliefs and principles, and it lived in the minds of all who shared those principles. So the Romans left the city behind and continued to fight until finally Hannibal lost a battle, and thereby lost the war."

Amanda smirked. "So you're calling the BrainTrust a great civilization? Don't you feel a little excessive hubris coming on with that fever?"

Colin settled back and closed his eyes. "And Dash has finally grown beyond what she thought were her limits. It will all be OK now. Even if something terrible happens to me—"

Amanda coughed loudly enough to break that train of thought. "Speaking of terrible things. You told me long ago to watch out for this headline." She lifted her tablet and began to read. "The President for Life regrets to inform his people that he has been taken ill with a minor flu and must cancel his monthly address. Rest assured that he is already recovering, and will be ready to address the nation in time for next month's presentation."

She put the tablet down. "You think he's dead, I take it?"

Colin's eyes flickered back and forth across the ceiling as he mapped out possible futures. "That's it, then. The Dance of the Dinosaurs has begun."

Amanda shook her head. "And while we're on the topic…"

Colin's face relaxed suddenly as he fell helplessly back to sleep.

"OK, then." Amanda smiled quietly. "And don't talk trash. You're too ornery to die. And more importantly, it's just not your style."

She kissed him lightly on the forehead. "Sweet dreams, General Scipio."

Dash pointed into the near distance where a patch of almost perfectly flat land lay. "That will be a good spot." She started walking.

With her mind still on Khalid, she spoke in a chatty tone, which was quite odd for Dash. "You know, Khalid is now part of a very interesting experiment. He has become Schrodinger's cat."

Ping decided to humor her. "He's a cat?"

Dash continued, "Schrodinger postulated that if you put a cat in a sealed box with machinery that gave her a fifty-fifty chance of living, the cat would enter an indeterminate state. She would be both dead and alive until somebody looked inside the box."

Dash waved her hand behind them. "Khalid is sealed in such a box, and I reckon he has a fifty-fifty chance of surviving. At this moment, he may well be both alive and dead." She stopped and spread her arms, reveling in the mix of approaching dawn, receding stars, and an unlikely physics experiment in progress. "Isn't that fascinating?"

As Dash started to walk again, Ping slowed down and Jam slowed beside her. Jam asked in a near whisper, "What's the crunching noise in your batpack?"

Ping grimaced. "While you were standing there like a statue facing Uwais, I was running around the room collecting the central controller boards from all the compute server racks. They're all in my pack."

She laughed softly. "So Khalid's got no compute power left except his personal machine. I don't know if that'll be enough to give him a fifty-fifty chance."

Jam chuckled. "It's worse than you know." She held up a hand she had kept clenched ever since falling against Khalid in the final moments of the battle. "Men are so easy, even the super-genius ones. I don't think he even noticed." She opened her hand. "This is the dongle needed to log into his personal machine. He has no compute power at all."

Now Ping had to cover her mouth to keep her laughter from disturbing Dash, who was still muttering in the distance. "You know, sometimes I think Dash is the embodiment on Earth of Ganesha, the Remover of Obstacles." Her voice turned darker. "But you and I, we sometimes embody Shiva the Destroyer." Ping thought it was good that Dash had not had to be Shiva. How damaging would that have been to her? Could she have ever recovered?

Jam giggled. "Oh, my. I just realized, we ruined Dash's cat experiment."

Dash had stopped to talk on her phone.

Ping offered one last comment as they came up to her. "Well worth the price."

Dash dialed her phone again, placing it on speaker. "Chance, I need your help."

Chance answered on a chipper note. "And I'm more than ready. You'll never guess where I am."

Dash answered, puzzled. "You're on board a space capsule in orbit, a capsule specially fitted with medical equipment—the newest vehicle from yours and Dmitri's company, Med Bays by Dash."

Chance's voice choked. "How'd you know that?"

Dash stated the obvious. "You told me." She paused, thinking back. "I guess not." She shrugged for no one in particular. "It was self-evident. I know you, Chance. Of course, at this moment, you would be in orbit with a fully equipped hospital, awaiting my call."

Ping whispered urgently to Jam, "If she can see us all so clearly and knows our actions so accurately, how could she not know what we did to Khalid and his computers?"

Jam gave her the answer that was, frighteningly enough, necessary and correct. "She does know. But she knows she doesn't want to know. And she won't really know until she asks. So she will never ask. So she will never know."

Ping responded with a kind of horror-filled wonder. "What's really scary is not that I understood what you just said. What's scary is that I already knew that that was what you'd say."

They turned back as Dash's next words compelled their attention. "Anyway, we'll need three moonsuits so you can contain us. Khalid infected us with something new, an entirely different virus from a different base virus. Smallpox."

Chance answered grimly. "Three moonsuits coming up as soon as we land. In a few minutes."

Ping asked, now sick to her stomach, "Smallpox? I thought we wiped that out generations ago."

Dash smiled gently upon her. "We did wipe it out, but when the permafrost in Siberia melted, frozen smallpox particles thawed and became available. Khalid sent someone to get samples."

Ping shook her head. "How do you know that?"

Dash just stared at her from a thousand miles away with cold, unseeing eyes.

Ping heard the unspoken answer: *I know he did because that's what I would have done.*

Dash put a hand to her left temple. Pain flared across her face "There's a hollow, aching place in my head where part of me should be." She wiped a finger thoughtlessly under her nose. It came away with a dark smear.

Ping gasped. "Blood. Is that blood?" She leapt to Dash's side, grabbed the finger, and examined it. The morning light was not yet bright enough to distinguish colors; Ping flicked her tongue across the blotch. "Blood!"

Dash stared at her own finger in bemusement. *Where have I seen this before?* she asked herself.

Like Ping, she licked a speck of the blood. "Oh, my. I seem to have a mild brain hemorrhage. I'll be fine." She blinked, and her eyes almost achieved full focus. "Although I must never again try for a state of hyper-awareness like that." She swayed and started to fall.

Jam and Ping both grabbed her. She wriggled in their hold until she got her feet under her once more. Dash smiled at the world at large. "I'm so glad we're all together again."

Jam and Ping put their arms around each other and her.

Suddenly Dash realized that the story would now end, as all such stories should end, with a group hug. She gave them a squeeze.

Ping jerked. "Ow!"

Jam grunted as something gave way in her shoulder.

Dash broke the hold. Driven by years of training, she snapped back to the self she had been before meeting Khalid. "What is wrong with you two?" She poked and prodded at Ping until she discovered what she sought. "Two broken ribs. We'll need to tape that."

She turned to Jam. After a moment's examination, she concluded, "Dislocated shoulder. Let me fix this real quick." She took Jam's arm in her hands. "This is going to hurt. On the count of three." She took a breath.

Jam steeled herself.

Dash began the count. "One." She twisted, and they all heard the sickly *thunk* of a shoulder being reset in its socket.

Jam grunted.

Dash turned back to Ping and glanced at the batpack. "You say you always carry rope and duct tape?"

Ping nodded.

Dash moved to get behind her. "I need the duct tape."

Ping spun suddenly until the pack faced Jam. "Let Jam get it."

Dash smiled ruefully as Jam groped around in the pack, accompanied by grinding noises. "I thought you said your batpack was mostly empty this time."

Jam raised her good arm high, duct tape in hand. She spoke triumphantly, saving Ping the need to respond. "Got it."

While wrapping Ping's chest, Dash offered them some scathing observations. "I can't believe you two! I leave you unsupervised for a couple minutes, and you get yourselves all banged up. How can I trust you to go anywhere on your own? You need to be more careful in the future."

Ping grunted in pain.

Jam offered a calm, logical defense. "Dash, we were fighting two of the greatest martial arts assassins on the planet."

Dash paused for a moment to glare at her. "*That's* your excuse? You call that a justification? Must I explain everything? It is exactly when you are battling the world's greatest fighters that you must be extra careful!"

That shut up both Jam and Ping.

At last, Dash finished winding the tape to her satisfaction.

Ping complained, "I can hardly breathe."

Dash rolled her eyes.

The need to administer first aid had indeed brought her

back to a reasonable approximation of normal. The ache in the side of her head faded, and the nosebleed ended. Earlier she had told her friends she would be fine to keep them from worrying. Now she examined herself with more objective clinical detachment and drew the same conclusion.

The only lasting side effect she would suffer was, she still had images and visions of how to cure the latest plague virus, a problem she realized she had been processing subconsciously the whole time she was hyper-aware. She smiled to herself. They were going to set yet another record for developing a vaccine in even less time than ever before. All would be well.

She reconnected with the normal reality brought to her by her senses and felt a peaceful pleasure as she considered how solid and reliable it was.

The sun rose, following the laws of orbital mechanics. The rocket descended, following the laws of gravity and motion. The sky filled with the thunder of engines, following the laws of acoustics.

Jam and Ping huddled around her, following the laws of friendship.

Then the story ended, as all such stories should end, with a group hug.

The story continues with Braintrust: Requiem, available now for pre-order at Amazon.com.

The World Economy Crashed and Burned. What's a BrainTrust To Do?

Having barely dodged an extinction level event, humanity now faces a new disaster: the world plunges into a Great Crash deeper and more cruel than the Depression of 1929. The BrainTrust has an answer. But the old, corrupt, dirtside Powers don't need an answer.

They need a scapegoat.

Soon an unholy alliance launches three mighty fleets, each individually powerful enough to destroy all the combined navies of WWII. Relentless and unstoppable, they bear down on the effectively unarmed archipelago.

Now Dash and her mentor Colin must face a last question.

It will be her Final Exam.

Can Dash even accept the only answer?

How terrible is the price she will have to pay?

Welcome to the thrilling finale of the BrainTrust saga!

Pre-order now at Amazon

Well, that was a long journey through a terrifying episode. You made it! Thank you for sharing it with me.

As always, thank you to my incredible beta and JIT teams, my wonderful editor (I have to say that, she's my wife, but I would anyway), Jake Caleb for creating an amazing new cover at the last minute, and Steve Campbell and his production team for always being on the ball.

But most of all, thanks to you, the readers, for being willing to step into my universe and take the journey with me. If you enjoyed *Ode to Defiance*, you will find links to the other BrainTrust Universe books at the end of this section.

About the story:

As Gina observes, "Let's face it: we'll do this because someone must, and only we can." I did not realize when I started this book that it was all about stepping up and transcending your limitations. I was sometimes as surprised as anyone when some of the characters did so. In the real world, I have personally had the privilege, just a couple of times, of witnessing when someone stepped up in this fashion, so for me at least, it all was quite credible.

It's been a while since I've reported on which parts of these stories are based on fact. The science, of course, is largely correct, except for errors committed by the author despite the efforts of his diverse community of experts to keep him on the straight and narrow.

Hukou, the Red Princelings, the web addiction rehab centers, and the social credit metric are very real parts of Chinese society. When I first wrote about it, the Chinese President had not yet declared himself President for Life, though of course now that part of the story has come true. The transformation of all powerful posts in the Chinese hierarchy into hereditary positions has not yet come to pass. Give them time.

The story of Qi Ru, the Hukou peasant who left the impoverished west to go to college at a Chinese university, got rejected, and went overseas to get a degree from a prestigious university, is true. Whether the real person went into high finance, I do not know.

The abusive power of civil forfeiture is not quite as real today as it was when I wrote *Crescendo of Fire*. The attorney general who vigorously encouraged this abusive practice is gone, and the Supreme Court, in a unanimous ruling, has imposed limits on its exercise. Of course, in the world of the *BrainTrust*, there are nineteen justices on the Supreme Court, ten of them selected for their slavish devotion to the whim of the President for Life. Clearly, in that world, civil forfeiture made a comeback.

The story of the Texas town of Roma on the border with Mexico is approximately true. As I write this, they are being "negotiated" by the Feds into deciding which homes to tear down for The Wall. I did include a couple of minor embellishments. I do not know for sure that the people to the south make excellent fish tacos, and I do not know that the people to the north like beer. However, based on my personal experiences in Texas and Mexico, that's the way to bet.

The character Diab is derived from another real person. The real person, born in Palestine, wound his way through the Mideast, went to college in Cairo, and in that more gentle and welcoming time, wrangled his way into America to become a much-sought-after engineer. He kept trying to retire, but no one would let him. He married another immigrant/refugee, a German who had survived the firebombing of Dresden. One of their children is a financier; the other, Jameela, is a Lieutenant Colonel in the US Air Force. I like to think that, had he been born a few generations later in the much more hostile world of the BrainTrust, he would have built the *First Chance*. He was certainly qualified.

The story of the mother and child who poop on the deck of the *Mt. Parnassus* is derived from a true story told by a retired Peace Corps worker.

The Israeli variant of the F35 that had a second cockpit where Dash could sit was on the drawing boards at the time of writing. It looks like that plan has been quashed, so it is true no longer. This is one of the risks in writing near-future science fiction. I don't regret using it for a moment, however. It makes a great part of the story, although perhaps I should have called it the F36 :-)

—Marc Stiegler, April 11, 2019

If You Enjoyed Ode to Defiance, You'll Also Like:

The President for Life has the Brawn; the young woman he must kidnap has the BrainTrust. Available now.

Game On!

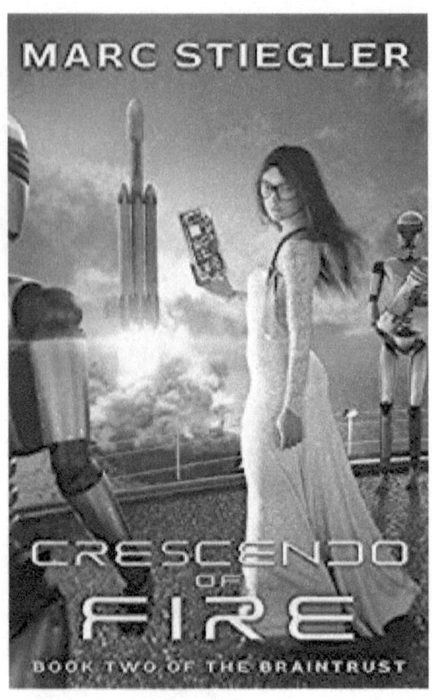

Who wins when a rocket ship dies?

Only the BrainTrust and the inimitable Dr. Dash can save SpaceR and the future of space travel. Available Now.

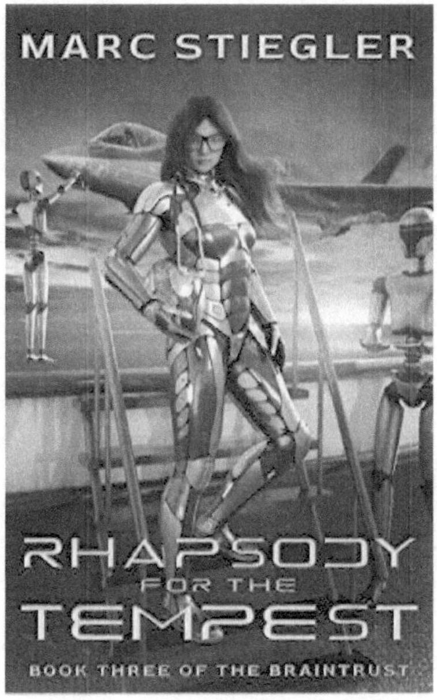

She's invading the Cradle of Civilization

The secret that powered humanity's first great civilization has lain dormant for millennia. Even with the help of her best friends Dash and Ping, can Jam bring it home to the BrainTrust, where it belongs? Available Now

Charlie was just doing his homework

But on the BrainTrust, homework can get you into a lot of hot water. Available now.

A novelette set in the world of the BrainTrust